HAILEY'S G

The Jenny Penn Collection
Cattleman's Club 2

Jenny Penn

MENAGE EVERLASTING

Siren Publishing, Inc.
www.SirenPublishing.com

A SIREN PUBLISHING BOOK
IMPRINT: Ménage Everlasting

HAILEY'S GAME
Copyright © 2010 by Jenny Penn
ISBN 10: 1-60601-827-2
ISBN 13: 978-1-60601-827-9

First Printing: August 2010

Cover design by Jenny Penn
All art and logo copyright © 2010 by Siren Publishing, Inc.

Printed in the U.S.A.

PUBLISHER
Siren Publishing, Inc.
www.SirenPublishing.com

DEDICATION

To Michele, for all her help.

HAILEY'S GAME
Cattleman's Club 2

JENNY PENN
Copyright © 2010

Chapter 1

Friday, March 28th

Kyle Harding believed in letting life come as it came. That especially held true when it came to a particular red-headed spitfire. Tracking the little savage through the crowd, Kyle felt almost every cell in his body start to vibrate. It had always been like that, and normally the sensation ended in disaster.

All the lessons of a lifetime didn't mean he could stop from crashing into that hole time and time again. Even now as she came too close, he knew he should just let her pass by him without incident. Not that he would.

Especially not with her so blatantly ignoring him. An invitation to "accidently" crash into all those luscious curves, that's what that was. Sweet feeling and smelling like cinnamon, even if her face puckered up into a scowl at the sight of him, Kyle didn't let that dissuade him one bit as he latched onto his prey.

"Well, well, well."

"Kyle."

Hailey Mathews' nose did that thing it always did when she said his name—crinkled in disgust. Far from menacing, the gesture made her almost irresistibly cute. It sort of enticed a man to pick on her a little more.

"Hailey Mathews at a Cattleman's event. Will life ever cease to surprise?"

Just as Kyle expected, her gaze narrowed on him in annoyance, and she didn't disappoint to come back with an immediate insult. "It already did. I'm not the least bit shocked to find you here."

They'd been eight. That's when this war started. It had been a sunny spring day. She shoved a firecracker down the headless body of his GI Joe figurine. He bombed her with dog-poo grenades on her walk to school. It had been a tit for tat kind of war that only kids got away with, except now they'd grown up and still nothing had changed.

Well, some things had.

Back then Hailey had been nothing more than a scrawny girl with a wild, orange halo around her head. Given the way dirt always clung to her clothes and a smart comment always tripped out of her lips, she'd earned her nickname as the little savage.

Just the memory had Kyle's lips kicking up into a grin, especially as her scowl darkened further. Annoying Hailey came like second nature to him, and nothing annoyed Hailey more than the fact that she wanted him. Well, at least her body did.

It always betrayed her. That ritual hadn't changed, either, from the way the puckered tips of her breasts panted out to greet him. Kyle let his gaze linger there, knowing it only made her burn more.

"I must say, you're looking very tempting tonight, Hailey."

In silent defiance to his ogling, Hailey's arms crossed over her chest. "You look as plum ugly as ever."

Kyle gave a true laugh at that. Hailey never changed. Wild, free, and untamed, God, but he'd love to get her beneath him. All those curves helped inflame that itch. Time had been kind to Hailey, filling out her body with very tantalizing dips and slopes. Yeah, they added a little more weight to her body and made her clothes look a little dumpy, but Kyle kind of liked that size.

He liked it since about sixteen when he started noticing just how good Hailey looked bent over a hood with that ass sticking out like an invitation. If any of the other fools in his shop class would have noticed then it might have been all right to show a little more interest in the girl. What had been a negative back then, though, turned only into a positive in Kyle's mind because the idiots still didn't recognize what they had right there under their noses.

"I see your charm hasn't changed, either, nor your fashion sense." He taunted her just to earn that look from her again.

"Never did take to the streetwalker style."

"Hmm." Kyle took another look. "Didn't your mama ever tell you covering everything up just makes a man itch to unwrap you? But," his finger reached out to stroke down her neck and Hailey flinched backward, "you seem to be missing something."

"Don't touch me."

Like he'd obey that command. "Ah, but you're so soft."

"I also have teeth, and trust me, my bite is a lot worse than my bark."

He might have taken that threat a little more seriously if her tone hadn't dipped into the husky notes of arousal. It just made the comment come out dirty. "I love a woman who bites...and screams and bucks with her passion."

"Passionate hatred."

"You protest a lot for somebody who could just walk away."

That hadn't been the brightest thing to say, Kyle realized as Hailey did just that. He'd forgotten how Hailey took to challenges. Never back down, which was something they shared. The little princess had to realize that all that running just tempted him all the more.

Why would she? You ain't done nothing about it so far.

That angry response echoed out from the cock that had finally started to harden for the first time that night. A real shame about that because there were a hell of a lot of women around who would be a damn sight nicer to his poor, pulsing dick than Hailey Mathews. After all, he might not mind getting bitten, but it all came down to location.

Shaking the empty beer can in his hand, he pitched it toward the open-barreled trashcan. Silently, he awarded himself two points as the aluminum rolled over the rim and fell in. The momentary glow of victory came and went as his gaze traveled over the dingy lip and up into the sparkling chaos of the party whirling around him.

Everybody and everything rolled on at full speed while he stood there feeling like an old man stuck in the mud. The bonfires raged high into the night sky, casting a warm glow over the half-naked women running wild through the fields. The half-drunk men chasing after them could easily have been mistaken for frat boys instead of the responsible, hard-working men they were.

That's what the Cattleman's Club was all about, a safe place to have some fun and not worry over the wagging of tongues. Not that Kyle felt any shame in any of his needs, and if somebody had something to say about that, they just talked on. Actually, he didn't know any man who'd have disagreed with him on that. It was the women who got funny about people knowing all their kinks.

Women also got funny about getting kinky with a man. They tended to want to believe that love had something to do with letting a man do *that* to them. The club offered Kyle an excuse to do just about anything he wanted without consequences. No names given, no obligations made, no woman could misunderstand that.

That had always been the best advantage of the Cattleman's Club, until lately. The endless sea of pretty women and constant flow of hot sex had actually begun to feel like monotony, a fact that shocked even Kyle. Not that he didn't want his pretty woman or night after night of sex, but Kyle just wanted to go home for that.

His mama always told him that a dog only had so many tricks in him. By the time he finished running through all his, he'd better have found a master who loved him enough not to mind that he wasn't so cute and lovable anymore. Kyle always listened to his mom and figured one day he'd end up chained.

That time felt like now. He'd come to the point where he should be getting off work to go home to a house that smelled nice and a woman that smelled even better. Ideally, she'd be one of those women who could actually cook and clean but not be one of those fragile kinds of ladies. What he really needed was a lady with an attitude.

Kind of like a savage princess.

For all the naked women running around, he didn't see but one who fit that description. On its own, his gaze found Hailey again, talking to the Davis brothers, and Kyle didn't have to wonder about that. He knew the inside scoop there.

A six-year-old with a crayon could have connected those dots. Hailey's best friend, Patton Jones, happened to belong to the Davis brothers. While the details had certainly not been aired publicly, nobody doubted anybody who touched Patton would be held accountable for touching what belonged to them boys.

Three boys. Three big boys. Very big boys. He and about everybody else had been warning Cole about just that. Cole, his best friend, didn't like to listen to reason. He especially didn't like to hear the word no, so Patton saying yes when he suggested they take a drive had been viewed as a good thing by Cole.

As Kyle watched Slade and Chase Davis make a rapid departure, he had to wonder just how long Cole would be holding that opinion. Hell, he didn't even know if Cole would hold on to all his teeth through the night, but it was his own dumbass fault for not listening.

That's why Kyle didn't make a single move to help out his buddy. Instead, his focus remained on the little spitfire trailing in the brothers' wake. He could almost hear fate calling him a dumbass for letting her walk away. He'd let her do that too often, but then again he really hadn't been ready to settle down.

Just the idea made him smirk because when he thought of Hailey, the last thing he thought of was domestication. Eight years of waiting and wanting hadn't dulled the primitive urges filling his balls as he tracked that sassy ass as it bounced its way through the crowd.

That is a mountain made to be conquered.

Before he could indulge in any gluttonous victory feast, he'd have to figure out just how to con the little princess out of her clothes.

He needed a plan.

A plan, a little luck, and certainly a willingness to sink to any level.

* * * *

Saturday, March 29th

"I told you, you ain't never had a chance at that woman."

Whatever it takes, whatever level I have to sink to, I'm going to bend Hailey to my will and keep her as a plaything. Cole Jackson had become quite tired of Hailey Mathews making him the laughingstock of Pittsview. About every man in the damn Cattleman's Club had a good laugh at his expense last night, this morning, and probably for the next few weeks out.

"Hailey would rather dance at his funeral than with Cole any day of the week," Jacob grunted, earning him a dark glower.

Not that Cole could deny it. Hailey didn't like him. Never had. That didn't change that he always had a boner waiting for the little darling. It'd been half-mast the first time he met her. Not that he'd been panting after the girl. Hailey might be cute, but she wouldn't be drawing any catcalls from the sidelines. He'd just been being his normally friendly self, trying to bring a little happiness into another person's life, and what did Hailey do?

She bit him.

God, but he loved a woman who bit, made conquering her worth every single eleven inches he could offer up to the job. Being hard for a woman didn't mean he intended to play the fool for her. Cole didn't chase what wouldn't chase him back. Waste of time.

Especially not when he knew Hailey would come his way eventually. He didn't care how much bluster and fire she put into her supposed dislike of him. Cole had a keen ability to tell when a woman wanted him, and Hailey's panties dripped, she lusted so hard.

A seasoned and successful hunter, Cole had long ago identified Hailey Mathews as a spitfire. They tended to burn hot and wild, fueled by their own passionate natures to go the extreme. That included hating and screwing.

That meant bagging Hailey wouldn't only be a very large notch on his bedpost, but it would be a hell of a ride to take. That made Cole's own cock go a little misty around the eye. Yeah, he imagined more than once all the fun he could have with Hailey Mathews under his direction. He just hadn't figured out a way to get in close enough without getting mauled.

He thought he'd seen a path, but he'd been blinded by his own driving need. It left him vulnerable to assault. That's just what happened last night when Hailey and her little gal pal, Patton, had set him up.

That stilled the fingers swirling the spoon through his mug. The sugar had long since dissolved into the hot liquid, but he didn't take a sip. Instead, he glared out at the world as he felt the fresh burn of Hailey's most recently delivered insult.

Cole knew who she was the moment he saw Patton next to Hailey. A legend almost in the Pittsview, she did her reputation justice. Not that Cole had really cared much about Patton. Sure, he'd have screwed her, but he'd really been after the hope of making Hailey jealous.

That they used his game against him only made him ache that much more to punish the fiery redhead once he got her beneath him. Then they'd see who liked to be bitten…whipped, spanked, fucked, and eaten out for hours.

Got to stop thinking about that.

It never helped him come up with a plan.

Trying to shake the dirty thoughts from his mind, Cole's gaze skipped over the remains of the Bread Box's morning rush. Barely nine in the morning and the little bakery already looked worn through.

Silent as a grave.

Except for the click and clack of plates being stacked as Heather scuttled about trying to rectify the damage. Cole's gaze narrowed in on her as he tracked her movements from table to table. Cute and petite, the fact that she had a kid didn't stop him or any other man from flirting her up whenever she came close.

Not that Cole would have gotten with a woman with a kid. Kids meant commitment, and he didn't do that. Not anymore.

"Hell, Hailey tried to bury him last night." Aaron laughed, drawing Cole back into his cousin's obnoxious poking. "Didn't I warn him that Patton was up to no good?"

"That you did." Jacob nodded at his brother.

"And didn't I tell him that Hailey and Patton were setting him up?"

"Hell, even I told him that."

"And did he listen?"

Jacob shook his head like a Sunday worshipper in the pew. "No, sir."

"And did they get over good on him?"

"His ass almost got beat bloody by Slade Davis."

Yeah, Cole's cousins had it right on every point. That didn't mean the story ended there. This story wouldn't end until he had Hailey so under his thumb she couldn't come without his approval.

"Look at him." His cousin's voice broke annoyingly through Cole's thoughts. "He got that goofy look on his face again."

"You mean that no good look," Jacob shot back.

"No, I mean that he got that screwed but didn't get any pussy—"

"Oh, *shut up* already." Cole knew they did it just to annoy him, but that didn't stop it from working.

"Go on, Cole, admit you got at least ten inches that's just aching to break ol' Hailey in," Jacob dared him.

"Don't be an ass," Cole snapped. "I ain't gonna break nothing."

Aaron snorted at that, smothering his laugh with a mouthful of new donut.

"I ain't." Cole glared at him for even suggesting otherwise.

Jacob rolled his eyes at that. "You going to tell me that you're just going to let the little woman get away with setting you up? 'Cause I ain't buying it."

"There is a difference between *taming* and breaking."

"Oh." Jacob's gaze went wide with comical understanding. "So you're going to *tame* Hailey Mathews?"

"You don't think I can?"

"No." Jacob couldn't get any blunter than that.

"Face it, Cole, you've been trying to figure out how to get in that woman's bed for two years, and all you've gotten were a bunch of self-administered hand jobs for the effort."

Cole didn't like hearing his failure so publicly aired. That was just another bone he had to pick with the little spitfire, and when he was done...

"Trust me, Aaron, I'm going to leave Hailey purring for weeks...years. You'll see."

"I'm seeing now." Aaron nodded over Cole's shoulder.

Shifting in his seat to track Aaron's gaze, Cole felt every muscle in his body tighten at the sight of Hailey Mathews sashaying across the bakery. As if he weren't there, and she didn't know it, Cole didn't buy that act for a second. He bought that she was arrogant enough to play it that way.

If he had any sense he'd turn around and give her equal measure. With his gaze narrowing in on that plump ass, Cole admitted that he didn't really have much use for sense. Reason and logic wouldn't get Cole what he wanted, the freedom to do whatever he wanted to every delicious inch of Hailey's body, and she'd be...

Wet, begging, on her knees and calling me master.

Just the stir of those kinds of thoughts had his Mr. Man swelling to the ready, eager as always to try and forge its way out of Cole's jeans and into the warmth it desired. Normally, Cole would have tempered that urge, knowing how hard Hailey would hit back. Today, though, he had enough of taking it easy on the little woman. His patience had come to an end.

Sliding free of the booth, Cole could hear his cousins quickly following in his tracks and silently cursed their presence. This was going to end up looking more like schoolyard antics than the intimidating threat it should be. At least Heather took the hint when her gaze met his over Hailey's shoulder. With a polite nod, she told Hailey to have a good day and hurried off.

Cole positioned himself so that when Hailey turned around her breasts grazed into his chest. So soft, so luscious, he liked feeling her pressed up against him. He especially liked the way her nipples hardened instantly, revealing the truth of the storms gathering in her gaze.

"Cole."

Caging her in against the counter, Cole leaned in as she backed up until he had her pinned. Savoring the moment with a deep, pointed breath, he inhaled the intoxicating scent of cinnamon that clung to Hailey.

"You know, darlin', if you start calling me master now, it might make me feel a little more charitable when it comes time to punish you for the little game you played on me last night."

Her lip trembled, curling slightly into a snarl. "You better back off, Cole."

"Or what? *Ow!*" Cole flinched back, hobbling on one foot as his other leg lifted in pain. "What are you wearing? Steel toes?"

"Always," Hailey snapped as she shouldered past him. Shoving between his two snickering cousins, she managed to make running away look more like storming off, but nobody could deny Hailey retreated quickly.

"Way to go, hot stuff."

"Shut up," Cole snapped at Jacob, about toppling him over as he pushed his cousin out of the way and took off after Hailey. He caught her as her hand curled around her Studebaker's door handle. Swinging her around, he started before their gazes even locked. "Listen here, Hailey—Ow! Damn it, woman, *stop doing that!*"

"Then stop annoying me!" Hailey roared back, kicking out again.

Cole anticipated the hit this time and managed to dodge to the side. Wobbling on one leg with the other still striking out, he caught her completely unprepared as he spun her around. Pressing her stomach over the bubbled hood with an arm in her back, Cole pinned her in place. He needed only that second to land the flat of his palm across her ass in a sharp smack.

"*Cole!*"

"That's for kicking me!" He spanked her again, totally ignoring her struggles or bellowed outrage. "And that's for trying to kick me again!"

A loaf of French bread broke across his cheek as Hailey finally managed to twist to the side. He got in one more spank before she managed to wrench around enough to latch on to his earlobe. At the first painful tug, Cole released her just as she released him.

Her teeth flashed bright white compared to the flush of her cheeks as she backed up growling. "You son of a bitch. I'm going to—"

"Do what?"

She didn't have a comeback to that.

"You started this, Hailey, and anytime you want to end it, you know what you got to do. Until then, you consider it game on, darlin'."

Chapter 2

Hailey still fought the echoing trembles her encounter with Cole inspired as she barged into her kitchen. Patton bore full responsibility for the nightmare unfolding around her. Up until this moment, she and Cole had maintained a tense truce. He annoyed her, and she did everything in her power to avoid him.

It was best that way because the two of them had some kind of chemical reaction when they got close. It started with that custom-made charm of his. Swaggering all around, dropping "darlin's" out of that wicked grin that had women sighing, wishing, *and fantasizing about sorts of things naughty and, oh, so nice.*

There lay the problem. No matter how much Hailey might despise the fact, she wanted the hard-bodied Cattleman. Something about him just got under her skin. It made her both burn with indignation and ache with a need she'd never confess to. Never confess because the last thing Hailey would become was one of his whimpering little pets.

Oh, she knew all about the women in Cole's life. He had his pick of any woman he wanted in town, which sickened her. God's honest truth, she got physically ill watching him smooth talk his way through every available bed in town while knowing he gorged himself weekly up at his precious little club.

It's not like he needed to bother her, but that didn't stop him. Nothing stopped Cole when he decided he wanted something. Who the hell was she to mess up that record?

Hell, not even Patton had resisted the man, and she'd resisted every other one up until him. Knowing Patton had only been using Cole to make the men she really loved jealous hadn't stopped Hailey from feeling the dark tinge of the God-awful emotion herself. Envious of Cole's interest in her best friend, that's how far the man had sunk her.

Hailey plunked the half a loaf of bread that hadn't been left in the Bread Box's parking lot onto her counter. Standing there, staring blankly at all the possibilities of what Cole could mean by "game on," Hailey knew she'd fallen into some very deep trouble.

The kind of trouble she honestly didn't know how to defend against. Hailey didn't kid herself when it came to her skill set with men. She didn't have the kind of experience that prepared a woman to deal with a man like Cole. It wouldn't just be him, either.

Kyle Harding and Cole Jackson were joined at the hip. They owned a house together, they ran a repair shop together, and they tag-teamed their women together. They'd be coming after her together, and she would end up both figuratively and literally screwed. Screwed in every kinky position they knew.

The blare of a horn coming down the drive echoed like a siren, snapping Hailey back to the reality of her kitchen. A peek out her window told her Patton had arrived, a good thing by Hailey's reckoning because she wanted to have some words with her best friend.

Not bothering to wait for her best friend to annoy her into answering the door, Hailey made it to it before Patton got out a single knock. Not dawdling to catch Patton's greeting, Hailey left her standing there by herself. To add to her silent statement, Hailey brooded all the way back into the kitchen, where she commenced slamming about as many things as she could.

She needed coffee now, but her patience would have to hold until it had finished brewing. Hailey never had been long on that virtue, and once enough dark liquid had gasped out into the pot, she yanked it clear. Ignoring the hiss and sizzle as more drops plopped onto the burning pad, she emptied the pot into her mug.

Pointedly rude, she didn't offer any to Patton but slammed the pot back onto the burner to finish filling. With the fortification of caffeine starting to hit her system, Hailey finally turned to confront Patton's tolerant smile.

"Rough night?"

"Worse day," Hailey shot back.

"I hesitate to ask." Patton got the clue and began helping herself to the coffee.

With narrowed gaze, Hailey tracked her movement, snarling when she came too close. "I can understand why, considering it's all your fault."

"My fault? How so?"

Patton actually managed to pull off sounding shocked. She even added to the performance by pausing to give Hailey that wide-eyed look of innocence. Like Hailey would let her get away with that shit.

"I ran into Cole down at the bakery this morning."

"Oh." Honest guilt flashed across Patton's features, wiping away the act. Concentrating on pouring her own cup of coffee, her hesitation shined through in her tone. "How was he?"

"How was he?" That was one step too far. She almost hit Patton for caring about the wrong side of the equation. Instead, her friend got saved as her cup smacked into the counter, nearly cracking.

"Was it bad?"

"Bad?"

"Look, Hailey. I can tell you're upset. Just tell me how bad he was hurt."

Hailey looked around the room in a desperate attempt to find some sanity in that moment. None came and so she snapped back at Patton in disgust. "He wasn't hurt at all, Patton. *That's not the problem.*"

"What do you mean he wasn't hurt?" Typical Patton, she didn't get it.

"Did I stutter?"

"But...I...are you sure?"

"Am I sure of *what*?"

"That he wasn't hurt," Patton explained as though Hailey was the idiot in the room. "Maybe Slade spared his face."

There would be no getting to the part where she got to cuss at Patton if she didn't get her friend over this speed bump. The annoyance at having to waste time though couldn't be hidden in her tone.

"Please, there wasn't a scratch on that boy."

"That doesn't make any sense. I saw Slade hit him."

Patton's head shook as she muttered to herself. Hailey began to get a sense that maybe, just maybe, Slade played Patton for a change. That had her smirking.

"Are you sure?"

"He hit him." Patton glanced up as if Hailey would offer her any comfort. "Maybe he hit him in the stomach, but he ripped him from the truck, screaming he was going to kill Cole."

"Why would he do that?"

"Because he was jealous. That was the plan."

This time Hailey grinned for real, glad that she wasn't the only one going to have a bad day. "He knew it."

"You don't know—"

"Chase figured it out at the bonfire and called me on it."

"What?" Patton blinked.

"They knew, Patton." Hailey waved her hands in the air. "The jig was up."

Hailey really did enjoy the way Patton wore her stunned expression. It didn't happen often that somebody got the better of Patton, which really made her friend's angry flush that much more funny.

"That sneaky son of a bitch," Patton whispered.

Hailey rolled her eyes at that and moved around to settle down at the kitchen table. Self-absorbed Patton was about to carry on as if she had any right. Banging her cup onto the counter to pull her friend back out of her own drama, Hailey snapped, "Are you listening to me?"

"I heard you." Patton settled down across the table, all regal but for the blush still lingering in her cheeks. "They played me."

"Not before you and I played them."

"Oh, I see." Patton reached across the table to give Hailey's hand a comforting squeeze. "Don't worry, honey. I'm not mad at you. You can't help it if you're not a good liar."

"Mad at me?" Hailey gasped, snatching her hand back. "Oh, no. You're not the one who gets to be mad. *I'm* the one who is mad at *you.*"

"Me?" Patton had the audacity to look amazed. "Whatever for?"

Hailey's jaw clenched back on the anger that snapped forward at that question. "You dragged me into this stupid-ass game, and now I've got the hounds of hell on my heels."

"Are you worried about Chase and Slade? Don't be. I can control them."

"Such ill-placed confidence," Hailey sneered. "But no. They're not my problem."

With an exaggerated sigh of patience, Patton asked her with all tolerance, "Hailey, will you just tell me what is going on?"

"Cole." Hailey spit his name out as if it was a sour taste in her mouth. "Cole Jackson and his two sidekicks, Beevis and Butthead. That is what is going on."

"Cole?" Patton laughed. "He's what's got you all concerned?"

It almost hurt not to go over the table at that. The last thing Hailey would have admitted to in that moment were the real details of her misadventure at the Bread Box, not that she wouldn't tailor it to prove her point. "He walked up to me at the bakery and said 'game on' with those two twits snickering at his side."

"What two twits?"

"Jake and Aaron."

"Doesn't ring a bell." Patton shook her head.

"They were two grades ahead of us. Remember? Aaron drove the black Malibu SS."

Patton blinked. "Malibu what?"

"It's a muscle car."

"Sorry."

"Jake had the beat up Chevelle they worked on in shop class."

"The Chev...what? Isn't that a rock band?"

Patton's ignorance had to be intentional given how much Hailey used to talk about that car. Either that or she really did think Hailey was boring. "It's an old Chevy."

"Don't give me that look, Hailey. I didn't take shop."

"Well, I did, and those two Neanderthals made my life hell," Hailey snapped. "They're Cole's cousins. They work with him down at his shop, and they're just as bad as Cole."

Patton snorted. "Cole isn't that bad. I wouldn't sweat him."

Hailey's mouth fell open. "Don't sweat him?"

"Yeah. So what if Cole has taken an interest in you. A woman could do worse. He's a hottie."

Hailey's head dipped to the side under the weight of her disbelief. "He's a walking advertisement for the convent. A woman could make him wear four rubbers and still not be sure she wouldn't get infected. Besides, he hasn't taken an interest in me, he's declared war."

"Just because of what happened the other night?" Patton looked doubtful and still completely unconcerned. Why would she be? It wasn't her ass caught in the crossfire.

"He's been ticked at me since I turned him down a year ago."

"He asked you out, and you turned him down?" Patton's mouth fell open. "Why am I just hearing about this now?"

"He didn't ask me out. The sleazy, arrogant bastard just wanted to get his hands—"

"—on your hot little body." Patton grinned.

"On my car." Hailey waved her hands in agitation. "Hello? Remember our conversation?"

"Your car?"

"You never listen to me." Hailey sighed. "I'll make this short. Cole has been lusting after it since I bought it. Thinks he's God's gift to wrenches and has been insulted ever since I told him where he could stick his ratchet. I take care of my own car."

"Sounds like the beginning of a beautiful relationship."

"There is no relationship!" Hailey shouted, provoked by Patton's dismissive attitude. "I'm telling you he's been lusting after my Commander for a year now. Oh, I've seen his eyes all over my baby, checking her out when my back is turned. I don't trust that man, and I know full well what the double dorks are capable of."

"Don't you think you're blowing this out of proportion?"

"No, I don't." Hailey crossed her arms over her chest. "You remember when somebody super glued my books to the shop table?"

"Oh, yeah, that was funny."

Hailey's eyes narrowed on Patton. Obviously she hadn't found any humor in the joke. "That was Jake and Aaron led by their then leader Kyle."

"Kyle? Kyle Harding?" Patton grinned. "He's hot, too."

"He's an ass."

"Oh, yeah, he certainly has one of the best."

"Patton, the man rivals Cole for the title of jerk of the century."

"Don't you think you're exaggerating?"

"No."

"I talked to him last night, and he was nothing but a gentleman." Patton pursed her lips and wiggled her eyebrows. "Much to my disappointment. I was hoping...you know. He and Cole appeared to be good friends."

"They're partners in the restoration shop in town."

"I wonder if they partner in anything else?"

"Patton!" Hailey's mouth fell open. "You have three men at home. Now you want two more on the side. What do you want? To die with your legs spread?"

"I wasn't thinking for me, sweetheart."

"Oh, no." Hailey shook her head at Patton's look. "That's your sick dream. Leave me out of it."

"Just think, Hailey—"

"Never going to happen."

"But—"

"I talked to Kyle, too, last night, and he was the same dickhead he'd always been."

"Were you a bitch first?"

That had Hailey's eyes narrowing and her voice growling, "If I was, I was justified. Remember the time when somebody rigged the exploding stink bombs to my locker door?"

"Kyle?"

"Or the time when somebody wired my toolbox to deliver an electric shock when I touched it?"

"Oh, yeah." Patton laughed. "Your pinky twitched for almost the whole day."

"Yeah, that was a great laugh. It was even funnier when somebody vaselined the path to the liquid recycling bin, and I busted my ass, knocked over a drum, and got covered in used motor oil. I almost shit myself. I laughed so hard."

"Okay, okay." Patton held up her hands. "I give in. But if you knew Kyle did all these things, why didn't you say anything in high school?"

"Because I didn't find out until years later when Kyle broke up with Mary Katherine, and she ratted him and his friends out. Besides, what would I have done? You're the master at these juvenile games. Me, I'm too mature to pull off those kinds of pranks."

"Oh, come on. Don't underestimate yourself." Patton smiled. "I'm sure you can do juvenile."

Chapter 3

Hours later, her conversation with Patton still echoed through Hailey's head. Working out her frustration as she always did in the shop, her anger wound slowly down. Cole was an ass, sure. Kyle might be a jerk, yep.

They also happened to be Pittsview's top-ranking bachelors now that Chase, Slade, and Devin Davis had been erased from the list. It seemed almost conceited to think they'd make a play for her, given her ranking on the bachelorette list had to be somewhere in the middle.

Average, that was her position in life. Men like Kyle and Cole didn't put any serious effort into chasing down women like her when they had porno queens out at their club more than willing to bend over and take orders. Even if they did come sniffing her way, what did it matter?

She wouldn't end up in any man's bed she didn't want to end up in. Not even if the idea tempted her. Not even Cole's. That would certainly serve as a shock to his arrogant ass. It would be fitting retribution if they did come after her. Then the whole town, and all their fellow Cattlemen, could see just who really mastered the control of their desires.

Hailey should have known not to issue even a silent challenge to fate. Fate always answered. Today it spoke back with the roar of Kyle's oversized pickup pulling into her drive all the way up to the garage door.

So it begins.

Chunking down her gloves, Hailey didn't dawdle to go greet her unwanted guest.

"The driveway is only for friends and customers. All others are supposed to park on the street." Hailey hit him with that before his feet had even finished touching down on the cement. Not that it gave Kyle even a slight pause as he slammed his door shut.

"Well, then it's a good thing I'm at least one of those." Casting her a grin as if she had only been teasing him, Kyle strutted on up. He had the body to back that walk. Something about the way the frayed and worn edges of his jeans hugged his hips drew a woman's eyes, seducing her with the smooth motion as he came closer.

All those muscles keeping his tummy hard and flat made sure a lady's gaze lingered, long and slow, before taking the easy trip up over that chest and the tanned tendons of his neck to curl around hard chin and fall into that smile.

It was pulled a little too much into a smirk at that moment, making her aware that he noticed just how long it took her to meet his gaze. Hailey's knees might have become infected with the same rubbery disease Cole afflicted them with, but Hailey had many more years learning how to get around that with Kyle.

"Get your truck out of my drive, Kyle."

"But I'm a customer." Kyle's complaint trailed very close behind her.

Hailey didn't even need the details. "No."

"Oh, come on, Hailey. I got cash, and what good business owner turns down cash."

"No."

"But this is serious business proposition."

"No."

"Aren't you the least bit interested?"

"No."

"Ah, come on, I come here hat in hand to seek your services as a professional. Now don't you think you could do the courtesy of at least hearing me out?"

Like a pit bull, he just never let go of anything, a trait that had driven her nuts in high school and still did. Flinging her wrenches back into the drawer, she slammed it closed before turning around and giving him one more, "No."

"What? What is it going to take to get you to give me a chance? You want me to go on my knees? I'll—"

"*Kyle.*"

"I ain't got no problem. See?" Somehow Kyle actually made kneeling sexy. "*Please, Hailey?*"

"Oh, for God's sake." Hailey left him there, heading for the open garage door.

If he thought she'd be stupid enough to fall for all his charm, then the man really didn't know her at all. *Or maybe he does* because her heart still raced, her knees still tingled, and worst of all, she could feel that vibration deep down in her soul. She felt alive in a way that made the sun brighter, the air sweeter, and the damn man in front of her almost irresistible.

"I'm begging you, Hailey." Kyle wobbled back and forth as he followed on his knees. "I need your help."

"Get out of my garage, Kyle," Hailey tossed back, completely unimpressed, "or I'll lock you in here."

"Damnit, Hailey. Why you got to be so stubborn?"

"Because I'm not dumb enough to fall for whatever trap Cole sent you over here to lay," Hailey retorted. Turning around, she confronted him. "So whatever prank you're planning, I'm not in the mood today."

"Cole?" Kyle either was a really good actor or honestly confused. Either way, the emotion carried him back to his feet. "What the hell does he have to do with this? Did he do something?"

"Did he do something?" Hailey coughed up a laugh at that, more from shock at Kyle' audacity. "Like you don't know."

"Know? Know what?"

"That Cole declared war on me this morning outside the Bread Box," Hailey explained calmly, waiting to see what Kyle had planned. It started with looking affronted. The grin fell from his features, and this time when he moved closer, he didn't have that swagger.

"I didn't hear about that."

"Bullshit."

"Serious, Hailey." Kyle came to a stop before her, all stern and concerned looking, but Hailey still didn't believe him. Why should she? They both knew that Cole couldn't get within a foot of her without danger to his person, so they sent Kyle, Kyle who had years of knowledge about how to get under her skin.

Just because she wanted to make sure she had a right to her anger, she held back, keeping calm as she asked, "Neither Cole nor Aaron nor Jake told you about how your asshole of a business partner took it on himself to spank me in a public parking lot?"

"Cole didn't come home last night, and I ain't seen those three all day. Been out shopping." Kyle's voice trailed off slightly as his gaze narrowed. "What did you do to Cole?"

The accusation in his tone, in his gaze, put her instantly on the defensive. For a second, she forgot this conversation wasn't real and responded from her gut. "Nothing."

"He just upped and spanked you for no reason?"

"He's an ass, what can I say?"

"Hailey."

"I kicked him, okay." Hailey raised her chin. "And I'm about to kick you if you don't get out of my garage because that's how little patience I have left today."

"Okay, here." Kyle fished his cell out of his pocket. Rapidly pressing buttons, he circled to her side, complaining every step of the way. "I was trying to build up to the moment, but since you're in such a crabby damn mood, just go on and take a look at that and then tell me to get out."

She didn't want to, but her eyes obeyed that command out of instinct. Dropping to the cell phone he shoved under her nose, her gaze locked on the thumb-sized picture of a rusted-out car. It took a second for it to register.

"*Oh, my God,*" Hailey whispered, awed despite herself. She couldn't help but to lift the phone a little closer as her gaze narrowed on the tiny details. "Is that…"

"A 1964 Studebaker Daytona." Kyle's dark purr tickled over her ear, igniting two passions at once as he growled, "An R4, Hailey, the rarest of the rare. Think about it, two four-barrel carburetors, original V-8, rated at 280 hp, but I bet we can crank more out of that bad boy."

Yes, we could. Hailey swallowed at that thought…*Ah, crap!*

Eyeing Kyle as she passed the phone back, she didn't know what he wanted. Her body, her humiliation, what price did he intend to exact for the prize he had dangled in front of her?

"What do you want, Kyle?"

"Help," Kyle snorted, doing a damn good job of looking innocent. "Shit, Hailey, I like Studebakers, but I ain't in love like you. I mean you can see the condition this car is in. It's been sitting down in Florida rusting until some guy passed and his kids went to unload the graveyard of cars in his backyard."

Backing the sincerity in his tone, Kyle gave her a level look, one that almost felt like an equal. "It might be a diamond one day, but it ain't going to get there without you. You know this car, Hailey. You know what it's supposed to look like, feel like, smell like, even sound like. I need your help."

"Huh."

Very impressive, his impassioned speech sounded good coming from him. It might have even sounded right if she didn't know the rascal lurking beneath that puppy-dog gaze. It didn't move her one bit, but it did make it hard not to smile.

"So, what? I'm supposed to come down to the shop and help you fix her up so you can sell her off?"

"Well," Kyle's shoulders rolled slightly, "I was going to have it hauled to the shop and sell out half the interest to Cole, but I thought maybe you'd like to take that half instead."

"You're offering me half a stake in that car?" Hailey smiled. "Why don't I just buy it outright from you? Hell, I'll pay you double and take it now."

"I don't think so, princess," Kyle smirked.

"Why not?"

"Why would I?"

"Because we both know once you put the time and the material into it, you ain't gonna double your cost at sale."

Kyle shrugged, a relaxed gesture that didn't match the predatory gleam in his gaze. "Not everything is about profit margins, Hailey."

Hailey froze. "So, you don't deny that this is a set up?"

"I don't deny when I saw it I thought first of you, just as I won't deny that I've considered the fact that you'd walk through hell for a car like this. I ain't asking you to go to hell, Hailey. I'm just asking you to work with me."

There came those puppy-dog eyes again. Kyle did sincere so well it almost scared her because it made even her question. Was it real? Hell if she knew, but Hailey knew she wouldn't be letting the Daytona go. He had her good and trapped, even knowing this might be a set-up.

Paranoid of the possibility, she gave in with ill grace. Turning, she stormed out of the garage without a word for him to follow or not. He did.

Kyle's footsteps thundered over her own softer steps across her porch, and the back door didn't slam shut behind her shoulder.

All the way to her checkbook in the living room desk, he shadowed her, making her feel more hunted than followed. The sensation put a slight tremble into her hand, and she scrawled out the check fast to hold it steady.

Ripping the check free of the register, she turned and shoved it at him. "This doesn't make us friends."

"But it does make us partners." The slow drawl matched Kyle's lazily satisfied motions as he took the check and folded it.

"That car comes here and Cole doesn't." Hailey didn't want there to be any misunderstanding on this point. "Not. Ever."

"It'll be here in the morning." The check disappeared into Kyle's pocket before his hands settled on his hips in a relaxed stance. "So you need help clearing out a spot in the garage?"

"Get out." Hailey added a point to that order.

"Don't you even want to talk about—"

"I'll see it in the morning." The mad rush she felt to get rid of him played well into her act. Hailey needed the time, the room to think. She couldn't do that with him here, grinning at her, infusing the very air she breathed with a musky, sexual scent that made her body just hum.

"But we have plans we have to—"

"Talk about it later." God, but she just wanted to test the strength of all those muscles. Shoving him toward the door seemed like a good excuse.

"You know this isn't a very gracious thank you. I certainly didn't agree to work with you, so you could make my life hell." Kyle carried on while she fumbled with the doorknob. Finally, it turned and the door swung free of its frame.

"Get out."

Laughing, shaking his head, Kyle got out. "See you tomorrow morning, princess."

Hailey took great pleasure in slamming the door on his smirk. The moment of victory didn't last but a second. Dissolving into tremors of need, Hailey leaned against the door. Even its hardwood surface wouldn't hold her up, and she slid down to the floor.

* * * *

Kyle still laughed at the memory of how flushed and fiery Hailey had gotten hours later as he watched GD's dart sail through the air before burying itself in the middle of the board. *Bull's-eye.* The clink and murmurs of Riley's bar didn't invade their little corner, perhaps because most of the nighttime crowd returned to the club to enjoy another night of revelry.

Tonight would be the competition and skills test that would rank the Cattlemen in order of abilities. Those rankings would carry over into auction when the men would get the opportunity to bid and win on the new crop of women waiting to be trained as slaves.

Actually, all those women were members. Far from being true virgins at the altar, they had the opportunity to request certain masters, or they could offer themselves up to the auction. Only one rule held at the club—during a woman's stay she only had one master, no matter how many lovers he shared her with.

Kyle had three such women in his corral until about a half hour ago when he told GD to take him off the schedule. He turned in his membership gladly because he only needed one feisty woman trying to defy him at every turn. Thank God, he now had at least one rope around her neck.

Kyle didn't doubt God's hand in his good fortune. Less than twenty-four hours ago, he'd been feeling itchy and wondering at that sense of restlessness that had invaded his bones. Then some force turned Hailey back into his life and gave him the leash to bind her there permanently. Kyle didn't tend to be a religious man, but he didn't argue with the spirits, either.

"I'm telling ya." GD stepped up to the board to pull his darts out as Kyle moved onto the line. "Cole's got his full focus set on Hailey now. I bumped into him out at the club, and he was freeing up his schedule."

"It won't last," Kyle predicted as he sent his first dart whizzing through the air. He wished it could because corralling a wild woman like Hailey would definitely be a fight to the finish without some backup. Cole, though, had set his bridge on fire when it came to Hailey, and Kyle didn't intend to get burned by those flames.

"You don't think?"

"I know." Kyle sunk his own bull's-eye. Cole would only be a negative in Kyle's column, and he'd earned enough of those on his own.

"And how's that?"

"Because you are going to make sure it doesn't." His third dart almost kissed the second one before Kyle looked over at GD. "Because you are going to find some Miss Double D to help keep him distracted."

GD swallowed down his gulp of beer before banging the glass onto the high-top table. "And why would I be doing that?"

"Because I'm asking you to do it."

Never one to hesitate to ask, the big bull rider considered Kyle for an unusual moment. "Why you working so hard to keep Cole from going after Hailey?"

Knowing nothing but the truth would satisfy GD, Kyle gave it to him. "Because I'm going after her."

"Then why ain't you going after her with Cole? You two share, anyway."

"Because Cole is a liability."

That brutally honest answer had GD's nose curling with distrust. "I don't know, Kyle. Cole and you are best friends, business partners, roommates, and you putting a girl in the middle of all that? This situation could get nasty, and I'm not sure I want to be sinking in a pile like that."

"I'm not asking you to." Kyle left his darts in the board to take the matter up close with GD. "Look, man, you know I've had a thing for Hailey since like the beginning of time."

Instead of being impressed, GD just snorted. "Why you saying that now? Huh? You got a thing that's burning all this time but ain't made no move until suddenly Cole's thinking of making his? You know how that sounds?"

"I know, but I didn't know Cole was making his move this morning when I turned in my membership to the Cattleman's Club."

That had GD snorting, not nearly impressed. "You didn't turn it in, Kyle. You suspended it. Whenever you change your mind, you know you're welcome back, so what kind of sacrifice is that supposed to be?"

"Damn it, GD. I'm telling you here and now, if this was just about a little pussy, you know I'd be game to let Cole join in. Hell, I'd be game still if I thought for a second he wanted something more than a little revenge, but what I'm after, Cole and his reputation is only going to get in the way."

"And you think you're going to fare any better? Because what? Your reputation is so much cleaner? Any sin Hailey can lay at Cole's feet she can lay at yours, too. Everybody in this town knows that you two are joined at the hip."

"That's my problem. I'm guilty by association."

GD snort rolled into a laugh at that. "Ain't that some bullshit. You're guilty all on your own, Kyle, or don't you remember the hell you rained down on Hailey's head through high school?"

"That was a long time ago."

"Time means nothing to a woman with a grudge."

Kyle scrunched his lips at that, unable to argue that point. "I guess I got some making up to do."

That mutter earned another smirk from GD. "Try some begging, boy."

"Trust me, my knees are already bruised."

"Is that a fact?" GD smirked. "Soon enough it will be 'yes, dear' and 'I have to check with Hailey—'"

"Shut up." Kyle shoved GD toward the line.

GD stumbled over toward the yellow line on the floor, barking, "Hey, you gonna get your darts out of the way?"

In his good time, and Kyle made that point silently. Annoyance didn't hold him quiet for the next few minutes. Dour contemplation did. Despite GD's skepticism, Kyle had always had a thing for Hailey.

A very special thing, and truth be told, it had annoyed him for most of his life—kind of like a dog who knew its owner's call meant having to crawl into a kennel for the night. Kyle had run as hard and fast as he could in the opposite direction in almost blind fear of being caged. Freedom had gotten lonely, and he tired himself out running.

"Your turn, lover boy." GD bumped him with more than that insult.

A hard shoulder had Kyle tipping back slightly as the mountain of a man cleared too big of a path for Kyle to avoid being hit. Kyle rolled with the motion, tracking GD around the curve of the table with his gaze.

"You ain't answered my question yet. You gonna help me with Cole?"

"And I was hoping you wouldn't ask it again," GD spat. "You know you're putting me in a shitty position, right?"

"And if there was any way to avoid it, I wouldn't ask. Hell, man, Cole's my best friend. You think I'd really do wrong by him? I'm just asking for a little time, and you can give me that. You control the schedule out at the club. Just make sure that enough of the right kind of women need his attention."

GD's jaw clenched before flexing outward. "You're a real son of a bitch, and you owe me, but yeah. I guess he can't complain about too much pussy, and God knows he got a pile of requests, but don't think I'm going to hold this dam forever. You say you got a thing for Hailey, then you better get your thing in gear."

That's just what Kyle planned to do. The belted bleeps of GD's cell phone cut off Kyle's intended assurance. As he listened and watched the big man, Kyle grew tense right along with GD's tone. Something had just come up. Not a happy something, but a bad one.

"I got to go." GD snapped his phone closed and reached for his dart case.

Like Kyle would let him walk out without an explanation. "What's up, man?"

"The Davis barn went up in flames." GD scowled. "Alex said somebody got caught in the backroom."

The pause there didn't take a genius to figure it out. Everybody knew what the backroom of the Davis barn was used for, and there would have only been one woman in it today.

"Everybody's all right, man, but I got to go." With that GD disappeared, leaving Kyle fumbling to call Hailey and get more answers.

Chapter 4

Monday, March 31st

Monday morning, Hailey stared through tired eyes at the tow truck backing down her drive. Eight o'clock and she managed to wash, dress, and feed herself, but Hailey still didn't feel awake and alive. The weight of worry fraying the edges of her exhausted body made watching the Daytona come home a bittersweet welcoming.

As wretched and unloved as the old Studebaker looked, it filled her with a sense of warmth to know the classic would be a beauty once again. That revival would come through her own hands and determination. She needed the work today. It would help deal with the stress.

The arrival of the Daytona and Kyle just emphasized how much stress she had coming toward her in the days ahead. He called Sunday night, sounding all concerned about Patton. Hailey believed he sincerely worried like everybody else in a small town who didn't plan too many untimely funerals. Thankfully, they wouldn't be this week, either.

Kyle could have found that out from any number of sources. He didn't need to call her to ask, but he had, giving Hailey the sinking suspicion he wanted into more than just her garage. The man wanted into her life. What remained a mystery was why.

"Morning, princess." Like a gladiator already claiming victory, he hopped out of the tow truck and strutted up.

"Morning, Kyle." Hailey managed to keep her tone even and her voice clear of emotion. Determined to start on a perfectly professional level with Kyle, she nodded to the space she cleared. "Go ahead and dump her. I cleared out a spot last night."

"I'm surprised you found the time." As if they had the kind of relationship that gave him any rights, he reached out to tuck a strand of hair behind her ear. "You're looking a little rough this morning, princess."

"Don't touch me." Hailey leaned away. "And I am tired, too tired, to deal with you, so could you just dump the Daytona and we'll roll her back into the garage?"

The grumpy rebuttal had him shifting back toward the tow truck, starting up the wench to angle the flat bed down toward the pavement. "Maybe you should have invested more time in sleeping than trying to clean out a spot for the car. You saved yourself, what, an hour of my company and still have a few thousand more to suffer?"

He said it like a joke, but Hailey could hear the honesty of his opinion embedded in the words. "I didn't clear it out just to get over on you," she retorted. "I just...needed to work."

The soft quality of those words seemed to penetrate Kyle's smirk, and his lips flattened. With a nod, he conceded. "I get that."

It took a good thirty minutes to lower the car and push its heavy ass back into the stall. Not trusting the breaks that had obviously worn through to dust, they braced her with thick wedges of wood under the tires. Toeing the last one into place, she came around the car. The only thing that disturbed her about the Studebaker was the man grinning over the hood at her.

"Ain't she sweet?"

"She's a rusted piece of shit." Hailey smiled.

That had Kyle's grin growing as he circled around the car to come stand with her at the front, staring down the long length of the rotted classic. "But she will be sweet once you and I get done with her."

Hailey knew where that kind of talk led. "Don't you even think about putting an arm over my shoulder."

"Well, there goes that moment." Kyle turned with his sigh as he began the long strut back to the tow truck. The man just had to look as good going as he did coming. "I'll be by tonight to start going over the details with you."

"What?" That had Hailey's eyes lifting off his ass to blink. "What do you mean by tonight?"

Kyle paused with his hand on the truck door to give her that straight look of his. "I mean, I'll bring the pizza."

"Don't bother." Hailey knew he wouldn't listen to her, but she intended to lodge her objection anyway. "I'll take a look at her today and then work up some plans. How about we just meet for lunch tomorrow?"

"Lunch tomorrow?" Kyle pondered that before shrugging.

He wanted her to think he said yes, but she knew he'd be on her doorstep at six. "I'll give you a call."

"You do that."

There came that grin again, a quick flash before he hoisted himself up into the truck. Hailey didn't trust that grin or the wave he gave out the window before rumbling down her drive. He'd be back, and she intended to have a welcome waiting for him.

* * * *

At 5:50 exactly, Hailey pulled off her gloves and stepped back to admire all she'd accomplished in one day. The frame didn't look too bad, but it didn't look too good, either. Not that she had the energy to tackle that problem now.

The long hours of non-stop work finally caught up with her. Her muscles ached, and her stomach started to revolt. She needed food, something beyond the last soda in the twelve pack she had stored out in the garage.

Thankfully, Kyle would be showing up with that pizza in ten minutes, not that she intended to rely on him. On the off chance she read his farewell wrong, a sandwich would be a good thing to be working on then.

Leaving her tools out and the lights on, she knew the first thing Kyle would see when he drove up—a naked car. The feeling of her life spinning out of control motivated her nicely today. She managed to get the whole car detailed out on paper, backed with pictures of just about every original inch, and still get all the body panels off, too.

For all the time it took, it didn't even feel like an hour to her. She'd been so focused on her task. Hailey loved the work. Letting lunch roll past and the phone go unanswered, she barely spared the time it took to pee for most of the day. It had all been worth it.

Not just for the car, but for Kyle. Scrubbing the grease and grime from her hands, she contemplated just how Kyle would take her answer to his arrogance. It'd probably have him a little upset and getting a little pushy. Hailey already knew her response. If he didn't like the way she did things, he could take his engine down to his shop and work by his damn self.

Slapping her sandwich together, Hailey kept her eye on the clock, getting more and more nervous as the minutes counted down to six. With her sandwich one inch from her mouth, the digital numbers morphed to six o'clock exactly the second her front door erupted in tremors as a hard fist pounded on it.

Struggling to put her grin in its place, she slapped her sandwich on the counter and went for the door. It shook before her very eyes as he pounded again. She paused to take a deep breath, schooled her features into a scowl, and opened the door.

"I brought the pizza."

A box smelling like heavenly delight to her empty stomach almost smacked her in the nose. Stepping back quickly before he physically ran her over, Kyle didn't even appear to take notice of how he all but shoved her out of the way. Passing by, he headed down the hall toward the kitchen calling out to her over his shoulder.

"Since you didn't tell me what you wanted this morning, I got what I want."

Hailey slammed the door in response before taking off after the man. Just as they had yesterday morning, her heart raced, her knees wobbled, and she skidded into the kitchen with a welcoming enthusiasm she hoped read like outrage.

"Meat lover's delight," Kyle informed her as though they'd actually been holding a conversation. Plopping the pizza on the counter, he cast her a dirty look. "You know, you could have at least showered, princess, because you're smelling kind of rank over there. Oh, sandwich."

Just like that, he picked up the sandwich she made and started eating. Holding it in his mouth like a dog, he just kept on acting like he owned her kitchen. Rifling through her cupboards and drawers as he amassed plates and silverware, Hailey stared until he glanced back over at her. Pulling the sandwich from his mouth, he even managed to make chewing look sexy.

"I'm not kidding about that stink, princess."

Like hot iron to the backside of a cow, his rudeness startled her back to the moment at hand and her role as the upset and indignant host. "What are you doing here?"

"I told you this morning, pizza and talk. We got plans to make, princess, so I'd really appreciate it if you'd get yourself cleaned up quick."

Ignoring that reference to her dirty state and not letting embarrassment catch her for smelling bad in front of a hot man, Hailey stepped into that argument ready to go. "I thought we agreed to make those plans over lunch *tomorrow*. Tonight, I haven't got time."

"Why's that? Didn't get all the body panels off today?"

Hailey smirked, feeling her moment coming. "It's half my car sitting in my garage. What, am I supposed to twiddle my thumbs until you get off work every day?"

Braving the foul air, Kyle met her in the middle of her kitchen to give back just as he got. "You could wait until we talked, which we could get to doing if you'd stop trying to rush me out the door, partner."

"And you should be thankful to have such a hardworking partner."

"I would be thankful for an honest one who didn't scheme behind my back—"

"Scheme? Behind your back? What do you—"

"And I certainly could ask for one who isn't so argumentative, not to mention the *smell*."

"Something smells all right in this kitchen, but it *ain't me*."

"You know, it makes me hard when you argue with me like this."

Hailey retreated instantly from that provocative statement. The grin weighing down on her had her taking another quick step back. She didn't trust him in that moment anymore than she did herself.

Kyle matched her step back with one forward, his grin running a little wild as his gaze traveled over her length. "You know, I could help you with that stink, princess. I'm actually known for making showering interesting."

The tremors beneath her feet warned her the scales had started to tip precariously in his favor. The slide had her feet stumbling backward in retreat.

* * * *

Kyle really hated watching Hailey storm off. He hadn't been lying. He could work some magic in a shower.

Ah, hell, another day.

Piling the plates, silverware, and napkins on top of the pizza box, he stuck the sandwich back in his mouth as he carried it all out to the living room.

The princess better hurry up if she wanted any food because Kyle didn't wait for anybody. Making himself at home in her house, he availed himself of the remote and settled in to enjoy his dinner. He enjoyed it all the more when he heard the shower kick on in the other room. The moment held the kind of domestication he'd been looking for.

One day, Hailey would come out of that shower wrapped up in a big fluffy robe. She'd settle down beside him on the couch for dinner, but it wouldn't be long before he had her naked and panting over the cushions.

"What the hell are you doing eating there? I have a dining area, you know. And get your boots off my table. What is wrong with you? Were you born in a barn?"

So much for that fantasy. Kyle sighed and glanced over at Hailey to give her a straight answer. "Yes, and I was raised by pigs."

The response earned him a classic wrinkled-nose look of disgust. Hailey mastered that expression around the age of nine. "Ha. Ha. Ain't you just a laugh a minute?"

Say what she wanted, the little woman sat down, which meant he won round two. That's probably why she got even crankier with him. "Listen, Kyle, we need to talk."

"That's what I've been saying since yesterday. All it got me was a shove out the door."

The way her jaw flexed at that provocation made it that much harder to keep a straight face while he said it.

"Yes, well, it would help if you did less talking."

"But you just said we needed to talk."

"I mean I need to talk, and you need to shut up and listen."

"Now see," he lifted his boots off her coffee table to sit up straight, "that's the kind of thing that doesn't make me real interested in listening. I have this rule. People insult me and, well, I get them back. You don't want me to be thinking like that given how many hours of work we have ahead of us, do you?"

"That's my point exactly." Hailey leaned in a little too excited for Kyle's liking. He had a sick feeling he knew what came next. "We don't even get along, Kyle. How are we supposed to work together?"

"Well, it would help if you'd start being nice."

She met that helpful suggestion with a glower that matched her growl. "Maybe it would just be easier if we didn't try at all."

"I ain't selling you the car, Hailey."

"I'm not asking you to. I'm suggesting that we lift that engine out and you take it down to the shop to work on and I'll—"

"Nope." Kyle cut her off with that simple, solemn protest.

"But you haven't heard what—"

"Don't need to." He knew it pissed her off when he interrupted her a second time. Her little ears started to glow red, and her lips thinned out to a tight line.

"Kyle—"

"Listen, Hailey." Kyle sat straight up and turned to confront her. "I brought that car here for both of us to work on, and both of us are going to work on it. That's what we're going to do. We're going to learn to get along and work together, and who knows? Maybe even have some fun."

"Like me falling into your bed."

"Oh, princess." Kyle sighed and risked getting bitten to reach out and cup her cheek. "If that's all I was after, you'd already be bent over the edge of this couch moaning how good I am."

Beneath his palm, he felt the delicate muscle of her throat contract with her swallow. "So, what is it you really want?"

"You." The flash of fear that shot through her eyes with that declaration didn't go unnoticed by Kyle. Sensing he pushed just as far as he should in the moment, he released her to flop back on the couch. "Just you eating my pizza and relaxing. Is that such a bad thing to want, Hailey?"

Giving in after a long moment, Hailey snatched a slice of pizza out of the box. She ignored him as he flipped through the channels, silently brooding in her corner of the couch. Kyle let her be, settling on some caught-on-tape show.

It didn't take long for the car chase to entrance Kyle with one near miss after another. Finally, as the suspect hit over 120 miles per hour, he lost control. Veering off the road right before a bridge, the car went airborne. Shooting over the gulley like a rocket, the car disappeared beneath the bridge's edge. Anticipating death, or at least some blood, Kyle leaned forward in rapt attention. A second later, a crash along with a large puff of dust had him laughing.

"Holy shit." Just out of habit, he turned to look at the person beside him. "Did you see that?"

"I've seen it before," Hailey grumbled. "The idiot lives, you'll see him running up the bank in a moment. Yeah, right there."

Kyle watched as the footage turned to a short foot chase that ended abruptly in a replay of the flying vehicle. "I bet they beat the crap out of that boy."

"Probably."

"Damn, if that ain't a *Dukes of Hazard* moment if I ever seen one." Kyle turned to grin at Hailey, who looked just a tad bit less pissed. "Hey, you ever get up any speed coming down Elm Lane and hit those train tracks?"

"Perhaps a few times, but I'm not going to break an axel just for a two-second rush."

"What's that supposed to mean?" He asked it, but he couldn't hold a straight face as he did.

"Don't even give me that look. Everybody knows what you did to Jimmy Harton's Alfa Romeo playing good ol' boy, and what made you think you do that with such a delicate car, I don't know."

"I was *sixteen*, Hailey."

"I was fifteen, and I knew it was dumb when I heard the story." That came back with the clear intention of just giving him grief. The hard edge of anger had worn down on her tone, and Hailey even leaned forward to help herself to his pizza. He took that as a good beginning and celebrated with his own slice.

"Yeah, well, just because something is dumb doesn't mean you shouldn't do it." Kyle settled back against the couch slowly, waiting to see if she'd snap at him for moving ever so slightly closer.

"Spoken like a true man," Hailey snorted.

Perhaps, but this man had gotten within an inch of his princess. That made him the smartest man in town by Kyle's reckoning

Chapter 5

Thursday, May 1ˢᵗ

"You going to stare at that man all night long?"

Rachel's pointed question drew Hailey's glower from Kyle's back toward her friend. Almost five weeks, that's how long she suffered. First pizza, then Chinese, take-out barbeque, fast food, sandwiches, night after night of food, conversation, working side by side out in her garage, it seemed every time she turned around, there he was.

They laughed, they argued, they just talked, and what the hell did that build into? What she really wanted to know was how a man worked so hard for so many hours and still managed to smell good enough to lick. Hailey could have sworn that Kyle went out of his way to make being sweaty and greasy too damn sexy.

"I'll take that as a yes." Rachel's tart response had Hailey realizing her friends had been waiting for an answer.

"Leave her alone." Heather waved her beer at Rachel. "Kyle's good to look at."

"But he ain't looking back," Rachel retorted. "And there is a point when a look goes from interested to pathetic. Now, wipe the drool off your chin, Hailey, and focus. I got a real problem here."

"I'm paying attention." *To the tight ass leaning over the pool table behind Rachel's shoulder.*

That's how bad it had gotten. She couldn't even blink and not look at him. Thankfully, she hadn't started panting, but Hailey wanted to. She wanted that and a whole lot of other dirty, little wicked things. The tempting ideas and luring fantasies nearly became obsessions, which was just why she ducked out of work for a girl's night.

She should have known the bastard would show up. He said it himself that first night. Kyle wanted her, he was coming after her, and he didn't intend to give her any room to hide.

"Hello?" A hand waving in front of her face played peek-a-boo with the image of Kyle and his buddies gathered around the pool table. "Earth to Hailey."

"I'm sorry." Hailey blinked, smothering down the heat of those unwelcomed thoughts to offer Rachel a small smile. "You were saying?"

"Oh, no." Rachel shook her head. "You're not getting off that easy. Say it again, and try a little sincerity."

Sucking in a breath to bring her straight up in her seat, Hailey met Rachel's gaze. "I'm sorry, Rachel."

"No, you're not." Rachel sighed and glanced back over at the men. "But I forgive you nonetheless. I know that puppy-eyed disease anywhere."

"Don't start with me, Rachel," Hailey warned her, not in the mood to take the teasing she probably deserved.

"You got it bad." Rachel leaned in to emphasize just how badly Hailey apparently had it.

"I do not."

"So bad," Heather echoed.

"*I do not.*"

"You're a stone's throw away from being like Marie down at the grocery store." Rachel's gaze cut to Heather. Both women gave a dramatic sigh as they fell back, speaking in unison.

"*Oh, Kyle.*"

"Oh." Hailey's head hit the table as she tried to hide from the truth. "I don't want to have it this bad. Not if he doesn't have it this bad."

"Oh, honey, he does." Heather patted her on the back. "It's just he's a Cattleman. Their whole thing is to control their wants."

Rolling her chin to the side, she gave Heather a one-eyed glare. "That really doesn't help."

"Nothing helps," Rachel groused. "Take it from me, Hailey, resist."

"Rachel." Heather added a look to that tone that left no doubt who the mother at the table was.

"I'm just saying we're fighting a war here. Look at me," Rachel gestured to herself, "I'm trying to establish my career as a credible reporter, and I have a man at home who thinks the most dangerous thing I should do with my life is bake cookies.

"You see, it's all my fault. I didn't run the bonfire story, and now he and Adam think they can just boss me all around. Well, I don't think so. I'm getting smart, and I'm not telling those bullies nothing about my next project."

Between ogling and brooding, Hailey managed to catch enough of Rachel's complaining to know what that meant. Smirking, she sat slowly back in her chair. "And just how long do you think you can hide your investigation into a prostitution ring? Hmm?"

"Long enough to get my story," Rachel shot back with no obvious concern. "Besides, I have a little help."

"Kitty Anne isn't going to save you from Killian and Adam," Rachel snorted.

"I'm not talking about Kitty Anne." Rachel smiled so smugly even Hailey tensed and she didn't know what the hell for. Hailey just followed Heather's lead as she straightened up in her seat.

Tapping Hailey on the shoulder, Heather nodded at Rachel. "What do you think Killian and Adam are going to do to her when that story hits the paper?"

"I don't know." Hailey shook her head, going along with the game. "But I'm thinking we're not going to be seeing much of her after."

"What do you mean?"

"I mean Killian and Adam are cops, Rachel." Hailey grinned, unable to help the mirth that bubbled up. "I'm thinking you're going to be wearing metal cuffs once they find out about your little project."

"And that's my point," Rachel shot back. "What am I supposed to do? Just give over because they're bigger and stronger?"

"And there are two of them," Hailey tacked on. "At least, I only have to deal with one."

She must have made a joke because both of Hailey's friends laughed at her response. Rachel's mouth crested on the edge of words, but they got cut off by the wild catcalls and howls as a group of boys who barely looked legal enough to drink fell in through Riley's front door.

Appearing already drunk, they piled in. Seven…eight…nine of them, and that was enough to make Hailey tense, right along with the other two women at the table. In that instant, Riley's went from the quiet comfort, almost reminiscent, of a library to the chaotic whirl of a near frat party.

"Well, ladies," Heather sighed. "I think that's the end of the night."

It would be best to go now before those guys noticed their table was the only one without a man in sight. Not to mention the dark looks the established locals lingering in the corners started to cast the interlopers' way. Hailey knew the smell of a bar fight coming. Like rain, it sweetened the air before it tightened down into violence. That made retreat prudent. Only one obstacle remained. It was Wednesday night, and Riley only hired waitresses for the weekends.

"So, who's going to wade in to the bar to pay?" Hailey had a sick feeling her name would be the answer to the question she put forth to the group.

All three women eyed the men who banded around it. None of them volunteered. Instead, Rachel threw Hailey under the bus she saw coming a mile away. "Let Hailey do it."

"Me?" Hailey shot Rachel a look as if she'd lost her mind. "Why me?"

"Because you got protection."

"And how's that?"

"Kyle's watching you now."

That had her gaze snapping back to the pool tables stretched out along the opposite side of the bar. Sure enough, Kyle's eyes locked in on hers, and even over the distance she could read the silent warning. He didn't want her going near those men. Finally, after five weeks, he was the one looking itchy.

"All right, I'll settle up the bill."

She might have been talking to Rachel, but her gaze never left Kyle's. In that instant when she shoved away from her chair, he straightened off the wall. Kyle shook his head at her as she started to move toward the bar. Hailey rewarded him by sticking her tongue out.

"Hey, darlin'. Is that invitation?" Before Hailey could fend him off, one of the drunk interlopers swept her up in a foul embrace.

* * * *

"You didn't have to hit him, you know. *I could have hit him.*"

"Yeah, princess, but it wouldn't have hurt him, and that's what counts."

That drunken slur ended with a yelp as Hailey reached across the seat to give Kyle the pinch he deserved for pissing her off so royally tonight. "Did that hurt?"

Whimpering back into the corner of the Chevy's long bench seat, Kyle gripped his arm and pouted. "You're mean, Hailey Mathews. Just mean."

"And you're an ass," she shot back without any heat. How could she take him seriously?

He'd just thrown down like an eighteen-year-old only to come up grinning like a drunken fool. Not that she believed his inebriated act for a minute, but she went along with it. Given he'd put some effort into the charade and even conned Killian into lying for him, Hailey thought the least she could do was play her part.

Besides, she suspected she knew how this play ended. He'd need help inside, probably try to sweet talk her into helping him all the way to his bed. Then, he'd strike. The very idea of which thrilled her.

"I am not." Kyle labored back into a proper sitting position with overly dramatic indignation. "I haven't had an ass since I was eighteen, and I'm now thirty-one. That's ten years that I have been officially assless."

With a sudden lift and turn, he presented his very hard rear up for inspection. "See, ain't nothing there."

Now that was a lie, not that Hailey looked. Not that she had to. She had years of staring to go by. "Oh, sit down, you damn drunk."

"That's your problem, Hailey." Kyle plopped back down on the seat. "You don't drink enough."

"Oh, yeah. I should aspire to be a bar-brawling alcoholic such as yourself."

"Well, at least if you were drunk, I'd have some grease when it came to conning you out of those clothes."

Hailey's heart almost stopped with that silky purr. He couldn't be more direct than that. The threat, or promise, put images in her head that held her response locked deep in her throat. All sound stayed there as the minutes ticked by and Kyle remained quietly in his seat.

It seemed like she almost escaped the moment when he grinned. "You know what I got?"

"VD?" That instant retort broke the tension.

"Ha. Ha. Ha. Ain't you just a stand-up comedienne."

Hailey rolled her eyes at the insult in his tone. "I ain't the one who belongs to the sex club."

"I don't belong to any sex club."

How he managed to pull off that bold-faced lie with sincerity amazed Hailey. "Kyle, *I* saw you there. Remember the night of the orgy?"

"Oh, yeah." Back to happy for all the wrong reasons, he tried to purr, but it came out a little comical sounding. "And just what were you doing at an orgy, Little Miss Hailey?"

"Don't touch me." She smacked the hand he snaked her way with that lewd suggestion. "And I think you know what I was doing there. I wasjust there helping Patton piss off the Davis brothers."

"Oh, yeah." Kyle clearly savored the memory. "You know, Hailey, I don't think any woman ever actually pulled a fast one on Cole until you and Patton got him that night."

"I guess I should be proud then, huh?"

"Or worried."

Hailey didn't like the sound of that, or how much Kyle enjoyed saying it. "What's that supposed to mean?"

"Nothing."

He made a lie out of that answer with just a look. Sending sparkles of something very dangerous dancing up her spine, his grin certainly didn't say "nothing." She shook them away by bringing Kyle's truck to another hard stop. This time in a driveway, his drive way.

Whatever he meant, he hadn't been warning her of what came next because Cole's truck didn't clog the driveway. Apparently, whatever Kyle's plans, they didn't include his best friend. That should have assured her, but for that good ol' boy grin, she still didn't trust him.

Keeping a stern eye on him, she leaned slowly across his lap for his door handle. Kyle got the message and held his hands up in surrender even as his lips quivered with laughter. They straightened right back out once she managed to shove his door open.

"Get out."

"Aren't you going to help me to the door?"

"No." Hailey snorted. "And I ain't gonna help you take your pants off, either. Now get out."

"It's my truck." Kyle sounded like he just figured that fact out.

"Yeah, and you can walk back to the bar to pick it up in the morning." Because that was the price he paid for this show.

"Mean," Kyle pouted. "And after all I've done for—"

His complaint got cut off as he whooshed out of sight, disappearing over the edge of the seat. Having already started to swing his legs out the door, Kyle fell out of the truck, banging his way down to the cement drive. Hailey closed her eyes and let her head hit the steering wheel.

"Ow."

It became almost painful in that moment to fight back the laughter. *The dumbass.* Kyle really would go to any length to win. For some strange reason, the idea that she was his prize warmed her in ways she would prefer to ignore.

"Hailey?"

Kicking the foot brake down, ripping the key out of its socket, slamming the truck door with more force than necessary, Hailey didn't have to act hard to pull off an air of high indignation. Stomping around the front of the truck, she towered over him, refusing to show any sympathy at all for his little boy, boo-boo expression.

"I knew you'd come."

"Oh, stuff it," Hailey shot back as she latched on to the hand he offered her. Yanking on his arm, Hailey couldn't have lifted Kyle if he hadn't helped by shoving upward. Ungracefully, Kyle managed to make it back onto his feet, what little use they provided him. Hailey bore most of his weight over her shoulders as he leaned into her and slurred.

"I take back what I said about you being mean."

That's because he hadn't gotten her to the edge of his bed. It just seemed a miracle that he suddenly needed her help when he managed to tackle the jerk who kissed her with the lethal agility of a sober man.

"You smell nice."

So did he. Just like that he had her thinking about how even the slight tang of alcohol only added to the spicy aroma of man. Drunk or not, ass or assless, the one thing Kyle would be to the day he died was tempting. With that mop of dark hair and those sparkling eyes matched up with his square chin and big grin, he had that fallen-from-Heaven thing going on.

"And you have the prettiest hair I ever did see." Kyle managed to tangle a finger in one of her curls, pulling on it when she about slammed him into the exterior wall. "Just as soft as silk."

"Yeah, yeah, yeah."

Hailey clenched against the internal melting that always happened when he got too close. As sweet as he was being now, it became a struggle to hold back the tide, but she managed. They wouldn't be playing along to his script where he lured her in with all the sweet compliments before he got his ropes out.

She let that message roll with a jerk of her head, pulling free of his touch. "I know I'm pretty when you're drunk. Now, which key is the magic one?"

His glazed-over gaze didn't focus on the shiny set of keys she clinked in front of him. Instead, he gave her a sickeningly sweet look. "You always been pretty, Hailey."

"And you've always been a good liar."

No denial, his grin just widened. "Yeah, but there are some things a man just can't bluff through. Not like a woman."

Unable to control the twitch in her lips, Hailey managed to bite back her snort of laughter. "You have a lot of women bluff through it with you Kyle?"

"If I say no, you'll think I'm just too dumb to know better." Yes, she would. "Real question is would you try to bluff it?"

Before she could answer that idiotic question, Kyle's grin twisted slightly as his gaze did a lazy once over of her. "Not that you'd have to. The real question is, could you hold it back?"

With a pointed roll of her eyes that hid the heat warming up through her veins at the suggestion in his tone, Hailey jangled the ring in her fingers. "Focus on the keys, Kyle."

"That's one of my favorite games, seeing how long I can keep a woman on the edge. Crying, screaming, babbling, completely at my mercy."

That stroked like fire over all the wrong parts of her, a warning roll of liquid heat that threatened to overwhelm without too much more provocation. "Fine, sleep on the porch."

"This one." He betrayed his sobriety with those reflexes. No drunk had the ability to snatch the one key out the dozen on his ring even as her hand had already started to retract. The move came and went in a blink of an eye, but still she let it hold her for a long pause, silently warning him his game slipped.

He struck back with a smile so goofy only an inebriated man would wear it. Just because he pulled the look off too well, she kept her own critical glance on him as she tried to jam the key into the lock. Not being her door, it actually required her to turn her attention to finding the hole.

"You know," Kyle started in what might have been an attempt at a philosophical tone, "I never did tell you what I got."

"I really don't need to hear about your syphilis," Hailey retorted as the front door swung in.

"There you go again, being mean when I was about to be nice," Kyle complained. That didn't stop him from giving her most of his weight as she helped peel him off the wall.

"Fine," Hailey grunted as she managed to get him over the threshold. Aiming for the couch just a few feet away, she really did wish she had the balls just to drop him on the floor. He deserved it. "Tell me what you got."

Like the magic words 'open sesame,' he'd been waiting for her to take the bait. In a sudden rush of motion too fast to distinguish the individual details, Hailey went from trudging his heavy ass across the floor to being pinned against him. The door slammed into its frame so hard she could feel the vibrations against her back even as a growl tickled over her breast while it worked its way through his chest.

"You."

"Uh, Kyle." She'd been expecting a move, but this one still threw her off. Knowing he'd be rubbing up against her hadn't prepared her for the reality of the delightful sensation. Instead of keeping to her game and putting a little struggle into it, Hailey only wiggled to entice the frenzy of thrills the delicious motion caused.

She certainly didn't argue with the head dipping down toward her. The gentle bush of his lips over hers robbed her completely of the ability to respond. Frozen in shock, she could almost hear the tinkling of alarm bells go off somewhere in the cold, dark recesses of her reason.

They warned her that she wasn't leading this game anymore. He was. All the worry of those internal whispers drowned under the smooth curl of Kyle's own husky growl.

"I got you, Hailey Mathews, and that's all I ever wanted."

* * * *

She doesn't stand a chance.

Kyle didn't intend on giving her the opportunity to find one. It had been a minor miracle that he managed to con Hailey through his front door. After five weeks of trying to figure out how to get around all her defenses, he lucked out tonight. There would be no backing down.

With the advantage of surprise holding her still, he forced her lips open for his invasion, intent on total domination. Plundering the honey depths of her mouth, Kyle growled when her own tongue rallied and tried to shove his out. It was a half-hearted attempt that didn't have the backing of the rest of her body.

Snaking, dueling, he lured her between the vise of his lips and then sucked. Like she'd been hit by electricity, Hailey arched, moaning and then gloriously snapping. He could almost hear the whoosh of all her uptight layers melting in that single moment. A man never knew what lurked beneath, and Kyle had bet the bank it would be a sensual woman of needs.

What he got was a wanton vixen rubbing against him as her lips pressed back and took command of the kiss. In that single instant, she robbed him of every rational thought. The feel of her teasing the hardened tips of her plump breasts against his chest had Kyle growling and doing some rubbing of his own. It felt so good. She was so soft. With that, all the well-planned stages of Hailey's seduction disappeared under the onslaught of lust so long denied.

Then, it was on. A full on battle of the tyrants as each warred for control. *Hard cider.* That's what she tasted like. A little sweet, a little spice, and the full-bodied flavor of intoxicating woman, she intoxicated him. If Kyle hadn't been drunk before, he sure as hell was now.

His whole body jerked forward, his thigh slamming through hers when she sucked his tongue like candy.

She shouldn't have done that.

All the fine plans of seduction he crafted over the past weeks wilted beneath the savage need to have her now.

Bedroom. He had to get her into the bedroom—as in *now.*

Not daring to give her a single second to find reason to deny him, Kyle spun her from the door, still trapped in his embrace. Stumbling, stepping on each other's feet, they crashed through the living room in the stubborn refusal to give up the kiss. His thigh bumped along the end of the couch before cracking into the hard, wooden corner of a table.

The sharp pain had him flinching enough to end the kiss. Annoyed at the delay and the perceived retreat, he barely gave Hailey enough time to gasp for breath before he put a shoulder into her stomach and lifted her up to be carried off. With a shriek and peel of laughter, Hailey chastised him.

"Put me down, you drunk, before you drop me."

He'd drop her, all right, on his bed a second after he kicked the door closed. Now, she was all his. Kyle didn't wait a moment longer to start enjoying his well-earned victory.

Chapter 6

A rolling bubble of laughter popped out of Hailey's mouth, eliciting a growl from Kyle, who appeared to take the giggle as a personal challenge. Fumbling in his rush, he began to tear the clothes off his body just like the barbarian he reverted into. Not that she had a right to cast any stone his way.

This was what she wanted, Kyle unleashed, in too much of a hurry to play any stupid games. She wanted him for all his power and his strength, but more than anything, Hailey just wanted to know what it was liked to be possessed by him.

Owned by him.

Hailey squashed that thought even as it growled out from her womb. Wet, heated longing dripped from her body defied her attempt to reign in lust with reason. Sex, it would just be sex, and that would be more than enough.

Even if it wasn't, even if things took a turn from here, it didn't matter anymore. There might be a million and one reasons that she would regret this moment for the rest of her life, but there was one single one that assured she'd regret not indulging in the moment anyway. The best one was stripping fast in front of her.

Boy, but he does look better out of his clothes than in them.

Kyle rippled, a graceful flow of flexing muscles as he bent and turned, working on his jeans and boots. Youth and stamina fairly glowed with his tan, but the fine layer of dark hair dusting over his arms and chest spoke to just how much a man he actually was. Hailey just had to touch. She'd regret it if she didn't.

Just once…so smooth…and hard…

Like satin stretched tight over heated rocks, that's what the sides of his waist felt like beneath her palm. Her fingers followed the vibrations of the rumble building in his chest, delighting at the purely male feel of the sound. God help her, she wanted to touch more, even if it was Kyle.

That just made the way he jerked and groaned when she tweaked his nipple all the more satisfying. Her attraction to him was undeniable, dripping out of her pussy in bold proof that the past antagonisms meant nothing to this moment but to make it even more thrilling.

It made her savor the power she had to make his muscles tremble as she slid her hand down to cup the heavy, pulsing length of his erection. Every single blood-swollen inch belonged to her, his master. Hailey's fingers tightened at the very thought, squeezing down on Kyle's cock hard enough to make it jerk.

With the snarl of a man gone rabid, she barely had a second to realize that he snapped his leash before he flattened her back into the mattress. She felt the almost painful press of his fingers into her waist a second before her shirt shredded up the middle, her gasp getting swallowed by the groan as she found the tender globes of her breasts instantly under attack.

The sound elicited a growl from Kyle, who retaliated simply by snapping the clasp at the front of her bra, and then she could feel every single callused ridge of his work-roughened hands caressing over the smooth skin of her breasts. Like electric sparks, the sweet friction had her twisting and moaning as she sought more of the delicious sensations.

"Now it's your turn."

The air for her question got sucked out in a shrill whimper as his thumbs stroked out over her nipples, pressing and rolling the tender tips with such excruciating slowness her whole body twisted trying to follow the titillating caress.

"Look at me, Hailey." She didn't want to heed that husky command, but her silent resistance only got her tender tip pinched. Groaning over the abuse, her eyes cracked open only to flutter wide when he released. Blood rushed into her nipple amplifying the sharp tingly sensation until it flooded through her body.

"Oh..." Hailey arched, wanting to try that again.

"I said look at me." This time, she offered no resistance as she tried to focus on the features chiseled out of the shadows. "If you don't want this, you got to say so now."

Like she could say no now. Hailey snorted. He was an idiot if he didn't realize that moment passed several minutes ago. Not that she thought he really meant to give her an out. If he had, he wouldn't have chased his murmur across the curve of her breast. Whispering kisses across her flushed skin, Kyle made the ripple of pleasure bloom into a flood as his lips closed over her nipple.

Pure, liquid heat rolled down her spine at the first velvety lick. Her muscles contracted under the sudden spiral of tension that twined in its wake, making her arch. Digging her head into the mattress, her legs bent around his thighs, capturing him as they flexed around the solid feel of his muscle. Right there is where she wanted him, there where the length of his erection pressed down on her aching flesh, making it burn against the denim rubbing against it.

Like a cat lapping at milk, his head dipped to let his tongue lick and roll over her tender tit, making her mew as she ground her pussy harder, desperate to feel him skin to skin. His tongue rolled her nipple, his teeth nibbling across the sensitive tip, teasing and tormenting, but always riling the carnal hunger cresting through her body.

It tore through her in a long, toe-to-head wave that crashed only to be reborn again as he sucked her tender tip deep into his mouth. The heated massage of his kiss caused her body to contract, winding tighter and tighter until she mewed and whined, trapped in the painful agony of needing more.

Like a call to the wild, he heeded her body's pleading gyrations. His travels took him from her breasts, and Hailey instantly lodged a complaint as the cool air pebbled her nipples painfully. Digging her freed fingers into the silken locks of his hair, she tried to yank him back into the position, heedless of the way he worked at the waistband of her jeans.

The only solace came in the form of liquid flames as his fingertips barely danced over the sides of her pussy, just flicking past her clit. Crying out in true pain, she rammed her cunt into his hold only to gasp as the rough caress ignited an uncontrollable inferno.

It didn't matter what he did then as long as he kept grinding that palm down just like that. Hailey panted through the sensations, letting the sugary vines of rapture twine around her, contorting her body as she fought always for just a little more.

* * * *

Kyle got clocked beneath the eye as Hailey's leg windmilled. Her heel glanced off his cheek and rammed into his shoulder as she almost unseated him. Grunting, he worked to get her damn jeans down her legs, having to catch them midair.

Lord, but Hailey was the squirmiest, loudest, most untamed woman he ever fucked. More wild and savage than he ever dared to dream, she lured his own feral nature to the surface. Snarling in annoyance as he finally jerked her jeans free, Kyle didn't bother to battle for her underwear, but instead shredded the cotton panties barring him from the cunt creaming all over his palm.

Smooth skin gleamed in the shadows, but it wasn't enough. He waited all these years to have Hailey naked and spread before him, and by God he wanted to enjoy seeing it. Clicking on the bedside light caused her to groan as if he somehow shattered her dream, but the yellow glow only illuminated his greatest fantasy.

Sleek, rounded with the softness of woman and the graceful lines of muscle, Hailey writhed like a sensual goddess across the dark folds of his comforter. The sight of her breasts, flushed and reddened from his mauling, had Kyle crawling over her to give them another taste.

As velvety soft and addictively sweet as he remembered, her tits were a delight he could have feasted on for hours but for the rapture of finally feeling her as he always wanted to—skin to skin. Kyle slid his cock easily through the plump, swollen lips of her pussy to be bathed in the sultry embrace of her cunt.

Reckless and impatient, it only took one teasing rub to have Hailey shrieking out and grinding up. Her nails dug into his hips as she began humping herself along his length in a mad dash to find her own release. The sheer audacity of her actions had the Cattleman in him snarling with annoyance as his head came off her breast.

That was his pussy, and it got pleasured when he pleasured it. A lesson he hammered home by letting her wind herself up into a fever pitch of panting and straining before simply lifting free of her hold. She damn near took a chunk out of his side in her refusal to let go.

Her instant reward for causing him to flinch had her nearly lifting off the bed with her scream. Open handed, he walloped her cunt, and it wasn't even as bad as it could have been given he didn't have her properly spread. They'd get to that once she calmed down because she reverted into pitching an outright fit. Her hands daring to come down and tend to the demands of her pushy pussy.

Having had just about enough of her attitude, Kyle brushed aside her hand as his own tunneled in to trap her clit in a firm pinch. The pressure had her going still, just he like knew it would. Even with the mews seeping out of her throat and the slow grind of her hips as he held her clit, Hailey settled down long enough to focus her fogged-over eyes in his direction.

"You going to need a lot of training, darlin'."

She surprised him with her ability to actually smirk. "I ain't never going to be trained, Kyle, so you might as well just get to the fucking. I hear you're actually supposed to be somewhat good at *that*."

That was a challenge if he ever heard one, and no woman, *ever*, had been dumb enough to challenge him on this. Especially not when he still held her clit in his merciless control. A fact that he reminded her of with a twist as he snarled out a vow.

"You're going beg, Hailey Mathews. Beg until you go hoarse."

He didn't know if Hailey heard him, but she could feel him. Pushing her legs wide, he settled onto his knees between her splayed legs and enjoyed the view. Naked, smooth, pink, and glistening with need, her little cunt showed him all her secrets, and he settled in to take a better look.

Thumbing back the slick folds, Kyle had just tilted his head to take the first lick of his newly claimed cunt when Hailey's hands jammed into his hair and shoved his face into her pussy. With a matching lift, she slammed her pelvic bone into him, making him bite his own tongue.

"*That is it!*" Kyle roared.

If he was coming out of this bruised and injured, she'd come out of it not able to walk for the next week. Giving into the urge to gorge himself on every single, delicate inch of her quivering flesh, Kyle unleashed his tongue to devour the pink folds in long, hungry forays that explored the deepest recess of her tender cunt. Barely minding the demand of her swollen bud, Kyle dipped down to fuck into the exquisite vise of her sheath, taking deep, greedy laps that had her screaming just as he promised.

"*Oh, shit*....Kyle! Oh, God, please."

God wouldn't help her. He wouldn't even dare to try and take what was his from Kyle. The very notion had him clenching his fingers into her thighs as he spread her wider to savage the spasming pussy at his mercy. Kyle had none. No compassion. Not for a second did he relent as he fucked her up and over the cliff in a screaming, writhing fit as her sheath clamped down and tried to milk his tongue like a cock.

The thought had his own dick jerking in an angry demand at wasting such a sweet release on a tongue. Kyle reigned in the tirading tyrant with the assurance that it was just the first, the first of many, and his dick would get its due and then some once he obliterated Hailey's control.

Already she was sputtering, whimpering, trying to shift away from the tongue he had curled around her clit. As her release relaxed from her body, Kyle teased her anew. Keeping his kiss soft and sweet, he gave no indication of just what hell he planned to wreck on her. Instead he waited, waited until she muttered a sleepy protest and brought her hand back to his head.

With a tug, she signaled that she had enough, and Kyle took it as his green light to give her more. Latching down on the clit in a sudden roll of his head, he buried his lips into her pussy and sucked that tiny bud over the hard edge of his teeth.

"*Kyle!*"

In a screaming buck, Hailey tried to unseat him as he unleashed his fury on her weeping cunt.

That's right, darlin', we ain't done yet. We ain't even begun.

* * * *

Hailey screamed herself hoarse. As the explosions of euphoric rapture continued to bombard her, they erupted now in nothing more than sobbing whimpers as her body desperately tried to escape the tyrant that savaged her delicate flesh. Kicking, bucking, she twisted in every direction as she sought a way through the catastrophic pleasure he measured out with each forge of his relentless tongue.

If only he held her bound with such a simple touch, she could have survived the rolling sea of orgasms he wrecked over her, but those fingers...

"Oh, God." Hailey squealed and panted through another press of his fingertip against that magical spot that made her light up like a sparkler on the Fourth of July. Whining through the torment, Hailey's body clenched yet again at the hard demand he drove into her ravaged sheath as he fucked that tender stretch of flesh.

With a squealed cry, she lost all control of her motions as he pumped her exhausted body to even greater heights. Sweet God above, she hated him for it. The damn barbarian waged war on her pussy, turning pleasure into a pain so fine that it could barely be endured.

Each breath had become its own carnal temptation, shocking oxygen back into the inferno to feed the flames that just scorched higher and higher as Kyle tirelessly drove her toward release. She ached even as she claimed her satisfaction, ached for the final climax that would bring this torment to an end.

For a moment, she tasted the faint sweetness of relief as his mouth lifted, leaving her a decimated mess over his bed. Limp with no energy to put thoughts into words, Hailey could do little more than roll her head in denial as she felt him crawling up her body. She just needed a moment, one moment, but Kyle gave her none as his hands pulled her hips down, holding her open as he settled himself into position.

Giving her a simple warning rub, he had her whimpering. Every grind of his hard muscles unleashed a torrent of tremors through her. The scrape of the coarse hairs tufted over his body felt like a pin prick against her flushed skin. Her body vibrated with need and panic as the head of Kyle's battering ram that kissed the weeping entrance of her pussy.

"Please, I…I," she murmured over and over again desperate now at the feel of her body rousing again to the thirst, the need. It would consume her whole this time. The very idea fed fear into her lust and she struck out blindly at Kyle. It only took one hand to restrain both of hers and one searing inch to have her legs clenching to a still as her whole body bowed under his invasion.

Her body went into full riot when he stopped, warring with itself. Knowing the pleasure would be the end of her didn't stop her cunt from trying its damnedest to suck him all the way in, or kept her legs from climbing his hips to clench and jerk in a not-too-subtle demand for more.

Bastard didn't give it to her.

Her eyes opened as her mouth searched for the words, but the sounds froze on her lips when she caught the look in his eyes. They gleamed out of the darkness of the night, shining with predatory intent. Pinned by his gaze, Hailey could feel the very words moving through his chest as they pierced through her lust to her very soul.

"This pussy belongs to *me*."

Hailey screamed as he took sudden and complete possession of her body. For that scorching second, she held a glimmer of hope that this might be the final act in a night wrung out way past her endurance. It sizzled into an aching revelation that he didn't plan to fulfill the promise his ruthless invasion had made. No. Kyle had only upped the ante in his war.

"Please, Kyle, just end it. Please, I can't."

Giving in to the begging he'd vowed to claim earlier didn't end it. It only seemed to provoke him as he knelt back, dragging her up his knees until his hard thighs cushioned her ass. With her spread out over his lap, he towered overhead, staring down at where their bodies joined.

Hailey couldn't even think for want, but when his thumbs brushed open her folds and his finger flicked her abused clit, Hailey managed to pop out a rational thought in the sudden scream that contracted through her body.

"*You fucking asshole!*"

He retaliated instantly by spinning her clit into a firestorm of unheralded proportions. Speared over the thick, hard length of his cock, her cunt spasmed and sucked before demanding her hips to fuck it against the steel rod. She couldn't stop it. Even knowing how he must delight at having her screw herself against him, Hailey needed this, needed him to fricken—

"*Move!*"

Intentionally misunderstanding, his hips sped up the little rolling motions, grinding his dick harder and faster against her clit, making her heave and scream as she tried to match the frantic motion with her bucking hips. So close…so damn close.

The tension had just started to leave her muscles as the roiling pit of need searing her cunt simmered down. Her pussy ached, pulsing against the unforgiving dick stretching her wide, but it was a bearable pain. Tolerable until the bastard plunged her into the darkened abyss of forbidden delights as he fucked two sticky fingers straight up her ass.

Her jaw fell as her eyes bulged. The sudden penetration sent a riot of sensual pleasures tingling with the strong claws of pain racing over her body in a physical quiver. Hailey tried to breathe through the sensation, unsure if she liked it or not, but held paralyzed by the sheer excitement of wondering just what happened next.

"Kyle?" Her voice quivered and broke on that barely audible whisper. No soothing, tender response greeted her. Instead, her gaze connected with the Cattleman she'd been dumb enough to crawl into bed with.

"Oh, yeah, darlin'," Kyle snarled. "I'm gonna stretch this ass good, 'cause one day, I'm going to be riding it hard, and you're going to be cussing, spitting, and *loving every damn inch.*"

In proof of that, he started giving her a few of them. Those wicked fingers pressed down on the thin stretch of skin that separated them from the cock pumping her sheath raw, making a symphony of pleasure sing out from her womb as she praised the gloriousness of fucking.

Sliding, grinding, she didn't care about the details anymore. Like a hound after a rabbit, she chased down her orgasm full-speed. Greeting each one of his measured thrusts with her own hard slam, she fucked herself against both dick and hand in an ever-spiraling rhythm that matched the tightening bands of tension bearing down all over her.

Then, sweet mercy, they snapped, and she went flying straight into the heavens, finally touching the stars that had always waned just out of reach.

* * * *

Kyle let Hailey get away with stealing an orgasm simply because she held him transfixed by her release. The little wanton took to his fingers like a duck to water, bringing to life his greatest fantasy. Having trained more than enough slaves' asses for the riding, he knew a virgin when he stretched his fingers into one.

Knew, too, the delights of being the first man to plunder such depths, but to carry that honor with Hailey, to be the man who tamed and controlled all her forbidden desires, that was a prize Kyle had only ever dreamed to hold. Dream of it he had, and all of those fantasies had him branding her pussy in a much different position.

It hurt to pull free of her cunt, so sweetly needy. Even in its already sobbing state, the velvety walls of her sheath clamped down in a vain attempt to hold on to him. A sentiment not echoed by its owner, who muttered and helped him by trying to roll away.

Kyle watched as Hailey crawled, righting herself along the bed until she finally reached a pillow. Then with a great shuddering sigh, she crashed down, no doubt on her way to passing out. The little thing really needed a lot of training.

She just didn't understand any of the fundamental rules, Kyle happily lamented as he crawled up behind her, pushing her legs out of his way. At least she'd done him the courtesy of falling down on her stomach. It made it very easy to reassume his old position, but this time, just as he always fantasized, with her bent over his knees and totally at his mercy.

He knew the second she got a clue. It was the same moment he took repossession of what was his. Sliding back into her pussy was like walking into Heaven. It cast a warm, homey, content glow over him that made him wonder just how long a man could live inside a woman's body. However long, it wasn't long enough, especially when the woman got grumpy.

"Kyle, I'm tired," Hailey whined into the pillow as she tried to pull away.

There was nowhere for her to go with the head board blocking her way. Instead of answering, Kyle gave her his response in the slow, steady sway of his hips as he finally settled in to fuck his woman good and proper.

Reveling in her pleas, Kyle gave himself over to the sweet friction that sizzled pure pleasure down the length of his shaft with every escalating pass of his cock through her cunt. Harder and faster, the burning in his balls drove him until finally the tension boiled up and popped, drowning him in ecstasy. Still, Kyle couldn't stop. The pleasure only spurred him on even harder as he savaged the cunt trying to milk the very need from his balls.

Freed of a sense of civility or decency, Kyle hounded after the release that sparkled in the horizon. Knowing that only Hailey could deliver him to such glory, he fucked her as no man had ever dared, forcing her to carry him where no other woman could.

Splitting her ass cheeks wide, he didn't give her a moment to wonder before he pumped his fingers back into her delicious rear. He was rewarded with a scream and soul-searing suck of her cunt even as her hips bucked that perfect ass up onto his hands. That's all she had to do, ask for it. Kyle was more than ready to give it to her.

Give it to himself really because that's what he did, gave in to his need. Unleashed, it consumed him, forcing him to strain every muscle as he rode her so hard the bed creaked, slamming into the wall in a rapid pattern that only ended with a deafening roar as his balls exploded under the strain. Over and over, he drove himself into her as he felt his very soul melting out of his body.

He flooded her spasming cunt until they both shattered, tipping over with the force of the aftermath to land in a sweaty mess on their sides. There, finally, Kyle managed to latch on to enough dignity to roll clear of her and issue one final, yawning warning.

"That was a good start, darlin'." He gave her an absentminded pat on the ass. "Take a breath and be ready to go again in thirty minutes."

Chapter 7

Feeling like she'd been flattened by a road roller, Hailey just laid there staring at the ceiling. The humid wind of Kyle's breath dampened her shoulder as he napped beside her. He might be all curled up and content, but Hailey wasn't. Not with Kyle's words echoing in her head.

Be ready to go in thirty minutes...ready to go.

It rang like an alarm bell, rousing her weary body with the panic. Had she just won? Or had he?

Be ready to go? Men only spoke like that to a sure thing. If Kyle thought she'd fallen enough off her rocker to land in that pile, he had another thing coming. She really didn't feel like getting up, and the idea of round two had a certain appeal.

That didn't change the fact that, for sanity and pride's sake, this probably should be the only time she rolled out of Kyle's bed naked and sore. Because next time, it might be Cole and Kyle's bed, her inner worrier pointed out.

As annoying as her inner voice might be, it had it right. She needed to get the hell out of here before Cole came home and woke Kyle up for the second round. The thrill that threat sent through her leaked down her leg along with the rest of their spent passion.

It didn't matter how much she wanted to rush, Hailey needed a shower. Hot, extremely hot, water beating down on her like a tiny million fists as it shoot out of a full-sized shower head, that's what Hailey dreamed of as she stood beneath the lukewarm trickle Kyle's shower put out. The thing had barely enough pressure to wash the evidence of spent passion from her body.

At least the pathetically weak stream didn't lure her into delaying. Breaking her record with a less than five minute shower, Hailey found herself stumbling over the next hurdle as she waltzed back into Kyle's room—clothes.

Hers lay in tatters across his floor. Her panties and shirt could no longer serve their function, which meant sucking it up and having to dig into Kyle's closet for a shirt.

Kyle's shirt. Hailey stared at them all in a row. Wearing one would probably be like being wrapped in his embrace, and just how warm and soothing would it be to snuggle into his hardness?

Swallowing down the weakness buzzing in her knees, Hailey considered she had a bad romantic streak showing through. In all likelihood, he'd be bragging tomorrow.

Who knew how Cole would take the news? If this was some kind of joke, he'd be around tomorrow to laugh. If not, he'd probably show up all sorts of pissed. Either way would be better than having him show up here now with her wearing nothing but jeans and a bra.

Hailey considered that she really needed to stop tempting fate with her thoughts as it answered with a squeal of breaks in the drive. Tripping over her feet as she stumbled toward the window, she prayed to a higher authority than the fickleness of fate.

*Oh, please, oh, please, God, don't let it be...*Cole. The sight of a street light glinting off the row of spotlights over the square frame of his mammoth truck had Hailey sucking in a squeaky breath. He hadn't come alone, which went to show that God was taking messages tonight.

Hailey stumbled back from the horrifying sight of a second pick-up crowding in behind Cole's.

Two Cattlemen? Try three, dumbass!

She was so beyond screwed now. If they caught her, realized just what she was doing here...and how could they not know? She was only wearing a fricken bra!

Unsure and beyond reason, protective instincts swooped in to save her as the heavy footfalls vibrated across the front porch and through Kyle's wall. The murmur of male voices harmonized with the scraping of the key in the front door lock.

Even as her frenzied fear crested, Hailey dove for the cover of the bathroom and the idiotic notion that it provided any more safety than Kyle's room. Clicking off the light, she sank back deep into the shadows of the far door as female laughter began to twine around the sound of the men.

They broke through clearer now as the group shoved through the front door. All too quickly, the voices separated, becoming distinct as they closed in on her location. Each click and clack of their footsteps treading down the hall sent another drop of terror rolling down her spine.

What the hell had I gotten myself into?

"Kyle?"

Cole.

"Where the hell is Kyle?" That sounded like GD, an old friend of sorts.

"Probably passed out drunk." Even at the distance, Hailey could hear the disgust in Cole's tone. "He's been acting all sorts of funny lately. I've been telling him he just needs a good screw."

"Leave him alone, Cole," GD barked. "Kyle don't want none of this or he would have come out with us earlier."

"There ain't no harm in asking." Cole sounded unnecessarily annoyed, muttering something else she didn't catch.

"Don't you worry about him, honey." That was the woman, giggling and making Hailey's stomach turn in outright revulsion as she continued. "I know how to take care of Kyle, just like I do you two."

Oh, shit.

They'd come home for an orgy. At that moment, Kyle's door banged open. Hailey knew exactly what they would see, the remains of an orgy already good and done. Even as they stormed into the bedroom, Hailey had already started to fumble with the doorknob behind her. Only one door separated her from Cole. That's how close she stood to having the worst night in all her years.

"See," Cole snorted. "Passed out drunk."

"But you were wrong about the screwing." GD sounded so damn smug. "Check these out, Kyle got himself a pink panty girl."

The door behind her gave way, and she was sliding through the crack even as heavy footsteps followed Cole's horrifying question. "Wasn't the bathroom light on?"

Hailey managed to make it behind the second door not a moment before the first one banged open. He didn't give her any time to shut it, and Hailey quivered as light flooded out of the gap between it and its frame.

"Why's that door open?"

Hailey didn't know what exactly happened next. Her mind stopped recording things the second her heart stopped, which was before he completed his question. All she knew was she dove, slid, and ended up tucked into the shadows of the wall, cramped under a bed.

"What are you looking for?"

That voice sounded so familiar, and if she could just get her heart to stop pounding so loudly she might be able to identify just who wore those strappy red heels.

"Nothing," Cole grunted, but Hailey didn't believe him.

"He was looking for Kyle's little girl." That was definitely GD's work boots pushing past Cole's. "He get's cranky when Kyle don't share."

"No need to get cranky, baby." Little miss pink toenails crowded next to Cole's black boots. "And you did promise to share me."

Crack.

The sharp spank followed a giggle as miss five-inch heels went teetering backward.

"I don't remember giving you permission to touch me, did I, darlin'?"

"No, master."

Oh, God, I'm gonna be sick.

"You know what you earned?"

"A punishment."

Hailey highly doubted that's what the woman expected, or she wouldn't have sounded half as thrilled at the prospect.

"Get your ass out them clothes, darlin', and get in position."

There were things worse than being caught, Hailey realized as the second man's T-shirt hit the floor. GD's and he pressed the bed down a good four inches when he settled in to work at the laces of his boots. When a woman's shirt hit the floor on the opposite side, Hailey smirked.

Well, at least that problem is taken care of.

She just had to wait until they all got good and distracted. Then she could steal the shirt and crawl for freedom. How long could it really take them? They were Cattlemen, and after her very recent experience, it seemed that in five minutes all three should be happily absorbed. Then she'd be good to go.

* * * *

It took them over *two hours*. Two hours of listening to Cole and GD put the poor woman though a hell that made what Kyle did to her seem like a pittance. Listening to the "paces they put her through" had a worse side effect than just being the most mortifying experience of her life.

With every second that ticked past, Hailey became more convinced that she was the real lunatic in the room. *She* had tempted *these* men? She'd half been joking when she said they were doomed earlier at the bar but now she felt it. It had been pure idiocy to come here tonight, stupidity in the extreme because now she knew. She knew and she desired.

Worn past the point of even being able to ask any mighty deity for help, Hailey just whimpered softly beneath the bed as her body twisted and convulsed with all sorts of perverted lusts. It didn't matter to her hormones that her body had already endured more than it could bear in Kyle's bed. Her imagination turned traitor, conjuring up explicit images to match the sounds she heard. It drove her arousal to the most shameful level—putting her in the image along with Kyle and Cole.

Oh, God, I got to get out of here.

Hailey swallowed hard and offered another, endlessly babbling prayer to her maker, hoping that He could deliver her from this hell. The only answer that rung back from the heavens was the high-pitched squeaks and groans as one of the Cattleman finally mounted the poor girl they'd been tormenting for the past couple of hours.

Threatening to come down on top of her, the couple went it at it like she and Kyle had, but there hadn't come a moment when her breath stopped and two men started grunting. The very fact that mere inches from her head some woman was getting double-stuffed had drool forming along Hailey's lips as she wondered...

Ah, got to stop that.

She had to get the hell out of here. She had to leave now.

That thought solidified with enough force to actually peel her off the floor. Snatching up the other woman's silk blouse from where it lay slightly under the frame, Hailey slithered very slowly, turning fully around so that she could peek just over the lip of the footboard to see that somebody hadn't taken his boots off to fuck. The other bastard still wore black socks, and that caught her enough to make her smirk.

Now that's sexy.

The snide comment echoed out of her soul, reminding her for a moment that she was Hailey Mathews and she didn't cower under any bed. What the hell would they do if she just popped up all of a sudden?

Probably shit bricks and freak out, and wouldn't that be funny as hell?

If it had been Patton instead of her, that's probably what she would have done. Hailey enjoyed the thought but remained focused on escape and not having to explain to anybody what she'd been doing under the bed for the past two hours. Fearing to look for the delay it might cause her, Hailey shoved back with her feet and slid nearly silently through the bathroom door. Staying on her back, she worked her way all the way into the shadowed safety of Kyle's room.

Through the bathroom she could still hear the clear sounds of spiraling passion. It fueled her panic to get out before they erupted into a loud enough frenzy to wake Kyle. He still slumbered peacefully, unaware of the chaos going on around him.

Just the sight of him curled up along his pillow distracted Hailey into a pause. But to be his pillow, Hailey sighed. Worn down, tired, and horny, none of that compared to the ache of being lonely.

Window or front door, Hailey? Focus.

Grinding her teeth at that harsh rebuttal, Hailey cut her eyes from Kyle to the window. It didn't even sigh was she shoved it up. A fact that disappointed her enough to glance back at Kyle and made her wonder if she didn't really want to be caught.

"Oh, God! Master!"

Not hesitating for fear of what the next moment might bring, Hailey swung a leg out and dropped the four feet to the ground. Then she ran, and kept on running until the residential street blocks faded into more barren fields and then back into the sudden cluster of commercial buildings that lined the curved main street of Pittsview.

She didn't slow down for all the ache in her muscles or the pain in her chest until Riley's gravel-pit parking lot crunched beneath her shoes. Long closed, only one truck remained, parked right up alongside hers.

Hailey slowed down, fishing for the keys thankfully still tucked in the bottom of her jeans pocket. Head down, already thinking of the shower waiting for her at home, she jumped about a foot when a male voice broke the stillness of the late night.

"Hailey?"

"Riley." Popping toward the right, she cast a wide-eyed glance at the bar owner walking down the side of the building. Headed her way with his keys out, Riley had obviously finished closing the bar for the night. Hailey figured that must have made it two a.m.

"What the hell happened to you?" Passing by his own hood and rounding around hers, he came in a little too close for comfort. Hailey knew what she looked like and probably still smelled like—a well-fucked woman.

"Nothing." Holding her hand steady, she worked the key into the door lock as fast as she could.

"Are you sure, Hailey?" Riley sounded too concerned and too close. "Because you look a little—"

"Tired?" Hailey managed to get her door open. Using it like a shield, it kept Riley from getting too good a look at her in the dim shadows of the street light. Plastering on a big, fake smile, she answered her own question before he could. "I am. Quite tired. And that's all I am, Riley. Good night."

Before he could argue with that bold-faced lie, Hailey slid in behind her Studebaker and made her escape.

* * * *

Cole shrugged into his jeans but didn't bother to button them. Claudia knew the rules. She had to get her skinny ass back in her clothes and out of his bed, 'cause he couldn't sleep with a woman in it, or a man for that fact.

"Hey, man." Cole smacked GD with a pillow to rouse him. With a snort and a single, stormy gray eye pinning him, GD awoke. "Time to get up and out, GD."

"You're a peculiar son of a bitch," GD complained. Swinging up to a sit, his feet hit the floor as his back arched in a lazy stretch.

"What? 'Cause I don't want to snuggle up to your hairy ass all night?"

"There's a woman between us…" GD shrugged off his glance when he took in the obvious fact that the woman had disappeared. "Well, there was. You send her running, too?"

"In the shower." Cole nodded toward the bathroom a second before he swung out of the bedroom. He didn't have any need to see GD dress or join him in the shower with Claudia, which is probably what the big bull rider would do.

Cole had had enough of Claudia. Sweet and well-trained as she was, she just couldn't put to rest the itch that had been gnawing on him for the past few weeks. He'd been trying to fuck it out of his system. The good lord, with GD's help, had certainly filled his bed to overflowing with the bountiful beauties piling up at the club.

Even the endless sea of prime and willing flesh couldn't appease that annoying part that kept him restless and looking for something more. Cole blamed it all on Patton James for bringing that spark back into his life. Pretty and wild, she reminded him that it could be fun to try to bring down an unbroken filly.

Not that Patton had really been his intended prey. She'd merely been bait. Very sexy, he-wouldn't-have-said-no kind of bait, but that would have been the dumbest thing he could have done. Forget the beating the Davis brothers would have rained down on his body. Fucking Patton probably would have screwed him out of any chance of fucking her best friend, Hailey.

In fact, just trying to screw her had probably not helped him a bit. Cole figured that out too late. He'd forgotten the cardinal rule—everybody blamed the man. A woman could make one man jealous using another because she knew the men would rally to fight over her. When a man got done, the woman was his prize and he took what he conquered.

Women, though they might fight between each other, still always blamed the man. Even if Cole managed to make Hailey jealous by chasing her best friend, she'd only be mad at him for it. Given that Hailey didn't need help being mad at him, Cole could see now that he'd been a little too rash in his plans for Patton.

The only excuse he had was that he'd become a little desperate in his pursuit of Hailey. Cole didn't like being desperate, not when it came to a woman. He knew from firsthand experience just how badly a man could get scarred by a woman when the cards stacked in her favor. He made that mistake once, and he wouldn't be making it again.

That's why you just spent the last two hours fucking Claudia and thinking about Hailey? Because you're just such a badass.

Cole told that snotty voice to go fuck itself, but it didn't take the advice. Instead, it pointed out just how much like a pussy he'd been acting for over the past month.

Cole twisted the lid off his water as he kicked the fridge door closed, not wanting to admit he had a point. Sure, GD had a scheduling nightmare at the club that kept him constantly on the register, but that had just been a convenient excuse.

He'd told the girl "game on" and then punked out. One thing he knew for sure, he wouldn't get Hailey beneath him if he didn't at least try at some point.

"Cole?"

Claudia came wandering through the arch that led into the dining room holding a towel over her breasts. *Not fully dressed, not ready to leave.* Cole held his sigh and his obnoxiousness in. "What, darlin'?"

"Have you seen my shirt?"

What a dumbass question to ask him. "No, darlin'. Where did you leave it?"

"On your floor," Claudia answered, as if that wasn't obvious enough.

In the hopes of moving things along, Cole ushered her back toward the bedroom, certain that the shirt wouldn't be found in the kitchen. "Well, I'm sure it's still there somewhere."

"I looked and it isn't."

Annoyed by that point and at the entire stupidity of their conversation, Cole released Claudia as they cleared the bedroom door. "It's got to be. Who the hell would take it?"

"I'm telling you, it isn't there."

GD gave him a smirk, and Cole knew then she'd already driven him nuts with looking. The two of them might not be able to find a damn shirt, but he sure as hell could. Probably under the bed and that lazy ass GD hadn't been willing to look. In the hopes of getting Claudia out of his house and his ass back into bed, Cole went to his knees.

Not that he found the shirt he was looking for, but he did find something that turned his attention—a very pronounced clean streak across the floor. Cleaning did not rise high on Cole's list. When he did put out the effort, it only extended to what he could see. Under the bed did not qualify, and the layer of dust had risen well over an inch in the past three years.

Something, though, had cut quite a swath through it and even pulled some back out at the foot of the bed. Rising up to his feet, Cole left GD to tune into Claudia's disparaging remarks as he tracked the trail to the open bathroom door.

GD's shower had left the room moist and disturbed, but that had only smeared the dirt tracks that lead through Kyle's door. Shoving the door wide, his gaze snapped instantly to the open window.

Son of a bitch.

Chapter 8

Friday, May 2nd

"*You slept with Kyle Harding!*"

That outraged shout cracked over Hailey as the blare of sunlight hit her like a cannon blast. Patton matched that overly loud proclamation with a yank back of her comforter, letting in a world Hailey hadn't been willing to confront so far that morning.

That's why when she heard Patton banging and yelling at the door, Hailey hadn't even twitched. She should have known Patton would just go around back to use the spare key in the little safety rock she'd given Hailey years ago. When Patton wanted to talk, there would be no hiding from her.

"I asked you a question, Hailey."

Groaning, Hailey rolled away from the light and her annoying friend. Pushing her head under the pillows, she waged a war with Patton over the soft sack. When Patton finally managed to yank the pillow free, she yanked it completely free, tossing it way across the room.

"Hailey! I want to know what is going on here."

Rolling over the bed, her feet slapped onto the cool wood floors, making her grimace that much more. Shoving up with a grunt, she ignored her friend as she trailed around the bed, rambling on.

"I mean, Riley calls in the middle of the night and now he's got Chase, Slade, and Devin all ready to go kick Kyle's ass, and if it wasn't for me—"

At the change of Patton's footsteps from clicks to clacks, Hailey came to a sudden stop. Turning with a hand out, she caught Patton in the chest as her friend barged into the bathroom behind her. The sudden flat-handed obstacle choked off Patton's words, and she let Hailey walk her back over the threshold.

It felt good to slam the door on Patton, but that small joy wore off quickly. She'd been hiding from this day for over an hour, unsure of what to do. Her plan unraveled on her last night. Neither a success nor a failure, it left her with no clear idea of what to do today or what to expect from it.

Patton's arrival certainly put the ominous thought in her mind that fate had just weighed in. Against or for her, that remained to be seen because Patton could be the best ally and sometimes the angel of doom.

It would help if doom didn't feel so damn good, but it did, at least in the fantasy forms that tormented her through the night. Dreams, memories, it all blurred into one sexual odyssey that left her with no place to hide from the ache. No place but maybe her shower, her last ditch hope.

She customized her sanctuary with her own hands, the curved stone wall, the over-indulgent number of high-powered spray jets, the steam. Hailey sighed as her shower flooded in behind her, trapping her in the momentary solitude of steam.

A very little slice of heaven, but even that morning it couldn't keep the demons at bay. That's because they came from within her, carried in by her own traitorous mind that refused to let the issue go. It couldn't let it go because last night hadn't been just sex.

Being scared of the truth didn't change the reality that she actually started to…like Kyle, just a little. Hailey's head hit the wall of the shower under the weight of that admission. Yes, she liked Kyle, kind of looked forward to just seeing him, messing with him, sleeping with him again.

Feed the beast and the monster just gets bigger.

Her mother's old warning about too much sugar seemed absolutely appropriate when applied to sex with Kyle. Look at what one taste did to her. Two and she'd be calling him master.

Dignity and pride be damned. If they wanted to avoid that future, they better stiffen up and save her ass now. Straightening off the wall, Hailey's mind solidified on a plan. She needed to get one, and sitting in her kitchen was the master of all games. Patton.

Hailey didn't have to wonder where Patton had retreated. The scent of sickeningly weak coffee greeted her the second she cleared her bathroom. Five minutes later, the sight of the yellow piss filling her pot confirmed her grim prediction.

"You know, if you're going to barge into my house and harass me first thing in the morning, the least you can do is make something stronger than a pot of piss."

Hailey greeted Patton with nearly the same complaint she treated Patton to almost every morning when she'd been staying with her a few weeks back. It earned her a typically-obnoxious Patton response.

"There's a bottle of motor oil over here. You want me to pour you a shot of that?"

Casting a dirty look over her shoulder at her best friend, Hailey eyed her friend's smug smirk. "So you know I slept with Kyle. Is that why you're over here breaking into my house and pushing me around?"

"No, I'm over here to complain about your love life invading into my personal time."

That Patton couldn't even get those words out with a wisp of sincere indignation had Hailey turning shocked eyes on her friend. "You did not just say that to me."

"Yes I did."

"After what you put me through this summer?"

"And I relished saying it." Instead of backing down, Patton grinned with satisfaction. "I get to complain now because I'm the one who was enjoying a pleasant interlude with my men when Riley called and riled them all up. Hey that rhymes, a little."

Hailey rolled her eyes at that and turned back to making her coffee. Behind her Patton prattled on. "He told them some wild story about a bar fight and you taking off with Kyle only to show back up later looking rolled over and wearing the wrong clothes. You can imagine, of course, how Chase took that kind of news. It wasn't pretty, and I'd say you owe me a good apology and thank you for keeping him at home last night."

Hailey laughed as she hit the button on the coffee maker. Turning to face Patton, she settled against the counter to grin at her friend. "You really expect me to thank you?"

"I really expect some juicy details," Patton retorted. "I did suffer for them."

"Yeah, you look it with that grin, too. Tell me, Patton, just why I should indulge your dirty little mind with details?"

"Well," Patton breathed in, considering that for a moment, "you could just leave me to fantasize, but then I certainly wouldn't have anything to say that might keep Chase on his leash. Unless, of course, this plan of yours is to have Kyle get the crap beat out of him."

"You know it's not," Hailey snapped. Her annoyance came out at Patton, but it focused more on her men. "This isn't none of their business. You can tell Chase, Slade, and Devin they'll be answering to me if they put a bruise on Kyle Harding."

"Oh, is that right?" Patton laughed. "And suddenly you care about marks on Kyle Harding's body? Tell me, you leave any last night?"

"Maybe a few." Hailey couldn't help the grin that spread out over her face. "I got to admit he left a few of his own."

"That's not juicy enough." Patton leaned forward in her seat, obviously eager to hear the answer to her next question. "Where'd he leave them?"

"Patton," Hailey groaned. Feeling the blush flood her cheeks at just the memory of where, she hid the tell-tale sign of embarrassment by busying herself with the coffee.

"Ah, I know where."

"Shut up, Patton."

Laughter peeled out behind her, coming closer as Patton carried her empty cup over for a refill. Sidling up alongside Hailey, Patton waited patiently for her to pour half a cup into her mug. Hot water from the tap filled the rest and then Patton sighed.

"Of course, I know other stuff, too."

Hailey didn't think she was talking about positions, not with that tone. Carrying her mug to the table with Patton trailing behind, Hailey gave over and asked. "What stuff?"

"Oh, like your brothers will be back in town in a few weeks."

"What?" That jerked her out of the moment. Shocked and happy, she just blinked at Patton. "How do you know that? They didn't call me."

"Yes, they did," Patton contradicted her. "Last night, apparently all night, until about 1:30 in the morning when they called Chase wanting him to go find your ass."

Hailey considered that for a moment as she tried to put the pieces together. "Then they called before Riley."

"Yes, but I told Brett and Chase that you were at Riley's with Rachel and Heather for your girls' night. He said he'd call you tonight. I suggest you answer that call, or you're going to have a set of really pissed off brothers on your door. That probably wouldn't help right now."

Hailey rolled her eyes at that understatement. "Brett can't just show up. He has to wait for the Marines to release him."

"They did. He's sitting out in California waiting for Mike to be released and then they're driving home for good is the impression I got."

"For good?" Hailey didn't dare to hope. Sure she knew Brett and Mike had decided not to re-enlist, but them spending the rest of their lives in Pittsview didn't sound right, either. Her brothers craved excitement and the most exciting thing going on in Pittsview? *Hailey Mathews sleeping with Kyle Harding. That could make the newspaper headline.*

"It makes you happy." Patton's hand covered hers as her friend misread her grin. "It'll be nice to have your family back together, won't it?"

"Yeah, but," Hailey looked around the kitchen. "What am I going to do about Kyle and Cole? Brett and Mike can be protective."

"No kidding." Patton released her to settle back in her seat with her coffee. "They'll have the shotgun at Kyle's back right after they pick his bloody body off the floor. Hell, you'll be Mrs. Harding by Halloween."

Hailey rolled her eyes at that. "Oh, for God's sake, Patton. It isn't like I was a virgin."

"And it isn't like Kyle considers doggie style kinky," Patton shot back, making Hailey snort.

"It isn't like my brothers know—" Hailey's words choked off at Patton's pointed look. She didn't need words to know what her friend meant. "Oh, God, no."

Waving that horrible truth away, Hailey looked anywhere but at Patton.

"Hailey."

"I don't want to hear it. If my brothers...are...what Kyle...ehhh." Hailey twitched true revulsion. "I don't want to hear it."

"Then let's talk about Kyle."

"Oh, him." Hailey turned back to give Patton her big, fake smile. "I figured it out last night. I'm doomed."

"Doomed?" Patton's brow arched. "Isn't that a little dramatic?"

"No." Hailey shook her head. "See, Kyle faked being drunk to try and con me into bed, right? And so, me being the genius I am, I decided to fall into it."

"Well, then, congratulations." Patton nodded, appearing more patient than sincere. "I take it this means you won."

"Won? I don't know about that," Hailey admitted. "I'm still waiting to find out the consequences of my actions. To be honest, I was kind of hoping if I stayed in bed they'd stay away, if you know what I mean."

"Well," Patton settled her cup onto the table and leaned in. "Maybe I can help with that."

"Really?" Hailey arched a doubting brow. "And how is that?"

Fluffing her hair in a gesture she never made, Patton settled back into her seat with all the stiffness of an insulted person. "I don't know if I want to tell you now."

"Patton."

"Fine." Patton studied her nails as if she really didn't have anything important to share. "It's just that according to what Riley told Chase, Kyle's got the word out all over town. He wants to know where you are and who you're with. Kyle asked everybody to keep it quiet, and Riley figured he didn't want Chase and them to get in his way. Hailey? You okay?"

"Sure." Why wouldn't she be?

"You want to talk about it?"

"What's there to talk about?" Hailey shrugged, except that the ground had just opened up beneath her feet. Patton wasn't doing anything other than stuffing her into the hole with her.

"Well, how about after I got Chase to agree to give Kyle a day to live, he went to throw Kyle out of the club, but Kyle had already resigned his membership over five weeks ago, Hailey, and isn't that about the time he started trying to worm his way into your life?"

Yes it was, but Hailey squashed that thrill. "It doesn't matter, Patton."

"What? That the man might actually like you? I mean, hell, Hailey, did you ever think the reason he picked on you so much in high school was because he liked you, maybe to a degree he wasn't comfortable with as a teenager, especially a boy. Shit, thinking about it, you probably—"

"None of that matters," Hailey snapped.

"Why not?"

Because Kyle didn't travel alone and this still could be set-up. "Cole? Remember him?"

Patton's ponderous response to Hailey's sarcasm ended with a shrug. "Chase called GD this morning to make sure that Kyle didn't piggyback into the club with Cole's membership, and you know what GD told him?"

"I'm not sure that I want to know," but she knew Patton intended to tell her.

"GD said that Cole had been working with Aaron and Jake *and* that Kyle had asked him to keep Cole busy so he wouldn't have time to come after you."

"Damn it, Patton! I told you I didn't want to know that. Now what am I supposed to think?"

"You're supposed to think that Kyle Harding is coming after you hard and strong. He's turned out his best friend to keep you to himself. If you think telling this man no now is going to save you, Hailey, you're fooling yourself."

Hailey glared at Patton for making her second guess what appeared to be an obvious conclusion. It felt dangerous and stupid to assume Kyle had any interest in her other than taking a few rolls through the sheets. She'd be a fool to believe anything else, but hope had no dignity.

"You think Kyle actually likes me?"

* * * *

Kyle could hear Cole smacking his lips as Cole came down the hall. A second later, he stumbled through the dining room toward the kitchen wearing nothing more than jeans he hadn't even bothered to button up. Cole didn't speak a word as he shuffled past. Just like every morning, he went to the fridge and pulled out his carton of milk to drink straight from the bottle.

That's why Kyle had his own bottle sitting by his bowl of cereal. Living with Cole was kind of like living with a teenager. He didn't cook, he didn't clean, but, thankfully, he bathed everyday and he tended to be funny as hell. Like this morning, when he wiped the milk from his lip and came to lean against the arch separating the two rooms.

"So, who'd you screw last night?"

Kyle choked on his cereal, washing the pain away with a quick gulp of his orange juice before pinning his best friend with an amused look. "What makes you think I got screwed last night?"

That had Cole's hand lifting in mid-air as he returned the milk carton to his lips. The instant speculation that crossed his face before he said, "Nothing," made a lie out of his words.

Kyle didn't like keeping secrets from Cole. Nothing had ever been worth the effort, much less the bother, but last night Hailey proved she was more than worth both of those. Grunting slightly as he shifted in his seat, Kyle felt a tinge of annoyance at the ache in his dick.

It had been a problem he'd been living with since he rolled over around three in the morning looking for his seconds only to find cool, empty sheets at his back. Sure he could have handled the problem himself then instead of lying there fantasizing about all the better ways his itch could have been scratched.

By the time he lumbered out of bed to take his morning shower, that itch had turned into a burning need that wouldn't be satisfied with a little hand-warmed soap massage. Kyle hadn't wasted the effort. Hailey put him in this position and he intended to save it all just for her.

He was thinking lunch and making a feast of—

"If you ain't got a woman, why you smiling like that?"

"I ain't smiling like nothing." Breakfast over even if he hadn't finished the bowl, Kyle lifted it up and shrugged past Cole as he headed for the sink.

"You so full of shit," Cole shot back.

"As long as I don't smell like it."

"That why your sheets smelled like cinnamon last night? Is that a new personal statement for you?"

"Why you smelling my sheets, man?" Kyle paused to look up from where he'd been stuffing the soggy mess he dumped from his bowl into the disposal. "You know, that's kind of like a sick thing to do."

"Because I'm like a bloodhound," Cole growled out arrogantly, making Kyle's eyes roll before he turned back to cleaning up his breakfast. "I'm on the hunt, buddy, and don't think I won't find out just who you had squared away last night."

"Whatever."

Cole could ramble on all he wanted. Kyle would be getting his while he did. If by some miracle measure Cole actually managed to charm his way into Hailey's bed, Kyle wouldn't object as long as he didn't get thrown out in the process.

"You know you got a black eye?"

"Bar fight." Actually, that idiot hadn't landed a punch. The bruise came from Hailey's heel when she clocked him. He'd wear it with honor, like all good hunters did their scars. Sure enough, he'd be bagging his prey a second time before the sun settled halfway over this day.

"You like getting hit or something?" Cole asked as he plunked his milk carton onto the counter. "Because you doing that idiot grin again."

"I certainly did enjoy beating the crap out of that man." Kyle bumped Cole's hip with the dishwasher door as means of asking him to move.

"What he do?"

"He touched what was mine."

"And just what the hell is that supposed to mean?

"It means what it means." Kyle straightened up.

Cole seemed to consider that for a moment. "You acting strange lately, and I'm betting you've gotten yourself into some no-good pussy, my friend. Bar fights? Drinking? Disappearing all night? This woman's got you all messed up."

"Who said anything about a woman?"

"And you ain't even sharing." Cole ignored his question. "Maybe I should be feeling insulted right about now."

"Maybe you should be thinking about Coldwell's Mustang and how we got to get that out the door today. Maybe while you're at it, you could actually put a shirt on and get your ass ready."

"Now, I really am insulted."

* * * *

Cole left Kyle with that parting shot as he swaggered off back toward his bedroom, taking his milk with him. Let Kyle try and keep his little secret. Even if nobody bothered to take notice at first, somewhere along the lines somebody would notice something. Somebody always noticed something in Pittsview. Nothing ever stayed quiet for long.

Even as Cole dismissed Kyle's sudden secretiveness, it bugged him to the point of obsession because he honestly worried about his friend. As he considered the matter, Cole began to see quite clearly just how right he'd been. Kyle had obviously gotten his head turned around by some drama queen who could easily wreck his friend's life. Except that Cole wouldn't let that happen.

Thirty minutes later as they clamored into his truck to head down for the shop, he just couldn't stop himself from needling Kyle. "So, you really didn't bring nobody home last night?"

That got him a dour look. "You still on that?"

"I'm just trying to figure out who the pink panties belong to. I mean," Cole gave Kyle's frame a divisive look, "maybe you're branching out, trying something new."

That got him instantly slammed into the door when Kyle gave him a shove. "I ain't wearing pink panties, you ass."

"What, you like them white?" Cole cringed from the punch before Kyle even landed it on his arm. Not that hard, it still left a sting as he straightened up laughing. "So if they ain't yours, then whose?"

"Tinkerbell's," Kyle retorted without hesitation. "*And* I want them back if you did happen to snatch them."

Cole smirked at that. "Whacha gonna do? Go try to match the panties to your Cinderella, Prince Charming?"

"Oh, God." Kyle's head thunked against the rear window. "You're never going to shut up about this are you?"

"Nope."

"Fine." Kyle sighed deep before turning in his seat. "Truth? I really like this girl and I just don't want to screw anything up."

"I see." Cole smacked the foul taste of that out of his mouth along with his annoyed response. "So, you going solo now."

"I really care about this woman and you...I know you got your reasons for keeping it just sex, but I can't risk that attitude messing up my future."

"Future?" Cole's head snapped around at that. "What are you picking out rings now?"

"Not yet."

"But one day..."

"I hope." Kyle nodded.

"Oh, Jesus, Mary, and Joseph, Kyle. Have you lost your ever-loving mind?"

"Spare me." Kyle snapped back in the seat to glare out at the road. "I know you got your reasons for being a bitter ass, but they ain't mine."

That had Cole's jaw clenching tight. Fine, let Kyle go down. It wouldn't be any skin off of his nose. No, he'd just have to be around to pick up the pieces. If they could even be picked up.

"I'm just concerned you're making a mistake."

"Well, I'm not, so you can shut up already."

That response just went to prove that Cole was too late. How that had happened just went to show how busy Cole had been the past few weeks. Hell, he should have seen this coming with all of Kyle's weird behavior lately, but, no, he'd been too wrapped up in his own problems to notice. Now anything he said or did would only get him bitten.

What a grim way to start a morning.

Cole shook his head as he curved the truck into the shop's back parking lot.

Chapter 9

The day wore on Kyle's good humor. Feeling Cole's brooding gaze focusing on him time after time added slowly to the tension he woke up to that morning. He really hadn't expected to find Hailey warming his bed, but it would have been sweet if he had.

That day would come, Kyle promised himself. One morning, he'd roll over to be greeted by all her soft curves, and he'd make sure it stayed that way for the rest of his life. Those kinds of thoughts didn't help with how painfully tight his jeans had gotten.

Nothing would but a quick trip to see his little princess at lunch. He didn't even bother to call and find out if she had plans, knowing she'd say yes no matter the truth. Skittish as she was, it would serve him better just to continue on as if they had a relationship than actually asking her to have one.

When the big and little hands finally collected under the twelve on the shop clock, Kyle didn't even wait a second before borrowing Aaron's keys. Knowing she'd very likely bolt if she saw him coming, Kyle even parked the car quietly along the curb one house up from Hailey's.

Sure enough, he caught her working in the garage. Intent on her project, she didn't even take note of him coming down the drive. With her back to the open garage door, Hailey couldn't see him as he snuck in without having to try to be stealthy.

Still, Kyle waited for the moment his arrival would have the biggest impact. He caught that second when she straightened up for a moment to stare down at what she'd been working on.

Smacking the garage door button, Kyle let the whine and clank of the lowering door announce his arrival. The sound had her jolting like she'd been struck with a lightning bolt. The grinder fell from her hand to clank down over the work table as she spun to take in the sight of him.

Hazel eyes going wide with worry, the fear in Hailey shined out of her gaze. It came through in the trembling of her whisper.

"Kyle."

Maybe he should go easier on her. *Then again, maybe I shouldn't give her any room to escape.* "I need to have a word with you, princess."

Kyle started forward, taking advantage of the stupor that had obviously caught Hailey. The warmth in her gaze only highlighted the wild sparks of green fire that ricocheted through the chocolate brown. The frenzy echoed down to her trembling lips. She really was just too adorable. The way her voice whispered, husky with desire but still squeaky with nerves at the high points fed the lust in Kyle.

"You shouldn't be here."

"And why's that?" He pulled up to a stop not an inch from her.

Smelling all alluring and looking so soft, Hailey didn't retreat. Neither did she meet his gaze, focusing instead on the crisscross pattern of his flannel shirt. "Because…why would you be here?"

Settling a hand on her hip, he couldn't help but enjoy a squeeze that had her shivering as he backed her up against her work bench. "'Cause you ran out on me last night, and I wasn't done with you."

"Last night was a mistake." Her ears went red right along with her cheeks as she blustered out that lie. Hailey had never been a good liar, which was why he ignored her rambling protest to rub a soft kiss over her lips.

"It can't happen again, Kyle. We're business partners, just partners, not even friends. It's just best that we don't confuse the—"

"Hailey?" Kyle lifted his head to give her a very tolerant look that had her swallowing.

"Yes."

"Shut up."

* * * *

Oh, the hell with it.

Denying the obvious only made Hailey look weaker than taking him on. Besides, retreat and withdraw felt like cowardice, and she didn't have a yellow-belly. This time, though, it would be on her terms. No more two hour long foreplay sessions.

Unless it ends with his ass begging.

That brought a smile to Hailey's lips even as she pressed them back against Kyle's, taking command of the moment. He tasted like sexy man mixed with the faint sweetness of juice…apple juice. Unlike some kiddy variety, his mouth held the full punch of hard cider, intoxicating her into more brazen behavior.

As her tongue beat his down with every twist and turn, she clenched her fists in his shirt and dragged him back into place. Now, that's what she wanted to feel, the hard, rigid press of his thigh between hers. Giving into the urge, she ground herself into the heated mass, making her pussy ache for a more intimate feel. Something like skin to skin.

Sucking down on the tongue Kyle managed to sneak past hers caught him off guard enough to let her shove him to her side. With a roll, she easily switched their positions, banging him into the work table so hard their lips broke apart as he groaned. Instantly bereft, her lips dropped, nibbling down his neck as her hands ripped through the rows of buttons that bared the delicious warmth of his skin to her touch.

The soft curls of hair that tufted over his chest felt silky beneath her fingers. They tickled as she explored the heated planes of his chest. Like satin stretched sensuously taut over bulging muscles, the feel of him tempted her into rubbing her cheek against his hardness.

So good. So damn good.

Hailey licked out to tweak the nipple that scuffed under her chin and delighted in the sudden breath strangling Kyle's throat. Tempted, she did it again. Lapping over him as he had done to her last night, the sweetly teasing caress ended in the sharp scrape of teeth, making Kyle groaned and jerked.

Oh, yeah, she remembered how he delighted in driving her insane. Well, two could play at that, and there was nothing more that she would delight in than riding this Cattleman like he was *her horse.*

* * * *

Kyle closed his eyes and gave the moment over to Hailey, more than pleased that she wanted to have it at all. He expected a lot more resistance than that soft mouth tormenting him. Clenching down on another groan as she bit him again, Kyle's smirk curled into a snarl when she sucked the little wound.

Hailey had a powerful mouth, and hopefully she knew what to do with it. Waiting for the answer to that question became painful as she taunted him. Slowly following the happy trail down, Hailey took her time before she started tugging on his jeans.

His control flexed with the need to take over and help his little princess. He would have given into the urge, but he didn't want to interfere with Hailey's revenge. He knew what those little nibbles on his nipples meant. If his little princess thought she could win at his game, then he'd just have to show her that no woman broke him.

Bring it on, little one.

Kyle smirked over that thought as Hailey finally managed to shove his jeans just enough down his hips to have his cock bobbing out. Anticipating a full-on assault, he cracked an eye when his poor dick just hung there hungry.

Concentrating on his jeans, Hailey didn't even appear to notice the erection a mere inch from her cheek. It hit him again that Hailey really didn't get around enough. She just didn't understand the principles of seducing a man because he sure as shit didn't care about his jeans.

Contracting just the right set of muscles, he managed to pop her in the cheek, leaving behind a sticky kiss. That got her annoyed gaze snapping up toward him. Kyle didn't even try to sound contrite, much less hide his grin, as he shrugged.

"Sorry, princess."

Silently, he waited to see if she could deliver the threat in her narrowed gaze as it stayed locked with his as her mouth flexed all the way open. That tongue rolled out and slowly licked down over his cock's head. Never once did her gaze flinch from his as her lips followed, brushing gently against his burning flesh before consuming it in her velvety embrace.

Oh, now that's hot.

He'd give her points for that, Kyle admitted as he sucked in a savoring breath, enjoying the way she drew out the moment. No need to rush, he intended to keep her there a long time because he had no intentions of—

"Sweet Mother of God!"

She bit him! Not hard, but enough of a nibble that the pain whorled the pleasure to piercing shards that broke the damn of his desire. Lust poured like molten lava out of the balls captured in her grip as she mercilessly fucked him with that glorious mouth.

Every drop of blood in his body rushed into his swelling dick, turning it into a living flame. Her wicked little tongue whipped the fires to muscle-spasming peaks at it heralded the sweet glide of her lips. Clamped down like a vise, her mouth pulled the already taut skin of his dick even tighter, making his head bang against the car as he fought for control.

She had him at the edge, but Kyle spent a lot of time there. Digging in, he panted through the rolling waves of pleasure, forcing his release back no matter the agony.

So damn close, so...oh, shit!

Kyle's heart froze even as his eyes went wide when Hailey's mouth popped free.

Those damn lips clamped down, sucking in a frail line of skin to catch between her teeth for her tongue to torment as they slid all the way down the side of his cock to balls. Tingly sprouts of pain shot up, infusing the rapture boiling through his system with panicked alarm. The feel of those pouty lips brushing open over the thin walls of his balls had the chaos going into full riot as the rush of ecstasy bore down on him.

"Hailey...*Hailey...HAILEY!*"

The hands gripping his cock choked off Kyle's roars. He had, no doubt, known what humiliation Hailey had in store for him, but, God help him, he couldn't save himself. Especially not when she began pumping his dick better than any woman ever had.

Hell, better than him, given the way she sucked his balls. Like they were candy, she tormented his tender sacks. Licking, sucking, even nibbling, she made him cry out in frustration. It hurt so much to hold back. Faster and harder, his heart raced to keep pace with the hands working him right over the edge.

The little witch! That thought popped out before the blinding white light consumed him. Piercing his control like a spear, her evil little tongue tickled down to toy with the ultrasensitive skin behind his balls. She shifted back up to milk the seed that exploded out of them as Kyle lost the battle.

* * * *

Hailey released Kyle to stumble back in a vain attempt to avoid the load he shot out all over her hair and shoulder. *Great.* Hailey's nose wrinkled as she gained her feet to stare at the big Cattleman panting and heaving as he clung to the edge of the work table.

Now, what was she supposed to do? He'd gotten his scratched, and she was still itchy. Hailey didn't blame herself for that problem, even if she'd intentionally set out to humble the arrogant ass. All she cared about then was that her good time had wilted back into limp sausage, leaving her to do what she normally did.

"Well, I guess it's a good thing the batteries in my dildo last more than *five minutes.*"

With that arrow shot, she turned and stormed off. Hitting the button on the garage door opener, she delighted more than a little in the curses and the sudden rush of motion she could hear behind her. That made her feel a little better. Storming out and slamming into her house made her feel even better, but locking Kyle's arrogant, useless ass out put the smile back on her face. Why in the hell was she even worrying about that idiot in the first place?

No reason, obviously. He might have come here looking to make trouble, but she'd definitely won that argument. For all the good it did her. At least it did one thing—shatter her illusions that Kyle had anything special going on. Last night seemed to have said yes, but obviously he wasn't any different than any other guy she jacked off.

Admittedly, masturbation only took things so far, but it never forgot to call, never stared at the waitress' breasts, never left dirty underwear on the floor or the toilet seat up and never, *not once*, shot its load five minutes into what should have been an hour-long celebration.

Hailey slammed through her bedroom into the bathroom, smacking the buttons to start her personal shower. That's all a woman really needed, a state-of-the-art shower system. Hailey installed her own. Dual rain heads for that idiotic belief that someday somebody might want to shower with her.

Well, that had been money wasted, but the three sides of full body jets, now that had been money very well spent. Better spent there than on a wedding, Hailey snorted to herself as she whipped her shirt over her head. It took her less than thirty seconds to strip down and her shower even less to heat up.

No dingy shower curtain or falling-off tiles led into her small slice of Utopia. Hailey had gone all out when she renovated her bathroom, mostly because she'd done all the work. The shower had been her baby, a curved stone wall that hid an exotic oasis in the middle of her traditional Southern white-wood house.

As she stepped into the shower, water sprayed out from the uneven stone walls, drenching her in liquid heat while fat plumps of water rained down from the ceiling. *Oh, yeah.* All worries and concerns just melted away as the steam wrapped itself around her.

This was Hailey's happy place, where she could close her eyes and dream of things she never admitted to, not even to herself. Today, as she settled into the full spray of hot water, Hailey's only problem was which fantasy would suit her best. All of last night, she focused only on Kyle, berating any slip of her imagination that injected any *other* man into her fantasy.

Now, though, it seemed almost fittingly spiteful to let Kyle be replaced by his partner. And just what would Cole do? Given last night, Hailey already knew. He'd torment her, make her turn around and lean up against the stone wall to put on a full show just for him.

Letting her eyes slip closed, Hailey imagined what it would be like to have those piercing blue eyes watching her, possessing her with just a look. Wickedly hungry, they'd linger where they shouldn't, where it wouldn't be decent. Just to tease him, she'd lift a leg.

Resting her foot on the little bench, she would slide her hand all the way up her thigh to bump over her pussy lips, giving him a little peek at the cunt hidden beneath. No lingering, she would make him sweat hotter than the steam shower and take her time.

That's why she just cupped her breast for the barest second before continuing on. Working the day's stiffness out of her shoulders, Hailey could almost hear Cole growling in her mind to get on with it. The impatience brought a slight smile to her lips as she imagined how eager he'd be.

He'd watch her, aching for her hands to touch as his hands wanted—down, slowly down, letting his palms roll her nipples into hardened buds, before sliding his fingers around to tease the sides of her breasts. Work roughened, those beautiful thumbs would swirl out in long passes, brushing against the edges of her tits before capturing them under the hard grind that had her back arching and little whimpers falling from her lips.

Pinch those tits for me, darlin'.

Cole's voice purred out of the shadows of her imagination, a husky drawl that echoed from the night before. She obeyed, aroused beyond caring that it excited her to yield. Twisting, pinching, lifting her breasts so her lips could reach the tender tips to suck, she obeyed every perverted command Cole issued, feeling the need boil hotter than the steam sizzling against her skin.

Her hips rolled and swayed, begging for the touch she ached most for, but Cole wouldn't let her take it. Not that she would. Instead, he used her hands as instruments of torture, letting only one finger slide down to flick her clit and send sparklers of delight rocketing through her.

Hailey whimpered to do it again, a little more, but he wanted something more from her. He wanted to watch her feed her little pussy, one finger at a time, having her fuck herself for his delight. Wild, abandoned, Hailey gave in to the urge, freed in her own submission, reveling in the delights of being possessed by another, especially someone as merciless as Cole because he wasn't going to be content with those shy little fingers.

He wanted to see her pussy stretched out over his dick, but the only one she had available sat on the ledge where she'd left it last night. It would amuse him, no doubt, to know that she used it thinking of his friend and he'd command her now to think of Kyle.

Thinking of Kyle fucking her on Cole's command, just like GD had screwed that woman last night for Cole's pleasure, Hailey sighed and whined as she pressed the dildo all the way in. Not nearly as long or as thick as the cock Cole had to give her, he taunted her with that fact, making her beg for something more, something that would put an end to the ache in her cunt.

Roll over, darlin', and spread that little pussy wide in front of the water spray.

Hailey cried out as she obeyed, taking the full force of the stream against her clit. It sent her into a frenzy, her hips swinging her pussy back and forth as she fucked herself between the dildo and the shower wall.

All the while Cole's voice haunted her. *That's it, darlin'. Think of what it'd be like to have me licking that little clit while Kyle rides that cunt to exhaustion.*

Hailey tensed, about ready to scream with the blinding explosion of release when the sound got stuck. Trapped in the same vise that held her heart still, Hailey's fantasy exploded into reality as a large, male hand knocked hers out of the way. Bringing the dildo to a stop fully embedded inside her, Kyle's shoulder pressed into her back, forcing her against the shower wall.

"I told you last night, this pussy belongs to me."

Chapter 10

Hailey didn't even have time to comprehend how the world shifted all around her. With barely a second between his warning and his action, she got half a breath in before, suddenly, the dildo was fucking into her so savagely that all she could do was scream.

His free hand curled around her hips to splay her pussy lips wide and expose her sensitive clit to the full, relentless blast of the water. In a destructive fit, her release broke hard over her, shattering her body beneath the force of the dildo slipping free of her cunt only to impale her ass. The sudden penetration ripped through her orgasm, making it bloom into unknown heights.

Hailey soared with it into the heavens, floating happy and free until the bastard spanked her back down to the hard wall he had her pinned against. Gasping at the shock of re-entering her own body, Hailey twisted, bucking against Kyle's strength.

He met her vain attempt to protect herself with another hard blow to her ass. The spank made that damn toy jostle, wrenching out a scream of pleasure from her already overwrought body. Panting through the aftermath, Hailey tried to ease her cunt away from the water stream blasting over her clit, keeping it painfully atwitter.

"You need a lot of discipline, Hailey Mathews," Kyle sighed. He shifted slightly, snaking a hand around her waist.

"You don't move unless I tell you to."

Hailey cried out as he delivered an even harder blow to her inflamed ass along with the grunt. Clenching over the convulsions that rolled through her, she could feel the tears forming along her lashes. That's how bad she ached, and Hailey knew Kyle didn't have any intentions of soothing her desires anytime soon.

"You certainly don't pet—much less fuck—*my pussy* without *my permission*."

Crack.

"Kyle, please."

Dignity be damned, Hailey cried out as the crest of rapture broke down over her. She couldn't survive this, couldn't indulge in this kind of wicked pleasure and still come out the same. The fear that scraped at the edges of her lust only fed the beast, fueling its rage as Kyle pounded through his list of complaints.

With each slap, he struck a new chord in the euphoric symphony singing through her body. The high notes squealed out of her in incoherent pleas as she approached the sweetest of summits. It figured he'd leave her to writhe there, cutting off all stimulation at once.

The dildo disappeared as did the spray of water as he cupped her pussy in his protective embrace. As much as it might have burned for her to admit it, disappointment crept in as the rioting balloons of lust deflated back into a simmering block of wretched need.

"You know, Hailey," Kyle sighed as if he wasn't standing in her shower fully clothed, tormenting her as if she were nothing more than a toy. "I think I spoiled you a little too much last night. Now, that's my fault. I admit it. I was just so excited to finally have you beneath me, I got a little carried away and gave you way too many orgasms.

"'Cause you see, princess, I didn't have to." Kyle's voice dropped into a dangerous growl as his lips nuzzled against her ear. "I can eat that cunt for twice as long as I did last night and never let you come once."

Hailey's heart stilled at the warning buried in that threat.

"You're going to have to be a good girl, Hailey Mathews, a sweet one to earn your reward." The humor in his tone assured her he didn't think she could do it.

* * * *

In fact, Kyle would have bet on it. He intended to give her more than enough rope to justify the things he wanted to do to her with it. Releasing her came as the first test, and the little spitfire surprised him by staying flush to the wall.

Perfectly still, so she had been listening, and worrying. Kyle enjoyed that victory. It made him eager to show her just how much he had in store for her. That wouldn't happen with her facing the wall. Stepping back to make sure he got a good look at her, Kyle ordered Hailey to turn around.

Obeying, she faced him, and he couldn't help but to take a minute and enjoy the view.

"You know, princess, I really liked that little show you put on for me." His fingers moved toward the buttons of his shirt, but his attention remained fixated on the puckered nipples pointing back at him. "I'm betting you had quite a fantasy going in that head of yours, so why don't you tell me just whose cock you dreamt of fucking."

The slight curl of her lip had his gaze narrowing even though she answered correctly. "You."

It had better fucking be him or he'd terrorize that cunt so bad it wouldn't weep for any man other than him. Hell, he intended to do that anyway. The reminder brought a smirk to his face.

"You ain't gotta dream, princess. Anytime you want, I got all the dick you'll ever need." His shirt slapped on the tile floor and he'd already reached for his belt buckle when she muttered back her heart's true response.

"For five minutes."

Kyle had known she wouldn't be able to resist for long, and she hadn't even lasted a minute before earning herself another punishment. First, though, he had a point to prove. Ripping the leather free of its buckle, he fought the wet jeans, trying to push them down. The old hound got in the way, but once he bounced free, Kyle's jeans dropped with ease.

He felt Hailey's instant reaction to the large cock straining over the distance to point at what it wanted. Alert, focused, and intent, just like a hound that had spotted its prey, Kyle's erection ached to get in touch with the smooth skin of Hailey's mound. Touch and then drill because that's really what the beast panting at the end of its leash dreamed of.

"Surprise, Hailey." Kyle moved in on the woman staring at his dick as though it had some magical power. Cupping her chin, he forced those wide, worried eyes back up to his. "I might be worth only five minutes, but the thought of you gets me ready to go in another five. That's what you do to me, princess. You make me ache to fuck you."

Brushing the trembles from her lips with his kiss, Kyle groaned out the truth. "I've been aching for years, Hailey. Back in shop class, I'd watch you bend over cars and get this pain in my balls from the need to just walk up behind you and plunge a hand down into your panties.

"I knew you'd hit me, just as I knew you would be wet as hell. I'd have tamed this pussy with an orgasm and then dropped your drawers and ridden you there in front of everybody. Every damn man would have known who you belonged to. No matter what you want to believe, I would have won.

"I just didn't have the balls to do it then, but I do now."

Instead of soothing the tension out of her as he actually hoped, Hailey stiffened slightly, pulling back to pin him with a gaze that had only darkened more. "This is just sex, Kyle. Don't bother trying to make it into anything more."

The slight rejection gave him pause, and he felt suddenly unsure of his entire plan. "Is that all you want? Just sex?"

"What else would I want from you? I don't even like you."

Kyle felt his ears go red at that blunt statement. Of all the possible reactions, he was still outraged at that comment coming now. "You have an odd way of showing your dislike, Hailey."

Needing to prove that point, he hooked one of her knees over his arm and bent it up, opening her pussy wide for the thick head he brought to its creaming gate. "Go on and say it again, darlin'. Tell me you don't like *this*."

Hailey's whole back arched with the scream he wrung out of her with one single, savage thrust. Her little sheath ate up his entire length with a greedy suckle, spasming all around him in obvious delight. For all that, Hailey still defied him. Even as her hips twisted and turned, rocking her cunt along his length, she panted out her rejection.

"It's just sex, Kyle. That's all. If I could figure out how to break this lust, I would because I don't want to like you."

Son of a bitch. "Fine," Kyle snarled, wrenching his hips back. "I'll give you your fucking, Hailey Mathews, but don't ever ask for anymore."

* * * *

It wasn't the ruthless thrust that punctuated that statement that had her heart clenching, but the sparkle that hardened over in his gaze. Hailey didn't have a chance to question it or wonder. With his fingers biting into the cheeks of her ass, he held her still for his savaging.

Hard and fast, grunting like a warhorse in full gallop, Kyle rode her. With every delicious slide of his heated cock over the wall of her sheath, he left a painful clench of need in his wake, driving her to beg him.

"Harder. Faster." Hailey's nails clenched into the taut skin of his shoulders as her hips began to flex with her demands.

The water went cool all around them, but it didn't matter. Nothing mattered beyond the sweet rhythm of the man grunting over her as he fucked her as savagely as she begged for. The overwhelming lust didn't protect her from the dangers of the heart. The bright bolts of ecstasy skyrocketing through her left a trail of rapture all the way to her soul.

Quaking out from the very center of her heart, her release triggered from the wrong spot. Too late, it catapulted her beyond reality, flying her into a world of warmth and comfort and soul-drenching pleasure. Like parched earth, she felt herself grow alive under the rainfall of her orgasm.

Biting down on Kyle's shoulder, Hailey hid the sobs that tried to wrench through her. Clinging to him, she sought safety from the frightening emotions billowing through her. The salty taste of him beneath her lips only worsened the pain.

As did his release. With a massive roar, he flooded her, pounding her brutally back against the wall as he lost control. Hailey cried out as she felt him filling more than her body. The bastard invaded her heart, merging into her very soul and making the pleasure that much more wretched.

Damn him. Hailey sucked in a deep breath, beating back the rapture to battle the unwanted emotions trying to cocoon her. This hadn't been a tender loving, but a rutting, just like she asked for. *It's only sex.*

As if he could read the thought in her mind, Kyle sighed heavily and jerked back. Stepping free almost before she even took a breath, he abandoned her, leaving her wobbling on her own two legs with a pussy that still ached for more. So did he.

He might have blown two loads, but Kyle's cock still stayed hard, glaring angrily at her with one eye. It matched the scowl on its master's face as he yanked his soaking jeans off the floor. Stepping into them had to hurt, but the pain of trying to get his erection back inside the stiff jeans didn't show in his tone.

That remained as cold and dismissive as his actions. "I hope that sufficed, Hailey, because that's all the sex you gonna get."

She didn't dare respond to that taunt, unsure of what her response would be. The tears burning behind her eyes warned her it wouldn't be the anger she needed to fortify her defenses. Instead of risking anymore in this moment, Hailey just stayed there leaning against the wall and watching as he jerked his sodden clothes back on.

Stomping back into his boots, he paused only to glower at her. "You can have the car, Hailey. You've earned it."

With that backhanded insult, he stormed off and she didn't even try to stop him. Staying in her safe little stupor until the door banged closed, Hailey didn't make a sound.

* * * *

Kyle had never been so fucking pissed in all of his life. If Hailey had been a man, he'd have beaten her to a pulp for making him feel this God-awful. *All she wants is sex.* What a bunch of crap that was? No woman fucked a man like she did him and didn't care.

She was just a bull-headed pain in his ass. Like Hailey didn't know the difference between fucking and loving. Screw her. Kyle didn't have to get all in a twist. He could have any kind of woman he wanted in less than a half hour and sure as shit they would be thanking God if he took more of an interest than just in their pussies.

Kyle jerked the Trans Am to a hard stop at the light and let his head whip back onto the wheel. *Oh, God.* He'd screwed that all up. If his goal had been pissing off Hailey to the point where she never let him touch her again, mission accomplished. Now what the hell was he supposed to do?

A beep from behind had him looking back up into a light that had gone green in almost ironic answer to his silent question. He didn't really have any choice but to roll through both the intersection and the disaster he created. Bluster or charm, those were his options because Kyle wouldn't honestly beg.

A blizzard would have to hit lower Alabama before he became any woman's pussy. Charm had gotten him along so far, but it would be what Hailey expected. In fact, she probably already thought he'd be showing up hat in hand to work on the Daytona the next day or so. Just what would the little spitfire do if he didn't?

Her pride wouldn't let her keep the car, that's for sure. She'd probably show up in a fiery whirl of indignation, but Kyle would bet money half her anger would be passion fed. His little honey would be horny, really horny, because that damn dildo wouldn't do what he could and they both knew it.

Just as sure as they both knew she would want him again. Next time though, Hailey would have to come hat in hand and on her knees begging him before Kyle gave her another thrill. A grin spread across his face just thinking of what the moment would feel like. Glorious, that's what.

It wouldn't be enough. All the pleading he could make her do wouldn't satisfy the pain aching in him. Kyle felt absolutely miserable and Hailey should have to pay for that. Leashing her to his bed and making her into his plaything wouldn't do. No. Kyle wanted Hailey as vulnerable and exposed as him. Equal measure, that's what he would demand if she ever came around looking for seconds.

If?

She would. She had to or he'd just made the stupidest mistake of his life and given her an out.

Which one sounds like realism, and which one sounds like desperate hope?

Cole's obnoxious voice echoed in his head. That's just what Cole would say too before he bust a gut laughing at Kyle. Not that he expected Cole to be all smiles when Kyle returned to the shop. Given how late he was, Kyle prepared to run the gauntlet as he bumped the Trans Am back into the parking lot.

* * * *

Cole breathed out slowly, glaring down the clock as it ticked one second off at a time. Thirty-two minutes and counting. That's how late Kyle was getting back from lunch. For a man who had not once in three years been late to work or from lunch, it stood as a stark statement for just how far his friend had fallen.

Cole didn't even hesitate to conclude that Kyle had ripped out of the shop to go be with his Pink Panty Lady. Kyle's lunchtime hook-up wouldn't have fazed Cole a bit if they didn't have Coldwell's Mustang due out the door in fifteen minutes.

Fifteen minutes. That's how long Kyle had to get back and fix the final short. Why the stupid son of a bitch hadn't taken the time to do that before he hauled for his pussy call, Cole feared he knew. Kyle had lost it.

Behind him, the Mustang cranked but didn't fire as Jacob and Aaron argued in a near frenzy to find the short only Kyle knew the location was on. That's just what he said before he left. He found the short and he'd fix it after lunch.

Thirty-five minutes. God help Kyle when Cole got a chance to have a word with him. Kyle could go solo in the bedroom if he wanted, but he was still a damn member of this team and they relied on him. This shit just wasn't cool.

"I'm going to kill Kyle." Cole meant it, too.

"Kill him after he fixes the short," Aaron nodded to the window as a flash of red streaked past. "He just pulled up."

Point taken because Cole surely did want to go out and greet his flighty business partner. Instead, he remained rooted in his spot, along with Aaron and Jacob. All three of them waited, gazes locked on the back door.

Whatever they expected, what crashed in hadn't been on the list. Slamming through the metal door, Kyle sloshed in looking like he'd trudged through a rain storm that hadn't darkened the sunny day. The shock held everybody, but Aaron, still.

"Holy shit, dude," Aaron yelled, jerking forward. "You didn't get in my car like that did you?"

"How the hell else was I supposed to get back here?" Kyle shot back.

"Son of a bitch." Aaron caught the keys Kyle threw and rushed out the back door. No doubt he'd be returning as soon as he got over his moment to carry on with Kyle. Cole didn't have time. No time for Aaron's shit, much less Kyle's.

Slamming the meter into Kyle's on-coming chest, Cole only had one thing to say. "You got ten minutes before Coldwell shows up."

Brushing past him, Cole moved as far away from temptation as he could. Slamming into his office, he just glared down at the paperwork, unable to shake his anger. A part of him knew it was out of proportion to the incident. So Kyle had been late, once. Hell, Aaron was late routinely, and Jacob never knew what time it was.

The seething in his gut had nothing to do with the Coldwell's Mustang and everything to do with the truth he had just seen in Kyle's eyes. That bastard had fallen in love. It wasn't jealousy that his friend might find happiness or might exclude Cole from it that had his muscles twitching with the need to punch something.

It was the sure knowledge that Kyle was going to get hurt. Hurt bad.

Chapter 11

Wednesday, May 7th

"Oh, shut up." Hailey whipped the pillow out from behind her to smack Patton's laughing ass in the face. "It's not that damn funny."

The hit toppled Patton over and almost sent her rolling off the plush edge of the couch. The convulsions of hilarity aided in her momentum, and they didn't stop. Not even when Patton tried to smother them into the cushions.

Hailey should have known that would be Patton's reaction to her confession. It had been nearly a whole week since Kyle disappeared in a snit. A whole week she held her silence. Using the excuse that Patton had her time filled with her three men, Hailey kept her misery to herself.

Now, though, she'd come to the point of breaking. Only two things would be happening in the next day. She'd either go totally insane with need, or she'd have to give in and call Kyle. Neither represented an acceptable conclusion to Hailey. An alternative solution, that's what she needed. It also happened to be Patton's specialty.

Of course she'd have to wait for Patton to finish belting out the laughter. The very fact that Hailey opened herself up to this moment went to show how desperate she'd become. That didn't mean she had to sit there and listen to it.

Leaving her best friend to ham it up on her own, Hailey marched into the kitchen in search of something to actually eat for lunch. Acting like she owned the place, she wrenched open the fridge door and began rifling around. Hailey helped herself to some yogurt, ignoring Patton as she came stumbling into the kitchen, still half drunk with amusement.

"Hey, grab me one of those."

"I don't know why I should." But she did. Snatching a second container, she dumped both on the island as Patton slid into a stool on the other side.

"Because I'm a good friend and I'm going to help you with your problem," Patton answered with absolute sincerity as she slid onto one of the island stools. "Given how big it is, I need sustenance."

"I don't have a problem, Patton." Hailey slapped a spoon down beside the container Patton drew toward her. "I am having a full psychotic breakdown."

"Oh, get over it." The tin top to Patton's yogurt splattered down on the counter as she dug in. "Kyle Harding is a hottie, and most women would be thanking God he'd taken such an interest in them."

"That's just my point," Hailey retorted, not about to be dissuaded from her position. "You know what Kyle's reputation is. He's easy."

"Of course he is. He's a man." Patton laughed. "All men are easy unless they're in love with another woman. You can't hold that against him, Hailey. You have to give the man points because as far as the rumor mill has it, he's been faithful to this relationship from the start."

Hailey rolled her eyes at that. "I am not having a relationship with Kyle Harding."

"Uh-huh."

"The only reason I'm stuck on thinking about him is because that damn car is stuck in my garage."

"Huh."

"If being in a relationship with that ass means getting treated like some cheap-ass whore to be bought off and paid for with some rusted piece of shit, then I'd rather die lonely."

"Hmm."

"And if he doesn't come and get it soon, I'm going to have it towed over to the front of his shop and set it on fire."

"Mmm."

"*Oh, will you shut up.*" Hailey ripped the tin safety layer off the top of her yogurt and chunked it into the sink. "Do I need to remind you of what he said?"

"You mean what he said after you pissed him off enough to say it?" Patton nodded. "Yeah, I remember."

"You're taking his side?" Hailey gasped.

Patton shook her head, licking her spoon clean before responding. "I'm just saying be as mad as you want about him being a jerk. That doesn't change the fact that he's cornered you. You either have to go on being horny and grumpy or give in."

"Give in?" The very idea had Hailey reeling. *"Give in?* That's the advice I came all the way out here to get? I've suffered the humiliation of you laughing your ass off at me just to hear you tell me to call him up and what? Apologize? It's been five days, Patton. I'm going to look pathetic."

"Have you lost your fricken mind?" Patton gave her a look as if she had. "Does that sound like me at all? Call him? Please, Hailey. The last thing you do with a man like Kyle is cave. You need a plan. A better one than just sleeping with him."

"Oh, for Christ's sake," Hailey muttered, totally disgusted. "Why did I even come here? I'm not interested in joining the revolution, Patton. I'm just trying to figure out what to do about Kyle."

"That's where you're wrong. You're already in the revolution. Look around this town, Hailey. There is a war going on, and we're losing women left and right."

"That include you?" Hailey asked pointedly.

Just the small reminder of Patton's position brought a satisfied smile to her friend's face. "I'm fighting the war from the inside."

Hailey snorted. "I'll bet you are."

"Look." Patton dropped her spoon into her yogurt container before meeting Hailey's gaze head on. "I chased my men. I got my men. You, on the other hand, are being chased. If you don't wise up and start taking control, you're going to be playing Kyle's game—with his rules—and trust me, you'll be screwed both inside and outside the bedroom."

Hailey scowled because that's just what she'd been thinking all week long. It would have made her life so much easier if she could just forget about him. Barring the reality of her accomplishing that goal, Hailey still floundered for a real plan.

"Let's just say I've totally lost my mind and would listen to *your* advice. What would you tell me to do?"

"Well," Patton pondered that as her spoon fell into her empty yogurt container, "I guess the first thing I'd say is you have to test his position."

"His position?"

"You can always tell who holds the power at this stage by which one is willing to follow." Patton shrugged. "It's the same as in high school when we used to move around a room or go outside and see if a boy follows you. Then you have the lead."

She knew she'd regret asking. "I don't think that really applies here, Patton."

"That's because he has the lead," Patton shot back. "And you should be ashamed of yourself for letting him take it."

That had Hailey bristling. "I didn't let him take anything, Patton."

"No, you just wigged all out when it felt like something more than sex." Patton's grin disappeared in an instant as she leaned over the counter. "But you got to stop thinking every man is like your dad, Hailey. They don't all leave."

Hailey flinched back from that. "That's not fair, Patton. This doesn't have anything to do with my father. Kyle's not interested in me for me. This is some kind of game Cole's set up."

Patton honestly appeared to consider her response. When she leaned in across the counter, Hailey expected a sincere, if not even compassionate, comment.

"Do you know what the definition of paranoia is?"

"Oh, screw you, Patton," Hailey snapped. "I'm not paranoid. Cole is out to get me. He said it himself. Game on."

"Eh," Patton waved that away, "that man's got a boner for you a mile long. The last game he'd play is where you ended up sleeping with his best friend and not him."

"Exactly." Hailey pounced. "That's why this thing with Kyle isn't just this thing with Kyle. They're trying to lure me in, Patton."

"Why you say it like that?" Patton scowled. "So what if they are? If you're not tempted, then...*oh*, you—"

"Shut up, Patton." Hailey didn't want to hear it, not even the rolls of laughter that came tumbling back out of her friend.

"You want to fuck Cole Jackson."

Hailey glared at her grinning friend, feeling almost betrayed. "Why you got to go there, Patton? You know how much I hate Cole. He's an absolute pig, and only the lowest class of low class women would ever crawl into his bed. You think I'm that sad?"

"I think you protest a lot for a woman who's not interested, and you kind of tried to steer me as hard away from Cole as you could."

"Because I was trying to save you," Hailey shot back. She could feel the heat seeping into her cheeks and hated the tell-tale trait that always gave her away when she tried to lie to Patton.

"Yeah, but if you didn't want him, you wouldn't be so worried about resisting him."

"I do not want Cole."

Hailey laid the lie down like a gauntlet. Straightening back from the declaration, Hailey waited for Patton to challenge her. She didn't but just sat there patiently, smiling as Hailey's blush consumed her face and she finally broke.

"Okay, fine. I might have some…primitive interest in certain *parts* of his body. That certainly doesn't change the fact that I can't stand the man."

"I'm just saying *maybe* you don't want things to be more than just sex with Kyle because if you actually had a relationship with him you might also find yourself getting closer to Cole."

"You're insane." Hailey shook her head. "Like some deranged cupid."

"I'm right, and you know it." Patton's chin rose, and Hailey could feel her heels digging in. "Now if you're smart, you will actually listen to me this time."

"Oh, really? And what does the ever-so-wise oracle have to tell me today?"

"First, I would advise you to be kinder to those giving you advice."

Hailey gave Patton a sharp look for that smart comeback but held her insulting response in.

"Second, I would tell you to stop worrying about Cole and relationships. You worry too much, Hailey. Just enjoy life a little bit and let this thing with Kyle grow on and in its own way."

Hailey arched a brow at that easygoing philosophy coming from Patton. "And, of course, that means manipulating him, but how?"

Patton made a face at Hailey's obnoxiousness but gave her a sincere-sounding answer. "Okay. Here's your next move. Go eat dinner at the Bread Box."

The sudden change threw Hailey. "What?"

"I'm telling you it's the follow rule." Patton's hand chopped through the air, highlighting her point. "You go to the Bread Box and park your car out front around the time Kyle's shop closes. That way, when he gets off from work, you'll know he'll see it. If he comes in, then you have the power. If not," Patton shrugged, "well, then we have a lot more work to do."

"That's just stupid." Hailey didn't care if Patton took insult at her response. "I'm not eight years old, Patton. I'm not going to go sit in the Bread Box and see if Kyle comes running. That's just...immature and stupid."

* * * *

So I'm immature and stupid.

Technically, though, she was here for her friend, even if Rachel hadn't shown up. Hailey hoped that didn't mean Killian and Adam found her, otherwise Rachel would never show. Without Rachel, Hailey didn't have proof of her legitimate claim that she was at the Bread Box to see Rachel and not spark any confrontation with Kyle.

Sure, she'd suggested the Bread Box to Rachel, but that was only because Heather owned the place. Given Rachel had thrown Killian and Adam out of her house, she would need her friends.

For fifteen long minutes, Hailey repeated those facts silently to herself, ready to spew them forth should Kyle come walking through that door. If Kyle arrived before Rachel, the gig would be up and her dignity would be in total tatters. Hailey's chin hit her palms as she stared gloomily down at the table.

I should have just called him and said I needed a quickie.

That defeatist attitude rankled as much as the good cheer swelling all around her as the dinnertime crowd grew. Slowly, the Bread Box packed in with locals cramming in around all the tables in search of some of the best fried chicken in Alabama.

Only Rachel's breakup let Hailey hold on to a four-person booth. Otherwise, Heather would have kicked her butt to the counter, friend or not. Only getting here pathetically early had secured her a parking spot out front not but a road-width away from the edge of Kyle and Cole's shop.

He wouldn't come. If he did, it would probably be just to gloat. Then it would probably be her turn to go down on bended knee because his ego would certainly have him holding out even more. Hailey didn't think she could take it.

God, but she ached, and even if her hand would never be better than good enough, it would be a hell of a lot more of a stable relationship than going through this torture. Why had she ever listened to Patton? These things never worked out, and, worse, they tended to explode all over the place.

Groaning at the mere impossibility of being able to come out of this with dignity intact, Hailey's head hit the table. She really should leave, but she wasn't going to.

"It can't be that bad."

Cracking an eye, Hailey frowned at Rachel's look. "At least not as bad as it is for you today."

Chapter 12

Kyle peered out the little window in the shop door before shoving it open. Cole, Aaron, and Jacob lingered around having an end-of-the-day beer. Not that unusual except that they weren't out back and they all stared across the street at the big, green Studebaker parked like a flag at the top of a mountain in front of the Bread Box.

Hailey had finally come. He wondered how long she'd make him sweat it out, but this? If the little woman thought he'd play along with the game, she had it all backward. He wouldn't let her duck out of giving him his victory, much less let her manipulate him into giving her one.

He knew. She wanted him to follow, to show just how desperate he was to get a glimpse of her by rushing across the street into the bakery.

Let the little woman wait.

He could afford to be that confident because she followed first.

She'd shown up, and just how close that meant Hailey had come to caving made Kyle a very confident and happy man. Instead of being ashamed to gloat over his victory, Kyle reveled in the moment of satisfaction. He earned it.

He collected more cuts, nicks, bruises, and even a burn mark thanks to being distracted by the angry tyrant in his jeans demanding he give over every minute for these past five days. It hadn't just been the unrelenting ache in his balls keeping him unfocused while trying to work.

Kyle honestly missed Hailey, missed all the little sharp comments and dry retorts. He missed watching her nose crinkle as she concentrated on something or the way she muttered to herself while she worked. Even the scent of cinnamon haunted him. He just wanted one more deep breath.

Kyle's eyes drifted closed as the need that almost had him calling her a million times a day rolled through him again. Like the wind of a hurricane, it made him wobble slightly. This time he bore it with the cool certainty that it would be one of the last times. Hailey would cave soon.

Real soon.

First, though, he had to go put a leash on Cole. GD kept Cole good and distracted for over the past month. Kyle certainly appreciated it, but the disaster that took place five days ago left Cole a little too alert and attentive. In a way, Hailey's tantrum helped cool the spark of tension between Cole and him back to normal.

That didn't mean Cole wouldn't accidently relight them by taking up the pursuit of Kyle's woman. If only Hailey liked Cole. That would have made Kyle's life so much easier. Sure as shit, Cole wouldn't have left her bed cold and empty for five straight days. He'd have righted Kyle's stupid blunder.

Life didn't work out that way, and as he locked up the door, Kyle gave up hoping it ever would.

"I know."

Catching Aaron's confident tone as he sauntered up behind the small group of men, Kyle's curiosity piqued. "What do you know?"

"That Hailey Mathews would sooner spit on Cole than smile at him," Aaron drawled out with a smirk.

"Hailey." Kyle kept it cool with only a hint of interest as he turned his gaze on Cole. "I didn't know you were interested in her."

Typical Cole, he shrugged at that as if showing any real interest in a woman would be owning up to a weakness. "I'm not interested in the woman. I want to fuck her. There's a difference."

"Hailey ain't the type of woman you just fuck, Cole." Despite knowing he should keep that reaction to himself, it shot out of Kyle with a reflexive instinct to protect his own.

Cole smirked. "You would know?"

"Kyle doesn't know more than a dog when it comes to Hailey," Jake responded.

"Hailey would sooner kick a dog like Kyle than she would smile at him."

Kyle would have rolled his eyes at Jacob's sense of humor, but Cole had trapped his gaze. He could feel his friend considering the severity of Kyle's comeback, weighing it for all that it could mean. One thing Cole had always been was predictable.

Whether the challenge attracted him or if he thought he might be able to distract Kyle from his Miss Pink Panties, Kyle didn't know. He did know his response just solidified Cole's intent to prioritize Hailey's seduction. There wasn't any point in trying to hide from that fact.

"Stay away from Hailey, Cole."

"You her man or something?"

It physically hurt to answer that one. "You know I ain't." But he damn well should be.

"Then you don't have the right to tell me what to do."

"She deserves better than you."

"There ain't nobody better than me."

"There's me."

"So that's the way it is, huh?"

"Yeah." It felt good to have it out in the open. "That's the way it is."

"Don't you think it should be up to the little woman to decide who is man enough to make her a real woman?"

"She'd never choose you," Kyle assured him, grinning at just how badly that would backlash on to Cole.

"Well, then," Cole grinned, "let the games begin."

* * * *

Before Kyle could give a comeback to that taunt, Cole turned and strutted across the street, feeling very enthusiastic about the coming confrontation. Sure, he'd put off chasing after Hailey for many good, sound reasons, but now he had an even better one for going after her.

This is for Kyle.

He'd face the hounds of hell for his friend. One little spitfire wouldn't intimidate him. He needed Hailey's help to save Kyle, and if that meant dooming both her and him, then so be it.

Whatever insane pussy Kyle sank himself into, his little Miss Pink Panties had withdrawn the past few days. Cole didn't trust that the crazy lady wouldn't be coming back. The crazy ones always did. There was only one thing that would fortify Kyle's defenses enough to see just how crazy Lady Crazy was—a better screw.

Cole couldn't imagine a better one than Hailey. Taking Hailey to his bed might end up destroying both his life and his sanity, but at least Kyle would be safe. Cole carried that vow through the Bread Box's door. It didn't even take him a whole second to locate Hailey tucked into a booth. If she thought she could hide from him in that corner, she made a fool's mistake.

The little brunette sitting across from Hailey, Rachel something-or-other, caught sight of him coming in their direction. He recognized her as the woman who took Killian and Adam off the market. That meant she knew quite a bit about the Cattleman way of doing things, and he could see that concern working from her eyes to her lips.

Not that she got a chance to get her warning out. Cole made fast work of the short distance, and he managed to catch Hailey completely off-guard. Pushing into her, he slid her ass into the corner of the booth as his landed down on the seat.

Just like that, he had her caged against the back wall. A fact that drained a lot of color out of Little Miss Hailey's cheeks. It rounded her eyes quite nicely, too, and Cole couldn't help but grin as he purred. "Hey, Hailey, been a long time since I seen you around here."

That pointed reminder to just how the last time ended kept his tone gloating. Cole especially enjoyed the way her features hardened. Gaze narrowing, jaw tensing, the little warrior growled at him.

"Cole."

"Hailey."

"Get out of my booth."

"I don't think so, darlin'." Stretching an arm along the back of the booth, he brushed the hair back from the side of her face. She flinched away, her face going red, and Cole didn't think it was half as much from anger as Hailey would like to pretend.

"Don't touch me."

"But you like it when I touch you. Don't you? Just a little?"

"No."

"You're a liar, Hailey Mathews." Following that growl with a hard slide closer, Cole pressed Hailey flat against the wall. With her breasts bulging against his chest, he gave her a little rub as he whispered out a truth he knew she wouldn't like hearing. "It's those hard, little nipples, darlin'. They give you away."

Before she could hit him or bite him, given as close as they were, Cole slid back and turned his full attention to the brunette who had the wide-eyed look of disbelief on her face. Intentionally trying to frustrate Hailey as much as humanly possible, he just started talking.

"I think maybe you need to leave us alone, darlin'."

That had Rachel's head cocking as her features tightened up. "Excuse me."

"There is no excuse for him," Hailey snapped from his side, shoving at him as she tried to force him out of the booth.

"I'm beginning to see that."

"Now why you two got to be so mean? Huh?" Cole asked. "And you...you don't even know the story, but you going to stick with Hailey just 'cause she's a woman, right? It don't matter at all that this little darlin' here almost got my ass beat. Three against one, that's the odds this little girl set me up against."

"You deserved it," Hailey retorted. "And you better get your ass out of my booth before I call up the Davis brothers and get them to issue another invitation to the dance."

Cole turned to give her a response to that threat, but his head snapped back as Rachel went flying cross her seat. Like a semi-truck flattening a compact, Kyle smacked into the booth. Without even seeming to recognize her presence, he slid into Rachel and bumped her down the bench.

"Hey," the little brunette objected with a hard bump back, "I was sitting here."

Kyle ignored her as he leaned into threaten Cole. "I told you to leave Hailey alone."

Straightening up and matching Kyle's snarl, Cole gave his friend back equal measure. "And since when do I take orders from you?"

"Do the two of you mind?" Hailey snapped. "I'm sitting right here."

"I haven't forgotten about you, darlin'." Cole curled in on her, brushing her ear with a promise only for her ears. "Or that challenge you issued."

"I didn't issue—"

"I'm going to be putting my hands all over that sweet body, darlin', and you're going to be begging." That came out loud enough for Kyle to hear. One bait, two fish, and they both snapped.

"Damn it, Cole," Kyle spat. Not that anybody paid him any mind.

"Maybe you'll be the one that's begging?"

Hailey's sharp retort had Cole grinning down at the defiant jaw lifting up. Hell, he could kiss her right now and then they'd see who was boss. "Is that so, darlin'—*ahhh*!"

Cole's head almost hit the side of the table, he bent so far over when Hailey's hand shot out to latch on to his nipple. The little witch twisted his tender flesh right through his fricken shirt, making shards of piercing pain shoot down his side.

"And don't call me darlin'."

Cole growled when her fingers curled even harder, trying to make him beg. Well, two could play that game. Shooting out his own hand, he managed to capture Hailey's tit. Shrieking, she immediately released him to smack at his hand.

"Damn it, Cole." The table banged into him as Kyle jerked forward like he was ready to come over it. "I told you not to touch her."

"Why are you sitting next to my woman?"

"What?" Kyle's head snapped in the direction of the shadow that growled that out, making Cole's gaze follow. He smirked at the sight of Killian in full deputy dress. The big man looked pissed. Too bad for Kyle, good for Cole.

"Get out of my way, Kyle. I need to have a word with *my woman*."

"Don't you take that tone with me," Rachel shot back at Killian over Kyle's head. "And don't you be calling me yours. I'm not a damn dog, Killian."

Smirking as his friend became trapped between the two squabbling lovers, Cole turned to issue his own soft warning to Hailey. "You twist my nipple again, darlin', and I ain't going to be held responsible."

"What? Can't take what you dish out, tough guy?"

"I can take it, darlin'. The question is can you?"

"Get out of my way, Cole."

"I said get away from my woman!" Killian's roar sliced through the diner. The sudden shock of the interruption held almost everybody still as the oversized deputy ripped Kyle from the booth. Almost everybody.

"Ah, hell." With a groan and an eye roll, Cole shoved out of the booth.

"Damn it, Killian!" Kyle shoved himself free of the deputy. "I ain't interested in Rachel."

Before Cole could even get in a smart comment to make fun of the scene they started, Killian's little fireball blazed out of the booth with sharp words for her macho man. That drew a lot more attention their way and good deal more embarrassment for Killian, which Cole enjoyed just watching until he noticed Kyle wasn't doing the same.

Kyle was having his own private, silent conversation with somebody. It was there in the slight eye movements and the little facial twitches. He was talking fast, all right, but not to Cole. With a breaking sense of doom, Cole turned in amazement to Kyle's partner in crime, and, sure enough, Hailey was bitching at Kyle the same way Rachel mouthed off to Killian.

It couldn't be. Cole leaned into her shoulder and got a good, hard sniff before she shoved him away. *Cinnamon.*

"What the hell is wrong with you?" Hailey demanded, full vigor. "Were you raised in a barn?"

"You're Miss Pink Panties?" Cole couldn't even believe his own words, and they tumbled out in a confused question.

Hailey's response didn't make him feel like a fool. Every drop of color faded from her flaming face as she stilled into a stupor, her shock falling from her lips in a squeaky whisper. "What?"

"Oh, my God." Cole reeled back slightly, trying to figure it all out as amazement wore into horror. "It was you hiding under my bed while GD and I screwed Claudia."

The fact that Hailey had gone silent along with the rest of the diner didn't register in Cole's whirling mind. Neither did the fact that he started yelling. All that mattered was the most gut-wrenching truth of all.

Looking over at Kyle, he could see it already on his face. "Now, Cole—"

"You fucked Hailey Mathews, and *you didn't even share!*"

Chapter 13

"Now, Hailey—"

"Don't 'now Hailey' me!" Hailey roared over Patton's too calm objection. She had enough. "You're the one that's been conning me into thinking Kyle wasn't up to any good. Don't worry about Cole, everything will work out. *Damn romantic*. Worst thing to have as a best friend."

"I know you're upset, but—"

"Upset? *Upset?*" Storming past the console table with enough force to make the glass lamp shake, Hailey cut a sharp right around the couch to loom over Patton, making sure her friend heard her loud and clear. "I'm not upset. I just want Cole Jackson to be so humiliated that his reputation *never* rebounds. That's what I want. I want to be the instrument of his destruction."

"You don't think that maybe that's a *little* dramatic, Hailey?"

"No."

Hailey didn't. She'd almost gone for Cole then and there in the middle of the Bread Box dinner crowd. Rachel held her back from the brawling men. Rushing Hailey out the door, Rachel stuffed her in her tiny tin can of a car before Hailey's scream of outrage ever had a chance of clearing the shock in her throat.

All the practical details of seeing to her car, retrieving her purse, even killing Cole, had been overwhelmed by Rachel's Genghis Kahn style management. Hailey hadn't been given any choice but to be rushed home and locked up in her house.

Patton showed up not thirty minutes later, called in by Rachel to help. Patton had helped enough according to Hailey's way of thinking.

"You're right."

"What?" That calm admission from Patton caught Hailey off guard. It brought her to a stop at the edge of the couch, where she could loom over Patton as she asked, "What do you mean I'm right?"

"You were right. It was a set-up. Cole and Kyle obviously had this planned." It must have hurt her to admit it, but Patton didn't show any strain. She just stared at Hailey with a sincerity that deflated Hailey's anger.

Collapsing into the couch beside Patton, Hailey groaned. "I'm never going to hear the end of this."

"It's not going to be that bad, Hailey." Patton smirked. "After all, what do you think people are going to be saying? That poor Hailey had to fuck a loser like Kyle Harding? I don't think so."

"No, they'll say Hailey's just another set of spread legs, didn't you hear Kyle got between them?" It left a foul taste just saying it, but she knew the truth. Hailey had spent enough years in enough shops surrounded by men to know. "I bet in the next week I get asked out by a bevy of eager pricks looking for a quick dip."

"Hmm, maybe, but then again maybe not." Patton shrugged. "I'd expect the first person in that line will be Cole. I don't think he'll be taking kindly to a crowded field, so—"

"You think Cole's going to come after me?" It seemed like a strange conclusion to Hailey.

Apparently not to Patton. "Oh, yeah. I mean, you're the one who thought he'd go ballistic when he found out Kyle slept with you, and he did."

"Yeah, but that's because I figured the game was to get me into *their* bed, not to humiliate me." Hailey hated having to air her own mistakes, but she couldn't avoid this one. "I was obviously wrong."

"Or maybe this is just the way they always planned it," Patton suggested. "Now they got every right to put you in the middle of a war between the two of them. And just think, two Cattlemen fighting over the same woman? Two best friends? That's the kind of gossip that could run for months."

Hailey just stared at Patton, realizing just how bad she was at these games. She never considered this move. They had her now, whether or not she participated. They could run all over her life and nobody would lift a finger to stop them as long as it didn't get violent.

After tonight, everybody would think they were involved, and so everything that came next would be a "private" issue. Something to be talked about but not involved in.

"Oh, God." Hailey's head dipped. "What am I supposed to do?"

"I don't see any choice but to go on the offense." Patton would say that. "This time, though, we've got to get serious."

"We?" Hailey lifted her gaze.

"Well, this is going to be your game, Hailey, but you need help. The first thing I suggest is for you to figure out what Cole's weakness is."

"He doesn't have any, Patton," Hailey groaned. "Don't you think I've already looked? The man doesn't care about anything beyond cars and fucking."

"Cars?" Patton arched a brow. "Kind of like that rusted thing Kyle lured you in with?"

"Oh, great. Let's play copy cat," Hailey snapped. "I'll go find a car Cole can't resist and then what? What good does that do me?"

"Well, I just got off the phone with Adam." That interruption had both of them turning to watch Rachel come in carrying a proper tray of tea. Over the clink and rattle of the cups, she continued her report. "I'm sure you'll be pleased to hear that Killian arrested both Cole and Kyle and is in the process of dragging them down to the station. What?"

Hailey stared right through Rachel, seeing the answer to her own question. "Cole would give his left nut for Bavis's Fastback."

"What?" Rachel scowled, glancing from Hailey to Patton. The motion turned Hailey's chin in Patton's direction, too.

"Rachel and Kitty Anne are running an investigative story on a whore house down in Dothan." Hailey's grin grew through those words, curling faster than the slow smile spreading across Patton's face.

Rachel wasn't smiling. "Why am I nervous at hearing my name mentioned?"

"I think see a plan."

* * * *

"Sit down." Killian shoved Kyle into one of the plastic chairs along the wall of the police station.

"Hey," Kyle objected as he kicked himself upright in the chair. With his wrists cuffed behind his back, sitting became awkward. "Don't you think the cuffs are a little overkill, Killian?"

"It's Deputy Dog to you, scumbag," Killian shot back, whipping out his baton to slap it threateningly. Always a smart ass and never one to show much compassion to another man, Killian clearly enjoyed the moment.

"You know, Killian, I'm going to enjoy when it's your turn."

"Never gonna happen." Killian shook his head. "'Cause I already got my lady, you see, and I don't plan on humiliating her by screaming out the intimate details of our sex life in a public building before engaging in yet a second brawl in about week."

"Your woman? That little brunette that called you a prehistoric baboon? That one?"

"Yeah, she's *feisty*, ain't she?" Killian smirked. "'Course it won't take me long to get her settled down and then she'll be back to purring. I'm thinking naked, on her knees, and asking me how she can serve her master. You know those kinds of fantasies. The kind you won't be indulging in with Hailey anytime soon."

Kyle snorted at that. "Well, ain't your shit just all shiny and sweet-smelling."

"Hey," Killian tilted Kyle's chin up with the end of his baton, "consider this, you jackass. My girl is good friends with the girl you're trying to get with. You know what kind of position that puts me in?"

One that gave him a hell of a lot more power than a simple pair of handcuffs. Kyle jerked away from the hard wood under his chin and glared.

"That's right, buddy. You just remember that, and maybe if you sit here nice and quiet, I'll just be suggesting to the judge a little anger management therapy instead of suggesting to Hailey you got serious issues."

Kyle stilled at that threat. "You wouldn't."

"I'm talking psycho, dude. I'll have that woman convinced you're one twitch away from going all postal." Kyle glowered at that but kept his anger locked in behind clenched teeth. "Now sit there and be a good boy, okay?"

"That goes double for you, dumbass." Killian gave Cole a similar push that had him crashing into the seat next to Kyle.

Saying nothing while Cole jerked about and righted himself in the chair, Kyle brooded. Everything had gone to hell. No doubt Hailey was out buying a gun to come after his ass after the spectacular scene Cole helped put on. He could just hope the only thing she did was kill him.

"You're a real bastard. You know that?"

"Me?" Cole gasped as if he hadn't rightly earned that title a thousand times over in one day. "You're the one that's been holding out on me."

"You just ruined my *life,*" Kyle spat back, turning on his best friend.

"Oh, God, don't get all dramatic," Cole huffed.

"I swear to God, Cole, if it wasn't for these cuffs…"

"What?" Cole swung around in his seat, pinning Kyle with his cold gaze. "What did I do? You're the one who's been lying this whole time."

That had Kyle bristling. "Only because you made me."

"Me?" Cole's brows shot straight up.

"Yes, you. Do you think I wanted things this way?" Kyle shot back with just as much astonishment, turning Cole's wide-eyed look of shock into a narrowed one of disgust.

"That's funny coming from you 'cause all you had to do is tell me the truth. That you'd boned my woman."

"She ain't your woman, Cole. Hell, Hailey doesn't even like you." Kyle delighted in informing his friend of that obvious fact.

"Oh, bullshit."

That had Kyle choking on his indignant laughter. "Where the hell do you come up with that response? Name one time Hailey's even been *civil* to you."

"It's not—"

"Because you can't." Kyle cut off Cole's excuse, not interested in hearing it. "Because Hailey doesn't like you, and it's taken me six weeks to just get in close enough to the girl to even hope that I might be able to get her into my life. I don't need you coming in now and screwing that up for me."

"Screwing it up for you? How about just being flat-out screwed by your *best friend.*"

Kyle muscles flexed, aching so badly to pound on Cole. With the cuffs on and Killian's warning looming over his head, Kyle had nothing left but to growl out his frustration.

"I didn't screw you, Cole."

"Yeah, right." Cole spat that almost apology back at Kyle. "You going say next that you didn't know I put a mark on Hailey?"

"*Over two years ago.* Shit or get off the pot, Cole. You can't hold a mark on a woman for two years."

"Well, it's not exactly easy to get close to a damn fireball."

Kyle couldn't help but smile and rub it in. "It only took me five weeks. Maybe you're just not her type."

"We're the same damn type, Kyle."

"I quit the club six weeks ago. Five weeks before I finally brought the trap down on Hailey. I'd be set to selling her on how reformed I am if it hadn't been for your ass scaring her off at the Bread Box."

"That's when this all started?" Cole's head tipped as if something just hit him. "That night she left her panties? That's it? That's the only time."

Looking away, Kyle let his silence be his answer. Cole swore in response, snarling and pouting all at once. "I guess I should be thankful it hasn't been the full six weeks that you quit the club. Why did you quit the club six weeks ago? If you just...*you son of a bitch.*"

Kyle cringed at that. Cole was putting the pieces together, and it probably had been a stroke of luck that they were already in cuffs at the police station. Otherwise, Cole would have come at him for a second round.

"You set me up. All those distractions at the club and overloading the damn work schedule at the shop. You knew I was going to go after Hailey, and so you cut me out."

They were going to have this fight sometime, so it might as well be cuffed in a police station. Owning up to it, Kyle met Cole's gaze head on. "I also got my hands on a nineteen sixty-four Studebaker R4 Daytona five weeks ago and used it to bribe my way into Hailey's shop. We split the interest on her and have been working together every night for the last five weeks."

Cole surprised him when he didn't come back at Kyle. He just sat there, jaw clenched, eyes narrowed, and a muscle actually twitching in his cheek, but he didn't say anything. That's how mad Cole was, and Kyle hadn't ever seen him that pissed.

In fact, he'd never seen Cole pitch a fit over a woman the way he had today over Hailey. He never cared enough to bother. The thought vibrated down his spine, weakening his muscles as he began to understand.

"You care about Hailey."

Cole flinched at that. With a wrinkle of his nose and a soft growl, he looked away.

"Holy shit," Kyle whispered.

"Shut up, Kyle."

Chapter 14

Cole studied the tips of his boots as he sipped the cold tea. He wouldn't have bothered if it hadn't been for the very strong scent of brandy coming off the cup. Hailey liked her tea strong. For all that she might as well drink it straight up, Cole thought as he shifted his feet.

Damn, I need new boots.

He really hated doing things like that, buying boots. It was just a waste of time, and it really made him think of the positives of keeping a woman around. Despite Kyle's gloom and doom attitude, Cole could see some good in having a woman.

It would be nice to be fed and have a clean house, have things smelling nice and not having to worry over the small print in insurance policies. Cole could get behind having a good, dutiful woman at home if that's really what Kyle wanted. A sweet, quiet woman who took care of the house and performed as needed at night—a well-trained one.

Cole figured Hailey would be that when she died because he couldn't honestly see her in a kitchen making cookies with the kids. Kyle's head must have been overruled by his heart if he saw that in his future. Cole wouldn't have laughed if Kyle said he did because that's the kind of fool love made of people. That's just why Cole could see Hailey doing some major damage to Kyle. That's if he didn't get this situation under control and quick.

All Hailey had to do was help him out with showing up. Tilting his head to glance at the clock on the mantle, Cole could see clearly an hour had passed thanks to the streetlight coming in through the windows. A whole fricken hour and Cole hated waiting.

It made him itchy, especially because by now Killian would have let Kyle out of the cell. Cole bribed the deputy to hold Kyle back for an hour, but by now his friend should be looking for him. Eventually, he'd show up here, and Cole really didn't want to have that conversation in front of Hailey.

It had been bad enough there in station house. All that arguing had gotten them nowhere. Cole even offered to be a good, dutiful gentleman and assist Kyle with Hailey's seduction. Given that what he really wanted to do was tie her ass to his bed and ravage her for several days in a row, Cole considered his offer quite a compromise.

That had been gracious in Cole's mind, but Kyle wouldn't agree to anything until Cole agreed that he cared about the woman. Why Kyle had to harp on that, Cole didn't know. The only thing worse than caring about a spitfire like Hailey was admitting to actually caring about her. Give a woman like that a weapon of that size and a man might as well just volunteer for prison because that's how much of his life he was going to spend being bent over.

Cole wouldn't go out like that, and he wouldn't watch Kyle fall into that fate, either. He'd figure something out once the damn woman got home. Unable to resist, he glanced at the clock again. Thankfully, this time a flash of headlights pulling into Hailey's drive illuminated just what time it was.

Swallowing down the last of his tea, Cole's boots plunked onto the floor as he rose to meet the moment. No longer the time for threats, the time had come to deliver.

* * * *

Hailey grinned her way up the drive. They had a plan. It might be as confusing as Patton complained and likely to fail as Rachel ominously predicted, but at least they had one. Even if her role in it consisted of next to nothing, Hailey would still get all the glory when the crap storm rained down on Cole.

Ah, but she already savored the coming moment of glory when Cole figured out she'd been the one who set him up. Hailey grinned as her key slid into the slot. It would just be a shame to put any real distance between her and Cole and Kyle. Then she'd miss out on all the fireworks as they happened.

Besides, Hailey could see the advantage of a second game. One she hadn't actually shared with Patton or Rachel because they'd have nagged her. The last thing she wanted was to have to justify her completely irrational need to put herself in the middle of the action.

In the middle was exactly where she intended to go because Kyle would be back in her bed within a day. It ground on Cole's nerves that she'd sleep with his best friend. Given just how much she enjoyed sweating up the sheets with Kyle, it seemed a waste not to eat her cake and flaunt it in Cole's face. It would only make the burn of his humiliation more scorching. A fact she laughed over as she pushed the door in, following it as she turned around its edge to shut it.

"About time you got home, darlin'."

Hailey shrieked at that soft drawl. Whirling with the door as it slammed closed, she found herself pinned against it as Cole came out of the shadows. Blue jeans, black T-shirt, and the smell of the shop on him, everything about the man turned her on. Her heart pounded through her shirt to thump against the hard wall of his chest, betraying just how bad she had it.

"What's wrong, Hailey?" Cole's whisper brushed over her cheek as he scrapped his jaw against hers to murmur in her ear. "You didn't think we'd finished our conversation, did you?"

Every breath he drew rubbed his hard muscles into her tender tips, making them swell with lust. Unable to control or hide the need boiling in her, Hailey panicked. All her grand plans, all her strategies didn't save her from the urge to grind back into the subtle rubbing motion he used to tease her.

"What do you want?" As if she didn't know. Hailey just wanted, needed to hear him say it. The answer would remind her why hers had to be no.

"Aren't you listening, darlin'? I want to talk."

By the mere strength of the last fiber of her dignity, Hailey managed to focus on his words and not the heated hands settling in to grip her waist.

"Then say what you got to say and be done with it."

"You got it backward, darlin'." Cole scraped that retort out along her neck as he sent spasms straight down toward her fluttering heart, making it that much harder to breathe. Then, with a tiny bite, he took that capacity away from her for a hot, splintering second.

"You're the one who has some talking to do because I'm really interested to hear how you ended up in bed with my best friend."

That hadn't been what she expected to come out of those beautiful lips. Curling her head to the side, she offered up more of her neck for his tasting. "What's wrong, Cole? Jealous?" The last word gasped out as he bit her again.

"Try pissed, little lady."

That deserved a look because even if he had her wet enough to forget all reason, Hailey couldn't hold back the shock of that. "What gives you that right?"

"How about the fact that you almost got me pulverized by the Davis brothers and then immediately turn around and seduce my best friend behind my back?" Cold, clear, blue eyes met hers. "Tell me honestly now, Hailey, are you screwing with Kyle to get revenge on me? 'Cause that ain't right."

"You really know how to ruin a moment. You know that?" Hailey snapped, stiffening up to meet his hard look with her own. "First off, you almost got your own ass beat messing around with Patton. Second off, I didn't go behind your back because it isn't any concern of yours who I sleep with. And third, Kyle seduced me."

"But you were willing every inch of the way. Weren't you, darlin'?"

"So what if I was," Hailey demanded. "It's still none of your damn business."

"It is." Cole pressed in that claim, bringing his nose to rest almost on hers. "Everything you do is my business, Hailey, because you belong to me, darlin'."

"I belong to no man."

It was like she hadn't even spoken. "I've looked the other way while you dicked around with all those little wimps you like to control, but you stepped over a line this time, Hailey."

"And I'm going to keep on stepping over it because you ain't the boss of me."

Cole growled at that, a warning blast that barely gave her a second to react before his head dipped.

Don't let him kiss you.

"No, Cole."

Barely audible, the heat of her whisper washed back against her chin as it crashed into his mouth not even an inch away. She could almost feel the violence clenching his muscles as he held back at the last second. Not daring to tempt his control even a hair further, Hailey held herself as flat against the door and as far from his heat as she could.

Not deterred, Cole lips settled on to the very tip of her chin to brush down its tensed slope with the gentlest of butterfly kisses. Barely holding on to the gasp of air that ached to be freed, Hailey clenched her jaw. Her eyes closed as she fortified her will.

He didn't make it easy, nibbling on the sensitive skin just below her ear as he growled. "Give me one good reason why not, Hailey."

"Because I said so." She didn't need a reason beyond that, which was a good thing because then she didn't have one.

"You say it, but you don't mean it." Cole drew his head back and gave her that little curl of a smile that made her heart do that double beat thing she hated him for. "You're standing there dripping wet, and we both know all it would take is one kiss and I'll have you coming before it's done."

He was daring her. Daring her because he knew that her pride would always foul her up. It always had. Tonight, though, she had blind fear to fortify her dignity.

"I won't be tricked into giving you what you want."

"What about what you need? And if that isn't the truth, then what harm would a kiss cause?"

Lips gone dry from the steady beat of ragged breaths, Hailey's tongue peeked out to wet them down, drawing Cole's darkened gaze like a beacon. The predatory gleam in those jeweled eyes flared with unbridled intent, making her cunt clench with anticipation.

There was no stopping him now. Isn't that just why she pushed him? Because it would be as glorious in the moment as it would be devastating in the aftermath.

"I don't even like you."

Cole's tongue tickled over her lips, wetting them for her and making her sigh slightly when he withdrew to whisper. "Now that, darlin', that's a lie I'm going to make you pay for."

"Cole."

"I dare you to say no again."

She couldn't. Not with his lips brushing against hers, rubbing, teasing, luring hers apart. Hailey never stood a chance. When the warmth of his big hand folded around her neck and pulled her from the door, she went willingly. Trapped in the heat of his body, she could not ignore the eruption of lust fueling through her body, and her lips parted with a sigh.

Instantly, his tongue invaded. No longer a soft, sensual lure, it ravished the inside of her mouth, mingling his taste with the sultry scent of musk that already intoxicated her. He possessed her mouth with a hunger that ate at her restraint until her own feral need overwhelmed the last of her reservations.

No longer the timid captive, Hailey became the aggressor, losing herself in the primitive wildness of raw lust. He tasted so good, so much better than she ever imagined. Darker, more male, and she couldn't get enough. Spearing her nails into the soft strands of hair clinging to his neck, Hailey refused him any retreat as she sucked down on his tongue and made him growl.

The thick vibrations crashed against her breasts as he flattened her along the hard wall of his chest. Ruthlessly, his hand plunged beneath the waistband of her jeans, branding her ass with the rough scrape of his flesh as he lifted her into his hardness.

Gasping for air as her world ignited, Hailey released his lips. The oxygen seared through her lungs, fanning the flames of the inferno burning in her cunt as his hand slid down to curve between her legs and boldly laid claim to the pussy weeping for his possession.

"Cole."

"Just as wet as I knew you'd be," Cole growled before splitting her legs wide with one single thigh. Hailey gave a strangled shriek as he dragged her up the stretch of bulged muscle, making her hips grind down and capture those wicked fingers in the creaming folds of her cunt.

"That's my pussy you're pawing, and you didn't ask permission." Kyle's snarl broke the sensual snare Cole had wrapped her in.

Chapter 15

Just like that, Cole dropped her back down onto her wobbling legs. With the speed of a predator Hailey often likened him to, he turned to confront the man who cast their forbidden world back into the cold light of reality just by clicking on a lamp.

Kyle squared off against Cole as she slid down, down, until her ass plunked onto the floor as her legs refused to perform any useful service. Panting, confused, and collapsed, she stayed sprawled there, the puppet watching her two masters square off.

"Permission?" Cole growled like a junkyard dog as he moved in steadily on Kyle. "I don't believe I need your permission. I had Hailey's agreement, and as far as I see, she ain't wearing your collar."

"Hailey's permission isn't that hard to get." Kyle snorted. His next pearls of wisdom had her ears starting to heat up as indignant brain cells started to fire, rallying to the insult. "It doesn't really take much more than a kiss, does it?"

"Maybe it takes you that much," Cole smirked. "But that girl gets wet enough for me without even a touch."

Indignation flared to outrage and put the steel back into her legs. Not that either one of them noticed her as she struggled back to her feet. Hailey could have interrupted, but the pissed she had brewing wanted to be fueled. It held back, letting the dumbasses before her build the bonfire of her temper upward toward a massive explosion.

"Is that a challenge?"

"Ain't much of a challenge if all you're bringing to the table is a fricken kiss."

"It's all a matter of where you kiss," Kyle retorted with smooth confidence that had Hailey clenching with the need to hit him. *Men.* Hailey breathed deeply as she found her footing.

"Trust me, Kyle, when I'm done with Hailey, she wouldn't even remember your name much less what it feels like to have that twig you call a dick inside her."

Hailey blinked at the cold revelation of just what kind of challenge they were building toward.

There's only one way they can end that argument.

With her naked, probably tied up and begging for mercy. The very idea made her muscles contract with just little a pop of pleasure, promising the explosion for the real thing would be well worth a try.

What sane woman volunteered to be stuck between two Cattlemen warring over which one could give it to her the best? What sane woman let two men argue over her like she was a piece of meat? Hailey might want them, both of them, at the same time, but that didn't mean she'd bow over her pride.

"Why don't we just let Hailey decide?" Kyle's sharp retort had her stiffening up.

As if that half measure would save him. It did twist her budding anger back into the heated measure of her refueling need for revenge. Especially when it came to Cole and that smile. He wore his special one, the one that made just about any woman act the fool.

"You're gonna have to choose, darlin'." Cole came on all smooth, closing the distance he opened up between them. If he thought pressing that hard body into her still tingling one would persuade her...Well, he almost had it right, but this time she had the sanity of light to keep her focused. "Who's your master? Me? Kyle?"

Hailey already knew her choice, but she enjoyed making both men squirm. "How about none?"

"Sorry, darlin'." Her hardened tone must have worried Cole. Even if it didn't show in the silky purr of his drawl, his hand coming to cup her breast told a different story. "That ain't a choice you get to make."

Warm, strong, and way too nimble, his fingers tried to persuade her to see things his way. Hailey knew she only had moments before that hardening nipple led her forward into his touch. Meeting his gaze straight on, she gave Cole what he probably never had in his life—a rejection.

"I say it is." Shoving him back, she broke his hold on her tender flesh. "I ain't sleeping with you, Cole Jackson. Not tonight, not any night, not ever."

"You gonna eat those words, darlin', and I'm going to enjoy feeding them to you."

"You might be that good," Hailey conceded. Stepping up into him, she backed her next statement. "But I don't sleep with every woman's whore."

Shoving past him while he still reeled from that blow was a mistake. Even as she cleared his shoulder, his arm latched on to her wrist, making her turn back around to face the livid heat of his gaze.

"What did you say?"

"I said you're every woman's whore," Hailey repeated slowly and distinctly before yanking her arm free. "And don't look so insulted. There ain't nobody in this town that doesn't know that you ain't nothing but a two-legged dog with a boner free to any cheap pussy that willing to demean herself and spread her legs for you. You're a joke, Cole, and you always will be."

A second hung in the air, expiring slowly, only to give over in a rush as Kyle suddenly appeared between them. He ran into Cole in his attempt to get to Hailey. Hailey didn't really know what she said that triggered that dark expression in Cole's eyes, but she knew danger when they narrowed on her. That insult apparently hit the sweet spot.

Kyle shook his head at Cole. "I told you not to come here, Cole."

"You don't want to stand between us, Kyle."

It stood against the tradition of the Cattlemen that Kyle didn't give over and side with his partner. A good omen for Hailey because she had plans for Kyle. Plans that involved using him to torture Cole the same way Cole used Patton to rub her raw.

"I'm not going to let you get your revenge for that one."

"She earned it," Cole snarled.

"But you ain't earned the right to give it to her."

Hailey didn't have to wonder at what that meant. She had a two hour tutorial on just how Cole defined punishment. Revenge just took it up a few notches. What it did leave her wondering was how long it would take Cole to respond to her challenge. He didn't do it then. Instead of giving into the fury in his gaze, Cole relaxed suddenly. "Then why don't we ask the darlin' just what it is that I need to do to earn it."

Both men turned to look at her as if they actually had the respect to be talking to her instead of about her.

"Earn what?" Hailey snorted. "The right to crawl into my bed?"

"Yes." Cole's answer was as unapologetically blunt as that.

"There ain't nothing." Hailey delighted in lying.

"Darlin', we both know that if push comes to shove I can have you laid out like a feast before me." Cole stepped up to stand beside Kyle, a silent reminder that Kyle would eventually fold. Then her problems would be doubled. "I'm showing you more respect and consideration than any other, but don't think my patience is endless. Name your price, Hailey, or I'll set one myself."

Hailey's eyes narrowed down on that threat. Her pride wanted to throw it back in his face, but her wisdom held that urge back. Cole had it right. She didn't have the defenses to hold him off. If Cole wore a leash it would be one he put on himself. Only one thing could make him accept that fate.

"Okay, Cole." Hailey smiled slightly. "You want a mark to meet, I'll give you one. Four weeks, no sex. Meaning no kissing, no sucking, no petting, not even flirting or dancing or checking out every woman's breast size when you first meet her or at any other point. You need to be not a dog, Cole, but an actual decent man for four straight weeks."

That had his head shifting back a little. Those sparkling eyes even widened a tad, but he didn't jerk back with an immediate dismissal. Hailey had to give him one for actually thinking it over before Cole stuck his foot in his mouth.

"And that no sex rule? That apply to you?" His eyes dipped pointedly to where her nipples still strained against her wet shirt.

Crossing her arms over her chest, Hailey's response popped out of her without thought. "You must really love the taste of that foot."

Like she hit him with a bolt of electricity, Kyle jerked with a shot of laughter that drew Cole's annoyed gaze his way for a second. "Shut up, Kyle."

"Sorry." Kyle's grin made a mockery of that apology, but Cole seemed to accept. More like his interest still remained focused on her.

"I'll take that as a yes."

"I would." Hailey couldn't help but to let a little smirk slip.

Cole didn't return the gesture. Instead, he jerked his head at Kyle and asked, "What about him?"

She knew exactly where he was headed but took a perverse amount of pleasure in making him say it. "What about him?"

"You gonna be sleeping with him for the next four weeks?"

"Would that bother you, Cole?"

Her gloating tone hardened his scowl as he snarled. "We're a package deal, darlin'."

"Oh? And here I thought the options were him *or* you."

"That's as your master, darlin'." Cole grinned. "Make no mistake, Hailey, there's going to come a day when it'll be both of us in your bed."

Hailey matched his smug smirk with her own. "And if I say no, you really think Kyle's going to follow you out that door?"

The both looked to Kyle for that answer. Helplessly, as if he actually couldn't make up his mind, Kyle looked between them before settling his gaze on Hailey to ask a very reasonable question. "Am I really going to be getting sex out of this deal if I say no?"

"*Son of a bitch,*" Cole muttered in absolute disgust.

Pissed beyond anything she'd seen before, Cole circled in a motion born of pure agitation. He made it a full three hundred and sixty degrees to pin her with a look so heated she knew if he made his mark he'd be leaving it on her body. Fortunately for her, Hailey already knew he wouldn't make it. She'd already seen to that.

Of course, he might be demanding that payment sooner, as in now. The threat came through in feral growl that vibrated out of his chest. It mated with the predatory gleam that hardened his eyes back to pure jade. When he reached out to curl a hand around her neck, Hailey held still like most prey not daring to startle the hunter with sudden motion.

Tilting her head back, he held her still until the heat of his gaze made her swallow. "You can have your four weeks, Hailey, but when your time is up it's going to be my way, anyway I want it, all night long. What you heard that night under my bed," his lips quivered up ever so slightly, "darlin', that's going to pale in comparison to what I'm gonna do to you."

With that, he released her. Shrugging past her and giving Kyle a shove that toppled him over the back of her couch, Cole stormed off down the hall. A moment later, the back door slammed closed, leaving her staring after him with one single thought in her head.

She'd better make damn sure Cole didn't make it those four weeks. If the plan fell through, she might be regretting giving in to this moment. It felt good, though.

And the punishment might feel even better. Hailey shook her head at that thought.

If Patton heard about this, she'd wig out. From the perspective of the grand plan, Hailey's little mini-bet with Cole could be seen as an act of sabotage. The master plan relied on Cole giving in to Kitty Anne's seductive powers, but now she'd just given him a reason not to.

Not that Hailey really expected Cole to resist Kitty Anne. He'd try for both and get nothing but that much more humiliation heaped on in the end. That almost had Hailey laughing as she turned back to Kyle. The laughter snorted out of her when she caught sight of the man already naked from the waist up. With his navy blue T-shirt hanging from the back of her couch, Kyle had his chin tucked into his chest as he focused hard on working his buckle free.

"What are you doing?"

That had him pausing and blinking and looking at her as if he had the right to be confused. "I thought we were going to have sex."

He couldn't get that line out without the edges of his lips quivering upward, drawing Hailey's narrowed gaze, even though she felt a similar tremble of humor in her gut.

"Nice try."

That had him straightening up and his lips flattening out. "You know, considering your unappreciative attitude, I just might make you wait four weeks before I scratch any itches."

"Yeah, I'll be losing sleep over that every night."

That brought his grin back. A sight that had hers dipping as he swaggered over. A woman just couldn't take a shirtless Kyle too lightly, especially when he came within touching range. Her hands managed to stay crossed over her chest even when one of his lifted to brush a thumb under her eyes.

"Looks like you're already losing sleep, princess."

"You really like calling me that."

"Because that's what you are, all spice and spit with that attitude that thinks she's too good for any man."

"I never said—"

"Too good for Cole, right?"

Hailey snorted at that and jerked back from his touch. "Any woman with a smidgeon of dignity would be too good for Cole."

"There's the spit." Kyle backed off with that, reaching for his shirt. "But then again, maybe you're one of *those* people."

"And what people is that?"

She had to wait for him to pull his T-shirt down over the rippled wall of his stomach to get her answer. "The kind that bites when they get hungry."

He actually had that one right. Not that Hailey would give him the satisfaction of agreeing. "No. I'm one of those people who get upset when two men break in to her house and then assault her."

"Assault?"

"Molest."

That earned her a nod. "Yeah, that was kind of hot." Kyle's gaze darkened slightly as it did a lazy stroll down her body, igniting a wave of heat that tempted her to say "yes" to his previous offer. "You sure you don't want to have sex?"

Toughening up her reserve, Hailey even managed a chin lift with her retort. "I thought you were going to hold out on me to make me beg, but yet you're the one who keeps bringing it up."

"Well, princess," Kyle moved as he talked, looping an arm around her waist to steer her down the hall along with him, "I am a man, and we are always hopeful."

"As in you never say no, and you wonder why I called Cole a whore?" Hailey couldn't let that opportunity pass by her even as Kyle maneuvered her into the kitchen.

"Nah, princess, not a whore. We're willing to give it away for free. That's more like a slut, just to be technical. I got to admit it was funny seeing Cole's reaction when—"

"Uh, Kyle."

Hailey latched on to the doorframe as Kyle tried to steer her through it. That brought them both to a stop, but one that Kyle didn't really recognize. Continuing on, he pried her hand free and used his hold to force her out through the door.

"—you called him a whore. I don't think any woman's ever rejected Cole, let alone insulted him like that." With her wrist firmly trapped in his grip, he tucked her into his side while he shut her back door. "Now if you'd been a man, he'd have hit ya. He still might. Cole's definitely into spanking.

"And I ain't talking no ass here, either, princess. Cole's specialty is packing a pussy full of dick and then whipping the hell out of that cunt. Normally, he forces at least two orgasms out of a poor woman. By then they're so hard up for a fucking or a breather they'd agree to just about anything."

Hailey pointedly refused to respond to Kyle, even if his words sank beneath her to inflame a wicked curl of delight that she'd never own up to experiencing. Not that Kyle asked. Bringing her to a stop by his truck, he pointedly ignored her ignoring him as he rambled on.

"I'm sure Cole is going to be quite thankful, then, that you gave him all the excuse he needs to be relentless and push you further." Kyle hoisted her up into the truck like some kid. "In fact, it just wouldn't shock me at all if he drove you through four orgasms that way."

That sounded like a promise more than idle speculation, but that might have had something to do with the door slamming shut. Sitting there almost humming with need thanks to Kyle's dirty musings, Hailey didn't even think about getting back out of the truck as he went around the front to open the driver's door.

"Then he'll probably eat you out." Kyle slammed the door, leaning in unnecessarily far to growl, "You're gonna love that, princess."

Straightening up, he jammed the key into the ignition with one hand as he pulled his seat belt across his chest with the other. "Hell, we might have to change your name to Kitten because after Cole finishes with you, you'll probably mew and purr at just the sight of him. Of course, he'll probably be drooling and desperate to get that tongue back in your pussy because, princess, you really are a decadent treat."

It just got worse from there as he popped the truck brake free and took off down the road. Pittsview being Pittsview, she really didn't have to wait long to figure out what Kyle's intentions were. Less than ten minutes later, they were rolling through the Mickey D's parking lot, angling for the drive through.

He intended to stuff some food into her but didn't even ask her what she wanted. Assuming all control of the order, Kyle didn't even give Hailey the chance to object. The lust Kyle had been stoking in her gut with all his lewd contemplations sizzled into annoyance that only grew as the truck rolled up to the window.

That's when she realized just how thoroughly she'd been played. The moment the little blonde attendant's eyes widened at the sight her and Kyle, Hailey knew what rumor would be added to the pile they already built today. She, Cole, and Kyle were working on the saga of the summer, and Hailey had a big bang ending planned.

Kyle probably thought he boxed her in good with this move, but Hailey honestly objected. She just played at it as he shoved the oversized sodas into her lap and then pushed hot, greasy bags in her direction. He left her to fumble with everything as he pulled out of the lot, going back into his monologue.

"Now I could offer to help you, train you. Trust me, it'll go a lot easier, and you really do need the training 'cause unless you noticed you gave me a nice shiner that first night. Kicked me square in the face, you're so damn squirmy. And that was just me trying to get your clothes off.

"You squirm like that with Cole and he's going to start getting out the ropes. He's not as tolerant as I am on a normal day, and you got him so riled up it would just be wrong of me to let you go into that situation without a little preparation."

The flat click of the turn signal clucked out for a moment as he turned the truck down the lonely road that divided the state park from the Cattleman's Club. It gave Hailey a slight pause wondering just where he planned to bring his truck to stop next.

"Of course, I'll be helping you through the moment, and I'll certainly try to keep Cole from making you come too many damn times, but you got to know that I just might enjoy the show enough to kind of get distracted. Either way, if it gets to be too much, you can always black out. That's what the weak ones normally do.

"Here we are."

Whatever here was. Hailey looked around as Kyle killed the engine and threw his door wide open. The clear, reflective surface of the lake gave her the only reference she knew in the tree-laden view. Kyle pulled down some dirt lane, and Hailey began to get a better sense of just what mischief Kyle devised.

Why he bothered with such an elaborate seduction setting, she didn't know. He could have gotten away with just a kiss and then they could be doing it in a nice comfortable bed. She didn't bother to ask him why, either, just silently sat as he wrenched her door open to grab the bags of food from her lap.

When he disappeared, Hailey stopped bothering with her statue impersonation and conceded defeat. Leaping down to the pine-straw-laden ground, her gaze caught on the sudden flash of a light to her right. A pink blanket, of all things, floated out through the air as Kyle spread it out across the bed of his truck.

Smoothing it out while she came around to the open gate, Kyle just kept on going. He didn't stop until their gazes finally connected as he turned to take the drinks from her. In the reflected sparkle of moonlight, Hailey could see that his little game backfired on the big, rugged Cattleman.

The hunger darkening his eyes made her own primitive lusts abate as humor slipped in to lighten the edges. A smirk pulled at her lips as she cocked a brow at him.

"A pink blanket? What, you keep that around to show what a sweet and sensitive guy you are?"

That had his gaze narrowing as he considered that for all of a second. "Have you ever had your nipples clamped?"

"Oh, stop it, Kyle." Hailey handed off the drinks and crawled up into the bed, forcing him back. "If you wanted to have sex, we could have done that back at the house and been a hell of a lot more comfortable. Then I wouldn't have to worry about mosquitoes biting my ass."

Kyle stilled, his gaze darkening as his voice lowered. "Don't you think I know that? Don't you think I know how to get you wet, naked, and leg-spread in five minutes whenever I want?"

Hailey swallowed, wanting to defend herself from the predatory hunger in his gaze, but fear overwhelmed her, and she remained silently still. Kyle didn't wait for a response.

"You're trying to play me against my best friend, and you either think I'm dumb enough or besotted enough to let you get away with it." Not a warm gesture, the grin twisting across his face was pure wickedness. "All those things Cole's going to do to you going to *pale* in comparison to my revenge.

"But that's in four weeks, and right now," Kyle fell back into the seat, letting all the tension drain out of him as he returned to his normal, easygoing self, "after all you said about the sex, I think I'm going to hold you to your word, darlin'."

He'd been messing with her mind, Hailey decided then. Kyle might threaten and strut, but he didn't have it in him. At his core, he was a good guy. Breathing out a sigh of a release, Hailey felt safe enough to crawl up into the truck bed beside him.

She even managed to tease him.

"Oh, yeah right."

"You don't think I can hold out?"

"Kyle, there are a good ten inches of cock bulging out of your jeans right now that says 'no' or 'yes'. You know what I mean."

"I ain't a slave to a single one of those inches, princess, so you better be real careful before betting on that dog. Burger?"

The scent of meat and cheese wafted up her nostrils as a wrapped delight suddenly floated in front of her. Too hungry to argue, Hailey still managed a complaint as she snatched the burger from him.

"And no pink blanket is going to woo me out of being annoyed that you didn't *ask* what I wanted to eat."

"Fine," the burger jerked out of her hand, "then don't eat."

"Give that back." Hailey lunged for the burger, but Kyle stretched his arm all the way up to hold it out of her reach.

"Not until you say please."

"You know I could just bite you, don't you?"

"And you know I bite back, and I expect a thank you when I hand it over, too."

Hailey straightened up, meeting his amused gaze with her own scowl. "Please, Kyle, don't make me have to spend years in prison for assault with intent over a cheeseburger."

His lips quivered at that, but he kept the laughter in as he lowered his arm. Bringing the burger to hover just above her hand, he paused. Hailey rolled her eyes and gave him what he wanted.

"Thank you for not making me have to spend the night at the hospital worrying over your ass."

The burger dropped into her hands as his brow shot up. "And you would worry?"

She gave him a dirty look for even asking that question before she focused her attention on stealing fries from his container. "Of course. The difference between assault and murder is quite a number of years in jail, so any sane person would worry."

"But you're not sane, are you, princess?"

Obviously not. Didn't this entire day stand as testament to that fact? If not the fact she actually kind of—just a little—enjoyed herself did.

Chapter 16

Kyle sighed and flexed his arm, curling Hailey closer into his side. Perfect, that's just what this moment was. Well, actually, it could have been refined. They could be naked, worn out. That would certainly elevate the moment. Not that he couldn't have gotten Hailey there with much difficulty, but getting her here took a lot more finesse.

After the past week, a lot of pieces had started to fall into place in this one day. Kyle could finally understand what had gone so horribly wrong in Hailey's shower. It wasn't the commitment that scared her but the loss of control that would come with it.

She might not ever admit to it, but Hailey was vulnerable. That made her very, very dangerous by Kyle's reckoning. It would be easy to take Cole's approach and consider simply overwhelming Hailey with lust, but that path dead-ended. For all the pleasure they could give her, all it would do was strengthen the wall of her defenses.

Kyle knew, he understood. Hailey needed to learn to trust them first. She couldn't let go of that control until she trusted them to take care of her. Despite what some men might thought, trust wasn't earned between the sheets. It developed slowly, strengthening every minute they spent together just talking.

Or cuddling.

Here, she couldn't hide. Not like she had when she called Cole a whore. Defensively attacking Cole, Hailey had been trying to re-enforce her own reasoning more than hurting Cole. It had been the same way she tried to reduce him down to nothing more than a sex toy in her shower.

Hailey didn't want to admit that it was the men and not the sex that lured her wicked passions out. Well, she set a timeline on her revelation because in four weeks Kyle would be helping Cole prove Hailey wrong. They'd seduce the most primitive desires out of Hailey. When they finished, she'd be bound to them because she would trust no other men, love no other men, enough to enjoy those lusts with.

Hailey was smart. She'd figure it out. Figure out it was about hearing a good joke and turning around to tell it to the person he most wanted to share a laugh with. It was about finally getting something fixed after pulling his hair out for four days and reveling in that victory with somebody who understood.

It was just about enjoying life with the person he knew he'd most enjoy it with. That had always been Cole, but Kyle could see now that he needed Hailey in that picture for it to be complete.

"It isn't going to work, you know."

Hailey's voice intruded with the sharp dryness that clearly challenged the cozy warmth of their snuggled embrace. Kyle smiled as he awarded himself two points for being right. Real intimacy terrified Hailey. He shared that victory only with himself, keeping her curled tight into his chest as he responded lazily.

"What isn't, princess?"

"Just because you're being all sweet, and that's quite a contrast from that ass you live with, it isn't going to make me forget our last conversation. You remember? The one where you paid me for my services?"

Kyle snorted at that. "I didn't pay you for nothing."

"You said I earned the car."

"And you did, or you going to deny you love it more than I do?"

"You said it right after we had sex," Hailey retorted, pulling free of his hold. "It was rude."

Kyle sighed, reluctantly pushing himself to a sit. "If you don't want the car, give it back."

That caught her off guard, breaking up the tirade he could sense her building toward. "What?"

"You heard me. You don't want the car. You're insulted by the way I gave it to you. Nobody's making you take it, so give it back."

Hailey's clenched jaw rolled as her gaze narrowed. "You're intentionally missing the point, Kyle. You made me feel like a whore."

"I did?" Kyle blinked in mock shock. If they were going to fight, then they'd have a good one. One worth having. The one he wanted to have.

"Why are you trying to piss me off? You're doing just what you did in the shower. Everything is going nice and fine, then all of a sudden you get as prickly as a cactus. Why?"

Her features clenched with tension as her arms crossed over her chest, and Hailey appeared almost to hunker down. He found a way to actually piss her off. True anger growled out at him now.

"I don't know what you're talking about."

Perhaps a considerate man would have taken the hint and let the subject go, but Kyle didn't worry about politeness. He worried that he might not ever be able to break through this wall Hailey erected. If he failed, it wouldn't be from a lack of trying because Kyle would get a jackhammer if need be.

A dark glower wouldn't deter him. In fact, Kyle returned it, letting her see the steel of his determination. "You really do think I'm stupid, don't you?"

The sudden accusation caught Hailey off guard. "What?"

"You think I can't see the obvious in front of me. I get close, you get bitchy."

"Gee, you think that means I don't like you?" Hailey snapped back. The defensive attack. Kyle could still see and hear the fear in her tone.

"I think it means you like me too much." Kyle slid to the side, crowding her back toward the wall of the truck bed. "I think it means you like me so much it scares you."

He fully expected an all-out assault for that one. He even braced himself to be hit, but instead Hailey just sat there glaring as if she hated him. Rage and pain echoed in a molten mass of green and brown shards swirling through her gaze, and Kyle knew it wasn't him she hated.

"It's because of your dad, isn't it?" Kyle knew the story, just like everybody else in town. "It's because he left your mother, and now you're afraid you'll get left, too."

Pausing for her response, he could see it forming on her lips. They parted, halting, before her voice finally came out sounding perfectly calm and too rational to be sane.

"My father didn't leave my mother. Nine years ago, he walked out on our family, and do you know how many times I've seen him since?" Hailey didn't wait for an answer but held up two fingers that ironically made the peace sign. "Two. First time was after my mother died in the lawyer's office, and the second was when I bumped into him at the mall. I'm not afraid of being left, *too*, Kyle."

"You're afraid of being left again," Kyle finished for her when she didn't. "Here's the thing you're forgetting, Hailey. I don't have anywhere else I want to be. If I did, I'd be there, but instead I'm here."

"For now," Hailey tacked on as if he hadn't finished.

Kyle gave her a little smile that dipped when she flinched over the hand he lifted to her cheek. Not letting her escape the touch, he followed her the inch back, making her accept his small bit of comfort.

"I don't see that changing, Hailey."

"Not until you're done playing whatever game Cole and you cooked up." Hailey hopped to her feet, taking that accusation to a full, arms-crossed-over-chest stance

"You think this is a game?" Kyle rose to his own feet to glare down at her. "I didn't take a beating to help Cole set something up on you, and I sure as shit didn't sleep with you to help him."

"You're a Cattleman, Kyle," Hailey stated, her chin lifting defiantly toward his.

"So?"

"You really expect me to believe you're going to side with me over your partner? Weren't you going on about how you were going to get revenge for me playing the two of you?"

"I get it." Kyle didn't want to touch that one. Hailey obviously didn't believe his promise earlier. She'd taken it as a hollow threat, which would just make her shock all the greater when he made it come true. Kyle intended to savor that moment.

Letting it go with a smirk, he started pulling the blanket up and cleaning out the bed. "You're scared. We'll take things slow."

"Slow?" Hailey repeated behind him, obviously annoyed at his dismissal of their argument. "What does that mean? You going to start bringing flowers by the house?"

"Would you accept them if I did?" Kyle cast her a grin, hoping to lighten up the moment. Slow meant keeping Hailey completely in the dark about what she had coming. It would be more fun that way.

"I don't know. Guess it depends on whether you bring food."

Kyle just laughed at that. Hailey didn't have to repeat herself because he learned his lesson these past five weeks—a hungry Hailey was just a mean Hailey.

"I'll remember to come bearing gifts."

"I'm not for sale, Kyle."

"It would be easier if you were," he retorted just as flippantly.

She didn't come back at him but held her silence for a minute. When she finally did speak, her tone held a distinctive pout to it. "You're serious about this slow thing?"

Pausing to straighten up and turn to confront her, Kyle nodded. "Oh, yeah. It's like I said. I'm not dumb. You put Cole on a four-week probation period. Well, princess, you can count me in on that deal because I want in on the big finish."

"Well, that just sucks." It popped out of her as an honest enough response to make him laugh as he turned back to folding the blanket. She didn't let it go but snorted behind him. "I'm going to have to object to that."

"Object all you want." Kyle flipped the truck gate up. "It doesn't change the fact that your bed is going to be cold for the next month."

Hailey sighed with a shake of her head. As if she felt the weight of the world settling on her shoulders, her back arched and her gaze lifted toward the heavens.

"Tell me something, Kyle. I've always wondered what's it like having such a big family. I mean, you're the one with, like, eight kids and three different dads. That's gotta kind of be an odd thing."

Her sudden interest in his twisted family line gave him a pause. Leaning back against the truck, he followed her gaze to the stars above. "It is an odd thing, but it's kind of a fun thing, too. For the record, my mom is on husband number four, and if you want to talk about weird, she's still friends with the first three."

"That's impressive."

"Ah," Kyle rolled his shoulders, "it's just the way she is. Don't get me wrong, my mom's side of the family is great. A little weird and definitely chaotic, but great."

"Then why didn't you move with her when she left town?" Hailey asked a question he'd been asked a million times, though not once in many years. "I mean, everybody knows you chose to stay with your grandmom."

"I don't know." Dropping his gaze back to her, he simply absorbed the beauty of Hailey in the moonlight. "I guess the thing is in a family that big it's just sometimes hard to feel like you belong in the same way just having one parent dote on you all the time makes you feel like."

Hailey grinned. "You're saying you liked being spoiled?"

"Yeah, well, who doesn't?"

"I don't know. I wouldn't recognize the feeling. I'm more smothered."

Kyle laughed at that characterization. Hailey could only mean her brothers. "Ah, Brett and Mike aren't so bad."

"Yeah?" Hailey's head dipped until her gaze met his. "I guess we'll see what they have to say about you when they get back into town in four weeks."

With that gun blast blown through his center, she left him watching her as she sashayed toward the truck door. If the little princess thought her brothers would save her from Cole's reckoning, from their reckoning, then she placed a bad bet.

Kyle considered what move he should make next as he lumbered up into the truck. Hailey clicked on a radio station, leaving him to his thoughts as he drove her home. One thing for sure, he'd be taking back his interest in the car.

That had just been a stupid, angry moment on his part. Getting back in the shop with Hailey would help get her past her fears or at least under them. Kyle could do with some help, though, because he bet Hailey planned on being stubborn.

He already knew she could hold a grudge. It figured her fear would last even longer. One would think she could get over it and be thankful that a man like him would be interested. And she should be thankful.

Kyle didn't drink too much, didn't gamble too often, he wouldn't run around on her, he earned a good wage, and he even happened to be a neat, clean kind of man. What more could a woman ask for? Hell, he screwed her like no other, and that had to be worth its weight in diamonds.

In fact, he bet he could ace any boyfriend test in any girly magazine Hailey threw at him. That's how perfect Kyle was. All he had to do was get her to agree. That started with opening her truck door for her, even if he technically caught it because she didn't wait for him.

At least she let him escort her up the path and even unlock her door for him. His sudden onset of perfect manners had him smiling as she stepped past him through the door.

"Well, thank you, kind sir. I—"

Catching her just as she turned to say goodnight, Kyle trapped her between his embrace in the door, following her back until it banged into the wall. Every step of the way, he kept his kiss bound her lips, making her go wild in his arms. Becoming the aggressor, her tongue toyed with his, her lips sucking on it as her nails bit into his shoulders and her legs rubbed along his.

Only with words could she have said it better.

Fuck me here, now, I don't care who sees.

That's all he wanted to hear. Releasing her, Kyle basked in the glory of having been the one to drain all the sour out of those pert features and leave them looking flushed with desire.

"Now it's a good eleven inches of meat I ain't gonna give you. See ya tomorrow, princess."

* * * *

Smacking his lips, Cole released the metal bar in his hands. With a whoosh and a clank that vibrated down the bench, the weights fell back into place as he sat up. Swiping the towel across his forehead, he chugged down almost a whole bottle of water. After a whole hour of working out, Cole still hadn't stilled the restlessness prowling in him.

The four bedroom house he and Kyle owned had a massive master bedroom suite. It had probably been the original one room house back in the late eighteen hundreds. Like most older country homes, it had evolved from one room to two and onward. Somewhere along the line, somebody modernized the room with a closet and bathroom.

Instead of fighting over the bigger bedroom, he and Kyle had opted to turn it into a gym. It had been a great compromise because both of them really liked having the equipment so readily available. Like having a good therapist on call, working out normally helped both of them work through their problems.

Not tonight. Not with Kyle still out there with Hailey doing God knew what.

Like I don't know what that bastard is doing.

After his battle with the ever delightful Hailey Mathews, Cole decided to console himself with a great deal of alcohol at the club. Actually, the plan had been to find the best looking redhead in the club and wear out some of his mad, but he only ever made it as far as the parking lot.

That probably was for the best, Cole thought as he swallowed down another gulp of water. Not that he worried Hailey would find out about anything that happened at the club and use it to violate his four-week pledge.

It hadn't even been his honor that saved him from making that mistake. No, it had been his burning need to wreak as much revenge down on Hailey's ass until it glowed as red as her hair. Nobody and nothing would drain the Mr. Man for the next four weeks, and that would make him a hungry beast when it came time for Hailey to pay up.

Oh, yeah.

Cole stretched his arms out. He promised Hailey she'd pay like no other, and Cole intended to deliver on that. The only thing that would make it sweeter would be her fearing her coming fate for the next four weeks.

The next four weeks.

Cole grimaced at that and straightened up. It would be hell for him, too. He hadn't gone one week without sex in the last four years. Now, suddenly, he had to prove himself?

Stupid ass, piece of shit that is, and for what?

For Hailey, like she was some prize.

You're a joke, Cole...You're just not the type of man a woman takes seriously.

An old familiar voice echoed out of his past, trailing on the heels of Hailey's comment. *Serena.* That's who Hailey reminded him of. Just the thought had him wrenching off the bench seat and stomping off toward the kitchen to refresh his water and outrun his past.

It just wouldn't let him go. Like an angel, Serena glowed to life in his mind, transfixing him even in memory with how beautiful she'd been. Tall, toned, tan, she bore herself with that regal bearing that had other women whispering that she was too confident, too arrogant. All they'd ever been was jealous over the way Serena demanded the attention of every man in a room.

Even if she hadn't been half as well endowed or blonde, men still would have noticed her. She just had that "it" factor. Hailey...Well, Hailey tended to be along the lines of a Smurf. Cole almost laughed at that thought. Comparing Hailey to Serena was like comparing an orange to a banana. Short, little, and rounded, Hailey didn't draw a lot of notice from the men.

Nah. Hailey and Serena didn't bear much resemblance at all. No resemblance except for the fact that they both had the power to ruin a good man's life. Serena had come damn close to succeeding with him. In a lot of ways, some might say she won, but Cole would disagree.

One day Kyle would understand why.

"That's a hell of a look."

Kyle's dry comment had Cole blinking back to the reality of the kitchen and the cool container in his hand. His so-called best friend strolled past, chunking his keys onto the dining room table before veering for a beer in the fridge.

"It's been a hell of a day," Cole retorted, moving out of Kyle's way. He tracked his friend, studying the way he moved with a critical eye. "You didn't sleep with her."

"Huh?" That had Kyle glancing over as he slid his beer under the old-style, wall-mounted bottle opener.

"What happen?" Cole felt his mood lighten slightly as that fact became firm in his mind. "Hailey back out on you?"

"No, wise ass. I backed out on her." Popping the top free with a gasp, Kyle relaxed into the arched opening to the dining room and gave Cole a grin.

"Why? She give your last performance that bad of a review?"

That earned him a snort. "Don't be a dick, Cole."

"I think I've earned that right, Kyle," Cole shot back, more than ready to pick another fight. Kyle thought didn't appear to want to give him one. Instead of turning into a scowl, Kyle's smile dipped only into an expression of honest regret.

"I guess you probably have," Kyle sighed. His gaze lifted to meet Cole's, and he could feel the bad forming behind that gaze. "I never would have cut you out if I'd known you actually cared about Hailey."

"I do not *care* about that woman," Cole stated as clearly as he could, "I just want to fuck her."

"Really? That's it? Just sex?"

Just sex? Just the idea made Cole grin. "Oh, no, the little darling could wish it would be that simple. Trust me, Kyle, I'm going to make that woman scream, make her beg, make her promise—"

It just all rolled out of him too fast for his mind to censor. The only thing bringing the flow to a sudden stop was Kyle's smirk. Bastard thought he knew what Cole had been about to say.

"Make her promise what?"

"To call me master." Cole wouldn't be tricked, lured, or annoyed into anything else. All he wanted was Hailey's submission. Once he had it, the damn knot growing in his gut would unwind.

"Uh-huh." Kyle nodded at that, looking a little too thoughtful as he straightened up. "You know, Cole, that's the woman I love you're talking about."

"The woman you what?" Cole couldn't stop the laugh at that. "Have you lost your fricken mind?"

"Knew you'd understand."

"What the hell else am I supposed to think?" Cole didn't intend to apologize for his honesty. "I mean, seriously, how am I supposed to believe you are in love with this woman when you won't even fuck her when she wants you to?"

"Whatever, Cole," Kyle snapped in obvious disgust. It was the insult buried in his tone that really had Cole clenching. "I ain't going to argue with you. I'm just saying I'm going for the long term here, and I know that's just not a journey you want to take. I'm asking you, man, as your friend, don't screw this up for me."

"Ah." Cole rolled that crap around his head until his natural response popped out. "God, you're such a pussy. That woman's going to have you trained in two weeks flat."

"Thanks for the help."

"No," Cole shot out as Kyle curled around the edge of the archway to walk off. "Damn it. Fine. If that's what you want, I got your back."

"Yeah?" Kyle didn't look terribly convinced. "And just how you going to get that?"

Cole sucked it in and did what he knew he had to. "By working with you, man. Between the two of us, you'll have that ring on Hailey's finger in no time."

"And you?"

"And me?" Cole smiled, already anticipating the day. "She can wear my collar."

Kyle scowled at that. "That's not what I meant, Cole, and you know it. I'm not going to let you treat my wife as some kind of mistress you avail yourself to whenever the itch takes you. She's either your wife or you can get the hell out of our bed."

"So I'm supposed to just know now if I want to marry Hailey?" Cole shook that question out of his reeling mind. Kyle apparently didn't see anything wrong with his demand. In fact, he appeared annoyed at Cole for even asking such a rational question, which just proved how far gone his friend actually was.

"You're supposed to be committed to trying to build a relationship," Kyle retorted. "You have to actually admit to wanting to have one of those with Hailey."

"Fine." Cole would do what he had to for Kyle. He'd help him build this relationship all the while trying to find a way to show Kyle it would never work. "We'll do it your way."

That caught Kyle off guard and it showed in his surprised expression. "Really?"

Cole shrugged, hating to have to say something sappy but knowing the moment called for it. "You're like a brother to me, man, and you're right. I like Hailey. I like her a lot, though I really want to fuck her more than that. Still, if you want more, I'll try it. I'm just not making any promises."

"I get that."

"Especially not if she calls me a whore again."

That had Kyle rolling his eyes before shaking off his smirk to offer a hand. "Friends, man?"

"Always." Cole gave Kyle's hand an unnecessarily tight squeeze that had him snorting. Releasing Kyle, Cole smirked. "So, why didn't you tap the little darlin's honey?"

"'Cause I got a plan." Kyle smiled a grin Cole knew well. Boy had been thinking, which normally meant some woman should be sweating. Hailey was going to get it, and Cole couldn't wait to help give it to her.

"Yeah? And just what—"

The flash of headlight streaking through the front windows slashed over the dining room wall and matched the squeal of breaks going down hard. The sudden motion from their driveway turned Cole's attention as both men looked for an answer from the other.

"Maybe Hailey?" Cole offered as he shouldered past Kyle.

"Maybe with a gun," Kyle retorted as he trailed after Cole. "And maybe you should put something on other than gym shorts and sneakers 'cause I wouldn't give her that much of a target to hit."

"That ain't Hailey," Cole commented over his shoulders.

Those pounding stomps came from a man, probably a big one, but that didn't have Cole hesitating to open the door before the first knock finished hammering down on it. That didn't mean he mistook the fist that rained down onto his face as an accident.

"Ah, *shit!*" Cole stumbled back as his hand came up to catch the blood coming out his nose.

"That's for Hailey." Slade Davis stepped into the room, following Cole to slam him with another punch. This one folded him over and had him teetering backward before falling to his ass. "And that's for making me get out of my warm bed and leave my woman to come hit you in the first place."

"You gonna hit me, too?" Kyle, always the pragmatic one, backed up.

"I should," Slade spat. "No doubt you earned it, but I'm just here to hit Cole."

"And are you done hitting me?" Cole asked, finally releasing his nose to see if he could breathe through it.

"Yeah and quit sniveling. I didn't break anything."

"Well, that's a relief," Cole snapped as he scrambled back to his feet. "Now you want to tell me why I shouldn't hit you back?"

"Because I warned you once, Cole. You upset Hailey, you upset Patton, you upset me."

"Hailey sent you?" That didn't sound right to Cole. Hailey always struck him as the type of woman who did her own hitting.

"Don't you worry about Hailey." Slade's gaze cut over to Kyle. "Either of you. Let that be the last time either of you says her name or even thinks about her and we won't have to be having this conversation again."

"You got balls, you know that, Davis?" Kyle shot back. "Who are you to tell us what we can and can't do?"

"You can consider me standing in her brothers' stead." Slade's head dipped in Cole's direction. "You told him about her brothers, right?"

"I've heard." Cole didn't take to being talked about, and he could answer his own questions him damn self. "She got two at least as big as GD."

"And two who will be returning home in about a month," Slade finished for him. "Until then, it's my job to come over here and hit you for anything that would have them coming over to hit you for. Trust me, Cole, they'll make sure they break something, especially if they hear that you've gone and torn up the bakery, screaming on about how you want to fuck their sister."

Cole couldn't help but grin at the red stripe of anger flushing through Slade's cheeks. "I'll tell you what, Slade. In the future, if you think I need to be hit again, you just call me up and I'll come out to your place and then maybe we can just go with the one punch."

"You really are a bastard, Jackson."

"I really ain't going to be leaving Hailey alone."

Slade should have brought at least one of his brothers if he really wanted to fight, and it looked like he did. Especially when the large cowboy stepped into Cole's face. "Is that so?"

"We're business partners," Kyle interjected, probably trying to stave off anything that would result in a messy, bloody living room. It worked, too, once he added on, "I mean, Hailey and I are business partners."

Cole smirked at Slade's scowl, but that didn't stop the Davis brother from turning first his gaze, then his head, toward Kyle. "Run that by me again?"

"We both have half interest in a car we're working to restore together," Kyle shrugged, "so we kind of have to see Hailey again."

"Are you being smart with me?"

"No. I'm telling you Hailey and I are working together, and believe it or not, Slade, she's grown up enough to make her own decisions. You need to come over here and hit Cole? Fine, then hit Cole."

"Hey!" Cole flashed a glare at Kyle.

"Just don't be thinking that you can then start issuing orders." Kyle stepped up to flank Slade, completely ignoring Cole's outburst. "Otherwise, you need to be bringing a few more brothers to help you with this fight."

Cole could see the way Slade took that suggestion. The big man was barely holding back, and Cole didn't need any second guesses to know who held Slade's leash.

"You really got to think here, Slade. How much this is all worth to you? You came, you got your punches in, now you can go on back to that warm bed and warmer woman, or you can get bruised and bloodied with us only to have both your woman and Hailey pecking at you tomorrow, annoyed with you for all your efforts."

That had Slade looking thoughtful for a moment. Of all three Davis brothers, Slade actually tended to be the more reasonable, level-headed one of the bunch. If his older brother, Chase, had shown up, he'd probably still be pounding on Cole.

Of course, they are brothers.

That thought popped out as he flinched back from the slug Slade hammered into his arm. "You can consider that one a gift."

With that, the man stormed out of their house much as he stormed his way in. Kyle trailed him to it, kicking the door closed behind Slade as he disappeared down the steps. When Kyle turned that grin on him, Cole couldn't help but return the gesture despite the throbbing in his arm.

"I always knew going after Hailey would be trouble," Cole lamented.

"Yeah?" Kyle gave him a pat on the shoulder as he strolled on past. Heading down the hall, he tossed back, "But it's worth it."

Chapter 17

Thursday, May 8th

Hailey stood over her sink the next morning and stared at her reflection in the mirror, wondering if a crazy lady looked back at her. After another sleepless night, she'd come to some conclusions.

She needed sex like she needed food or water. Until she got laid, her ability to function and think rationally would be diminished. That's what made it so hard to figure out if she was terribly excited or horribly afraid of what she started yesterday, of all that she started yesterday.

The countdown had begun. This was day one, and come day twenty-eight, the world as she knew it would be inevitably altered. For the good or the bad, either way, she wouldn't be in any condition to handle day twenty-eight if she had to survive the intervening twenty-seven days sexless.

Despite all the games already in motion, Hailey stilled needed another plan. One that got Kyle out of his jeans. Hell, at that moment, she'd actually begun to consider how to get Cole out of his. As crazy as it sounded, the idea had grown on her last night as she lay in bed.

Cole would jump at the chance to give Kyle a taste of his own medicine. It would certainly drive that wedge Kyle worried over. It would even add to Cole's degradation in four weeks. Not only would he be taken down by women, but the pack would be led by the very woman he'd been sleeping with.

So much for the king.

He'd be more like the jester then. The only problem was it sounded good in theory, but she didn't think it would work in reality. Getting Cole to do the deed wouldn't be the problem. Getting him to do it without all the kink and bondage would be an almost impossible goal. Better not to even flirt with that danger.

So, she needed a plan to get Kyle back in the buff. That concern shifted sharply to the side when bathroom started to vibrate with the grumble and whine of something way too big and heavy backing down her drive. A peek out her window confirmed the commotion came from a tow truck.

Just why some fool backed it into her drive before eight in the morning, Hailey didn't know. She did have some thoughts about the matter, thoughts she intended to share with the driver.

Clenching the edge of her robe tight in her fist, Hailey secured the gap over her chest as she stormed through her house. Flying out the back door, she had the rude words already formed on her lips, just waiting for the driver to open up his door and hear them.

"Morning, darlin'." Cole hopped down from the cab, cutting every single one of her dirty comments off. As if he had all the right in the world, he set about unleashing the wench's chain as he hollered back. "Will you open the garage for me?"

"What the hell are you doing?" Stunned went straight into outrage, and that had her forgetting all about her robe as she tore off the porch after Cole.

Cole tossed the straps aside and turned to greet her as Hailey came up on his heels. "What am I doing? What are you doing? You ever heard of clothes, Hailey? You're supposed to put them on before you leave your house."

"No, shit," Hailey snapped. "And I should be able to finish brushing my teeth before having to deal with your ass first thing in the morning, but I didn't exactly get a vote in that, either. So what are you doing here, Cole?"

"I've come to get the car."

"The car?" Hailey blinked at that as he pushed past her, heading down the little stone path toward the garage's side door. Having to race after him again in her bare feet didn't improve her mood. "What do you mean you've come to get the car? And where do you think you're going?"

"I'm going to open the door," Cole retorted, coming to a sudden stop that had her slamming into him from behind. He did it on purpose, and she knew it the second he turned to catch her in his arms. "Why don't you go get them clothes on now, Hailey, because it just ain't wise to run around that close to naked near me."

Wrenching free, she growled in response to his smirk. "Don't even try that shit with me, Cole. I ain't in the mood. Now you better get to explaining what it is you're doing here, or I'm going to get to calling the cops."

Cole's nose wrinkled at that threat. "You're cranky in the morning."

"I'm cranky whenever I'm the hell around you. Now will you answer the damn question?"

"I've come for the Daytona." Cole shrugged, turning back toward her garage door.

"The Daytona. That's my car." Hailey delighted not only in reminding him of that fact but also offering no assistance when he jiggled the door knob. It was locked, and all she offered at his questioning glance was a smirk.

He responded by giving her his back as he went to his knees and started rooting around in the flower bed to the side. Even as his hand closed over the fake rock hidden under the foliage, his words already started her snarling.

"Yeah? Well, it's half mine now."

"What do you mean? And give me that." Hailey tried to snatch the rock Cole lifted up, but he turned with her motions, keeping her at his back. "Damn it, Cole."

"Don't cuss me, little lady. Your lover boy is the one who sold out his half interest in the Daytona to me, so you can just save all our gratitude for him." Cole didn't sound upset as he tossed that defense over his shoulder. Far from it. The man sounded outright cheery, and that just made her flush hotter.

"What? He gave you the car? He can't give you the car. He already gave it to me!"

"Ah, yeah." That had Cole turning around, her garage key in hand as he dropped the fake rock back into the planter. "About that. You got a contract?"

"What?"

"Money, like a check, anything that proves Kyle actually gave you the car?"

Son of a bitch knew. Hailey could see that in the wicked humor swirling through those eyes. "You think you're just so damn funny when you know we had nothing more than a verbal agreement."

"A verbal one, huh?" Cole's grin dipped closer. "And did you shake on it?"

"No." Hailey wouldn't let him embarrass her. "We fucked on it. Now give me my garage key."

Cole's reflexes were amazingly faster than Kyle's, and he caught her hand before it every got close to the key. "You see, darlin', I just don't believe you're willing to get up in a court of law and explain just how it is you paid for your half of that car. Unless, of course, you want to be labeled a whore."

"Fine." Hailey had enough. "No car is worth this shit. Just take it, and I'll take a check for my half."

"Yeah, that's not happening." What apparently was happening, though, was Cole breaking in to her garage in front of her eyes as he put lock to key and swaggered on into her shop as if he owned the place. Not about to be run over as if she weren't anything more than speed bump, Hailey went in after him.

"Then you're not taking the car." Slapping the garage door button a second after he hit it had the gears whining as they tried to make the sudden reverse.

"I'm taking that car, Hailey. It's half mine." He hit the button as if that were some kind of gavel coming down on His Highness's edict.

"And it's still half mine, and I say you ain't." Hailey smacked the button.

"You're going to break the garage door."

"I'm going to break you, boy."

"Mighty big words for a little woman in a fluffy robe."

Hailey had had enough of Cole, enough of his threats, enough of living in fear of what he might do. She had only one response left for him. Ripping at the tie to her robe, she flung it off in a full fit of temper to ask proudly, "What about a naked one? Are they too big for that?"

"Holy shit."

Cole didn't even try to fake the decency of not staring at places he shouldn't ever have gotten a look at in the first place, but that didn't dent Hailey's temper in the slightest. He could stare all he wanted. Better yet, he could get a move on to something that would at least take this damn edge off, but if he didn't do either, then the least he could do was get the hell out of her garage.

"Damn, Hailey," Cole whispered, his gaze still locked way south of hers. He sounded like he was talking from a distance and not at all sure of his words. "You got like five seconds to get that robe back on."

"Or what? What are you going to—"

Her five seconds came up, and his answer came not with words, but with action. Like the sudden blast of a warm wind sweeping in rain, she found herself drenched in his heat. Surrounded by the hard strength of his muscles, the world floated away as he dragged her up his long, rigid length to smother out the last of her challenge.

Hailey didn't even bother to fight it. Not that Cole gave her any chance. Covering her lips with his, his tongue took outright possession of her mouth even as his hand swooped down the curve of her spine. Leaving a trail of liquid heat eating up her flesh, that calloused palm dipped over her ass and slid down between her legs.

Just as wonderful as last night, there could be no doubt that Cole knew how to work with his hands. Slipping two fingers along the seam of her pussy, he opened her wide for the rough assault of his third finger as it came in to molest her clit.

Fiery shards of pleasure raked up her back and broke her lips clear of his to let the moaning gasp of pleasure leak out as her legs lifted. Cinching her thighs around his waist, Hailey didn't bother to worry as she began riding that hand to a very glorious pinnacle.

"Sweet Jesus, darlin'," Cole grunted as his other hand slid down to palm her ass and hold her up, "you're wet enough to fuck now."

"Oh, yeah." Hailey liked the sound of that. Just the idea of having him ride her hard and ruthlessly made her fingers dig even tighter into his shoulders as she rubbed that joy all along his front. The scratchy flannel of his shirt teased her tits, making her grind even harder against him as her hips bucked in silent demand.

Hailey didn't let the words fail her, though, as she demanded more than begged. "Fuck me. Just go on and fuck me, Cole."

* * * *

That's not the victory Cole planned on taking, but this entire morning had veered so far off track he didn't really have a plan left. No plan, just instincts that smoldered into ragged need with Hailey flaunting all her sweet curves at him.

As tempting as her breasts had been, bouncing with their hard little tips as she boldly flashed him, it had been the pink folds of her cunt that held him transfixed. She'd been so smooth, like velvet melting all hot and creamy over his hand. That's what she felt like, and it was no different today.

Hailey's greedy little pussy humped against his hands, forcing her clit down against his touch and making her moan out more demands. She hadn't conceded defeat. She'd taken control, testing his as she began ravaging his neck with her mouth, whispering all sorts of dark and dirty things while her fingers made very quick work of the buttons down his shirt.

Never before had Cole been caught so off guard by a woman that he'd been rendered still, but that's just what happened as Hailey's voice began detailing out fantasies that she wasn't making up on the spot. They were wicked, twisted, and involved not just him.

Even as the words poured out of her, her body began flexing faster and faster. Her breath shortening, she abandoned his hand to rub her pussy along the bulging ridge of his jeans, faster and harder. Hailey wasn't waiting for him to obey. She intended to take her satisfaction herself, and that had the primitive in him rushing forward to cry foul.

No woman took. He gave. Cole let her ride herself up to the moment when those hazel eyes went wide and he could feel the first ripples of her release rolling down her leg muscles. Just like that, he lifted her off of him. The sudden denial made her scream, which he expected.

The fist that pounded him in the cheek caught him off guard as she started to holler all sorts of crazy things at him.

"You son of a bitch! What the hell is wrong with you? You been threatening all this damn time to lay me out and now look at you—"

Hailey's tantrum whipped out into another ear piercing scream as Cole lifted her back off her feet. Whirling her around, it didn't take him but two steps to have her pinned against the hood of her precious Studebaker. Squashing the breath out of her, he flattened her breasts with his chest as he leaned in to snarl in her face.

"You don't come, little darlin', until I let you."

"Wanna bet?"

Hailey's neck stretched up to deliver that threat, and he barely managed to dodge her kiss as her hand wrenched free and snaked down between her spread legs. He caught her by the wrist, but the motion cost him as she managed to snake those damn legs back around him and begin grinding her way back to bliss.

"Damn it." Where the hell was a rope when he needed one? Nowhere close enough to help.

That only left him with one option for controlling the little wild fire going up in flames in his arms. Grunting against the strength she managed to exert, Cole still broke the clasp of her thighs. Not giving her a moment to come up with some new way to drive him nuts, he shoved her straight up the hood until her swollen, sweet, glistening cunt hovered under his nose.

"You wanna play, darlin', then let's play," Cole muttered to himself as her fingers swooped in to show him just how she liked to be petted. No shame, that's what Hailey had, and God help him, he loved her for it. He should be tearing up that little pussy, but he had to enjoy watching those skinny little fingers try to do the work of a man's thick hands.

All hungry and creaming, her cunt glistened just the way he'd been dreaming of since the moment he met Hailey over two years ago. He didn't intend to let her masturbate her way out of his control. Instead, he teased her with just how pathetic her own administrations were. Tilting his head, he dipped down to give her clit a little lap, brushing over her fingers in the process.

"*Shit!*" Hailey squealed and jerked like he struck her with pure electricity.

"You like that, darling?" Cole asked as he gave her another teasing lick.

"Oh, God, *yes*," she gasped, her hips arching up as her greedy little pussy followed the trail of his warm breath.

"If you want more, why don't you put those fingers to better use and spread that little pussy wide open for me?" Cole didn't know if he should expect to be hit or cussed at, but she held him spellbound when, instead, she actually obeyed.

Those slender, pale fingers looked so dainty holding her delicate lips open and letting him see it all. That was just an invitation not even Cole had the ability to control his reaction to. He intended to tease her, make her beg and plead, drive her up to the peak of climax again and again until he broke her, but at first taste, it was Cole who broke.

* * * *

Hailey's breath caught, freezing her lungs as she watched Cole hover over her spread sex. The ragged pants falling from his lips washed a warm breeze over her delicate flesh, making it shiver and pulse in angry demand for a more intimate kiss.

She must have lost her mind to offer herself up in such a vulnerably wicked way to Cole, of all people, but that's probably why it thrilled her like nothing else had. Especially when his gaze burned up her length to spear her with the feral lust glowing in his eyes. A sane woman would have whimpered and moved to protect herself.

Hailey just purred. "What's wrong, Cole? Need me to call Kyle to teach you how it's done?"

Pure rage flashed in his gaze and singed across the tips of his ears before exploding over her cunt as his head dipped, and devoured her. Hailey screamed as he sucked the swollen bud of her clit past the hard ridge of his teeth. Trapping her sensitive flesh, he tormented it with relentless rolls of his tongue.

Her body twisted and writhed as he circled over her clit. With each decadent lap, the binds tightening down on the rapture blooming through her grew a little more strained until she could feel the release vibrating through her muscles.

From a distance, she heard him curse but didn't cry out when his lips lifted free of her burning flesh. Too far gone to track reality, instincts had her fingers taking over, and she folded her legs around her hand as she stroked herself ever closer toward sweet oblivion. She'd almost reached that blissful edge when Cole returned.

Rough hands pried open her legs, forcing them wide as the sticky bluntness of a cock head came to press into her fingers. Not bothering to wait for her to move them, Cole pushed them up into her sheath as his swollen head stretched her entrance wide, almost to the point of pain.

But what delicious pain it is.

Hailey's head rolled along the Studebaker hood as she fed more of her fingers in along with the velvety rod burning up her inside muscles. Absolutely perfect, that's what taking Cole deep felt like. It felt even better to hear him mutter and cuss as her palm came down on the several inches of solid steel he had waiting for her.

Pressing down along his smooth length, she managed to both pump his vulnerable flesh while stroking her fingers down the over sensitized walls of her sheath. They both jerked, and she couldn't stop from doing it again as Cole cussed even harder.

* * * *

"Son of a bitch."

Hailey was undoing Cole like no woman ever had. The untamed passion burning through her went unrivaled by any other he ever had, matched only by the very perverse fantasies he always had to hold back even at the club. Not with Hailey.

He could give free reign to his desires, and she'd challenge him to go further. Even now, she captivated him as his eyes went dry staring at where their bodies were joined, her hand caught in the act. More erotic than watching her screw herself was feeling her doing it.

He touched heaven at the first kiss of his dick into her sheath. Nothing had ever felt this hot, this tight, made so perfectly for his possession. Hailey's pussy loved him back, sucking him deeper, rippling around every single inch he fed her in a desperate plea for more. When he wouldn't give it to her, she tried to take it.

Stroking those fingers in and out of herself, up and down his length, she lured her hips forward, until, inch by inch, Hailey screwed her way down the full length of his cock. Her fingers didn't have room left, but even as they abandoned her pussy, they slid down to find his balls burning with need.

"You know, Cole, this would go a lot easier if you would help a little." That dry comment had his gaze snapping up to meet her smirk. "I mean, after all the talk, I'm kind of disappointed at your level of participation here."

She held him transfixed, but all he'd been was an easy fuck to her. God, he hated when Kyle was right. Growling out all his frustration and self-hatred for doing what he had to, Cole wrenched himself free of Hailey as fast as possible and stumbled as far from temptation as he could get. Not even trusting himself to watch, he turned his back on her as she went about taking care of the edge he'd driven her toward.

Leaning against a support pole, Cole panted through the cries coming from behind him that only added to the misery coming from his own cold, lonely cock. He might have done the right thing, but he felt miserable for it. That he added as another large debt to Hailey's column.

Chapter 18

Hailey's fist pounded into the hood of her baby as her frustration roared out of her in a scream. Finally, she gave up, recognizing all her attempts to gain release were only making it that much more painful not to find one.

"Cole, you damn bastard!"

Hailey sat up, fully expecting to find Cole watching her with humor in his eyes. No doubt this was some sick domination game, and now she was supposed to beg him for release. Well, he'd be the one—

Her silent tirade cut off sharply as she spotted Cole leaning against one of the black poles. Even with his back to her, she could tell from the way he slumped over that he was in pain. It didn't take a genius to figure out from what, but it might take one to figure out why.

"Cole?" He flinched at that, but made no comment, which had Hailey sighing. "What the hell is wrong with you? Why are you over there whimpering when you should be over here screwing? What? Do you need me to say that I want you? Because I do. In fact, I need you, so if you don't mind…"

She waited and after a second he finally moved, albeit very slowly and nothing more than his head. Lifting his chin over his shoulder, he pinned her with a look so full of rage and lust, Hailey felt her voice follow her thoughts in a massive retreat.

"I'm not your whore, Hailey," Cole growled from behind clenched teeth. "And I ain't going to violate your rules. Come four weeks from now, there is only going to be one whore in this room."

Hailey should have taken insult at the last bit, but she'd gotten stuck on the first part. The words, the challenge in them, matched the angry glow in his gaze. Kyle had been right. She'd hurt Cole. Despite everything, that didn't sit right with Hailey.

"Cole—"

"Get your robe. Get dressed and help me with this car."

As guilty as she might feel, that only made Hailey lash back harder. "I ain't going to get my robe until we talk this out. I didn't mean—"

"Fine. We'll do it your way." Cole cut her off, slapping the garage door button. Hailey shrieked and dove for her robe, not about to get in another war over the button that might leave her naked ass flapping in the wind.

"Damn it, Cole." Hailey wrenched her robe tight before belting it.

"You listen when I tell you something, darlin'."

"And you should listen when I have something to say because—"

"I haven't got the time, darlin'." Cole waved her off as he moved toward the Daytona. Pulling out the wooden blocks they used as tire stops, he worked his way around the car.

"Will you stop calling me darlin'?"

"Whatever you want, sweetness." Cole flung the driver's door open and leaned down to begin pushing the car out.

"Damn it, Cole." Hailey wasn't about to be ignored and moved in front of the damn car to block him. "Will you listen to me?"

Cole straightened up, not appearing the least bit amused. "Get out of the way, Hailey."

"Not until you listen to me."

"I've been listening to you, woman, and I must say, you're not that interesting."

"Why you got to be an ass? I'm trying to apologize here."

"Apologize?" Cole scowled at that word, coming around the door as he repeated it. "Apologize? For what?"

"For calling you a whore."

"Huh?" He came to a stop not inches from her to act as if he actually considered her apology with any sincerity. "Is that because you didn't mean it? You don't think I'm a whore?"

"Well, maybe slut would be a better description."

"Gee, thanks." Cole turned around at that.

"Oh, come on, Cole." Hailey raced after him. "You got to be kidding me with this attitude. This is what we do. We insult each other."

"No." Cole did that turn thing that had her basically stepping into his hold. "*I* don't insult *you*, Hailey."

"Like hell." Hailey searched for one instance when she could prove that outright lie. "Damn it, that's not fair, Cole. You're insulting with your attitude, not your words."

"My attitude?"

The fact that he actually looked appalled at that had her jerking back and getting over her guilt. "Don't give me that look. You know what I mean. What about when we first met, and without any consideration for how much work I put into my car, you had the audacity to suggest that I bring it by your shop?"

That had Cole advancing on her. "First off, I didn't know anything about your hobbies or interests at that time. As you just said, we'd only just met, and all I knew was you were hot and had a cool car. It was a pick-up line, Hailey. Not an insult."

"Even if I were dumb enough to buy that excuse, what about Brody?" Hailey ran toward her other point, not able to argue his first one. She honestly didn't know if he was lying or actually telling the truth.

"Brody?" Cole's shoulders lifted with that confusion. "What about Brody?"

"You use him. You outsource all your fabrication to him when you know I can out weld that jackass any day of the week."

"You're right. I do use him even though I know you're a better welder, and you know why? Because he never pinches my nipples!"

The pulsing vein in Cole's neck had her own straining as she yelled back, "You deserved that!"

"For what? Coming on to you?"

"Try threatening me."

"If you're so afraid of me, then why the hell did you rip your damn robe off?"

"To get it the hell over with!"

That had them both stepping back. She had not just said that. It sounded outrageous to her ears, and she didn't have to wonder if Cole concurred. His slow smile assured her his amusement had blunted his annoyance.

A real smile this time. Not one of his practiced grins that made every woman go weak in her knees, but one that made warmth seep into her. It was like they were friends in that moment. Understanding that their relationship was too warped for any normal definition didn't change the fact that it held them in a special bond.

Cole sighed. "I guess we just like to go after each other."

"Maybe it's just all this sexual tension." Hailey didn't mind offering that with a heavy hint of hope in her voice.

That had Cole laughing and shaking his head. "I think maybe we ought to start off with just trying to be friends."

"Well, that's…awfully decent of you."

"I'm trying here, Hailey." Cole caught her up in his solemn look. "It would be nice if you would, too."

That had the guilt coming back and her gaze snapped over to the Daytona. "So Kyle sold you his share of the car, huh?"

"He seems to think we'd get along if we're forced to spend some time together."

She smirked at that and shook her head. "I guess he wants us to be friends."

"Make no mistake, Hailey, he wants us to be more than that." That had her chin shifting back in his direction. "Outside of his kin, there's only one person Kyle's ever loved, and I think you're about to make it two. I'm sure he's got some fantasy going where he hopes we fall for each other."

Just that kind of talk made Hailey shift uncomfortably. "So what? I'm supposed to indulge this fantasy?"

"You could at least give it what I'm willing to. A chance," Cole suggested. "I mean, what can it hurt? We try to be civil and polite, work together, and who knows? Even if we don't find love, maybe we find a few good laughs, maybe a few wicked nights, and, hell, maybe even a future business relationship. You never know where things end, Hailey, but you know you ain't going to get there unless you're willing to take the journey."

"Well, isn't that very philosophical of you." Hailey rolled her eyes. "You get that from a greeting card?"

"Actually, high school graduation, but I think it applies here."

"All right, Cole." Hailey didn't see any point in continuing the war. Not that she believed his peace offering, either. Cole was up to something. It would only be a matter of time before she figured out what. "You want to play it nice. We'll play it nice. For now."

"For now?"

Hailey gave him her polite smile, the one she reserved for difficult clients. "Until I figure out just what it is you're really after."

"Not much." Cole shrugged with a smirk. "Just one night, four weeks from now."

Hailey could grin at that because she knew what was headed for Cole. "You're never going to make it."

She expected for Cole to come back with some overly arrogant threat, but as part of his apparently newfound attitude, he just shrugged her taunt off. "Yeah, well, even if I don't, it will still work in my favor if I can convince you to come down to the shop and maybe take a look at a few projects we're looking on."

It wasn't the prospect of getting to work on Cole's cars that bribed her but the show of respect. Finally, he offered her some token of an apology. A token might be all it turned into, too. "You offering me a job?"

"How about contractor, 'cause I'm really not interested in having to put up with your shit on a daily basis."

That she took as honest. Appearing to consider it as payment for his tagged-on insult, Hailey finally caved. "I guess I could put on some clothes and take a ride down to your shop."

"Yeah?" Cole appeared a little caught off guard by her acceptance. True to nature, he recovered quickly. "I don't think the boys down at the shop would mind if you didn't bother with the clothes, and let me just say, congratulations, Hailey. I didn't think you'd look half that good naked, but damn, girl, if I had known what you been hiding under all those boy clothes, I would have been much more aggressive in getting you out of them these past couple of years. Now, we'll just consider that comment grandfathered in."

He didn't wait to see if she agreed to his anointing himself with forgiveness for that crass observation. Hailey really probably should have taken a chunk of his skin for it, but she showed her own willingness to play his new game by following his lead and turning around without comment.

All her nasty thoughts evaporated quickly, her mind turning to what he'd said. Finally Hailey found something to smile over. Cole had been impressed by her naked body. That had to count for something.

* * * *

At exactly eleven fifty-five, Kyle's truck cracked into the lip of the shop's drive. Paying no mind to the damage he might do, Kyle flew over the drive's brow and banged up into the little parking lot out back. He didn't have time to worry right then over his truck.

Not when he knew that exactly at twelve Cole would be leaving to pick up the Daytona with or without Kyle. That's what they agreed on that morning. Getting Cole to wait until noon, when Kyle got back from the parts run, had taken some finesse, but he really wanted to be there when Hailey found out.

He just couldn't trust Cole yet. Hailey would probably pitch a fit when she found out he sold the Daytona, and he wanted to be there to make sure Cole didn't overreact. The two of them could be gold together, or they could be fire and gas. Kyle hoped to steer them away from that dangerous explosion.

It cost Kyle a good thirty seconds to maneuver around the tow truck clogging up the back parking lot. Pulling his truck up to the garage doors, Kyle didn't waste any more time screwing with the parts. He parked his truck there and flew out the door.

Fully expecting to be greeted by Cole, it took him a moment to register what was wrong with the image before him as he rushed into the shop. All that urgency drained out of him as his feet stumbled to a stop. There were four cars, not three, crammed into the shop. One didn't belong there, yet.

Son of a bitch!

He should have known Cole wouldn't have waited. It had occurred to him, but given everything he'd done already, Kyle accepted the risk. He never should have. That's what the sickening feeling in his gut told him as Aaron and Jacob sidled up alongside him.

"Well, look who decided to finally show up to the party." Aaron's smirk grated on Kyle's barely held temper.

"Shut up, Aaron."

"Oh, ain't he cranky."

"I'd be cranky, too," Jacob drawled. "Especially if my best friend was wooing my pussy."

Not in any mood to put up with the Tweedle Dum and Tweedle Dee act then, that comment still had Kyle hesitating as he stepped forward to go find Cole. "What the hell you talking about?"

"You should have just shared, Kyle." Aaron shook his head.

"Now you got to go head to head with Cole."

"You got like two seconds before I hit you," Kyle warned Jacob. "Now what the hell is going on that has you smirking?"

Jacob didn't answer. He didn't need to. A wafting roll of laughter floated by, and Kyle knew that sound. It had him stiffening straight up as Jacob's grin got bigger.

"No."

"Yeah," Jacob nodded. "You didn't really think Cole would let you steal his woman out from under him and not return the favor."

Ignoring the point of Jacob's comment, Kyle held his breath as he read some hope into it. "They've been getting along, then?"

"Of course," Aaron snorted. "Ol' Cole's been on his best behavior, showing her around, talking to her about what jobs we might need help on. Hell, he ain't even darlin'ed her once. Trust me, Kyle, you going down."

Kyle shot Aaron a dirty look for that last part, but the rest came like music to his ears. Cole promised he'd try to be nice, and it sounded like he actually managed that goal. Kyle still wanted to see it with his own eyes.

Shoving away from Cole's cousins, he made straight for the office to find just what it sounded like he would. Cole and Hailey hovered nearly in each other's laps as they leaned in over the desk. From behind he could still catch glimpses of white paper edges and colored pencils rolling all around.

"That's sweet," Cole murmured. "Where did you learn to draw like that?"

"Kind of just came by it." Hailey's answer drew out as she obviously concentrated on what she was doodling. Cole's attention caught along with Kyle's as they both scanned over her hunched frame.

"That's cool. You know, I always got these ideas in my head for cars, but I can't ever draw them out. Makes it kind of hard to build something when you can't show the others what it is you're trying to build."

Hailey sorted at that. "See, that's why I don't like working with others."

"I thought that was because you didn't work well with others."

"Apparently, she's working well enough with you." That came out a little too loudly as Kyle stepped into the office. Even if it had all gone well, he didn't appreciate Cole jerking him around that morning.

Not that Cole bothered to look up and take note of the scowl Kyle sent his way. "Hey, man, what's up?"

At least he recognized Kyle's greeting, which Hailey didn't even appear to take note of. Her silent insult annoyed him into kick-slamming the door in an attempt to rattle her. He got nothing but a look from Cole.

"Something wrong, buddy?"

"I don't know." Kyle gave a pointed look at Hailey's hunched shoulders as he stalked around the desk. "You tell me."

"I ain't got a problem. Hey, Hales," Cole nudged Hailey, "you got a problem?"

"Don't believe in them," Hailey retorted without even a glance in Cole's direction, which just went to prove how big of a problem she had.

Kyle glanced down at the car Hailey worked on detailing out. He had to agree with Cole. She really did draw well. Though he'd never seen the car before, he heard Cole's description often enough to identify it as Cole's dream car. Cole's dream, not Hailey's, which meant her ignoring him held meaning.

"So you two are all friendly now, is that it?" Kyle asked, catching Cole's gaze. Cole just grinned before giving Hailey's shoulders a quick squeeze.

"We talked out our differences, didn't we, sweetness?"

That had Hailey's head lifting, looking only at Cole. "We had sex. I don't remember there being much talk."

"We didn't have sex." Cole dismissed her claim instantly, but just like Hailey, his gaze didn't track toward Kyle. This wasn't a confession. This was Hailey's way of letting him know he pissed her off.

"I beg to differ. There was penetration."

"Oh, you wanna get all technical now, huh? Well, there wasn't any stroking, so no screwing. That would mean no sex."

"Excuse me, I was stroking, and just for future reference, Cole, when a woman is massaging your dick while she finger fucks herself, you do a little more than just lay there."

"I was just laying there because you ain't got no manners, little lady. You don't just strip down and start molesting a man."

"A man, yes. A weenie, no." And they all knew who fell into the weenie category as far as Hailey was concerned. Not that it appeared to bother Cole. He caught Kyle's gaze and offered up a grin.

"Hailey's a little moody because she can't get nobody to scratch that itch for her."

"I wouldn't say nobody." With that muttered threat, her head dipped back toward the paper.

Sharing a look with Cole, Kyle understood one thing. Cole had listened. Whatever happened between the two of them, Cole hadn't taken it all the way. Instead being his normal perverted self, Cole had put something besides his own pleasure first—Hailey. Of course, Hailey couldn't bothered to be pleased with all their efforts, specifically all of Kyle's efforts. If she thought he'd tolerate her snotty-little-girl routine, then perhaps he shouldn't wait four weeks to teach her a much-needed lesson.

"So, how you doing, Hailey?" Kyle asked her very loudly and pointedly.

"I'm fine, Kyle." She responded in the same near shout he had but didn't even look up to give it to him.

"Just be thankful she isn't twisting your nipples." Cole's snicker ended in a wince. "*Ow*! Damn it. Or kicking ya."

"You deserved to be kicked on a regular basis," Hailey shot back.

"And here I thought we were finally getting along. What happened to the love, sweetness?"

That had her rolling her eyes and snorting over her laugh as she pretended an annoyance that none of them believed. "Stop calling me that."

"Whatever you say, honey." Before Hailey could respond to that, Cole's cell phone lit up. Checking the number that flashed on its screen, Cole gave Hailey a surprised look. "Well, what do you know? I guess you'll have to excuse me."

With that, he shoved back from the table, flipping the phone open as he headed for the door. "Hey, Bavis. I'm surprised to hear from you."

Hailey's head snapped up and around as she watched Cole disappear out the door. Kyle wondered if she actually worried about being left along with him. She should.

Settling down on the edge of the desk, Kyle waited for her attention to shift to him. It didn't. In the rudest of snubs, her head dipped back to the picture she'd been working on without once connecting with his gaze.

"So," Kyle forced his jaw to relax enough to let the words come out easily, "you and Cole have come to an understanding, huh?"

"Yep."

"Now you going to be working around our shop."

"Just on a contract basis, not as an employee. After all, you know me." Hailey's head lifted to finally pin him with her frosty gaze. "I got issues with commitment."

That was it. Kyle didn't intend to play anymore. Before she had a chance to see him coming, Kyle latched on to Hailey's arm and ripped her right out of the seat. Surprise aided him in turning her so fast she spun completely around.

"What the—"

Her words ending with an *umph* as Kyle switched his grip from her arm to her waist and pulled her onto his lap. Her plush ass bounced into his erection, and he pinned her against him, making damn sure she felt him.

"You got something to say, Hailey, say it," Kyle snarled into her ear. "Otherwise, I'm going to I'm going to fuck this Miss Snotty attitude out of you right here, right now, and I don't give a damn who sees. Got me?"

As tense as she was Kyle knew Hailey had started to believe him. Started, but the little spitfire just didn't know when to save herself. "I thought you said no sex. You were joining Cole's deal and all that?"

"Right you are," Kyle agreed easily, sliding one hand from her waist to press down on her stomach. The tips of his fingers dipped below her waist line, causing her to suck in a breath and give him the room to slip in and cup the pussy already weeping into her panties.

"Of course there are other things we could enjoy." Kyle pressed in against the cotton crotch to tweak her clit and made her jerk so hard she almost bolted out of his hold. "What do you say, Hailey? Forget the four weeks. It's almost lunch time. We could make ourselves quite an interesting sandwich right here in the office. All I got to do is call your new best friend, Cole, back in."

"Fine," she snapped, caving, "you want to talk, then get your hand back above my waistline."

Kyle obeyed, for the moment. Not only did he give her the room to think, he waited a moment for her to catch her breath before pressing. "Well?"

"Why did you send that man over to my house at eight o'clock in the morning? Selling the car out from under me? Sending Cole to steal it out of my garage? Hell, you are lucky I don't twist your nipples for that."

Instead of directly answering, Hailey went on the attack. Obviously annoyed with the memory, she stiffened, pulling as far away as he'd let her—about a whole inch.

Kyle smirked, not about to be cowed by her indignation. "First off, I didn't send Cole over there. We'd agreed to go together at lunch time, so that's all on your newfound friend. Second, I didn't sell you out. I sold my stake in that car—"

"Which you had given to me."

"And which you accused me of treating you like a whore for. You can't have it both ways, Hailey."

"This from the man holding me hostage and threatening to molest me in front of his juvenile co-workers," Hailey shot back. "Like you have any decency. If you did you'd have at least told me you were going to sell him your share, given me some time to gather a defense."

Kyle rolled his eyes at the word decency coming from her. "I'm getting the sense that you handled your defense just fine, or was Cole lying when he said you stripped down and molested him?"

"You really should have been there. I just tossed off my robe and took him completely by surprise." With no shame, her tone dipped into heated amusement, and he knew she intentionally taunted him with her words.

"I'm sure." Kyle snorted, knowing just how good Hailey was with those kinds of right hooks. "And I'm sure he recovered fast enough."

"I don't know." Hailey considered before giving a shrug. "Honestly, you handle my spontaneous gestures a little better, which is kind of shocking. I mean, who would have thought Cole was the reserved one?"

Kyle would, but he spared her the answer. Appeased with her honesty and glad that they were moving forward again, he decided to let her go and hopefully leave her misconceptions intact. "I guess I'll take that as a compliment."

Instead of stepping away, Hailey turned on Kyle, pressing her hard little nipples right into him. "You can take it as an invitation if you want to give me a lift home for lunch."

The little rub that came with her tempting smile had Kyle growling at her. "What? I can make everything up to you with maybe a quick thirty minute roll through the sheets?"

"I was thinking an hour, but whatever you think you can give to the moment."

She taunted him in the hopes of making him take up the challenge, but Kyle wouldn't be so easily led. "And what about Cole? You gonna invite him to the party?"

"No point." Hailey shrugged. "Even if I did, he'd say no. He made that quite clear this morning. He's going for his four weeks so he can have his one night of superiority."

"It's called domination, Hailey." Kyle couldn't help but smile at the roll of her eyes. She could dismiss it all she wanted. "If Cole's dug in and decided to suffer for four weeks, you realize that means he has some very specific ideas of just what he wants to do to you."

"So I've gathered."

"It also means he doesn't think you'd give him permission to do them otherwise."

That comment triggered some thought, something Cole must have said or done because she flushed and stepped back. "I've gathered that, too."

"You really ready for that, Hailey?" Kyle straightened off the edge of the desk and giving his Johnson a little room to breathe. "Because I don't think you are. In fact, that's why I sold Cole the car. You can try to pretend to be as detached as you want, but what Cole's going to ask of you will require trust. That he's going to have to earn for the next four weeks."

"And what about you?" Hailey gaze came back to his. "Don't you think you have to earn it, too?"

"I know I do, princess. Trust me, I got my plans."

Hailey just stared at him for a long moment, and he could see she couldn't tell which way to read that statement. Punking out, she decided to just ignore that comment all together.

"The two of you are going to drive me insane."

Kyle nodded at that. "Probably."

"I'm not totally convinced in Cole's sudden reformation."

"I wouldn't be, either."

"Or that you aren't up to no good."

He should have expected that. "I gotta rank a little higher than Cole, right?"

"Just a little." They shared a laugh that got cut off as Cole swaggered back into the room.

"You two playing nice now?" That question went to Hailey, who shrugged with her normal lack of enthusiasm.

"Apparently."

"Good, 'cause I'm hungry and it's lunch time. Let's say you make us a sandwich, huh? Sweetness?"

Chapter 19

Wednesday, May 14ᵗʰ

Cole watched Hailey pull her mask off and arch her back. His gaze tracked the graceful lift of her breasts, giving the Mr. Man reason to growl for about the millionth time that morning. The little beast had become obsessive in its demands for a taste of that pretty, little redhead.

It didn't understand these games they played, and his cock really didn't care. The only thing it worried over was the six-day dry spell it suffered through. Going solo for six days wouldn't have been that big of a deal if he didn't have to be constantly tormented by so much lush and readily available flesh.

Cole cleared his throat as he adjusted himself. This was the best moment, when Hailey shrugged her paint suit off and bent over to pull it all the way down. The woman just had to know what kind of invitation she sent out by waving that plump ass in the paint booth's window.

Just three more weeks, Cole whispered back to the Mr. Man. Three more weeks and he'd have his revenge. The more Hailey teased and tormented him, the deeper he dug into his imagination as he fantasized about just what he'd be doing to the little princess in three weeks.

"She does know how to slop on paint, huh?" Kyle's slow drawl drew Cole's gaze from the window to his best friend's knowing look. "We already got three calls for custom work asking just for Hailey. We better hope she doesn't decide to set up a paint booth and cut out on her own."

"Hailey isn't going anywhere." Cole shrugged past Kyle, giving up his gawking for the moment. Hailey better not even think of skipping out until they settled up on their bet.

"I don't know." Kyle waded in Cole's wake, hounding him back into the office. "I mean, it isn't like we got a real contract with her."

"What?" Cole rounded the desk with a snort. "You want to make everything legal now? You think that's going to bind the girl to you even when she decides to split."

"It's not like that. I'm just suggesting we handle Hailey like we would any outside contractor. What? Why you looking at me that way?"

"Because you're crazy," Cole snickered. "She's been working here for a week now, every morning, no problems, so what is this sudden treat-her-like-any-other-contractor crap really about?"

"Man, you are about as grumpy this morning." Kyle shook his head as he dumped the work orders he'd been holding onto the desk. "But I ain't your bitch, Cole, so if you got attitude, take it elsewhere."

"Well, it's not like I can do that," Cole grumbled, causing Kyle to pause on his way out the door. Instead of clearing over the threshold, he gripped the knob and slowly closed the door before turning back around.

"You're horny."

That hadn't been the accusation Cole expected. It took him a moment to finally shrug in agreement. "Well, duh. It's been *six days*."

"Six days of staring at Hailey." Kyle nodded.

"Six nights working with her side by side."

"Lunches."

"Dinners."

"And she likes to bend over a lot, don't she?" Kyle grinned that question out.

"About enough to make a man mad with need." Cole didn't grin. He didn't find it the least bit funny. He'd known Hailey would try to drive him nuts, but this went beyond the pale. "I'm telling you, man, it's like my balls are on fire, and I don't even think any other pussy would do at this point."

That had Kyle's smile evening out. "And you thought about it?"

"No." That had been the first time he ever outright lied to Kyle. Sure he thought about it. Of course he thought about it. What man wouldn't? Especially given Bavis's soon-to-be niece-in-law.

The picture the old man had given him. Kitty Anne. Cole sighed as his mind went over the image of the blonde goddess in his mind. The woman even sizzled in two dimensions, so why the hell hadn't he made his play?

All he had to do was seduce Kitty Anne, prove that he had to be her fiancé, write a check, and then, finally, after all these years, the Fastback would be his. All he had to do was say yes and betray his agreement with Hailey. He could do it. Hailey would never need to find out.

Cole collapsed into his chair feeling about as defeated as he ever had. "I'm just saying, working every morning and then spending damn near the whole night cramped in this shop with that girl is too much. I ain't going to make it three more weeks."

There. He said it. Hailey won because he couldn't take any more. The bend in his pride didn't hurt so much as the idea of losing all the fantasies he'd been dreaming up. If he wanted to save them, he could always wear himself out on Kitty's blonde cunt.

Cole scowled at the very idea. It didn't feel right, but God, how he wanted his one night with Hailey, one night of her submission. The Mr. Man, on the other hand, only wanted the pussy. All the ceremony didn't mean much to him.

"What if you didn't have to?"

Kyle's suggestive question had Cole glancing up. "What do you mean?"

"Well," Kyle settled into his seat on the other side of the desk, "I'm just taking note that the circles under Hailey's eyes have gotten kind of dark and her mood more than a little bitchy at moments, and she certainly likes to stare when she thinks nobody's looking."

"So she's horny, too," Cole scoffed. "That's not exactly a news flash."

"Nope, but that doesn't make it irrelevant. It seems to me what we have here is a mutual coincidence of desires that could be resolved with a well-defined, short-term treaty."

Cole blinked all that in. Typical Kyle, he didn't make any sense. "What?"

"I'm talking porno-date night."

"Now that, I get." And so did the Mr. Man. Already stiff, the damn tyrant just had to swell that little bit more to make Cole's entire day even more painful. "You think you can get Hailey to agree? She's been lobbying you pretty hard these past few days, and this is just going to be an open door in her mind."

"As they say, there isn't any 'I' in team. Hailey's lobbied, and I've made it clear we're a package deal from now on."

"Hmm." Kyle's impressive stance only drew more doubt from Cole. "She won't bite. She's intent on driving me insane and winning this damn race. Trust me, Kyle, Hailey won't call it quits."

"She doesn't have to. The war can go on. I'm just talking about a temporary cease-fire, so we can all regroup and rejuvenate—"

"With a night of sex?"

"Kink-free sex," Kyle corrected him immediately.

"What? You going to go negotiate missionary-only position now?" Cole smirked.

"I doubt it will go that far," Kyle snorted. "Though I'm pretty sure Hailey will come up with some list."

"I can see it now," Cole muttered, and the sad thing was, he could. Hailey would be that type. "What's the point? She wouldn't let us have any real fun."

"The point? The point is that none of her rules will matter," Kyle retorted. "Seriously, if we can't find a way around, over, or under whatever obstacles she thinks up, then we should just be ashamed of ourselves."

"Whatever, man." Cole didn't expect this would go well, but it might be entertaining. Reaching for the phone as it rang, he gave Kyle a hard look. "You better make sure the little princess doesn't take sandwiches off the list. Hello?"

"Cole Jackson."

"Bavis." Cole knew that scratchy voice anywhere. The devil had called for his due.

* * * *

Hailey snapped her cell phone closed and just stared at it. Bavis's chuckle still crept down her spine, making her jerk sharply after a moment as she tried to throw off the sensation.

"Everything all right?" Kyle's question, coming around a mouthful of food, had her glancing back up to where he settled in at her kitchen table.

"Fine."

Her smile felt forced, and from the deliberate way he finished chewing, she didn't think Kyle bought it. That didn't make her answer a lie.

Everything was fine because everything was going just how she knew it would. No unexpected surprises in life today.

In fact, today just went to prove how right she'd been. A reminder she needed after spending the last six days nearly tied to Cole's and Kyle's hips. The constant contact started to wear down her defenses and her doubts, giving a little bloom to a thing called hope. Also known as stupidity because Cole hadn't changed.

Kyle wiped his hands on his jeans before seeming to remember she'd given him a napkin. The small, masculine slip made the moment that much more depressing. When he just shrugged it off and finished wiping his hands on his jeans, she could almost see her future with him sitting there through the years. A fantasy, that's all that was.

It had been a long time since Hailey had to feed a man, and every day that Cole and Kyle labored up to her kitchen table to eat, she felt that tug. The sort of homey feeling that brought a strange glow back in her life. Maybe that's why it seemed so dim today because without Cole there she could see the fractures forming in her fantasies. She'd been a real fool to ever start putting him in there in the first place.

The clink of Kyle's plate going down in the sink had her snapping back to the moment. Her chin led the turn toward the sound, and she found herself nearly snuggled into Kyle's chest with the motion. He completed it for her, stepping up to wrap one arm around her waist to pull her the rest of the way in.

She probably should have fought it, but he just felt so good and smelled so comforting. If she could just convince him to lie down for a moment, she probably wouldn't even need the sex to get to sleep. Boy, but she missed sleeping.

"You know, you don't look fine," Kyle commented as if he could see anything with her face tucked into his shoulder.

Hailey didn't offer up that argument but deflected his concern with an easy excuse. "It's just business. You know I got other jobs to get done."

She tried to interject a bit of lightness into her tone, but the attempt didn't distract Kyle. It might have explained, though, why he wrapped one of those big hands around her neck and tipped her chin back.

"No. That ain't it." Branding her skin with the rough, calloused feel of his own, Kyle slid his hand up, over her neck to cradle her jaw. One lone finger stretched out to rub her cheek. "You're not sleeping, Hailey."

"I sleep just fine, Kyle."

"Liar."

That had her hands coming off their rest at his hips to try and push off his chest. It was like trying to move a mountain. He didn't even have to flex a muscle to keep her in place.

"Kyle—"

"We both know what's keeping you up, so why don't you just own up to it."

"Don't you have work to get back to because I certainly do."

There came that slow-crawling smile again. She really hated when he did that. Normally because it followed with an entirely too reasonable and utterly annoying response, which it did.

"And don't you think that maybe this problem," his finger smoothed back over her cheek, "is going to get a whole lot worse in the coming weeks?"

She should have known. A man with a boner wasn't much different than a dog looking for its bone. Maybe she should consider that, Hailey thought as she began to reverse her attitude. Slipping her arms back around his solid sides, she let hers rest on his rump.

Like a man, she used her hold to jerk him into the cradle of her thighs. She even added a little rub with her purr as she tried to tease him into folding.

"Well, you know, Kyle, there is something you could do to help me with that."

"Is that so?" Kyle growled, pressing a big palm against her ass to hold her still while he did a little of his own grinding.

Hailey couldn't stop the need driving her body's subtle motions, and that just made the moment all the more painful. Under the weight of her own misery, her eyelids closed out the world, letting her live only in the pleasurable sensation.

"Now see, princess, just think how much better all that grinding would feel without no clothes on."

"The bedroom's down the hall." Hailey groaned out that encouragement.

"I don't need a bedroom, princess. I just need to call Cole."

"Ah!" Hailey shoved back as hard as she could, breaking his damn spell before she said something stupid. "Why you got to be like that, Kyle? Ruin my moment?"

"Because I have a compromise to offer you." The little bastard made her feel like the mouse in a cat's house with that smile. Hailey didn't trust that smile.

"An offer?"

"Something to help with them bags, princess, because, honestly, they ain't attractive."

She should have known. "Kyle, do you want to die today?"

"Okay, okay." He held up his hands in defense but didn't slink back out her door. "I was just going to suggest a porno-date night, but—"

"A porno what?" Despite her best efforts not take him seriously, that caught her off guard on the preposterous scale. Kyle proved his willingness to go extreme as he stepped back into her and growled out in that husky way he knew made her knees wobble.

"You know, a porno-date night. You dress a little slutty, come on over to the house, and Cole and I will show you what 'just sex' is all about."

Just the mere idea had her heart racing, and blood flushed through her veins, warming her up for the meltdown. "You're serious."

"Like a pitbull after his bone, princess. See, I've been thinking, and it isn't right to use sex as a weapon. That's what we're all kind of doing and it's hurting us all, so I say we wise up and call a temporary truce."

"Truce?"

"A porno-date night," Kyle repeated.

He meant a three-way, porno-date night, but he couldn't understand why she had to say no to his offer. Only a fool would sleep with a man she'd already set up to seduce by another woman. Right? It had almost happened a week ago, but a week ago she hadn't liked Cole, but now she kind of feared what she'd done, worried that she might end up hurting herself.

"What do you say, princess?"

Hailey's jaw clenched because she couldn't tell him no, even knowing Cole was setting up to betray her. "If I said yes, it would be a no-thrills kind of deal. Straight sex. None of your deviant games."

Almost immediately his head tilted as his eyes glanced down over her shoulder. "Well, we probably should start stretching that ass. You'll be thankful for it when Cole's leash comes off."

Hailey shivered at that blunt comment, but she refused to let that distract her. "I'm not just talking about that. I'm talking no ropes, no ties, no binds, no toys—"

"No toys?"

"Nothing that I don't own."

There came that wicked grin. "You gonna bring your collection with you?"

"Nothing beyond a dildo and lube."

"Boy, your collection sucks."

"I'm serious, Kyle."

"I know and that's what's so depressing. You gonna tack on no form of bondage and domination of any kind and really suck the joy out of my day?"

Kyle's laughter didn't infect her. Hailey's mind still stared down the realization of what she'd just agreed to. *And why not?* Cole might be a bastard, but that didn't change the fact that she wanted him. What it would change was the level of his humiliation.

Hailey's mind latched back on to the argument she sold herself on in her garage a week back. Sleeping with Cole would only add to his shame, not hers, so she might as well enjoy the ride. Especially given that Kyle had just negotiated away all the bells and whistles Cole liked to threaten her with, though one rule remained to be stated.

"And no means no."

"Doesn't it always?"

"There will be no more of this just kiss her and she'll forget about that stupid objection. No means no. Got it?"

"You know, Hailey, you're really taking all the fun out of porno-date night."

"Kyle."

"Fine. No means no. No bondage. No domination. Can I at least still get a blow job?"

"Sure. I can spare the five minutes. You want it now?"

The second the words broke the air, Hailey knew she'd regret them in the very near future. At least they took the smirk off Kyle's face. Still, that comfort seemed a little hollow as he leaned in to issue only one challenge.

"Let's see if you have the balls to show up first. Seven o'clock. " With that he straightened up to give her a quick, almost dismissive look. "And see if you can actually find something appropriate to wear, princess."

Hailey delighted in slamming the door on that one. It felt better because she almost nailed him with the solid wood punch in the process. Kyle got out of the way, though, and from the whistling she could hear trailing off her porch, the near miss hadn't bothered him at all.

Chapter 20

"Are you nuts?" Aaron leaned in to whisper across the table at Cole. The dinner crowd still lingered in the restaurants and at home, leaving Riley's place pretty much empty. That didn't stop his cousins from matching Cole's hushed tones as they deliberated over a back table.

"You know Bavis is just screwing with you," Jacob added. "You can't trust him. Even if he just asked you to pay him some number that would be a risk, but this has setup written all over it. That puts you in the sights to either get beaten or killed. You need to stay away."

"And I agree." Though not because of any of the reasons his cousin just listed, logical as they were. No, Cole didn't want to waste time and energy on Kitty Anne when he had the more entertaining prospect of Hailey and their porno-date night.

"Then why you smiling like that?"

"I ain't smiling like nothing," Cole snorted, tightening up his features.

"He's thinking about Hailey," Aaron grunted. "That's his real problem right now. Kitty and the Fastback or Hailey and Kyle. And you know if it wasn't for Kyle, he'd be trying both pussies and the car."

"And that ain't no lie, but as you just pointed out, I'm a little jammed up here." Cole shot back the expected answer.

Truthfully, he just wanted Hailey and the car. Kitty Anne didn't even rank as a side benefit at the moment. She'd become more like the weight dragging him down.

"I get the feeling this is the part where he asks us to do something stupid for him," Jacob murmured to his brother.

"Why should we do it for him?" Aaron grunted. "Why can't we just get the same deal from Bavis? I mean, if it's not a setup."

"Even if it is, I think I'd take a beating to own that c—"

"Holy shit and mother of God, is that the Kitty?"

Jacob and Aaron bent over the picture Cole had gotten from Bavis. Like two teenage horndogs looking at a nudie magazine, they drooled over the blonde. Just as he suspected, that shut them up. Jacob and Aaron had always been into the Marilyn Monroe types.

"I think I'd take a beating for a piece of that," Jacob whispered as his head lifted. "Damn, Cole, what the hell is wrong with you? You can't pick between this woman and Hailey? You gone blind or something?"

Before he could respond to that taunt, Aaron elbowed his brother. "Don't be a dumbass. We're about to get ourselves a piece of this action, and you're trying to convince the seller not to sell."

"I didn't mean it like that, dummy. I'm just saying we really should go talk to Bavis and maybe even Hailey." Jacob's gaze rolled around toward Cole. "I mean, you got to figure she'd be interested in—"

"You might get the beating and no reward for it," Cole growled out. "Now will the two of you stop playing and listen up?" He didn't wait for his cousins to obey but rolled on over them. Cole did snatch the picture back to help keep them focused.

"As I said, Bavis's nephew's going to marry this woman in three weeks, and Bavis is convinced that she's whoring around—"

"God, I hope so," Jacob whispered.

"—*and* Bavis wants the proof. So I'm thinking one of you jackasses seduces her and the other takes some pictures. We give them to the nephew, take the beating if needed, then get the damn car."

"As in, we get the damn car? Or you get the damn car?" Aaron shot back instantly.

"Well, you are getting the pussy."

"So, what," Jacob turned to consider his brother, "three-way split, man, thirty-three, thirty-three, and thirty-four. We'll give you the point."

Cole snorted at that. "How about twenty-five, twenty-five, and fifty?"

"Why you get fifty?" Jacob demanded to know. "You ain't doing none of the work."

"Well, I don't think Bavis would give you this deal, and I know you are going to go after this woman no matter what. So why don't I give you squat and just sit back and let you do what you're going to do anyway?"

That had Jacob and Aaron sharing a look that ended with Jacob shrugging. "Fine. We'll take the quarter each and the picture."

"You do drive a hard bargain." Cole smirked as he handed over the image. "Just remember her name is Kitty Anne and she works at the library over in Dothan."

"Librarian." Aaron nodded in approval. "I've had a few fantasies about those. You think she got the keys to the library? Always wanted to do it in a public place."

Cole rolled his eyes at that but refrained from egging on his cousins as their conversation dipped into outright perverseness. Kitty Anne wouldn't know what hit her once Jacob and Aaron got done with the little gal. He could almost feel sorry for the woman but definitely felt better for himself.

Aaron and Jacob were the miracle answer to all his options. Now all he had to focus on was Hailey, their porno-date night, and figuring a way around all the stupid restrictions Kyle had agreed to. Hailey might have thought she covered her bases, but Cole could do a lot with just a dildo and a little lube.

Even if she didn't let him get out the ropes, there were two of them. One to hold her ass down while the other had his fun. Yeah, they'd give Hailey Mathews a few lessons tonight, and with Jacob and Aaron doing all the grunt work, he'd have both Hailey and his Fastback…and Kitty, well, would have Aaron and Jacob to enjoy.

A sharp bolt of sunlight illuminated the yellow dinge of Riley's bar. Snapping out as quickly as it broke through the building, the darkness chased the main door back into its frame, washing shadows over the mountain of a man who shouldered into the bar.

Snapping the picture over, he gave a sharp nod toward GD as he bore down on them. Speaking a little loudly and very pointedly, he greeted the man.

"Hey, GD, what you doing in here at this time of the day?"

"Looking for you." GD came to a stop at the edge of the table, barely sparing a nod toward Jacob and Aaron.

"I'm taking it, this isn't a social call."

"I hate to do it, man, but I got to ask for your club card."

"What?" Aaron's head dipped to catch GD's gaze. "You're kidding, right?"

"No, he ain't." Cole had expected this all day, and he didn't offer up any resistance as he pulled his wallet from his back pocket.

"Them Davis boys are pissed because of what happened at the Bread Box last week, and they've finally scrounged up a rule to kick Cole's ass out without it looking like what it is." GD snatched up the card Cole offered him, giving him a hard look in the process. "You'd do well to remember that Hailey has a lot of friends in this town and none of them want to see her get hurt."

Cole straightened up at that threat. "You talking for yourself or for somebody else, GD?"

"I'm just saying, Cole."

With that, GD turned to storm off, saying quite a bit more as he slammed back out of the bar.

"Well," Aaron sighed as he turned back to gaze at Cole over the table, "it seems to me Cole's flirting with his own kind of beating, huh, Jacob?"

* * * *

"I can't wear this, Patton."

"Let me see."

"*No.*" Even though Hailey couldn't see her friend through the bathroom door, she still gave it a dirty look.

"It's not like you got something I don't, or do you?"

"Patton." Disgusted, Hailey wrenched back down the tank top she'd worn over to her friend's house.

Thankfully, Patton had the perfect red, floral skirt to go with it. With its fitted waistline and flirty, mid-thigh length skirt, it looked very girly and very down-home sexy when matched with the white tank. The problem came from the underwear, which Patton insisted really made the outfit.

"I'm just saying, Hailey. I won't judge."

Hailey wrenched open the door and shoved the lacy garments into Patton's hand. "You know, I think I'll just stick with white cotton."

"What is wrong with these?" Patton dangled the little lacy camisole and matching panties from her fingers. "They're one of my best sellers, and you said you wanted something sexy and not lewd."

"They're black, Patton."

"So?"

"So, only six-foot-tall, all-tanned models look good in black. I'm only five-foot-six and pasty white. They kind of make me look short and fat." Hailey snapped the words at her, annoyed at having to point out her own flaws.

She didn't believe in belaboring the downfalls of her looks because she was not a vain person. That's why these girly kinds of things Patton always enjoyed irritated Hailey. The only reason she'd come was because Kyle laid down his stupid challenge about wearing something appropriate. It certainly hadn't been to become Patton's lingerie model.

"Oh, you are not short and fat," Patton groaned as she moved off to hang the garments back on the rack.

The new barn the Davis brothers built to house Patton's business glowed all white and ultra modern, making Hailey even grumpier. Seeing Patton study the racks with that look only worsened the condition. Hailey felt like the experiment trapped in some kind of weird scientific chamber.

"And I don't look it in my normal underwear."

"But what kind of statement does that make?"

"Oh, spare me."

"Seriously, Hailey." Patton turned to drag Hailey back over to the long line of skimpy outfits. "Underwear makes a statement. It sets a mood."

"Mood? It's just sex, Patton."

"Just sex is so boring."

Hailey grimaced. Ever since Patton wrangled her way into the Davis brothers' bed, she'd become a little deviant. "Don't start with me about all those kinky little fetishes. I like my sex straight up."

"Which just makes the underwear so much more important," Patton countered. "I mean, if you're not setting the mood with whips and chains, then you might as well be wearing some, right?"

"Underwear is like a yield sign, Patton. Men just pause long enough to see if they're going to get stopped before taking it off you."

"Only if they're boring and uncreative," Patton retorted in disgust. "A good lover is like a grandmother trying to save wrapping paper—they know how to savor the unveiling."

Hailey's head dropped at that. She'd asked for it. Give Patton one metaphor and she'd give you back another. There would be no winning this argument, but she sure as shit wasn't going to show up on Kyle and Cole's door in a hoochie-mama outfit.

"I don't know why I'm bothering." Hailey sighed out all the frustration holding on to her in that moment. Not that Patton helped.

"You're bothering because this is your big victory over Kyle Harding." Patton plunked the discarded lingerie set back on the rack before turning her grin loose on Hailey.

"I have to admit, I wasn't too keen on this idea when you brought it up last week, but seeing as how you actually got Kyle to agree to sleep with you and leave Cole on the sidelines, all I have to say, Hailey, is congratulations. You're the Queen Bitch now."

Hailey didn't smile back or laugh or enjoy the moment in any way other then feeling even sicker. She wanted Patton's help, but she didn't have the balls to tell her she upped the ante on her original plan. Perhaps she didn't want the help after all because she knew Patton's only advice would be to call her an idiot and tell her not to go through with the porno-date night.

"Of course, you've won the battle, not the war." Patton shrugged and turned back to sifting through the rows of cotton, lace, and leather. "The war takes place tonight, and your opponent has a much higher shock factor than the average male. You better keep that in mind, given you're walking into your own funeral."

"It's not going to be a funeral." Hailey rolled her eyes. "It's going to be sex, Patton. Just plain sex."

"Hmm."

"What's that mean?" Hailey paused to glare at Patton before imitating. "Hmm?"

"I'm just thinking." Patton paused to consider a green and blue silk teddy. "I mean, Kyle has to know this will upset Cole, and he agreed anyway. Kind of like he did before."

Hailey closed her eyes knowing just where Patton headed with that thought. As nice a trip as it would be to take, it would be a fantasy because Kyle hadn't really forsaken Cole. "It's nothing, Patton."

"Nothing but betraying his best friend a second time for you." Patton's gaze rolled into her with a pointed accusation.

"It's nothing, Patton."

Patton didn't jump into the argument Hailey's tone prodded for but continued on down the racks. "It's been nothing for a whole week. Every time I call, who are you with? Morning, night, lunch, dinner, *and* breakfast, who are you with? Oh, Cole and Kyle."

Hailey groaned, hating the way her friend dragged out her smug observations. "Get to the point, Patton."

"Well," Patton released a panty and bra set to swing back into line as she turned on Hailey, "I guess when you called this afternoon, I figured you'd come over here for dinner and tell me that you wanted to call the game off."

"Why would I do that?" Haley scowled in honest confusion. The game was going to save her from making the biggest mistake of her life. It was her safety net.

"I don't know." Patton shrugged. "Maybe because you're falling for them?"

"You think I'm falling in love with *them*?" Hailey gasped, taking a step back from the big, smug smile spreading across her friend's face.

"Yeah."

Hailey almost laughed at Patton's confident response. "Are you insane? Fall in love with Kyle Harding and Cole Jackson? If you honestly believe that, then you should be calling the loony doctors because I need to be locked up for my own protection because what fool falls in love with men like them?"

"You do."

The quick, calm response had Hailey sobering up. Attempting to impress Patton with the truth, Hailey walked up to meet her scowl to grin. "Okay. First off, I'm not falling in love with Kyle or Cole. Second, I'm spending so much time with them because that's part of the plan."

Patton's brow arched. "And that's all?"

"That's all." Hailey held firm.

"And sleeping with Kyle?"

"Just part of the plan."

Pausing to consider that, Patton's grin faded. "So you still want to go through with the plan."

"Absolutely."

"Even if that means that Cole and Kitty might hit it off and end up in bed. That wouldn't bother you in the slightest."

Hailey couldn't answer that one, and she knew Patton had her. So, she cared. It didn't change who or what Cole was. If Cole was a cheater, then Kitty Anne was a just a placeholder. Take her out of line and another woman would step up to fill Kitty's role.

"Yeah," Patton nodded. "That's what I thought."

"It's Cole's decision to make, Patton. I might be the one putting the offer on the table now, but someday some other woman will make him the same offer."

"And you just need to know that he isn't going to make the same decision as your father, right?" Patton finished for her before snorting. Shaking her head, she glared at Hailey. "This game isn't supposed to be a test, Hailey. You can't test men like that."

"I'm not testing Cole," Hailey snapped. "I already know his answer. That's why I'm not falling in love with him. Do you think I'd be that dumb?"

"I don't think brains have anything to do with it. You fall in love with your heart."

"I'm not in love with Cole." Hailey repeated it slowly, clearly, assuring Patton could not misunderstand a single syllable. "I'm not even falling in love with Cole."

"Hmm." Patton sighed and finally let it go, sort of. Turning back to the racks, she began rummaging through them again before letting her next bomb slip. "Let's just hope he isn't, either."

"What do you mean by that?" Hailey's head felt ready to pop, Patton drove her so far up the wall.

"It's just, what if he doesn't lose? What if you're wrong and he chooses you over the car? You are going to owe that man a whole night, his way, and I'm not sure you're ready for that or that you would ever be if you're not in love with the man. I mean, seriously, Hailey, I've read Cole's Cattleman file and you—"

Hailey couldn't help the curiosity that piqued at that. "You looked at Cole's file? I thought Chase put down a serious threat if you broke into the Cattleman's database again."

Shooting her back a smug smile, Patton fairly glowed. "Like that would stop me. Seriously, if those men think that punishing me is some kind of deterrent, then they shouldn't make it feel so good."

"Never mind," Hailey cut her off before Patton could go any further down that road of thought. "I don't want to know."

"Well, first they have to catch me, and then I'll just call it taking one for the team. Because, trust me, it was thick and it was juicy."

The knot in Hailey's gut tingled to life as threads of pure excitement snarled in with the dread she'd been carrying the last few minutes. Like being tempted with a peek of the fate she'd be coming dangerously close to within hours. Hailey waited as long as she could for Patton to continue.

"Well?"

"They call him the Denier. He's a legend for toying with women for *hours* and never letting them come once."

"Hours?" Hailey swallowed.

"Hours." That didn't sound good. Neither did the rest of what Patton had to say. "The women love him for it. He's rated at giving some of the best orgasms and known for making women do whatever he wants, even if they said they wouldn't before they stepped into his chamber."

The very idea echoed through her head and out her lips. "Whatever he wants?"

Patton thrilled at the wicked gossip. Her voice dipping low, Hailey could hear the giggle popping up in her words. "When women join the club, they fill out forms saying what they don't want to experience, like anal sex. That's a common one that is listed on many of Cole's pets' lists. No anal sex unless it's Cole because he's that good at making women beg for things they said no to an hour before.

"You get anywhere near that man's bed, Hailey, and it's going to be you begging, forgetting all your own rules, and letting him do whatever he wants to you. I'm telling you now, you better pray to God that man chooses Kitty Anne, or he's going to own you."

She shouldn't ask, but Hailey found herself doing all sorts of things she shouldn't be lately. "What about Kyle? You look at his file?"

Stupid question. Patton's grin already made Hailey regret giving in to her curiosity.

"I wouldn't trust him in a bedroom even if I had him chained to a bed." Patton delighted in exaggerating, but this time Hailey had a sickening feeling her friend told the truth. "You know what they call him? Trojan."

Not sure how to take that name, Hailey scowled. "As in condoms?"

"As in a charming gift that sneaks past a woman's guard and then ravages her mercilessly. He's smooth, Hailey, charming right up until you're leashed to his bed. But, then again, you already know that."

No, she hadn't actually. Anxiety and fear made Hailey ignore her friend's knowing look. They were going to eat her up tonight, and she didn't have enough sanity to not offer herself up for their feasting. Boy, would it be fun.

"I'll tell you what. I just won't wear any underwear."

Patton blinked at that shift in the conversation before her gaze narrowed. For a moment, Hailey braced for a sharp comeback, but when Patton whirled around stating, "I've got the prefect thing," Hailey's gut tightened with fear.

"Patton." She didn't want to follow her friend, but she did.

"I just made them the other week, and I've been playing with a design for a top, but," Patton paused along with her words to cast Hailey a considering look, "I think braless will work well with these panties."

"How come I get the feeling these aren't just panties?"

"Ah, here we are." Patton pulled something wrapped in tissue from a plastic storage box. As she began folding back the paper, Patton babbled on. All the while, Hailey's eyes just grew wider and wider.

"I got this idea from watching *Fresh Prince*. I catch it at night sometimes in reruns. Anyway, the mother...What was her name? Oh, I forget. She was telling somebody about how she wrapped herself up in saran wrap to seduce her husband, and it gave me this idea. It took me forever to figure out how to get it just right, but, well, what do you think?"

Hailey blinked at all of that, but only one thought came to mind. "I'm not wearing plastic panties."

Chapter 21

Cole barely noticed the flash of headlights pulling in to the drive. On his third beer without any food, he staked a place out on his bed to spend the night at least watching porn if he couldn't participate in any of the fun.

The little digital numbers on his DVD player blinked nine at him. Two hours later than when Hailey was supposed to show up. That just made him the biggest fool walking around Pittsview. He cleared his calendar of a sure thing and abided by Hailey's rules like a good boy, and for what? To play with himself all night?

It just went to show that the woman wouldn't ever hold up her end of the bargain. She probably planned to waste the next three weeks making him play good boy to her leash just to welsh on her end when it came time to pay his bill.

She overplayed her hand this time. He could see now so clearly what Miss Hailey's game was. Well, she had better have a contingency plan because Cole intended to rewrite her rules to his liking.

He drank to that only to find his bottle coming up empty. Grunting, he rolled out of the bed. Might as well go get a new beer and a slice of the pizza Kyle brought home with him. Not bothering to put on shoes or a shirt, Cole managed to button up his jeans as he padded down the hallway.

Instead of being greeted by Kyle coming in the door with the pizza as Cole expected, a knock welcomed him into the living room. Not really in the mood for a visitor, he clunked his bottle down on the console table behind the couch and moved in on the door without any enthusiasm. It took him long enough to earn another knock.

That earned the unwanted visitor a cuss in Cole's head, and he moved even slower in response. Smacking his lips and scratching his belly, he took his time before he bothered to get the door. Intent on chasing off whoever disturbed his brooding, Cole's smart-ass comment got caught in the back of his throat.

In the dull, yellow glow of the porch light, a fiery-headed princess glanced nervously around. As the door whined wide open, the sound drew her gaze up, but not before she already started shoving her way past him.

"Why are you dawdling? Let me in."

A horn honked behind her as a truck he recognized as one of the Davis brothers' prized possessions started backing out the drive. Cole let Hailey slide beneath his arms, letting the waft of cinnamon and the brush of feminine curves chase away his bad mood. In fact, he even found a smile as he watched the truck take off down the street.

"Don't tell me one of those boys drove you over here?" Cole would just love to hear that. He'd love rubbing it in their faces even more because their interference would certainly explain Hailey being late by two hours.

"No."

Hailey's answer offered nothing more than disappointment and a strong reminder that as happy as the Mr. Man might be to have his playmate show up, he still had a grudge to settle with her for making him wait.

"Patton gave me a lift over. That's why I'm late. It's hard to get anywhere on time with Patton in tow."

Turning as he closed the door, he tracked Hailey as she shed her sweater, finding a new reason to grin. The little princess actually put on a skirt. He didn't remember ever seeing her in one of those before, and he would have remembered.

As sexy as her legs looked spread out on the hood of her Studebaker a week back, that little skirt made all her rounded curves look even juicier. Soft, smooth skin, and just the sight of her invited his touch, and then he could wrap his hands around those thighs and wrench them open. That little skirt would pop up around her waist.

The little princess really should wear it like that, like a belt, and show off her smooth little cunt, all pink and swollen. It had been a long time since he tasted something that decadent. Tonight he'd gorge himself and forget about the damn pizza.

Shifting slightly with that thought, his cock pulsed angrily in demand, and he quickly assured the Mr. Man he'd get to gorge himself, too. His dick really didn't care to wait.

"One of you is going to have to give me a ride home tonight." Dropping the sweater over the back of the couch, she glanced all around as she rambled on with obvious nerves. "I didn't bring my car because I didn't want it sitting in your driveway advertising anything."

He'd just have to make her scream loud enough to be heard all the way down the street because Cole definitely wanted every man in Pittsview to know who put the smile on her face come tomorrow morning. That smart retort got caught in his throat as Hailey turned back around.

The damn woman hadn't worn a bra. There went all the blood in his brain. It rushed southward, flooding into his balls until they burned with a need he couldn't wait to satisfy. It took every bit of control he possessed to stay there, leaning against the door, when what he really wanted to do was tackle her to the ground and ravage her there in the middle of the living room.

He didn't give in to that savage urge. Even with all his thinking being done below his belt, Cole still managed to have a few rational thoughts. For starters, he figured out in that moment she'd done this to him on purpose.

Making him wait, knowing it would make him harder by the second, not to mention angrier, and then showing up half dressed. All of it had been intentional in the hope of triggering him into rash action. Rash enough not to make her reconsider any of those stupid rules she had Kyle agree to.

His gaze stayed caught and stuck on the dark shadow of her nipples beneath her tank. Cole couldn't help but grin as they puckered and strained forward under the heat of his gaze. *Oh, yeah.* He'd be enjoying all the delights Hailey's body had to offer tonight, and she wouldn't be rushing him.

"Cole?"

"Huh?" Lazily, he lifted his gaze to catch Hailey's scowl. It matched the sharpness in her tone, and he knew he already irritated her.

"Where is Kyle?"

"Getting pizza." Cole shrugged. "You know it's porno night."

"Pizza?" That darkened her frown. "I would have thought the two of you had eaten by now."

"I would have, but you know Kyle, always wanting to play the gentleman. He only went for pizza once he gave up hope of you showing up." Even if he gave it to her in a smooth tone, he could still see Hailey bristling at that comment.

"I told you I got held up."

"Ever heard of a phone, Hailey? It's this really neat invention that—"

"I would have called, but I just lost track of time."

Cole snorted at that. "I can understand how that would happen. It's just because you didn't have anything like a setting sun to remind you."

Hailey didn't jump on that bait, but she did start to look a little concerned as she backed up. "Are you drunk?"

"You could wish."

That didn't lighten Hailey's glower or tone. "You've been drinking."

"Not enough to pull the dog back from his leash, princess." Cole grinned as her gaze snapped down to where his erection pushed out every single button down his jeans. With a lick of her lips and a quick swallow, Hailey gave away every thought in her head.

"Don't worry, princess, this is porno night."

His reassurance had her looking more agitated than ever as her eyes darted toward her sweater. "I don't know what the hell that's supposed to mean, but maybe I should just go."

"Go?" Cole moved quickly under that provocation, catching her wrist in his grip before she could even lift the sweater off the couch. His other arm circled her waist, dragging her flush against his body as he pinned her with an arm around her waist.

"You can't go, princess. You just got here," Cole murmured against her neck before giving her a little suckling kiss. He felt the shudders race over her and gave her another taste.

"Cole." The breathy way she whispered his name stroked like a liquid flame over his body, making every muscle tighten. Trapped in his hold, her hands came up, protecting the racing heart he could feel pounding beneath the soft press of her breasts. "I don't—"

"That's right, Hailey, don't." Because he didn't want to hear anything but her panting his name in that sexy little way that made him ache. Sealing any protest she might make, Cole whispered a gentle kiss across the smooth arch of her lips. Seducing her with the slow rubbing caress, he teased her with tiny nibbles and quick nips that had her mouth sighing open.

"Cole."

Yeah, just like that. All husky with want and need, she moaned out his name as her body began to melt around him. It triggered every ruthless urge he possessed, unleashing a primitive instinct that demanded he take, conquer, command the luscious landscape of curves rubbing into him.

It became almost painful to hold back as her nails scraped through his hair and tried to force his kiss hard against her lips, but Cole held on. It would be an easy delight to take her hard and fast, there in the living room, but other victories would hold even greater satisfaction.

Lassoing his desires in, Cole took it slow. Refusing the wicked taunting of her tongue and aggressive press of her lips, he gave her only teasing licks, soft nibbles, forcing her to his pace until she melted down the front of him and gave up the battle.

Slow...go slow. Silently chanting that thought welded it into a single purpose, the fortitude of which was tested as his palm fanned over the lush curve of her rump. The thin fabric of her skirt offered no protection to the heat of her flesh. It seared his hand, branding him with one single thought.

Sweet mother of God.

The damn woman had come to his house without any panties on. Sharp spikes speared through his simmering lust, flexing every one of his muscles in a blind attempt to break Cole's control. Fighting the savage whip of raw desire, his fingers crushed the hem of her skirt in his tight fist, a hair's breadth from ripping it clear and giving in to the pounding drive of his cock to plunder what sweet flesh lay below.

"Cole?"

A tender curl of warmth unfurled inside him at that soft, sexy pant. It grew, infusing his lusts with a thicker, deeper emotion as he lifted his head to gaze down into Hailey's wide eyes. They'd gone molten chocolate with her arousal, a beautiful contrast to her red lips, all swollen and pouty with his kiss.

This was how she should always look at him, with the flush of a woman's desires staining her cheeks and the flutter of lashes as her lids sank with pleasure. Just the slight tremble in her lips made his cock pulse with demand.

This is what he'd been missing, what he'd been looking for so long, the pleasure of just watching a woman coming undone in his arms, watching and feeling the soft velvety resistance of skin, so smooth under his fingers.

The slight brush of the back of his hand against the inside of her thigh had Hailey gasping out a little pant as she jerked forward.

He couldn't resist but to tease her again, luxuriating in the way her breath caught. A second later, she sucked in air, heaving her temptingly against his chest. Breath by breath, stroke by stroke, he dismantled Hailey's reason until she quivered beneath his touch.

Slick with sweat and the thick cream of her arousal, her skin grew damper as he traced the trail of desire up to the soft, swollen brush of her pussy lips. There he hesitated, teasing the delicate seam where her leg dipped in before flaring out into her sweet heaven.

He kept her suspended in that moment until she quivered and mewed before collapsing against his chest. There, in a husky pant against his skin, she gave him what he wanted most of all.

"Please, Cole, please…" The soft murmurs faded away into ragged draws of breath. Her body told him what she wanted. Clenching against his jeans, her leg rubbed his, opening her most intimate flesh to his touch as she gave him another plea. "Please, Cole."

Savoring the moment, Cole didn't intend to let Hailey get away with anything short of total surrender. She'd call him master or he wouldn't give her what she wanted. Tilting his head down, he took a taste of the delicious stretch of neck she laid vulnerable to him.

"What, princess? What do you want?"

"Touch me," she whimpered. Her leg strengthened her plea into a demand. The hard curve of her knee bit into his waist as her whole leg flexed in a pointed display that she opened herself to him.

"Where?" Cole indulged in the decadence of having Hailey at his mercy, giving her only a single pass of a finger over the curve of her swollen lip. "Here?"

"Yes." Gasping, her hips arched in blind search of his finger. "Please, Cole."

Smothering his chuckle against her neck, he gave in to her pretty pleas. Stroking his fingers up her pussy, he didn't pause or linger but petted her like a cat, making her preen and mew as she arched helplessly into his touch.

"You're so wet, Hailey. You walk around like this or should I take it as a compliment?"

"Cole." Not amused, not appeased, her cries took on an anguished demand as her nails dug into his shoulders and she lifted up, rubbing that hot cunt down the front of his jeans.

Just like that morning, Hailey tried to take what only he had the right to give. Just like then, Cole was left wishing he had a rope. Then he could really have some fun with his sweet Hailey. He had binds in the bedroom and the skills to make her forget all of her stupid rules.

Pinning her leg in place with his arm, Cole gave Hailey the pleasure she sought. Burrowing one thick finger through the parted folds of her pussy, he trapped her slick clit beneath a roll that had her whole body twisting. Slow and steady, he watched the climax build in the darkening swirls of her gaze. He could hear it in the squeaky gasps.

He could even smell it thickening in the air until she tensed and stiffened, her muscles trembling with the power of nearing release. That's just where Cole left her, on the edge. He didn't give her time to object to his hand's retreat but caught her lips in a hard kiss. Again, just when she began to respond, he lifted his head.

"I think we better finish this in the bedroom." With that heated promise, he released her. Knowing that she'd fallen too far into his spell to do anything more than obey, he held his hand out. "Come."

Even though he knew she would, Cole couldn't help releasing a slight breath of relief when her hand slid into his. Tightening his fingers, he assured she wouldn't escape by sealing her hand in his fist. Not that Hailey fought even his firm hold.

The click-clack of her strappy sandals echoed all around him as Hailey followed docilely after him. How many times had he heard that sound? How many small hands had he held in his and led down this hall before? Too many for Cole to count, too many for him to remember, but he knew he'd never forget Hailey.

This ritual had always been just a moment, not even worth a thought. Tonight, though, he savored every sound of her heels on the wood floor, the heat of her palm pressing into his, even the delicate arch of her fingers as they twined through his.

It all filled him with a sense of satisfaction he'd never touched before. Hailey was not just another pussy to be conquered and tamed. She was a delicacy to be devoured, consumed, and possessed. By the time she left his bed tonight, she would be his true slave.

Not another toy to be amused with, but a pet to be leashed and kept for the rest of her days. Never before had Cole felt such a driving determination to make a woman want him not just for the moment but forever. It should have scared him, but instead it fortified his control, strengthening against the desire to simply ravage.

"Oh, Tina, you have such a wicked tongue."

"What is that?" The shrill cries of the porn still playing on his TV must have acted like a bucket of cold water because Hailey's tone sharpened in an instant back to its normal vigor.

Ah, hell. He always did like a challenge, Cole thought as he released the hand now tugging for freedom. He knew why. He could see it there on the television where three blondes were all eating pussy in an almost triangular position of naked bodies and silicone inflated breasts.

"Well, now, that's porn." He didn't see any way around admitting the obvious. It earned him a dirty look, and he began to reconsider just how far gone Hailey had actually been a moment ago. Maybe he underestimated his opponent because she didn't look very subdued now.

"Maybe I *should* go."

He should have known. Hailey would never have folded that easily. She *had* been playing him, playing it all weak and sweet, trying to dupe him into giving her what he wanted. Cole had underestimated her. Pity for Hailey because that just meant he'd have to step it up a few notches.

"Well, maybe you should." Cole shrugged as he settled back into his bed. "I'm sure that dildo you got at home works just fine."

He didn't bother to look away from the interesting threesome on the screen to see how Hailey took his calling her bluff. Not that he needed to. Cole had ears and even over the panting moans of the porno babes, he could hear Hailey's growl.

"Well, will you at least turn that off?" Caving with ill grace, she stormed in front of the flat screen hanging on the wall. "I didn't come here to watch porn, Cole."

Just because he knew it would piss her off even more, Cole smirked at that. "You came for porno night, princess, and in man's land that means pizza, beer, porn, and jacking off."

"I didn't come here to watch you play with yourself, either," Hailey snorted, rolling her eyes.

"I could play with you," Cole offered. Daring her with his grin to back down, he upped the ante on her without waiting for her to chip in. "We could act out the scenes."

Almost as much as he savored watching her face go all soft with desire, Cole really couldn't help but be thrilled at the way anger flashed over those delicate features. The raw emotion sparked green terror through her gaze as it narrowed dangerously on him. It made him go a little tense and even harder as he anticipated her come-back.

He shouldn't have been surprised when, instead of giving in to her smart mouth, she called his bluff. Stepping to the side, she visibly relaxed as she studied the girls on the television. He didn't buy for a moment that she enjoyed it any more than he fell for the sweet smile she turned back on him.

"Really? And which pussy are you going to play, Cole?"

He could have laughed at that just because he knew she wanted to antagonize him into action. Giving her the hope that her sad attempt worked, Cole slid his legs off the bed and strutted right up to her toes. Keeping his features grim, he towered over her.

"Well, then, I guess I'll get one of Kyle's DVDs. He has all the dick in his."

Chapter 22

Kyle glared at the darkened shadows of Hailey's house over his white knuckle. Gripping the steering wheel tighter and tighter, Kyle tried to vent out all his anger and frustration and break the damn things in his hands. He looked everywhere for her. The bar, the diner, everywhere he could think of.

He'd even cruised past her friend Rachel's house, and now he sat there drumming up the anger to drive out to the Davis ranch. As riled up as Kyle felt, he could take on all three brothers if that's what he needed to find Hailey.

Or I could just sit here. She's got to show up sometime. He'd about tired out of this hide-and-seek game Hailey got stuck on. That had been the whole point behind tonight—to give her what she wanted and show her that she'd never be done needing it.

Of course, the damn woman hadn't shown up. Cole had given up on waiting, but Kyle took this affront personally. Hailey played him for a fool, and worse, he let her. The last thing Kyle would do is sit at home and lick his wounds, or more precisely play with his dick.

No doubt Cole had already settled in for just porn night. Part of the oddity of Cole was that he took these kinds of evenings almost like a rite of passage. There were rituals to be maintained. More precisely pizza, which Kyle hadn't procured yet.

Braced for Cole's bad mood, Kyle fished his phone out of his pocket and hit the speed dial button on his cell.

"Where the hell are you, man? That must be some fucking pizza." Cole answered the phone just the way Kyle anticipated.

"I'm at Hailey's."

"Yeah?" Cole paused and Kyle held his breath, waiting for the hit. "She there?"

"No."

"Sucker."

That seemed unusually mild for Cole given Kyle owed him food. Instead of easing Kyle's tension, Cole's response only agitated him more. "Yeah, I know, but I think I'm going to wait a little while and see if she shows up."

"Huh." There came that hesitation again, and Kyle growled with his impatience for Cole to just go ahead and be an ass so they could fight, because that's what Kyle really wanted. "You gonna be long?"

"No," Kyle snapped. "I'm just going to give her a half hour."

"If you want," Cole conceded easily. "Just don't forget my pizza."

"Okay, Cole, just give it to me."

Cole had the audacity to sound confused when he asked, "Give what?"

"Whatever smart ass thing is making you smile through this fucking phone."

Cole laughed outright at that, clearly enjoying frustrating Kyle. "If you expected me to be a dick, why'd you call?"

Because he needed to relieve some of his tension before Hailey got home and he took things too far. Cole had probably already figured that out. Bastard that he was, Cole wouldn't give him an out.

"Never mind," Kyle muttered. "I just wanted to let you know I'd be late with the pizza."

"Yeah, well, I got a beer in my hand and a movie to watch, so if you're done? Good. Don't forget the pizza."

Kyle glared at his phone when the line went dead. Something weird was going on.

* * * *

Hailey felt like the cat that had wandered into the dog house, only she'd been dumb enough to walk in with way too much arrogance. Patton had been right. She didn't have the defenses to take on Cole. If it hadn't been for the shock of the porno he'd been watching, she would probably already be bound to his bed, begging him to do whatever he wanted.

Just like Claudia.

Shivers raced down her spine as memories of that night flashed through her. It made sinking into the heated musk of Cole's sheets that much more thrilling. For all the fear and nerves that plagued her as she stayed hidden, this time, pure excitement coursed in sporadic tremors through her muscles.

If she had any sense, she'd leave, jump out the window again if she had to. Hell, if she had any sense she wouldn't have come here in the first place. Hailey thought she'd proven quite well in the past two days how very little sense she had.

As easily as that could have been taken as an insult, Hailey took it as a compliment. Everything may have gone completely off kilter, but it would definitely go down as one hell of a summer. It was only looking to get better as Hailey settled into Cole's spot on the bed.

All of the pillows had been stacked into a small mountain on the right side. Still indented from where Cole had obviously been spending the past two hours, his outline spanned at least two inches on either side of her as she settled into his place. Recognizing he'd take it as a challenge, Hailey fluffed up the pillows and adjusted the sheets before making herself comfortable.

A bold move, no doubt, but it didn't stop her from having to take a deep breath every five seconds as she tried to force the anxious trembles from her muscles. The only thing that chased away the chill of fear was the warmth inspired by the sight of Cole strutting back into the room.

He still hadn't bothered with a shirt or even to buckle his belt. There was just something about the sight of fuzzy hairs rimming his belly button and fading down into the weathered waistband of his jeans. It made her tingle in all sorts of wicked ways. Just like the deep drawl of his voice did.

"You know that's my bed, don't you?" He hadn't even paused as he paced up alongside the bed.

Hailey couldn't help but smile with her anticipation of his coming response. "So?"

That had him hesitating a second before he set a cold beer down on the nightstand at her elbow. "So, it'd be nice if you took off your shoes before you got in it."

"Yeah? Well, it'd be nice if you picked up your dirty underwear from the floor before I came over."

That finally earned her a dark look. "Hey, I pick up my dirty underwear once a week."

"Laundry day?"

"Get your shoes off my bed." With that proclamation, he strutted off with the DVD box he had in his hands. It gave Hailey quite a delight to kick her sandals off at him. One even popped him in the ass, provoking a giggle she couldn't help.

"Kyle called. He's running late."

Those grim words coming out of that smile being cast over his shoulder had her nerves kicking back in. It kicked her arousal up another notch, too, because now there was nothing stopping Cole from doing his worst. Just like the idiot she was, she just had to egg him on as the player's tray slid open.

"I guess that explains the beer. Figure it makes your charm any smoother, Cole?"

That got a chuckle. "Beer, pizza, porn," he held up a DVD box as he pressed the tray closed, "and masturbation. You can't leave out any ingredient, Hailey. The tradition is that sacred."

Hailey snorted at that bit of wisdom. Something about what he said kind of made her go *ick*. "Have you ever jacked off in front of a woman before?"

Clearly caught off guard by that question, he straightened as he turned back toward her. Considering it for a moment, the answer came to him with a shrug. "I don't think ever."

"Figures," Hailey snorted and just like that he jumped on the bait.

"Why's that, princess?"

"Because masturbating for a woman, letting her just watch your pleasure, that would be a vulnerable position for a badass like yourself. Right, Cole?"

Coming to tower over the edge of the bed, he smirked down at her. "See, now, I'd have just said it was a waste of time. What fool plays with himself when he has a pussy to keep him entertained? Set and match, princess."

Before she could respond to that arrogant declaration, he scooped her off the bed. "*Cole.*"

"You know, Hailey, you really need to gain about another hundred pounds to back all that sass you got in you."

Going from captured in his arms to trapped in his lap, Hailey's ego smarted at how easily he could just claim victory. "You know, Cole, I really am going to need that beer to help me believe you're charming."

One blink and the dew-covered bottle floated in front of her eyes. "You know, Hailey, if it only takes one beer, you really are a cheap date."

Not about to let him get the last word, Hailey snatched the beer out of his hand. "You know, Cole—" Her words got cut off in her gasp, as his cold touch sizzled into her thigh.

"And these legs, princess, they stay spread in my bed." Growling those words into her neck, his hands settled onto her thighs and wrenched them over his. In less than a heartbeat, he bent his knees and folded them over hers, pinning her into position.

The heavy, rough press of his jean-clad legs against her bare ones scraped tingles of pure electricity straight to the cunt that barely remained covered by the thin edge of her skirt. She could feel herself split open, the cold air tantalizing her most intimate skin. Swollen and creaming, it begged for what it knew came next.

"Now you just relax with your beer and watch the movie." His voice dipped again into a sexy growl as his lips nuzzled the delicate skin beneath her ear. "You just let me take care of masturbating this pretty little pussy."

Hailey choked on her own breath as, with that little warning, Cole's big hand covered her mound. No tender seduction or gentle teasing, he claimed her cunt with a ruthless invasion as two calloused fingers slid in to force her lips wide.

Her pussy greeted his touch with a spasm of pure rapture. The sensation hummed through her clit, vibrating back in magnified ripples of delight as his palm settled over her throbbing bud. The rough scrape of his hardened skin against her delicate flesh had her gasping into a shriek as he fucked two thick fingers into her.

No pause, no hesitation, he screwed her hard and fast, igniting a riot through her system. Those magical fingers drummed over the walls of her sheath, beating out spasms that racked her body, making her writhe as she cried out.

Panting, bucking, Hailey dug her head into the hard ridge of his shoulder as her hips lifted in a desperate plea for more of the ravaging grind of his palm over her clit. Digging her nails into his thigh, Hailey held on as her whole body lost control, riding his hand toward the glorious conclusion she could feel cresting.

"*Son of a bitch!*"

Hailey would have bolted out of the bed at the first contact of the ice-cold bottle against her molten flesh if it hadn't been Cole holding her down by the waist. Even as he pressed into her heat with that bottle, Hailey tried to push herself up his lap in an attempt to escape.

"Damn it, Cole!"

"You were going to spill it," Cole cut back as he tilted the bottle till the hard ridge of its bottom started to massage over her clit.

Too wound up by his petting to be put off by a little chill, the cool only made the sparks igniting in her tender nub that much more violent.

"Nobody spills beer on my bed."

"Oh, God," Hailey panted, falling forward as she felt the first sparkly tension of her impending release.

"You ever fuck a beer bottle, princess?"

Even as strung out on pleasure as she was, Hailey didn't fail to respond with full honesty. "Don't even think about it."

"Oh, come on, Hailey. A woman who only owns a dildo and a little lube has to be creative."

"Cole." Hailey groaned only his name because no other words could form through the blooming pleasure.

"That's why I picked you up a few gifts on the way home today."

Just like that, the cold bottle disappeared, leaving her there on the edge, again. It didn't take any more than the one brain cell Hailey had left firing to figure out that pattern. She needed more cells to start working, though, if she wanted to do anything more about it than just listen to Cole gulp beer.

The clunk it made as he settled it back onto the nightstand had her head rolling to the side. The near miss of a splendid orgasm held her still as she watched him pull open the nightstand drawer and start to pull out a crumpled up, brown bag.

"Now come on and settle back." A big hand came to span over her stomach and press her back into place against his chest. "This night is all about relaxing, and what's more enjoyable than getting a surprise gift?"

A few more brain cells kicked in as he settled the bag between her splayed legs. A gift? If this had been a horror movie, she'd have expected to open it and find a dead rat. This was porno night, though, and that meant only one thing could be in that brown paper bag.

"Nice gift wrapping job."

Even with her tone still brooding with the husky tones of desire, Hailey managed to at least align the words for a decent come back. Her damn voice just dulled the edge, earning her a chuckle.

"It seemed appropriate."

"And did you have to park behind the building to go in?" There, that sounded a whole lot more biting.

Not that it dented the gloating sound of Cole's voice one bit. "Are you going to stall all night, princess?"

Swallowing back another retort, Hailey braced her soggy defenses and slid a hand into the bag. Hard, rounded plastic, that's what her fingers curled around, but it wasn't the cock she had been expecting. Pulling the small bottle out, she squinted slightly through the daze still in her gaze to read the bottle.

"Edible warming lotion?"

"Oh, yeah." Cole pulled the little jar from her fingers. "I like this stuff. You ever use it?"

"I've heard of it," Hailey answered as she dug into the bag. Trying to ignore Cole unscrewing the cap, she couldn't stop the shiver as he poured some of the cool lotion onto her shoulder.

"Well, princess, there isn't anything like feeling it."

One single finger silenced her response as it dipped into the lotion and traced a line of liquid heat up the side of her neck. The warmth sank deep into her skin, liquefying her muscles as Cole's moist kiss ate up the tremors tracing back in the wake of his touch.

"Mmm." His growl echoed her groan. "You're just the sweetest thing I ever did lick."

"Cole." Hailey moaned out his name as he took another taste of her tender skin. This time his teeth scraped over her flesh, singeing her shivers with pointed sparks of electric pleasure.

"There's more in the bag, princess." In what he obviously intended to become a ritual, Cole leaned back. Setting the lotion down on the nightstand, he changed it over for the beer. "Go on now. You ain't an old lady with gift wrap. Tear on into that bag."

"I'm screwing my best friend."

"What?" Cole caught that muttered thought as it popped into her head.

"Nothing." Except that his comment made her see it all so clearly now. Patton and Cole had a lot in common, which was kind of sick to think about then. Instead of turning away from the idea, Hailey embraced it and the fortification it brought to her defenses because it made it really hard to want Cole then.

"I ain't your best friend, Hailey."

"No shit because no best friend of mine would give me, what? Stimulation gel? Where the hell are you going to use this?" That insult had her squirming. Not that it did any good. His legs still pinned hers in place, and his hand around her waist made sure that all her motions did were rub her ass harder into his erection.

The only response she got to that question was the whirl of the cap being undone. A second later, another cool drip hit the indention where her spine and neck connected. Cold tingles quaked out in every direction, making her shoulders hunch as her skin tightened with sudden sensitivity.

Moist heat flooded, washed away the chill as Cole's lips closed over the tender spot, sending searing lashes of pleasure radiating straight down her spine. With a suckling kiss, he had every bit of her anger gasping out as she bent forward.

"Anywhere I want, princess." Cole released her to set the second bottle down.

With a deep pant, Hailey steeled herself and settled back against his chest. Cole would take her out. There could be no getting around it now. She didn't even want to. Despite all the suffering she knew Cole intended to put her through, Hailey would be enjoying every moment.

Patton had been right. If the men really wanted a woman to obey, they wouldn't have made punishment so much fun. Hailey studied the soft, little gadget in her hand. She'd heard about these things but had never actually seen one. Unsure, she asked, "A butterfly?"

"Oh, yeah." Cole enjoyed whatever ideas that gift put in his wicked head. "A must-own for every woman."

"A blindfold?" Hailey turned as much as he'd let her to give him her best *you wish* look. Not the least bit contrite, Cole just shrugged.

"You never know."

"I do know, and the answer is no." Tossing the thing across the room, she pulled out the next hopeful item Cole wasted his money on. Before she could fling the pink, fuzzy-lined cuffs far away, Cole snatched them out of her hands.

"I'll take those."

That earned him a dark look over her shoulder. "The answer is no, Cole."

"I'm aware of that."

"As in, not even if you deny me an orgasm for the next five hours and I'm begging you to bind me up, the answer is still no. That's part of the agreement Kyle and I made."

"And you also agreed to let me use whatever toys you owned and now you own them."

"Cole."

"Fine. No for tonight. I'll just put them here in this drawer." Hailey watched as he tucked the cuffs into his nightstand. "Just so you know, it's going to take a lot of persuasion for me to be getting them back out, princess. No means no, after all."

Hailey didn't miss the threat in those words. It didn't amuse her half as much as it so obviously did Cole. "Very funny. Don't think just because you bought me all this crap that I'm going—What is this?"

Her thoughts got sidetracked as she pulled out the last item, a bag of thin chains, as far as she could tell. Cole didn't give her a chance to read anything before he snatched it out of her hands and dumped it in the nightstand drawer.

"Why don't we save that one for later, too?"

Not mollified by that response at all, Hailey reached for the drawer even as he banged it closed. "What were those?"

Clamping his hand around her wrist, he kept her still with more than just his hold as he growled out his answer. "Clamps and they're for four weeks from now, princess."

Clamps? Hailey's hand fell away as she tried to consider just what Cole thought he'd be clamping. The answers didn't help with the nerves that lit up her stomach. In that second, she realized the stakes were so much higher than she anticipated.

The shrill ring of a phone danced down the hall. At the sound, her gaze cut back to Cole. They both went stiff as they silently shared the same thought. Kyle, and he was her only hope now, but there would be no getting to that phone. All she could do was sit there and listen to her lifeline fall silent.

Cole's grin barely broke when the landline gave a shout out. Both of them flashed into motion. Hailey lunged for the cordless resting on the nightstand, but she remained caught in the steel trap of his legs. A thick hand smothered out her objection as it covered her face.

No amount of squirming or fighting could free her. It didn't even cost Cole a huff in his voice as he answered the phone. In fact, the bastard sounded downright cheery.

"What's up, man? No, I ain't gonna get out of my comfortable bed just to get an update on your sad status. Now, why the hell are you bothering?"

Hailey managed to bite him. It didn't gain her a second to call out. All it earned her was a spank. Wedging the phone between his shoulder and ear, Cole freed his hand to deliver the electrifying blow to her vulnerable cunt.

The impact shot a bolt of ecstasy up her spine. The river bloomed to an all-out flood as his finger rediscovered her quivering clit. Jerking under the merciless lash of pleasure, Hailey forgot all about fighting as Cole's words faded into the distance.

"Oh, really? What a shock? I could have told you the princess wouldn't have shown up, but why ask me for the obvious answer? No, I don't give a shit about the pizza. You can hang out there as long as you want. Hell, wait all night if you want to play the fool that long. I got other things to eat."

Hailey lost the thread of the conversation there. Too consumed with the pounding glory vibrating through her body, she sucked in massive breaths as she tried to survive the sensation. It helped when his hand disappeared and let fresh air in.

"Now," Cole's voice growled into her ear, "I believe I owe you for all the squirming."

Punishment. He's talking about punishment.

That sent a bolt sizzling through her. Enough fear mixed into the excitement that she found the words she needed to have then.

"You promised, Cole, no punish…ahh!" Hailey arched into her scream as he fucked those two amazing fingers back into her. Nice and thick, they stretched out as they began pounding into her. Giving over to the imploding pleasure, Hailey's hips lifted and rolled, fucking his fingers back as they squished in and out of her.

"No punishment, Hailey. Only pleasure."

Chapter 23

Pleasure. Cole didn't know if he could hold his at bay as Hailey went wild in his arms. Good God, but he wanted to fuck her. The tight bind of his jeans had become an excruciating vise as the Mr. Man rebelled. As his cock fought to outgrow the width of his waistband, he could feel the rebellion leaking onto his stomach.

That only angered him into screwing his fingers harder into Hailey, making her scream and writhe. Digging her heels into the mattress, she rubbed that ass against his bulge and took the war to the Mr. Man.

Cole knew he didn't have the fortitude to win that battle and punished her by leaving her creaming cunt to spasm empty and on its own. At least he got to watch, savor the sight of her beautiful pink pussy glisten with her desire. He had Hailey Mathews in his bed with her legs spread-eagle, and the little princess didn't even realize he could see her perfectly in the closet mirror.

Maybe she did. Cole wouldn't put anything past Hailey in that moment, but she hadn't looked in that direction once. He would have known. He'd been watching her the whole time, savoring the victory of finally having the sour little princess captured in his hold. *Defenseless.* Cole's lids closed on the sight, giving him the moment to take deep, steadying breaths.

They didn't work. His entire blood supply still pounded into his balls while his eyes just couldn't resist taking another look. God, but she looked good in that flimsy red skirt up around her waist just like he wanted. Good enough to screw just like that. Cole grinned.

That's just what he planned to do, put the little princess on all fours and fuck her hard enough to make that skirt flap over her ass. Then he'd fuck her there. Cole's gaze traveled up to the sweet tits trying to press through her shirt. First, he had other plans for little Miss Hailey.

"You're a real son of a bitch." Hailey sighed as her head settled back against his shoulder. She contradicted her harsh words by settling against him as if she had all the trust in the world. "You know that, Cole?"

"And you're a much stronger fighter than I anticipated."

That had a smile crossing her face as her droopy gaze lifted slightly. "Turning into more of a battle than you expected?"

"Don't go getting all cocky on me now, princess." Cole brushed her hair back from her shoulder. Moist from her exertions, it betrayed the true cost of her resistance. The way she flinched as his hand slid down her arm, brushing against the side of her breast, only deepened his growl. "After all, we haven't even gotten to the movie or the pizza."

In the mirror, he watched the delicate muscles of her throat work over a swallow even as her voice came out clear a second later. "You don't really need a movie tonight, do you?"

"But it's not for me. It's for you."

Assured that she'd have no ability to withstand what came next, Cole eased back into the pillows and relaxed. The fun had only started, and he wouldn't let the Mr. Man screw him out of it.

"Special? Just for me?"

He didn't need a mirror to see the skeptical look on her face. She gave it to him full force with a turn of her arrogant little chin over her shoulder. There. That was the Hailey who made his entire body clench to conquer her, to make her beg—beg for hours.

"Well, knowing you as well as I do," Cole said as he picked up the remote and hit the play button, "I figured this was just the kind of fantasy you'd get off on acting out."

Even as the music started and the intro rolled over the screen, Hailey's gaze remained fixed on Cole. "I'm not sold on this acting out thing."

"Well, you're always welcome to jack me off, but you seemed to object to that idea just a while ago. Now shut up and watch the movie."

With an overly dramatic huff, Hailey turned her glare on the television, though she did manage to put an elbow in his gut with the motion. Cole didn't complain. Nothing short of her setting his bed on fire would distract him from his plan because he hadn't been lying when he said he picked this movie out just for her.

The blonde that starred in it had about everything happen to her that he intended to do to Hailey. Better yet, no binds, so he didn't have to worry about her stupid set of rules. Best of all, it didn't even take as long as it took him to take a sip of beer before they got to the action.

Like all good pornos, there really was no plot. Boiled down, it revolved around a hot, slutty secretary interviewing for a personal assistant job to a lawyer. As a good porn star, she was willing to do anything. Of course, the lawyer took immediate advantage. She barely introduced herself before the man made everything quite clear.

"I hope Miss Lauder explained everything to you, Vanessa. While you are free to leave at any time, during this interview you will obey my every order without hesitation."

He felt Hailey stiffen slightly at that, her eyes rounding slowly wider as the scene played on.

"Yes, Mr. Hard, Miss Lauder explained everything, and I am eager to get this interview started."

"Very well. You may leave your briefcase by the door and hang your blouse and jacket on the coat rack."

The movie definitely had Hailey's full attention and so did he. The hypnotic pant that had her breasts bouncing froze along with her breath as he curled his fingers under the hem of her tank top. The muscles beneath her velvety skin quivered and sucked in, letting him slide the shirt off even as the naughty secretary let hers slide down.

Cole rolled the shirt, letting the folded layers of cotton brush and rub against her tits. Hailey mewed and arched, following the teasing caress as far she could before her arms lifted and the tank wafted over the side of bed. Now Cole could see all of her.

"Very nice. Very nice indeed." Cole growled out Mr. Hard's line, just as captivated by the sight of Hailey's flushed tits in the mirror as Hailey seemed to be by the movie.

"Cole." The soft plea whispered out with a rush of breath that had her lush globes lift and fall. Twisting in his hold, her hands came to push his up toward her swollen breasts. With their rosy peaks puckered to little nubs, they begged for his touch, his kiss, and Cole ached to give in to their demand, but he wouldn't be moved by simple lust. Not tonight.

"Shh, Hailey." Murmuring kisses up her shoulder, he hesitated at the delicate curve of her ear. "Just relax and watch the movie."

With a gentle tug, he had her settled back against his chest. Those little hands of hers still tugged at his, trying to budge them upward even as she twisted ever so wantonly in his arms.

"Please, Vanessa, have a seat. Legs spread at all times when you are in this office."

Cole watched the movie with his chin hanging over her shoulder, delighting in the way Hailey tensed as good old Vanessa spread her legs wide open and hinged them over the chair. From the way she went still, Cole knew the princess had just realized how badly she'd been set up because she and Vanessa were in the exact same position.

"Do you not regularly wear panties, Vanessa, or is this a special day?"

"I find underwear only gets in the way, Mr. Hard."

"Hmm, I would have to agree. In fact, that is a rule in this office. Personal assistants are to be easily accessible at all times. It's part of providing a quality service."

"I can assure you, Mr. Hard, I'm all about providing personal, experienced service to you or any of your clients' needs."

"Perhaps you would care to demonstrate just how you would go about, say, entertaining a client while I was held up in court?"

"It would be my pleasure." This time Cole copied Vanessa's line, letting his hands follow her actions and lift up to cup Hailey's breasts. Hailey's reaction was instant. Digging her head into his shoulder, her whole back arched as she pressed her heated flesh harder into his grip.

"Cole."

He loved the way she whimpered his name, all sexy and soft, all wet and restless with need. He watched, mesmerized, as he slowly undid her. Savoring every moment, he took it just as slowly as the blonde on the TV. Palming Hailey's breasts, roughing them up with the glide of his work-calloused hands over her sensitive flesh.

Beneath his touch, her skin heated with sweat as her hips began to roll in a silent demand for the fucking she needed. Need all she wanted, Cole took his time, letting his fingers press down only occasionally on her nipples to roll or tweak them.

Hypnotizing her with the rhythmic roll of his hands, he had her swaying to a beat. That made it all the more satisfying to watch her arch and gasp when her tender tit caught between the long edge of his fingers, giving it a little squeeze, a tiny tug.

Mewing his name with every panted breath, that single caress snapped her resistance. Ceasing their tugging, her hands started pushing his out of the way. Cole released her, letting Hailey drive her own pleasure as he savored the victory of having reduced the princess to nothing but a thing of wanton need.

The sight of her thin, delicate fingers working fast over her nipples held him captivated. Pinching, rolling until her palm flattened out over the tip and began to twirl, she didn't hold anything back from him. Not even the most intimate moment when her hand sank down between her legs.

Eyes going dry as sweat prickled down his brow, his own need swelled to volatile proportions as he watched her swirl her clit at an ever faster pace. With no will to bring an end to one of his greatest fantasies, Cole remained paralyzed as she wound herself so close to orgasm her legs tensed and clamped down on his thighs.

The feel of those muscles getting ready to detonate triggered an outcry from the Mr. Man not to miss that ride. Not about to give in to his cock's relentless demands or Hailey's, Cole snatched her hand out from between her legs, making her cry out. Jerking, fighting him, she tried to tear her hand free of his grip.

"Damn it, Cole! Enough is enough."

"But we haven't even begun." Tugging her wrist behind her head, she went still as he licked her fingers clean of the desire that dripped from them. Only once he tormented himself with a tease of the feast to come did Cole finish his warning. "Now watch your movie."

Temporarily defeated, but never truly conquered, Hailey gave him attitude even as she obeyed. With another pointed huff, she didn't try to put her hands back to good use, but glared at the TV before bitching at him.

"Oh, look, some woman's playing with her breasts. This is just so exciting."

Cole rolled his eyes at her sarcastic comment but didn't try to argue with her. Instead, he let her bitch on as he reached for the lotion.

"I bet those aren't even real. I mean, seriously, look at them. They look like water balloons—*ahhh!*"

Hailey's tirade whipped out into a moan as her whole chest lifted up into the warming lotion Cole massaged over her already heated skin. Nails digging into his thighs, she did that lift up thing. He loved that motion. It brought her pussy out of the shadows of his lap and into the glorious light so he could see every intimate fold.

See and hear because the hotter he wound her, the louder she became. Each cry fell out like a stroke to his already inflamed dick. With hips grinding down on his erection, the sensation became near painful. Each pound of his heartbeat flooded one raw wave of arousal swamping his system with searing heat.

Cole didn't cave to his lusts, keeping his motions slow as his hands rolled over her breasts. For all the restraint she cost him, he made her pay by tensing his fingers. Rougher, harder, he pinched and rolled her nipples with no wisp of tenderness, loving the way she grew more and more wild in his hold.

"*Cole*, please."

He grinned at that demand and tormented her with a flick of his thumb over the tip of one breast. Dragging out the motion to scrape the edge of his nail over her tender nub, he matched the action with an equally feral growl.

"Please, what?"

It took her a moment of panting and arching before another whine came out. "You said you were going to act out the movie."

That had not been what he'd been expecting or wanting to hear. He wanted her to beg. Her denial of his savage need had his hands pausing, his finger clasping her nipples in a warning pinch as he asked, "So?"

"Look…" Her demand faded into a whine as he punished her puckered nipple for her insolence.

Cole had put up with enough of her insolence and disrespect. She'd pushed, teased, and outright molested him. All for naught, but that still didn't stop her from trying to command him once again. This time the insult burned too hot to ignore.

Making her writhe as punishment for her ability to still follow the movie, he tormented her swollen breasts as a small reminder of just who controlled the moment. Unrelenting, he drove her back toward disobedience just for the fun of punishing her even more.

It didn't take much. Within seconds, her hand had slid back between her legs, but this time Cole didn't even hesitate. Releasing her breast, he slapped his hand down over hers so hard he made her spank her own pussy. Like he hit her with a bolt of lightning, she arched, screaming, and he just had to do it again.

Capturing her wrist in his hand, he used it like a whip. Smacking her own hand against her own weeping flesh, he punished her good, making her cry and twist until her fingers curled in, refusing to play as his toy anymore.

Growling out his refusal to be denied, Cole's own fingers wrapped around hers, keeping them elongated as he brought them back down toward her creaming cunt. Not to hit, but to penetrate as he fucked both their hands deep into Hailey's spasming sheath. She reacted instantly, arching her hips up as she began to screw herself against the invasion.

Cole didn't deny her. Using her fingers, he gave it to her good and hard until every breath he took tasted of her desire and every breath intoxicated him with the scent of her arousal.

"So good," Hailey panted out as her whole body bounced.

He loved that motion, loved watching her tits roll and sway, loved the slight sheen and the glisten as her body sweated hard under his fucking, and once he'd completely broken her, he'd see her rise over him and ride him while he got to play with any part of her he wanted.

"So damn good. Oh, God, *Cole*."

"Call me master," Cole growled, seizing his moment. He had reason to hope. Even as she denied him, the words came out broken and babbling instead of firm with resistance.

"No....no...Cole."

He pressed deep into her sheath, swirling her fingers so that his could brush over her sweet spot. He knew he hit it when she whined and her legs tensed with the shock. Pressing his advantage, he whispered his demand once again.

"Master."

"No."

Yanking her hand clear, he caught her other one before she could pillage herself. It didn't even take the second it took him to raise her hands up before the princess started pitching a tantrum. Screaming, she threw all the fight she had into breaking free of his hold, but the spitfire just didn't have that much strength in her. At least, not in her body. Her vocal cords, on the other hand, spit fire as only a true wild woman would.

"You stupid son of a *cow-licking bitch*!"

Cole had to raise an eyebrow at that. "Cow licking?"

"I wouldn't call you master if you were the last man alive. What are you doing?"

The wobble in her question revealed the nerves beneath her strident resistance. Cole didn't intend to offer any reassurance. Holding his answer until he pulled the dildo out of the nightstand drawer, he set it down next to the lotion before picking up the remote.

"Whenever you want to put an end to this, Hailey, you know the price." Breathing that heavy warning in her ear, he clicked the reverse button. "Now, where were we?"

Chapter 24

Hailey blinked in response to that. They'd come to another draw, but it had been a near thing. If only the smug bastard hadn't asked her to call him that, then she probably would have given in to any of his other demands. That's just how close it had been.

A sane person would take that as a sign to leave, but Hailey already condemned her sanity days ago. Not that Cole would have given her any chance. With her ankles pinned beneath his calves and her legs bent over her thighs, he had her bound to his bed without a single tie. That didn't make her happy, but it sure as hell excited her.

Hailey had issues with excitement. It didn't enter her life often, so she really didn't have the resources to cope with the emotion. For all the glitter and shine that drew her toward even more reckless behavior, it also terrified every logical thought in her head as she felt her control slipping. That fear had saved her so far.

These moments of calm when Cole eased back helped, too. Her frayed nerves, not to mention tattered body, needed these seconds to try and breathe in the rational air. The only problem was there was no reason left to find in this room, partly because the scent of her own desire mixed with the musky hues of the man behind her to create the sexual dew that fairly hung in the air.

Hailey couldn't draw a breath without inhaling another heavy dose of desire. It ping-ponged through her body, flaring pure oxygen over the simmering abyss of the wanton need pooled deep in her womb. The crackling embers flared with each passing wind, sending searing licks of nearly painful pleasure down her sheath.

She had to win this next round because she couldn't bear this burn anymore. This time, she'd take it all the way. That vow had no sooner sealed over her reserved energy when the sound of the movie kicking back in had her eyes lifting with an impending sense of doom.

"Oh, good God, no."

"That's right, princess," Cole growled behind her, a pinch too pleased and way too damn smug for her liking. "Every time we stop, we go back to the beginning."

Hailey swallowed because that wasn't a threat. Cole wound the movie all the way back to when Miss Vanessa walked in to shake Mr. Hard's hand. He really had gone all the way back to the beginning, which meant he intended to start all over on her.

Knowing what would come should have made it easier to bear when it did, but all those long minutes that passed before his hands lifted only made her that much more tense, that much more excited. When finally it came, his touch rolled over her like a warm blanket on a cold morning. Pure, liquid heat soaked through her chest to melt her muscles to butter.

That didn't stop them from contracting with the sharp whips of rapture that raced over her flesh as his calloused palms caught and rolled over her sensitive peaks. Already throbbing from his former torment, each new touch sent a pulse of ragged pleasure down to her throbbing clit.

There it collected, pooling into a massive wave of unrelenting need. All the while, Cole just toyed with her, playing with her breasts like he had no intention of doing anything else. It drove her mad. All she wanted was a little focus, a little focus on her nipples, but the bastard just kept rolling over them with his palms. Rolling and winding her tighter and tighter until her nails bit hard into his thighs, clenching down on his muscles as she fought the urge to take control. He'd never allow it. He'd punish her again and she'd break. She'd call him master and beg him to do whatever he commanded...*No!* Hailey bit back that silent scream as her back arched toward the hands that lifted teasingly away from her aching flesh.

"See, princess, see how your body obeys my touch. If only its owner would be so practical, then we wouldn't have to go through all this." Cole's heated breath teased over the delicate curve of her ear, sending sparklers of warning racing down her spine.

The sounding alarm didn't help brace her for the strong fingers that closed around her breast. Cupping her flushed and swollen flesh, he lifted it up, bending it back over the thumb he pressed into the upper swell of her breast.

"*Lick it.*" Cole's savage command sunk into the dispassionate tones of Mr. Hard.

Through the forest of her lashes, Hailey could see the blonde on the TV tilting down her chin to suck her own tit. There could be no mistake of what Cole wanted as his forehead pressed down on the back of her head, forcing hers down to her own captured flesh.

"Lick it."

Hailey swallowed, assured that obeying would lead to more pleasure than she could control. That didn't stop her chin from dipping lower.

"With your tongue, princess, lick it."

Her lids drifted closed as her tongue rolled out. At the first soft swipe, her whole body jerked. Banging her ass backward, it rubbed into the massive erection that bulged as a reminder that Cole wasn't half as uninterested as he tried to act.

Giving over to the moment, she took her time. Licking, rolling, teasing her own tender bud as she let the rapture start to wash over her. The rhythm of desire invaded her muscles, her very bones, until her whole body swayed and rubbed against the cock that came so close to being where she needed it most.

Lost in the winds of her own lusts, she didn't notice when his second hand disappeared, but she knew the moment it returned. Something cold dripped over her clit, injecting every single cell in her already sensitive bud with pure adrenaline. Like a party turning into a riot, the tender ball of nerves exploded with raw, unrelenting tingles.

"*Cole!*"

He didn't respond to that gasp as she jerked and twisted under the volatile lash of ecstasy pulsing out of her clit.

Calm as ever, the Denier shifted his hold to her other breast. Offering it up, he commanded, "Lick it."

"Ah." Hailey twisted again as the very air brushing against her open sex felt like an intimate caress. "What did you do to me?"

"It's the sensitizing gel. Like it?"

"Oh, God." Her head dug into his shoulder, her body flexing as the sensation intensified. The heated scrape of Cole's cheek along hers rolled back until his lips pressed into her ear.

"Wanna see what it feels like on your tit?"

She didn't even need to think about that answer. "No."

"Then lick, princess."

Something about the way he cracked that command ignited a primitive response deep in her soul. She'd go down, but she'd go down so hard she'd leave him scarred for the rest of his life—just as he did her. Swallowing down that grim reality, Hailey lowered her chin toward her own nipple.

At least he let her control her own torment, and she liked it slow. With easy motions, she rolled her tongue over her throbbing flesh before sinking her lips down to give it the tug she needed. Losing herself to the moment, Hailey didn't resist when his fingers curled around her wrist once again.

Knowing what came next, she welcomed the moment right up until he pressed her finger down over her clit, and the already over-worked bud detonated so strongly it ripped out of her throat with a scream.

Forgetting all about her breasts, not even capable of the concept of resisting, Hailey gave herself over to the chaos of the orgasm trying to rip through her body. It beat her hips at a steady pound against the fingers whipping over her clit, matching the second storm's eye building over her nipple as Cole's hand took over the task of driving her soul completely clear of her body.

A scream echoed through the room, but it wasn't hers. Not in that second. In the next, though, her cry pierced loud enough to pain even her ears. Cole punished her once again by leaving her so close that she could feel the climactic pulse already seeping through the walls of her pussy. They clenched painfully, demandingly. Before she could give voice to her commands, her face hit the mattress.

In one smooth move, Cole tumbled her forward onto her knees. Releasing her legs, he shoved her head all the way down so her back arched, leaving her ass high in the wind with her skirt flapping down her back. The voices coming from the television vibrated down around her.

"Very nice, Vanessa, but why don't you come on over here."

Her chin rose out of the sheets to lift her clouded gaze toward the screen. With every breath becoming that much more labored, she watched the blonde crawl up onto the lawyer's desk. Ass up, head down, skirt rolled up like a belt, she presented him with her pussy with legs spread wide—just like Hailey did Cole.

That's the image that burned through her mind, making her cunt shiver and pulse at the very idea that it lay open and exposed for Cole's enjoyment. She didn't have to wonder what he intended as she watched the lawyer spread the porno babe's pussy lips wide with his fingers.

"Let's see what we have here."

The scream that tried to rip its way out of Hailey's throat was too raw and brutal of a sound to actually resonate through the air as Cole's fingers stroked over her intimate flesh. Like a branding iron, they left a trail of sparkling sensation that pierced her flesh with so much pleasure she jerked forward, trying to claw her way to freedom.

"Oh, God, *no*."

It was too late. He'd already set her pussy on fire by dripping that damn sensitizing lotion all down the sensitive folds of her pussy. Panting out whines as her sex became a living, breathing thing of relentless pleasure, she tried again to pull her way over the edge of the bed.

Cole held her steady with a ten-fingered grip on her hips. Those steel bands bit down into her skin until her ass dipped and the warm wash of his breath had her mewing out babbling pleas.

"Oh, please, no. Cole, I can't. I can't take this."

"You know what I want."

Those dark words rumbled like thunder over her clit, making her breath catch as her whole body clenched under the impact. For all the power of the climax tempting her into doom, Hailey managed to hold on to one shred of dignity. She wouldn't do it. She'd suffer any of the fates of hell that the Denier could dish out before she would do that.

Not capable of the words needed to issue the challenge, Hailey delivered it by simply lowering down her pussy to the hungry mouth breathing against it. The scream she hadn't been able to get out before came through clearly this time as Cole met her with a lick straight down her slit.

The cry didn't end until she ran out of breath as he unleashed a torrent of suckling, nipping, licking kisses all over her pussy. With no ability to draw breath in to fuel the sound of her soul being sheared from her body, she couldn't stop her own savaging as she fucked herself against his mouth.

Then he bit her ever so slightly with the barest scrape of his teeth, but the small pain shot through her drugged flesh like the sharp edges of a spear. Jerking free of his hold, her hips whipped upward as she finally managed to gulp in life-giving air.

"Oh, God, Cole. You can't do that. I can't take that," Hailey panted out as her head hit the mattress again. Feeling washed over and wrung out, she could only pray he would put an end to this. She had reason to hope. Cole had retreated, but she only needed to lift her eyes to see what came next.

The pop of the button on the lawyer's slacks echoed behind her, just as the downward hiss of his zipper. The porn star's meaty-looking dick definitely matched the feel of Cole's bulbous head as he rested his cock against the entrance of her pussy. Just as the man gripped Vanessa's hips and stepped into her pussy, so did Cole slide slowly, deliciously, all the way home.

Whimpering over the sweet sensation, Hailey's head collapsed again. This was worth all the torment in the world. It had been so good that morning that she thought it had all been in her head, that her need and desperation had driven her to hallucinate. Maybe so. Maybe still, but what a dream it was.

Thick, hard, the steady thump of his vein came to a complete stop. The way he leaned forward and slid his hands over her stomach and up to cup her breasts actually had her sighing. This time the barreling pleasure was tempered by the soothing balm of being about to tighten down on something so wickedly strong.

"So good, so thick, you feel wonderful."

Silently, Hailey echoed that sentiment, though she didn't open her eyes to see if Vanessa had given herself over to the lusty pleasure of swaying up and down the cock impaling her. If not, Hailey would definitely recommend it. Hell, she couldn't stop doing it, and as much as she ached for Cole to add his own momentum into the game, she savored every enchanting grind as she rotated her hips slowly.

"You like that? And what about this, my pet?"

The air caught in her throat as one of Cole's hands traced back over her trembling stomach muscles to dip down between her legs. Tripping over itself as it restarted, her heart sent her lungs pounding out a whine as he rediscovered her clit. Her poor, tormented bud felt bruised by pleasure, stretched by the cock filling her pussy, and it still burned thanks to Cole's gift. None of that deterred him from trapping her tender nub once again beneath the calloused pad of his finger.

"Oh, sir, I can't take what you are doing to me!"

Hailey couldn't, either. Crying, she pumped her hips hard in both reaction to the intense pleasure his rolling touch sent reeling through her body and in desperate demand for him to get to the screwing she so desperately needed.

"You are wild, my pet. I can see it will require a lot of work to get you properly trained, but for now we'll start with begging. You want my fucking? Then beg for it."

That's just what Hailey did. "Please, Cole, just fuck me. I can't take this anymore."

That had Cole stilling. "You know what I want."

Hailey growled at that, annoyed back into her resistance even as she knew starting back at the beginning would about kill her. "Fuck your wants, Cole. I *know* you can't pull out of me, so why don't you start acting like a man instead of some childish kid playing games and *fuck me*."

That did it. Just as she silently bet it would. Cole lost it with a snarl. Bending over her like a beast in need, his chest slid to stick against her sweaty back as his arms came down in a cage of sinewy strength. He didn't just fuck her, he rutted.

With his chin bent over her shoulder, he panted out like a warhorse in full gallop as he pounded one deadly hammer of his hips after another, shafting every delicious inch of his cock straight into her. From the slick, suction sound of moist flesh being pillaged to the slap of his balls against her pussy, Hailey rode him back just as hard, loving every moment.

In all her years, it had never felt this good. *This damn good.* Even with Kyle, as amazing as he'd been, there hadn't been this sense of exhilaration as Cole's cock drove her straight into Utopia's brilliant horizon.

"Son of a bitch!" Hailey roared that out as the great reflection of beautiful perfection fractured and fizzled with a dose of searing pain. Flattening out on the bed, she tried to breathe through the sudden sensation of having her rear stuffed completely full. In one single second, Cole used all his momentum to pull free of her pussy and sink himself balls deep in her ass.

It was too much. The pleasure, the pain, it all overwhelmed her, and in that moment she couldn't tell what she was feeling. Through that din of confusion, warmth settled over her back, easing and soothing muscles strung tight with tension.

Cole's hands massaged over her back with the tenderness of a true lover as his voice trickled down from above. "I'm sorry, Hailey. I forgot for a moment. Please tell me you've done this before?"

Even through the pound of her own lusts and anxieties, Hailey registered the sincerity and guilt in his voice. She had leverage now. He'd forgotten himself in the wild moment of climax, and she could use that against him, to break his will and win the game.

The only problem with that logic was that then the game would stop and this moment would come to an end.

"Hailey?"

"I haven't." Hailey swallowed, not sure of exactly how to put that into words.

"Oh, God. I'm sorry." Those words followed a reflexive retreat that had him easing his pulsing length back down the tender walls of her passage. Sizzling sparkles of pain lit out of her ass. The tendrils ran into the fog of lust burning in her womb. Like cold air meeting hot air, rapturous thunderstorms broke out along the fissure of the two contrasting sensations.

"Don't," Hailey gasped as her muscles clenched down on the ragged pleasure, making it echo that much louder through her body as her channel trapped his thickness in a tight grip. "Oh, God."

"I'm so sorry." Cole was right there, leaning over her and feeding that precious inch back in as he smoothed his hands up over her shoulders. "I didn't mean to hurt you."

"Doesn't." She couldn't seem to get more than a word out at a time as the rolls of clashing sensations ricocheted over her muscles, constricting them and her ability to speak.

"Don't? Don't what?" Cole had never sounded like that before—caring. It made it that much harder to breathe. If only he could be the same ass he always was, then she could be mad at him. Instead, his remorse-laden compassion melted through all the raw emotions, soothing their ragged edges even as it smudged the line between pleasure and pain even further.

"Hailey?"

"I just..." Her eyes rolled back as that thread of thought faded under another intense wave of emotion. "Oh, God."

"You like it." As that revelation rolled out, so did his tone deepen into the hungry recess of a growl. "Don't you?"

Fear held her back from answering that. Fear that he would stop. Fear that he would continue. Hailey didn't know the answer because she didn't like it. She loved it. The pleasure, the pain, the sheer intensity, nothing had ever felt like this, and that scared her more than anything.

That didn't mean Cole would let her hide or even have a moment to recover. Apparently he'd gotten over his guilt because nothing but naked aggression remained when he murmured her name up against her ear.

"Hailey?" Tempting her, he slid a palm down her side, dipping over her hip. "You like it. Don't you, princess? You like everything I'm doing to you."

"Cole," Hailey whimpered. She didn't have the strength to fight the fingers fanning out over her mound, not with all her energy being dispensed to tense and tremble as she waited for him to offer up the final, killing blow.

It didn't come. Instead of delving back into the folds of her pussy, he caressed the naked skin of her mound. Massaging a seductive kind of warmth straight into her womb, he calmed her ragged desires but didn't soothe them in the slightest.

"Tell me to stop." Cole taunted her as he began placing heated, suckling kisses up her neck. "Tell me to stop and I will, princess. It's all you have to say."

"No." Hailey didn't question where that answer came from. Neither did she try to fight the truth it contained.

"Then you know what I want."

That should have brought a scream to her lips, but instead a smile tugged at them. Cole was as stubborn as a damn mule. Then again, so was she.

Seriously, if those men think that punishing me is some kind of deterrent, then they shouldn't make it feel so good.

For once, Hailey agreed with Patton, not that she'd ever tell her friend that.

She would thank her, though, because in that second, Patton's smart mouth saved both Hailey's dignity and sanity. Finding the power to lift her head off the mattress, she arched her neck back so that she could almost whisper directly into Cole's ear.

"No."

This time the growl that echoed out of Cole's chest was loud, ragged, vibrating out of his soul and across her body as every muscle tensed around her. He'd thought he had her. This had probably been his nuclear option, and it misfired. Victory was hers.

To the victor went the spoils and in her case that turned out only to be about five seconds of rejoicing before suddenly Cole lifted up. With his arms pinning her back to his front, he took her with him, igniting a wildfire of sensations as her ass rubbed along his erection.

"Cole?"

Panic set in as she felt herself falling back. Not into his lap, but onto it. If she thought thirty seconds ago that he'd done his worst, she'd been very sadly mistaken. With her weight sinking her down those precious last few centimeters, Hailey found herself captured and impaled.

The chaos erupting out of her ass flared blazing bolts of ecstasy straight up her spine. The glorious heat eradicated any concept of pleasure or pain. It annihilated thought of any kind, leaving her body nothing more than a whimpering shell for Cole to tuck back into a frighteningly familiar position.

"Well then." The motion of his arm aiming the remote back at the television drew her bewildered gaze in its direction. "I guess we start back at the beginning. Unless you're interested in changing that answer?"

Chapter 25

Kyle kicked down the foot brake with more force than necessary, just like he did the truck door. Hell he even kicked it closed because that's how pissed he was. That's how long he waited.

Two fucking hours, and what did he have to show for it? A pizza and a six pack because Cole had it right. Best to be refreshed for tomorrow, because the next time he saw her, there would be no polite conversation, no understanding consideration, no nothing other than her moans and him taking what he wanted, where he wanted—on the office desk.

What a breakfast that will be. Giving the back door a good kick just because, Kyle stormed into the kitchen. The rumble of the refrigerator greeted him along with the blare of porn coming down the hall. Loud as hell, people could probably hear that shit on the street.

It just pricked Kyle's foul mood all the more as he chunked the pizza onto the counter. "Cole! Turn that shit down!"

He didn't get a response other than the sudden silence. Well, not full silence. The fridge still gave him hell as he wrenched open the door. Half expecting Cole to come padding down the hall, he just started talking a little loudly as he stuffed the warm beer in and snatched a cold beer out.

"I got pizza and the damn refrigerator is grumbling *again*. I thought you fixed this piece of shit. I swear, man, it is just time—" Kyle's words cut off as he stood up to find nobody listening to him and no sounds of anybody moving in the house.

Snorting in disgust, he muttered to himself. "Can fix a damn car, but can't even fix a damn icebox to save his life. Too busy off fucking around with himself."

Working his temper back into a frenzy, he smacked the beer bottle down with undue force before shouting out. "I swear to God, Cole, if you don't fix this thing, and fix it as in tomorrow, I'm going to go out and buy a new damn refrigerator, and you're going to pay for it."

Nothing. Not even a fuck you, which probably wouldn't have pricked Kyle's temper half as much as when he yanked a bolt of paper towels clear off the roll. Flipping open the pizza box, he considered which one of them was more pathetic—Kyle for panting after Hailey or Cole for panting after himself. Stacking two slices on his paper-towel plates, Kyle figured it had to be him because he was about to be guilty on both counts.

Swiping up his beer in one hand and pizza in the other, he trudged toward his bedroom, intent on being just that kind of pathetic. He paused in front of his door to shout down to Cole's open one.

"Pizza's on the counter."

Only the muted blare of a porno murmured back down the hall. Rolling his eyes, Kyle nudged the light switch next to his door on with his elbow. Tracking across the room to dump the pizza and beer on his nightstand, he couldn't help but notice the little cabinet under his TV had been rummaged through. Kyle didn't need more than one guess to tell who had violated his privacy.

"You know, if you're going to borrow my shit, you could at least not leave a mess in your wake!"

Still no response from Cole, and that broke Kyle's last nerve. Not so much that he wanted to catch Cole doing the deed, but he certainly couldn't think of a better moment to ruin it for his friend.

"I'm talking to you, Cole, and don't pretend like you can't hear me." Kyle banged through the bathroom door loud enough to give Cole warning but stormed through too fast to give him any time to hide. "I don't care how many disks you've worn out tonight. I want my movie—"

He forgot the very word forming on his lips. It just froze there along with his ability to think or breathe as his eyes widened on the sight that greeted him. *Hailey.* There she was. He'd been waiting for her all night, and there she was, all but naked on Cole's bed.

Cole had her on display like some kind of prize. One dark, hairy arm spanned over the delicate flush of her stomach to pin her against him. The contrast looked as savage as the thick, masculine thighs pinning the plush curves of her sexy legs down. Down and open, spreading the beautiful folds of her pink pussy wide.

The swollen flower bloomed out, all glistening and shiny with the arousal it perfumed into the air. Just below it sat the dark, blood-swollen balls of an angry cock, but it wasn't buried in her cunt.

"Took you long enough, my friend." Cole's cool drawl drew Kyle's gaze up to Hailey's flushed features. A large hand camped down over her face, puffing up her cheeks, but he could clearly see the tears shining in them. "I was wondering how long you were going to play the fool."

For all the smoothness of his words, Kyle could see the truth in Cole's gaze as their eyes locked. He was hurting, and odds were he backed himself into a corner of some kind. Hell, he probably even thought Kyle's arrival just saved him.

That didn't dismiss the tears in Hailey's eyes.

"You forcing this?"

A look of disgust flashed over Cole's features at that question. "Nah. I'm just tired of—"

"You baboon-balled, monkey-for-brains asshole! *Fuck me.*"

"—that," Cole snapped along with a slap of his hand over her cunt.

"I swear to God, Cole, if you don't do me, and do me right now, I'm going to tell *everybody* you got a two-inch twig in your shorts." Fiery as ever, Hailey's words proved whatever had been going on, Cole hadn't bent her will in the slightest.

"Nobody will believe you, princess." Cole's hand shifted toward her breasts, and Hailey whimpered even as she arched into his touch. "Because as you pointed out, I've already slept with half this town."

"Fine, you son of a bitch, I'll tell them all it smells down there and looks like you got a fungal growth—"

Hailey's voice lit up into a shriek that incinerated the actual syllables as Cole bit down on her neck at the same time he twisted on a puckered nipple mercilessly. From the deepness of her blush to the glistening sheen of sweat coating her body, Kyle could tell they'd been at this for a while. A while, as in Cole probably had her naked in his lap while he'd been talking to Kyle on the phone.

"Why you got to be like that, princess? Now we're going to have to start back at the beginning."

Whatever that meant, it got an instant roar from Hailey. "Damn it, Cole! We've done this six times now. When are you just going to admit defeat?"

"When are you going to give me what I want?"

"Never!"

"Then we start at the beginning."

"The beginning of what?"

That had both of them looking in Kyle's direction with the sort of sudden start that clearly showed they hadn't been pretending to ignore him. The two of them had obviously gotten into a war over something and now they both looked at him as the intruder. That really pissed Kyle off.

They'd taken his truce, his porno-date night, and twisted it into something completely different. Then, of all the arrogance, they excluded him from it. That snapped his temper down to the very last withered thread. He held on to that frayed string only by the power of indecision.

He just had to decide which one deserved the brunt of the ill will he had brooding in his gut. Cole looked good for the fight. The feral look that normally took over his features during sex had become particularly savage tonight. Kyle had the distinct feeling that if he tried to take Hailey away, he'd get hurt.

Of course, he'd also get to do some hurting himself, and that idea held a great deal of appeal. If it had just been naked aggression fueling his temper, the scales definitely would have tipped in Cole's direction. His lust, though, couldn't let go of the sight of Hailey, bound, open, vulnerable.

If only she knew the thoughts brewing in his head, that wicked grin wouldn't be tugging on her lips. There was hunger in her gaze, enough to match the need boiling in his balls. The smug smile pulling at her lips didn't help, either. Kyle had worn out of playing nice with Hailey. She didn't respect nice and that smile proved it.

"We're acting out the movie." And that just made her grin all the more. "Oh, and look what scene it is on."

The natural reflex to obey that kind of command had his head turning. The moaning and groaning coming out of the television matched up with the image of a man licking some blonde's pussy while she humped his mouth. It barely registered for a second before the image was suddenly flying backward.

"Hey!" Hailey belted out, immediately drawing Kyle's attention back to the couple tangled up in the bed. "I liked that scene."

"We're starting at the *beginning*."

"But there isn't any role for Kyle in the beginning."

"He can watch."

"He'd rather participate, trust me." Hailey turned that grin loose on him, and Kyle felt every muscle in his body tighten. "Wouldn't you, master?"

Oh, she thought she had him with that one.

"You conniving wench," Cole spat, jerking up as his gaze snapped toward Kyle's. "Don't you listen to her, Kyle. She's just lying to you. She don't mean it."

"I'll do whatever you want, master."

Already the giggles of victory tickled around those words as her smile just kept on growing. As her sultry smile grew into a full grin, so too did the savagery of the burning pit of need in his stomach escalate. That smile made him ache to give her just what she asked for.

"I'm telling you, Kyle. She's desperate." And so was Cole from his tone. "You give me five minutes and she'll purr that on command."

"Five minutes, huh?"

The calm smoothness of his own tone appeared to unsettle both of them. They grew stiller yet as he strolled around the bed to pull the remote from Cole's hand. Cole gave it over with no resistance thanks to the calculation in his gaze. Given his position, Cole didn't really have any other option but to fold for the moment.

"It seems to me you've had a whole bucket full of 'five minutes.'" With that he clicked the stop button on the remote before tossing it onto the nightstand.

"Yes, he has." Hailey was all over that point and more. As quickly as she could, she tried to stack the scales of justice in her favor. "He's been at it for hours now, Kyle. Think about that? He lied to you twice on the phone."

"Like he wouldn't have done the same," Cole snorted, but there was doubt in his tone.

Doubt, too, in Hailey's gaze as she tracked him back to the foot of the bed. Kyle didn't ease any of their concerns. Tugging his T-shirt off as he went, Kyle considered Hailey's point. "And what about you, princess? Just where were you at seven?"

"Well, I got held up."

That got another snort from Cole. "For two hours? Don't even try to sell that load. You were playing a game. One of the oldest games in the book."

"*I got held up.*"

"You ever hear of a phone?" Kyle asked as he kicked off his shoes. Never make love with socks on, that was the rule, and so he toed them off as Hailey's grin started to fall.

"I got distracted."

"Hmm." Kyle worked his belt free. "Well, I think I'm about to get distracted."

That had her going pensive real quick. "This isn't fair." That grudge escaped Hailey with a pout as her gaze tracked the hand on his belt.

No more smiles for the princess, but Cole sure had a cocky one going on. "Ain't got nothing to do with fair, princess. Tell her, Kyle."

"No. It doesn't." Kyle whipped his belt off and let it clack down to the floor before he began the crawl up between her and Cole's spread thighs. Looking down at the glare Hailey shot back at him, Kyle found his first smile that night. "Because, see, in this house, might makes right. Not much a dainty little princess can do about that."

"Kyle." Hailey used that tone on him, the one she never used on Cole because she never expected better of Cole. "Think about this—"

"That's all I've been doing, princess, sitting on your porch thinking about it."

"But the rules—"

"Fuck the rules," Kyle bit back, letting his temper show through. "We all know you don't want to play by them, anyway, so why don't you just shut up about all these damn rules."

Before what looked like a blistering response could more than squeak out of her, Cole's palm flattened out the rest of the words into murmured roars. "Hold up there, princess, before you go off and think just how much worse this situation is going to be if you rile Kyle's temper up any more. Then remember that you only have one word to say, stop, and all this will go away."

From the thunderous bolts of green in her gaze to the dark scowl furling her brow above, Kyle fully expected her to give him that one word as Cole's hand eased away.

"Assholes."

"Smack her pussy for that one, man."

Kyle didn't need to be told twice. He did have to lean to the side to get a good wallop in on her open cunt. Hailey took the impact with a scream. The broken sound of pleasure fell from her lips as her whole body lifted in a glorious display of need for another. Just as quickly, she collapsed back down, panting so hard the plush globes of her breasts bounced in a near mesmerizing fashion.

He'd been too much in a rush the few times he had her naked. Too much in a rush and he hadn't gotten to indulge in the joy of playing with her. The blame for that lay on her shoulders because she was always pushing, demanding, outright forcing him to give her what she wanted, a crime that well deserved another spank.

"Damn, man," Cole grunted as Hailey went wild again. "Give a buddy some warning before you do that next time."

"She deserved it." Kyle settled back onto his knees, enjoying being let off the leash for once. It felt good to flex some muscles, especially when Hailey's molten gaze fluttered over him as her head rolled over Cole's shoulder.

"I didn't do anything to you, Kyle. I don't deserve anything."

"Now that's a load," Cole retorted with his natural cynicism showing through. "You been messing with that boy's mind for weeks. You've had him so turned around he doesn't know if he's coming or going. I'd say he deserves a little reward for putting up with all that. What do you say, princess?"

The glaze receded back as sparkles of green started to glitter in her gaze. Kyle could almost see the rallying call to battle growing in her eyes as Cole's words sunk in. Normally, this would be when he'd curse Cole and try to soothe Hailey, but Kyle had enough of playing nursemaid.

Hailey didn't appreciate tenderness or gentleness. She liked to pick battles, which is just why she was trapped in Cole's lap. Actually, in it because that son of a bitch had his cock fucked all the way in his princess' ass. That had been Kyle's territory. He'd intended to be the one to addict her to those delights. That just etched another notch in the tally of grievances he had to set right with Hailey.

"I'd remind both of you I won't be pressured into saying anything I don't want to say."

"Then we start from the beginning."

* * * *

Hailey swallowed at those words coming from Kyle's lips. This was not good. "But you don't even know—"

"I know every second of this movie," Kyle growled down at her. He started to sound like Cole, his voice going deep into husky range. It matched the wickedness darkening his gaze. Kyle looked hungry, and Hailey suspected she looked juicy.

Very much like the cat cornered by the dog, she remained tense. Every muscle arched, tightening even further with anticipation for what came next as she watched him reach for the remote.

"Yes, Mr. Hard, Miss Lauder explained everything, and I am eager to get this interview started."

Drifting closed on the world, her lids dipped as Vanessa's voice floated through the room. They were back at the beginning, and how she had grown to flinch when she heard that line. Feeling every pulse of her heartbeat tick by, the pace slowly built up as the dialogue progressed.

By the time they got to act one of her nightmares, her heart had reared to a gallop, pushing adrenaline back through her system. It flooded in with her desire, making her arch up blindly toward the touch she could feel coming even as she bit her lip in anticipation of the excruciating pleasure.

Instead of the whiplash she waited for, Kyle's hands settled over her chest with the warm rush of a mid-afternoon storm. Coated with the heated lotion, his fingers curved around the full slope of her breasts. Swallowing her swollen globes in big hands, his rough skin teased and prickled her tender flesh, sparking little thrills through the molten heat of her lust.

Rolling over her nipples, the scratchy pads of his palms elicited a sparkling shower of pleasure that fell like a mere spattering over the roiling abyss of unrequited lust built up in her muscles. Already overwhelmed and overloaded, Hailey's body hummed at such a high elevation that at any second she could almost touch the euphoric sky.

Almost, but not quite, and Kyle's hands didn't push her any closer. Instead, his touch vibrated out with a slow, deep pulsing wave that only thickened the morass of her desire, making her feel bloated with sensation.

Her gentle lover, Kyle didn't pull screams from her throat like Cole did but made her moan as her whole body slowly unraveled, giving over its command to his touch. For as surely as she knew she could take no more, neither could Hailey resist the luring temptation for more.

More she would have because Cole didn't intend to just watch. He intended to make her suffer. Nuzzling down on the delicate stretch of skin where her neck met her shoulders, he matched Kyle's slow pace as he took a nibble. The scrape of his hard teeth sent rivulets of rapture rolling down her chest to spark over her nipples. The sensation echoed back with harsher edges as Kyle's tongue lapped up the side of her tender bud to flick its puckered peak.

"Oh, God." Hailey groaned and twisted as both men licked her like dogs sharing a bone. Tracing the vein pulsing in her neck, following the furled edge of her nipple, two velvety tongues toyed and tormented her with the amazing decadence of having two men love her at the same time.

"You have such beautiful breasts. You know that, princess?" Cole murmured that compliment along the curve of her neck, leaving Hailey without the ability to respond.

"She never lets me have any fun with them." Kyle nipped that complaint out as he took a little nibble of her nipple. "Always in a rush."

"Trust me, I've been thinking about a rope all day long," Cole grunted back before pressing his lips to her ear. "You hear that, princess, because that's what is coming in four weeks. You think tonight is bad, then you think about me free to do what I want and you tied to this bed."

"And me, joining in the fun."

Hailey moaned over the very image they painted in her head. Just having the two of them like this now felt like an absolute marvel of gluttonous excess.

"You'll be playing by my rules that night, Kyle. This sexy body is mine to devour. You only get to feast on the scraps I throw you."

"Then I guess I better gorge myself now, huh?"

With that growl as his only warning, Kyle switched from Dr. Jekyll to Mr. Hyde just like that. Trapping her nipple between his teeth, he flicked it over the hard edge before settling in to suck and roll her poor bud raw. Ragged claws of need plunged down toward her already throbbing cunt, shadowing the finger span of the hand slipping down over her stomach.

Her breath caught as Kyle's hand cupped her pussy, not pressing, not teasing, just threatening there as he continued to cover her breasts with his kisses. Hailey knew the bastards wanted her to beg, and she fought it for as long as she could, but the ache in her womb couldn't be denied.

Stretched over Cole's thick dick, all the twisting and grinding Kyle drove her toward only made her suffering that much worse. As her own need mounted a rebellion, Hailey lost the reins of her control and her hips lifted. Desperate for a touch from those fingers, it was the throb the motion sent through her ass that had her pumping backward.

Cole's chuckle ground through her head as his fingers appeared to bite into her hips and hold her restless motion still. "I think the little princess is asking for something, Kyle."

"Well, that's a real shame," Kyle gave her nipple a strong, slow kiss that had her twisting in Cole's grip, "because I don't hear her asking for anything."

"Kyle." She managed to put enough demand in that whine that it didn't come out completely pathetic. It was a struggle with Cole's hand sliding in along the sides where her inner thighs dipped toward her pussy.

Three hands now paused at the threshold of her most intimate flesh. Her swollen folds pulsed and wept, desperate for the ravishment that waited like a threat a mere breath away. Sadist that he was, Cole stroked warning tremors down into her womb as his thumbs slid up and down the very edges of her pussy lips.

"Beg, princess," Kyle growled around the nipple he trapped between his teeth.

"Beg or we go back to the beginning."

"Ahhhh!" Hailey arched with aggravation. "I hate you both, and if you don't start touching me, I'm going to kill you both."

Instantly, everything stopped, and her eyes popped open with the fear of what that meant. Kyle's head lifted as all three hands retreated, and Cole started to say the very things she'd grown sick to death of hearing. "Back to the beginning it—"

"No." She couldn't take that. Not again. She'd do anything, absolutely anything, not to have to start over, even whimper out a plea. "Please, Kyle."

No give, not even a sparkle of humor stared back down at her. "Please what, princess?"

"*Please*, touch me."

"Where?"

He demanded more of her than she could give to those savage eyes, and her own closed, blocking out the sight of her sweet lover gone hard. "Please, Kyle, I need you to touch me."

"Where?"

Hailey whimpered as her head rolled onto Cole's shoulder. She wanted to hide from her own voice, but even as it whispered out she couldn't escape her own words. "My pussy."

Just like that, she fell off the cliff and spiraled down into the wicked wonderland Cole and Kyle toppled her into. The rush of warm mouths and thick fingers greeted her as both men instantly returned to tormenting her already tortured body.

The pleasure that ballooned to magnificent proportions already started to seep out of her body as it sweated, prodded on by the lovers devouring her body. Kyle's mouth consumed her, ravishing her breasts even as his fingers forged down between her folds to invade her most intimate recesses.

Cole's fingers were there, packing in her pussy as they both fucked her in unison. Thick, ruthless fingers stretched and tickled down the inside of her clenching muscles, sending blinding bolts of rapture searing up from the delicate stretch of skin separating them from Cole's cock.

"Oh...oh, I can't." Hailey didn't know what she could do because she did everything the sensations commanded. She twisted and ground herself along those tantalizing fingers and over that delicious cock, but it wasn't near enough, and the begging began to fall from her lips.

Through the fog of darkened delights, Cole's voice murmured through her head. "Call me master."

"No, no, no." She didn't know whether she said the words or not, too consumed with the fire raging over her skin. So damn close to the sun now and it felt beautiful, too amazing for words. If only she could touch it.

"Call me master or have Kyle eat this cunt until it's raw."

"No." She couldn't take that, but the words that fell from her lips didn't save her. All the pleas, all the begging, none of it stopped the slow tasting that brought Kyle's heated breath to fan over her weeping flesh. Just as Cole threatened, their hands retreated.

Nothing barred Kyle as he pressed in and gave her pussy one long, slow lick. The thorough inspection left no secret undiscovered before he finally trapped her clit beneath the flat of his tongue. Pausing there, he appeared to almost wait for Cole's sticky fingers to lift up and cup her breasts.

"One last chance, princess. Give me what I want."

Licking her lips, Hailey's eyes fluttered open to take in the cracked ceiling above. "Do your worst. I won't ever call you master."

That bold declaration ended in a scream as both men rallied to the challenge.

Chapter 26

Hailey screamed and squirmed, pumping her cunt into Kyle's kiss. He groaned as the sweet scent of her arousal flooded his head, right along with the intoxicating taste. *Delicious.*

Wet, hot, open for his feasting, just the way he liked his cunts. Any rational thoughts he had about tormenting her got rolled under the avalanche of his own need. Just as it had been the last time, Kyle lost himself in the greatest treat life had ever gifted him. Unconcerned with anything other than devouring her sweet flesh and driving her to the pinnacle of insanity, he sucked down on her swollen clit.

Keeping it trapped between his teeth, he toyed with the her magic bud, licking, rolling, sucking until her whole body tensed around him, and he could hear his name panting out as she stretched toward release.

"Damn it, man! Don't let her come." A heavy hand whacked his head off target, banging his chin into her thigh. With a growl that roared over Hailey's instant curses, Kyle dove back into that pussy.

This time he fucked his tongue up into her spasming sheath. Rolling and massaging the plush walls, he delighted in the way they humped him back. It thrilled him even more, though, when his thumb found her clit, and her whole pussy convulsed with one long pull that sucked his tongue deep.

Relentlessly he fucked her, becoming almost obsessed with the delight of having full command of Hailey's body. She was his puppet, and he controlled her with just his kiss on her molten-hot pussy, and God, but his own master wanted a piece of that action.

Twelve burning, throbbing inches of pain demanded their due. With no will or want to defy the hammering pound of lust boiling out of his balls and up his spine, Kyle ripped at his zipper blindly, face still buried in the soft, warm heaven of Hailey's cunt.

His lips wouldn't give up their prize that easily. Even as his cock fell free into the world, they locked down on her clit, determined to drive her screams before any dick got in the way. She offered him just the reward he wanted. Nails scrapping through his hair as she pressed his head to her flesh, Hailey begged for her release—begged for him to give it to her with his tongue.

The consolation prize of having his hand stroke over his swollen flesh did not soothe his angry cock. It jerked with the demand to make its case with Hailey's pussy, knowing it could make her scream so loud she'd go hoarse. That didn't persuade his mouth to give up its treat.

Kyle had always loved a good pussy, but Hailey's made him forget all control. All control, and as it began to seep out of him and onto the sheets, Kyle's sense of pride rallied. He'd not be reduced to jacking off between her legs.

With a snarl at that thought, Kyle shot up her length and drilled all twelve inches straight into her heat. Acting like he'd forged a hot iron into the heart of her, Hailey screamed, her nails scratching as she clawed her way up his body. Rising off Cole's chest, she plastered those sweet tits against him and clung to him, panting out how good it was as he fucked each full-length stroke into her.

As his swollen head rubbed down the velvety walls of her pussy, he could feel Cole's cock pressing back in from her ass. So tight, so hot, and she loved every inch of both cocks because her lush ass was bouncing. Kyle's hands curved around the plush curve of her cheeks and pulled that ass up hard, making her fuck Cole with the same wild abandon she did him.

Like the gates of heaven opening in the distance, a world of such pleasure spanned out around him, driving Kyle mercilessly deeper into the euphoric sensation. Grunting, his hips galloped at a near painful pace as he screwed himself as hard as he could into the one woman who had ever shown him these heights. A desperate and pathetic part of him raced toward the hopeless goal of binding her so permanently to him that this moment never ceased—but it had to.

With a crack of pure, white-hot glory, Kyle felt the release rip out of his balls. It was perfection.

* * * *

Cole grunted as he fought not to let the pleasure obliterate him. It had never burned this hot before, but then it had never felt like this, either. The sexy sight of Hailey and Kyle clinging together as they road off to their release should have only been a little extra kink, but he could feel the thickness of true intimacy coalescing around the couple, around him.

The fine, silken web of emotion blurred into the rapture clawing over his body. The thin, shimmering sensation should have been delicate, but it clung on, searing into his soul even as his seed boiled out of his balls. There could be no stopping the flood gates as his release barreled down his dick.

Above him, Hailey went wild with her own pleasure, making him ache in a way he didn't want to. His wants meant nothing, and in that moment he couldn't help but wish it was him she clung to, panting all those little sexy sounds as her breasts pressed in on him and her stomach rubbed over his. Cole groaned as he tried to block those images from solidifying in his mind.

It didn't work. It only got worse as Kyle and Hailey fell over into each other's arms, leaving him there alone with his cold, sticky cock. That didn't matter to him, Cole snorted. The only reason he felt any disappointment was because he hadn't gotten what he wanted. A fact that he felt the need to point out right then.

"You really screwed up my game, man."

From the opposite side of the bed came a snort. "Yeah, remind me to care about that later."

"Your knight isn't always going to be around to protect you, princess," Cole warned Hailey as he rolled out of bed. That got a deep sigh from the puddle of lush curves and tantalizing recesses all curled up along Kyle's side.

"I mean it, Hailey. You will be calling me master one of these days."

Sitting up, she cast him a dirty look. "You lost, Cole. Get over it."

"You want to start back at the beginning?" Hell, if he had the energy for it, but Cole knew he had the interest already growing down below.

"What I want is for the Cattlemen to teach you morons more than just how to fuck," Hailey snapped back as she started scooting down the bed. "Because you know what? There is such a thing called afterglow, and you two really, *really*, suck at it."

With that fiery proclamation made, she slammed the bathroom door on both of them. It was just the kind of trigger that normally would have had him barging through the door to take that argument up, but Cole could still feel the chafe marks of his release on his heart. He didn't like that sensation at all.

"You know I'm going to beat the crap out of you tomorrow for not telling me Hailey was here." Kyle didn't sound the least bit upset with either him or Hailey as he got out of the bed.

"Yeah? See, I was just thinking tonight made us about even."

"No." Kyle reached the bathroom door but paused to finish the argument. "Because you hit me. Now I get to hit you back."

"See, I remember you hitting me back when I was hitting you."

"Well, I didn't say you couldn't hit me back. Now, are you going to let a good shower go to waste?"

Cole scowled at that just because he wanted to say yes too badly. "Nah, I'm going to get a piece of that pizza."

He didn't wait to catch Kyle's response or be tempted by him opening the door. Not bothering with clothes of any kind, Cole paced down the hall. Sure, he flashed his neighbors as he crossed the entryway from the living room to the dining room, but nobody had ever complained before.

Heading for the greasy box Kyle had left on the counter, he flipped it open only to stare down at the cold pizza. The sight did not stir his appetite. Not in the least, though his stomach felt hollow enough to be hungry. It just didn't seem like food would fill that ache.

"Eh."

Cole popped the lid closed and turned to the refrigerator. It garbled back at him, earning it a few solid hits on the side until it stopped its bitching. That didn't stop it from punishing him for his abuse by being pretty much empty. Beer, milk, something that had been wrapped in tinfoil and sitting there for way too long. It didn't matter how long he stared in, nothing else but a ketchup bottle stared back out at him.

"Eh."

Cole closed the door only to roll his eyes a second later and rip it back open. Milk it was. Maybe it would help with his heartburn.

Where the hell did that come from?

Rubbing his chest as if he could somehow smooth away the awful sensation, Cole scowled.

It was probably Hailey's fault. It was all that stubborn defiance that got under his skin and those last moments—they hadn't meant anything. Cole had proof because he still felt restless. Itchy and unsure of what the hell would ever put the sensation to rest.

For God's sake, he'd just spent hours indulging in one of his greatest games with his biggest catch ever, not to mention having shot through an orgasm like some fucking shooting star, and look at him. Cole looked down at the Mr. Man. The cock stood tall and ready for round two.

"I think you've had enough tonight."

The Mr. Man didn't even blink. Glaring straight back at him, there only came one thought echoing out of his balls. *Pussy.* What would it be like to lose himself in Hailey's heat? Cole gulped down a large swallow of milk, trying to cool that thought.

He'd been there, on the edge of his own climax earlier tonight. Not even five minutes into fucking and he'd been there, on the horizon of something that had so shocked him with its significance he'd forgotten himself in that moment of fear and retreated to her ass.

Cole flinched from that memory. He'd never once caused a woman harm, never once lost control, and look what he'd done to Hailey. The mere fact that the woman loved it didn't change the fact that he could have really hurt her tonight. He might be all sorts of a bastard when it came to women, but he wasn't that bastard.

Shoving the milk back in the refrigerator, Cole tried to leave those thoughts behind as he traipsed back down the hall. The shower had stopped, and from the murmurs coming through Kyle's door, Cole figured the couple moved into Kyle's bed.

Well, that was good because he couldn't sleep with anybody in his. Hell, it was even better for Kyle. Shit, Kyle loved the girl, and all Cole had for her was a few inches of meat that would one day lose interest. Better he just be good sex and bad at afterglow because then nobody would get any wrong ideas.

Turning into his room, Cole hoped they'd closed the bathroom door on their side because he didn't want any kind of awkwardness. He knew how women could be, and she'd probably make it weird if she saw him. All his worries ended in annoyance as he saw the door was indeed closed.

Apparently, they hadn't been expecting him to join. Well, that was just fine by him, Cole thought as he wrenched on the shower. Of course, they could have at least left him a smidgeon of hot water, and why the hell did the steam smell like cinnamon?

He'd never been so grumpy after sex, but Cole didn't bother to fight the emotion as he took it out on his own skin. Between the hard scrubs and the cold water biting into him, he still glowed red when he stepped out and wrapped the towel around his waist.

Pausing for a second to glare at Kyle's door, Cole couldn't help himself but to open it. It was worse than he expected. Cuddled under the covers, they snuggled up together, their hands rubbing against each other as they talked. The smooth motion of those fingers interlacing caught him for a second, and he could already see the gold bands that would be shinning there one day.

"Hey, man." Kyle's happy greeting had him looking up to his best friend. Cole had never seen Kyle look like that. "You have enough hot water for that shower?"

That had Hailey giggling as she flashed that wicked grin at him. "Nice tent."

"Yeah, take a good look, princess, because tomorrow night we're going to be back at it," Cole shot back, turning to proudly display the deformity in his towel.

"Tomorrow night?" Hailey shared a look with Kyle. "What the hell is he talking about?"

"Oh, come on, Hailey." Cole grinned. "What's the point in that no-sex rule, now? Might as well enjoy the next four weeks, get you ready for what's coming. Unless, of course, you think you can't handle it."

That had her gaze narrowing back on him. "Ha. Ha. Cole. You aren't going to trick me into nothing. This was a onetime deal."

"Because you were horny," Kyle weighted in, and thankfully it was on Cole's side. "You really want to go three more weeks without sex?"

"Am I to assume this 'it's either him or me' has now been settled into 'it's either both or none?'" Hailey retorted.

The considering look Kyle cast his way reminded Cole of just all the reasons Kyle had to say no. The grin that crossed his friend's features didn't make him feel any easier.

"Well, I guess you might as well consider us a pair." Kyle's hand lifted where it had lain across her back. Brushing back the hair from her cheek, the look he gave her was so full of love Cole wondered if the idiot realized he was wearing his heart on his sleeve again. "What about just once a week? Kind of like a hold over."

Hailey's hesitation had Kyle's head dipping. He rubbed a yes from those swollen lips. With a sigh, she settled down against his chest and gazed over at Cole. She looked as content as a kitten, and for some reason, that really irritated the crap out of Cole.

"Fine. Once a week, but next time I expect to get some pizza and beer. After all, there are traditions to be kept. Right, Cole?"

That was his Hailey. Kyle's Hailey might be all sweetness, but Cole got the spice. "Yeah, I remember that, princess. You remember this, no panties and your legs stay spread. After all, there are traditions."

"You're such a perv, Cole."

"Back at you, princess."

"You two going to fight all night?" Kyle complained. "Because I actually need some sleep."

"Eh." Cole turned and strutted off. He didn't doubt Kyle would be doing more than sleeping with Hailey in his bed, but fine. Cole would leave him to it. He didn't like having anybody take up room or drape all over him in the middle of the night. The very last thing he'd ever want to sleep with was some spasmodic spitfire who might bite him in his sleep.

Much better to crawl into a nice, empty bed. Except that his bed smelled like Hailey and sex. There was some biological matter smeared about, too.

"Eh."

Chapter 27

Tuesday, May 27th

Hailey glared Cole down without blinking. "I said no."

"I said yes," Cole shot back. This was the problem that came from giving a little savage too many free orgasms. They got temperamental and pushy.

"That is an original R series 289 V-8. It's a classic."

"It's a rusted piece of junk." Cole leaned in to make sure she heard him good and clear, a move Hailey copied that just proved how very little she feared him.

"Then fix it. That is what you do, isn't it? Or are you just some parts guy, Cole? All you know is how to rip and replace?"

"Don't even." That had been an insult too far. Cole never just replaced a part to shirk his responsibilities. The suggestion that he would had his ears burning. "I'm telling you now, Hailey, this piece of shit can't be saved. It'll cost too damn much."

"Okay." Kyle appeared just about out of nowhere to push a good foot between the two of them. "I think maybe it's lunch time, and don't either one of you give me that look. You're not having that argument here and now."

"Tomorrow night then," Cole conceded, casting a smirk at Hailey's narrowed gaze. Tomorrow would be their third and final "do-it" date before the clock wound down toward Cole's day of ultimate victory.

"You ain't going to fuck me into agreeing, either," Hailey shot back.

"At least not here," Kyle tacked on with a pointed look at Cole's snickering cousins.

"Not anywhere." Hailey's gaze hadn't followed the clue but stayed locked on Cole.

"You want to take that test and see who passes?" Cole stepped into that challenge, easily pushing Kyle out of the way. "We'll let Jacob and Aaron declare the winner."

That had her nose wrinkling up as she finally cast her dirty look in their direction before laying it back on him. "That isn't even funny."

"I wasn't joking," Cole assured her with a grin. "You see, we got this tradition down at the club where we publicly compete—"

"Never mind!" With that snap, Hailey turned and stormed off toward the shop sink. Her retreat brought to life the chuckles that had been building in his chest, and he could hear them echoed from his cousins across the shop.

"Oh, come on, princess, you won't know if you'll like it until you try it."

"Fuck you, Cole."

Cole laughed outright at that as Jacob and Aaron brought their own bales closer. Clustering around Kyle and Cole, they all watched as Hailey started to scrub her frustrations out with her vigorous hand washing.

"I cannot believe you actually managed to get that girl into your bed."

"You're the king." Aaron's shaking head turned to a nod at Jacob's comment.

"What about me?" Kyle did a good imitation of a highly insulted man, not that Cole cared.

"You." Jacob sized Kyle up as if he had to consider his answer. That moment only had Kyle's gaze narrowing before Jacob's hand dismissed him. "You're kind of like the heir apparent or whatever they call them."

Cole had to shed a few chuckles for that insult, especially when it earned Jacob the same attitude he'd bought off Hailey.

"Fuck you, Jacob."

"Why you so cranky? Just be happy Cole shares his good luck with you, buddy."

"Try my good luck."

"Try proving it." Jacob's hand patted the top of the Daytona. "Right here, right now, and we'll all call you the king."

Like that would happen. Like Kyle would do that to his precious Hailey. Jacob knew it, too. He backed Kyle into a corner with that offer and then had the gall to smirk when Kyle remained sullenly silent.

"Yeah, that's what I thought."

"You done having your fun?" Kyle asked.

"With you, yeah." Jacob turned his gaze on Cole. "But you. Aaron and I need to have a word or two with you."

Cole bristled over that tone. "What the hell did I do?"

"How about we explain that to you at lunch?"

Cole cast his gaze over at Hailey. They'd eaten lunch every day, all seven of them in a week for the past three straight weeks, and he kind of liked the ritual. "But I got plans."

"We were thinking barbeque," Aaron stated clear and pointed.

"The Picnic Table sounds good to me." Jacob nodded.

"Cole paying sounds better."

"Well, it sounds like you have new plans, *sire*."

Kyle relished that one a little too much. Cole got the sick feeling he'd be hearing a lot of that in the coming days. Hell, Kyle would probably tell Hailey all about it over lunch, and he'd have to listen to her smart ass call him that, too.

Of course, it wouldn't be so bad if she were panting it, begging me to—

"Hey, dumbass." A slap to the back of his head pounded Aaron's rude interruption into his fantasies. "We're talking to you here. Lunch. The Picnic Table. You're buying."

"You're rude." Cole glared at his kin. "Didn't your mama ever teach you any manners?"

"Yeah. She taught us family always comes first," Aaron shot back.

"Which means you do about any dumbass thing for your blood," Jacob tacked on.

"Even taking a beating or helping a buddy out when he's in a jam."

"But there *are limits*."

"And apparently whatever you asked them to do hit theirs," Kyle concluded as if he had any place in this conversation. "Which kind of makes me wonder. I mean, what would be something these two would object to, given they're pretty much game for anything?"

"Nothing." All three Jacksons gave him that answer at the same time.

"Yeah. Okay." Kyle shrugged. "I'll pretend to be that dumb and go have a pleasant lunch with my lady."

"My lady?" Aaron repeated in total disgust.

"What the hell, man? Next you're going to be baby talking to some purse-sized dog." Jacob shook his head. "You just got demoted from heir apparent."

That didn't seem to bother Kyle at all. "Say what you want, Jacob. A least I ain't got to go begging around town for my meals."

"I ain't got to beg." But he did have to shout thanks to Kyle strutting off. It made Cole's cousin sound a little too defensive. So did the look Jacob turned on him. "We gotta talk."

* * * *

"You really know how to rock a sandwich." Kyle got that out from around a mouthful of bread, cheese, and meat as he hunched over Hailey's kitchen table. The sub she placed in front of him not minutes ago had already started to rapidly disappear, and he was already eyeing the second one she worked on.

Normally that would have Cole's name on it, but today it was all his. Kyle shoveled in the last chunk of his first sandwich just to clear his plate, so she had a place to put the sub. Hailey didn't even recognize his compliment as she settled the new sandwich down in front of him.

Kyle eyed her over the wheat roll and decided she looked a little too thoughtful. A little grumpy, actually. Over the past three weeks, he'd gotten pretty used to Hailey's moods and considered it nothing short of an epic accomplishment that he and Cole had kept her away from grumpy.

Not that it took much effort these days. Kyle's plan to simply insinuate himself into every facet of Hailey's life worked. All three of them ate breakfast together every day at the Bread Box, they worked all morning, then went to lunch, dinner, worked all night in the shop.

About the only time they weren't together was the afternoon and the few hours of sleep they got every night. Even then, once a week for the past three weeks Hailey had been at his side for those moments. Those were the best moments, and in six more days, they'd become permanent.

Six days, that's all that stood between Cole and his reckoning. Kyle fully expected that event to change everything. Once Hailey had truly given herself over to them, learned that she could trust them, she'd settled down.

Before, though, she looked to get prickly. That's just how she sounded, too. "You know, I think tomorrow we should do lunch at your place and maybe you can do the cooking."

"Cook? It's just a sandwich." Kyle knew the minute he heard his own words he stepped full on in it. Snapping his head to the side, he caught her dark look. "But really, Hailey, you rock the sandwich."

"Oh, shut up." Hailey snapped the refrigerator door closed and shot him a dirty look. "That's not what I mean, and you know it."

Not willing to give in to criticism for fear it would spur her ill temper, Kyle just widened his grin. "I do?"

"Look." Hailey took a deep breath as if she were heavily burdened by this issue and began slowly. "I'm the one having to come up with two out of three meals a day."

"That isn't fair," Kyle objected around a mouthful of food. "We chip in."

"Money, not time," Hailey snapped. "I'm the one who always has to go get everything and then clean it all up. That's sexist. I'm not your waitress, Kyle."

That had his jaw stilling in mid-chomp. Looking down at the half eaten chunk of sandwich in his hand, he glanced back up uncertainly as he held it out to her. "I think maybe you need this, princess."

"I think maybe you're asking to get hurt," Hailey retorted in a calm voice, letting him know she didn't find any humor in his attitude.

Kyle got the message and labored under it as he finished chewing. Deciding it might be best to put down the sandwich and start groveling just a little, he dropped the sub to clap his hands free of crumbs.

"Okay, I got an idea. Instead of just going into porno-date night tomorrow, I'll cook you dinner." Bringing his plate around to the sink, he paused to offer that to her as a humble apology.

Hailey looked skeptical as she turned to watch. "What about the pizza and the tradition?"

"Screw the tradition." Kyle shrugged, highly doubting Cole would object.

"I'm not talking microwave dinners here or warming up Chinese food."

That had him thinking again before he offered, "I can grill."

"Gee, that's a shock."

"Nah, seriously, Hailey. I'll go by the grocery store after work and get some ribs, then stop by Henry's Market and get some corn and little red potatoes. Hell, I'll even swing by the Bread Box and get Heather to make up some corn bread so that you don't have to..." The narrowing of her eyes at where that comment led had him backing off. "I mean, to finish out the meal. We could even watch some movies."

"You're talking about a date, Kyle."

Yeah, he was. "So?"

"Don't you think you should ask your partner first? I think he kind of likes porno night the way it is."

For some reason, she just couldn't seem to let the issue of Cole go. Leaning against the counter, he shrugged off her comment even as he considered its significance. "If Cole's so obsessed with porn, then he can go jack off on his own, and we'll join him after our date."

Hailey snorted at that. "Easy enough to dismiss the sire when he isn't here, isn't it?"

"Is that what's got you all sour today?" Kyle grinned, thrilled at the idea. "You missing Cole, Hailey?"

"No." She shouldn't have said it so fast because the speed made a liar out of her.

"I think you are, princess." Kyle laughed, pushing off the counter to close in on his prissy little princess.

"Don't get all giddy now, Kyle." Hailey held her ground, that chin rising up. "I'm just saying you might want to consider asking Cole before you promise him to anything."

"Ah, come on, Hailey." Kyle wrapped his arms around her waist to hold her in an intimate press of hips. "Why don't you just admit you like Cole? Or don't you think I haven't noticed the way you stare at him? Kind of reminds me of the way you stared at me back in high school."

That had her stiffening up, her eyes going wide.

"You didn't think I noticed?" Kyle guessed, given her look. "The way you stare and get all wistful looking, it's these eyes that give you away, Hailey."

He followed that comment with a gentle sweep of his fingers across her cheek as he tucked the hair back behind her ear. Lingering, his palm slid down until he cupped her head. Using his hold to keep her captive, he backed her around to the edge of the counter even as he kept her pelvis pinned to his.

"You know they go all chocolaty when your aroused, and little lightning bolts of green shoot through them when you're mad, but when you get that wistful look, they get all muddled and gentle looking. That's when I know you're thinking about sweet things, Hailey. Sweet things you don't ever want to own up to."

With the gentle brush of his thumb over her cheek, Kyle leaned down to whisper against her lips. "All you have to do is say the words."

He could almost feel the truth brushing back against his mouth. "I'd love to have sex with you, Kyle."

With a groan his head lifted. "Why you gotta be so difficult, princess?"

"Why do you?" Hailey's hand slid in between them to curl around his erection and give him a little tease. "Come on, Kyle. All the other kids are doing it."

That had him wrenching back before she managed to talk him out of all his good sense. "You're evil, Hailey Mathews, just evil, and you know what? I'm going to enjoy what you got coming to you in six days."

That sharp reminder of Cole had her smile fading and her gaze getting lost over his shoulder. It shouldn't surprise him, but it did when she went back to what obviously worried her too much.

"Why does Cole want Bavis's Fastback so bad?"

"What?" That question caught Kyle off guard. "Why you asking about that?"

"Well," Hailey shrugged, but her tense muscles betrayed the casual gesture, "everybody knows that Cole's always panting after it and, so I just thought, with the way he ran out today..."

"What? That Bavis had yanked his chain?" Kyle snorted at that before releasing her to turn back to the plates. He didn't want to be accused of any more sexism. "Trust me, Hailey, if Bavis gave Cole any reason to hope, he'd have been crowing it from the rooftops, but I take it you'd like that to be the answer."

"What?"

"I get it, Hailey, but you don't honestly need to be worried. If Cole had some interest in another woman or anything going, I'd know about it."

"And you'd tell me." Hailey laughed outright at that.

"Actually," Kyle straightened up as he closed the dishwasher door as his cell phone went off. Adam's number flashed on the screen, but Kyle hesitated before answering to finish reassuring Hailey.

"I would. I wouldn't like being caught between the two of you. There ain't no lie about that, but I wouldn't let Cole hurt you anymore than I'd let you do the same to him. Trust me, Hailey, there isn't another woman."

Chapter 28

"I ain't messing with that woman no more, Cole."

The Picnic Table had emptied out of its lunch-time crowd, leaving just a few stranglers. Big barreled garbage cans overflowed with paper plates and plastic silverware as Doug and his family began going from table to table, dumping almost everything left into the trash.

Jacob and Aaron had been insistent that they eat and he pay before they coughed up the reason for this impromptu meeting. As if Cole hadn't already guessed. They wanted more than twenty-five percent, and he should have seen this coming.

"What's wrong, Jacob? Did the pretty, little Kitty scare you?"

"She's crazy, man." Cole might have been kidding, but Aaron wasn't. "I'm talking full-on feminine Nazi kind of psycho."

"You want a woman like that playing with your balls?" Jacob snorted.

"I sure as shit don't," Aaron answered for Cole.

One week until both the Fastback and Hailey were his, and his cousins knew he was vulnerable. They had leverage, and Cole knew exactly what Jacob and Aaron would do with the precious commodity. "Okay. Fine, she talks to ghosts. What percentage gets you over that hump?"

"Percentage?" Aaron scowled, looking for guidance from his brother.

"He thinks this is about money."

"It's always about money with you two," Cole cut in, not interested in taking the long way to the point. "So how much?"

Jacob and Aaron shared a look. Cole could almost hear their silent communication as they assured each other on the number. When Jacob turned to meet his gaze, Cole could tell by the set of his jaw that number was high.

"Let me ask you something, Cole. How much would you charge to let some woman tie you up and paddle your ass?"

"What?" Cole's head bent back slightly as he scowled down that statement.

"I'm just asking, what percentage you'd take to suffer that humiliation."

"Ain't no woman tying me up, Aaron," Cole growled. Not for any amount of money or even a damn car would that ever be happening. "Now you telling me that's the kink Miss Kitty Anne's into?"

"That's just the start," Jacob snorted. "I'm not shitting you here, Cole. The woman's involved in some kind of club where they tie the men up."

"Well." Cole blinked, not at all certain what to say to that. "Have you suggested maybe a porno-date night?"

Now it was Jacob's turn to give him an exasperated "What?"

"I mean, so she has some kinks. We all have some, but that don't mean we always give in to them. Just charm her into the old missionary, and get it done with."

"You ain't listening," Aaron growled.

"This club," Jacob glanced around at the empty tables but still leaned in to whisper, "men pay to have sex with the women, as in pick the woman and by the hour. You know what that is?"

Yeah, Cole knew exactly what that meant, and it was good news, too. "Well, hell, Bavis called her a whore, but I thought he was just being a prudish bastard."

"He wasn't." Jacob settled back. "And I ain't getting involved in nothing like this, Cole."

"Not for no twenty-five percent, right?" Cole had to admit, his cousins had a right to want more.

"Not for a hundred fricken percent, you twit. No means no," Aaron shot back, sounding like he meant it.

"Oh, come on." Cole had enough of this. They couldn't back out on him. Not now. "You don't have to go to the damn brothel or whatever. Seduce her the old-fashion way in the back of your pick-up."

"She doesn't do it for free. Okay?" Jacob snorted. "And we ain't paying for it."

"But just think how good this is," Cole pleaded. "I mean, hell, it don't matter now if you do the deed or not. Bavis wants something to chase her off his nephew, and what would be better than proving that she's actually whoring?"

"And how you gonna prove that?"

"How did you figure it out?" Cole shot back at Jacob.

"I used my noggin, okay? I'm telling you, the girl's in the trade."

"But you don't have proof," Cole concluded for him.

"We don't need it," Aaron retorted. "This isn't no court of law. The only jury here is my gut, and it says the girl is up to no good."

"Spare me lectures from your gut," Cole snapped. "You can't back out now."

"Why the hell not?"

Cole growled. Even if he didn't want to say it, he didn't have much choice. "Hailey—"

"That's what I thought." Jacob leaned back. "You so damned whipped, Cole."

"I ain't whipped! I just have six more days and then—"

"Your deal with Bavis expires in six days because little Miss Kitty will be walking down that aisle." Aaron's hand lifted to give his best impression of a beauty pageant wave. "Say bye-bye to the Fastback."

"This isn't just about Hailey," Cole shot back. "It's about Kyle, too. If I choose the car, then I screw him up. So I gotta choose Hailey no matter what I want."

"Yeah, that sucks for you," Jacob agreed as he stood. Digging into his pocket, he flipped a business card on the table. "If you don't want Hailey but choose her anyway, you'll eventually screw Kyle over anyway. If you don't want Hailey, just tell them both, and then go get your damn car yourself."

"It's not that simple."

"It is if you don't want Hailey," Aaron grunted, shoving back in his own seat. "Either way, it's your problem now. That's Kitty's number."

With that fatal shot, his cousins lumbered off, leaving Cole completely screwed. He had less than a week and didn't know a single man who would be willing to let some woman tie him up just so Cole could get his hands on a car. Not to mention the whole paying thing.

Staring at the number Jacob left, Cole wondered just how far he'd have to go. Bavis hadn't actually said he had to sleep with the woman. He just had to break up her pending nuptials. If he could get proof that she turned tricks, that would be more than good enough.

Hell, if her fiancé didn't dump her then, at least he'd go into the marriage knowing the truth. Cole would be sort of doing a good deed. All he really needed was to get her propositioning him on tape. It would have to be good, leaving nothing to doubt, for Bavis to come off that car.

The worst he might have to do is kiss the woman and maybe a little petting, but that really wasn't that bad given the rewards. As much as Hailey loved that Daytona, she'd understand that he had to flirt a little to get the Fastback.

No, she won't.

Understanding and Hailey didn't really go together. As much as she might like to think of herself as a rational, sane person, Hailey's emotions ruled her reactions. It made her unpredictable in so many ways but this one.

He'd be lucky if she didn't rip his nipples clean off. Not that she'd have any right. After all, she made it quite clear she *expected* him to cheat. The damn woman slept with him while still betting against the fact that he couldn't be faithful, and how insane was that?

He thought about it the whole distance from the table to his truck. Nothing Hailey did or said gave him any reason to think she'd ever feel anything more than sexual attraction and friendship toward him. He'd be an absolute fool to let another woman cost him another Fastback.

Serena...and look how that battle had ended.

Cole tried to fight back the memories for the past three weeks, feeling the rush of an old fate crashing in around him. He couldn't avoid it anymore. It stared him in the mirror as he slid into his seat.

He'd never really loved Serena. He'd been obsessed with her beauty, but that hadn't been what had driven him to sell his Fastback. No, he sold it for their child. When she told him she was pregnant, Cole's whole world exploded with amazing possibilities for his future.

Possibilities that snapped out in a blink and left him grieving for somebody he didn't even know. His child. Cole sucked in a deep breath at the thought. In all the years, he let himself focus on Serena because it had been easier than facing the truth. His baby had died, and he'd never stopped grieving.

The idea of another child, another woman felt worse than betrayal. Being that vulnerable again filled Cole with fear. Somehow, though, the idea had started to slip in. It came in moments when Hailey would give him that look, and he could almost see it on the face of their child before she said "Daddy." Said it in a way that expressed absolute annoyance and total impatience with him.

Sometimes he and Hailey would share a smile behind Kyle's back, a quick roll of their eyes, as they worked together to intentionally drive the most even-tempered one of them into a fit. He could feel the future where that would be their kid, Cole sinking down to the juvenile level as he teamed up with a young, punk version of himself to help torment the responsible father.

He could so easily see them staring back at him. Little hellions that savaged the world with too much attitude. They'd wear him out. Keeping the boys alive until their eighteenth birthdays and the girls from popping out any babies of their own would be a full-on, non-stop ride.

Hell, his daughters never would be old enough to have sex. It would be kind of fun to teach that lesson to the young bucks who would come sniffing around. Cole so wanted to go on that trip, but he knew he wouldn't be getting there in the Fastback.

He would be getting there, though. Sitting and staring at his own reflection, Cole realized he had it all backward. It didn't matter what Hailey felt. Hailey could spit, hit, and cuss all she wanted, but she belonged to him. That's all that counted.

Cole's daddy taught him that. There was nothing his mom could have ever done to break his father's love for her. Nothing Cole could, either, because his father loved unconditionally.

To that moment, Cole feared that side of himself, feared the pain that kind of emotion could cost a man. Being afraid didn't make Cole any less of a man, but letting that fear turn him into a coward—there was no excuse for that.

Certainly none existed for letting that fear be the justification for hurting the woman he loved. Cole looked down at Kitty's number and watched as he balled the little sheet up in his fist. He'd told Hailey once, but now he meant it clear to his soul. *Game on, princess.*

* * * *

Cole's happy moment came to a stop, along with his cocky swagger, as he stepped into the office and found Kyle waiting with one of Pittsview's finest. Seeing the deputy didn't automatically raise Cole's alarm, but the tension in the air he could read well enough. Something had happened. Something big. Kyle was smiling.

"Hey, man, have a good lunch?" The good cheer in Kyle's voice only made the dread thicken in Cole's stomach. Always up for a good time and letting laughs roll easy enough, Kyle knew the line. The Trojan, on the other hand, ignored it. That bastard gleamed out of Kyle's gaze, and Cole had to wonder who unleashed the beast.

No. He didn't have to wonder. Sighing, he asked the most obvious question. "What did Hailey do?"

Kyle didn't deny she'd done something, but instead nodded at the door. "Why don't you close that and have a seat. Adam's got an interesting story to tell."

"I got a feeling I might like to take this one standing," Cole commented as he shut the door and waded into the incoming disaster he could sense unfolding.

"Probably." Adam nodded. "But if you're not sitting then you won't be able to jump up and stand when Kyle tells you his half."

"His half?" Cole settled into the metal chair set off next to Adam's and gave Kyle a dirty look. "I can't wait to hear that part."

"Well, why don't we start with this," Adam shifted forward. "Kitty Anne is a good friend of Rachel's, who is a good friend of—"

"Hailey." Any conversation starting off this way guaranteed Cole couldn't relax now.

"Yep." Adam nodded.

Cole could do the math, but what he couldn't do was see where it added. The problem being he got stuck on the obvious fact. "Hailey knows Kitty."

"Oh, I don't know about that." Adam shifted forward, pulling his little notebook off the desk. Nose in it, he talked more to the paper than Cole as he shifted through the pages. "I do know that Kitty Anne is helping Rachel investigate a prostitution ring. They were working on getting Kitty Anne set up to play the role as whore and wanted to find a "friendly" male to help them in their charade and then…"

Adam's voice faded off as his fingers flipped faster through the pages, but Cole knew what came after. Then somehow Rachel, Kitty and Hailey came together, but with Bavis? They had to be working with the old man. Hailey working with Bavis to set Cole up. He just sat there stunned and somewhat numb.

"Ah, here." Adam held the page up as if Cole would actually read it. Pointing to a cluster of writing, Adam smiled. "This is it. Wednesday, April thirtieth, Rachel made notes about some kind of meeting involving Patton, Hailey, and her with old man Bavis."

"Remember that day, Cole?" Kyle nearly sang out from the other side of the desk.

His best friend's good humor polished Cole's shock into annoyance. "Should I?"

"It's the day you humiliated Hailey at the Bread Box when you told the whole world she'd fucked me. Remember now?" Kyle drawled. "It's the same day—"

"She made the deal with me." *Damn!* She'd set him up from both ends, and he'd never seen it coming. A bolt of pure, heated aggression sizzled through Cole, snapping him to his feet as the need to hunt down one feisty, little redhead flooded him.

"He's on his feet, Kyle." Adam's warning came nearly a second after Kyle rushed to block the exit. The deputy helped, putting one hand on Cole's shoulder to bring him to a temporary stop.

Glancing up at Adam, Cole lifted a brow. "I don't want to waste any of this on you, man. Let me go give it to the woman who earned it."

"Cole—"

"And she did earn it," Cole snapped at Kyle before he could find some reasonable, sensitive explanation for waiting. "Damnit! I have every right to deliver. Every right! That woman set me up to what?" Cole turned to Adam. "Be a headline in her friend's story?"

"Um," Adam swallowed. Cole really hadn't been expecting an answer, but by the way Adam's eyes darted to Kyle's, he knew. The story was only half done.

"What?" He had to know now. Releasing Cole, Adam took a healthy step back, which only made Cole turn on him as he waited. "Come on, man, what?"

"From the notes I read, I'd say it was they expected *you* to be the headline."

"Rachel's been leaking information to the Dothan police," Kyle filled out for Cole, sounding all too happy about everything. "See, they know about the game, but because the women rent the rooms, they could never get to the actual motel's owner. Rachel's been helping them build their case."

"I'm going to kill her." Cole meant as in now, as in Hailey. He could see where that train led.

"It gets even better. Tell him, Adam."

"Tell me what?"

"I'm not sure of this, Cole, but," Adam shifted another few inches back. "From what I can tell of Rachel's notes, Bavis sold Hailey the Fastback. He delivers the car when she delivers, well, you."

Son of a bitch. Cole stared at Adam, trying to digest everything he'd been told with everything Hailey had put him through. It didn't matter. It didn't change anything. Not one of his feelings. He still loved the damn woman, and Cole knew for a fact she loved him back.

"Cole?"

He must have been silent for too long because Adam sounded a little worried as he prodded Cole. Smiling from the deputy to Kyle, Cole straightened up. "If you'll excuse me gentlemen, I have to go talk to a lady about a car."

Talk as in tying Hailey's ass to his bed and torturing the truth out of her. Maybe if she caved early, he'd find some mercy and release her in a day or two. Otherwise, Cole would keep her there as long as he wanted. Hailey had just volunteered to be his slave for life.

"Now, Cole." Kyle didn't budge from where he guarded the door. Only it wasn't Kyle leaning there, arms crossed over his chest, smirking. The Trojan, master of deception, straightened up and finally stepped into the game. "There are many better things than punishment, like revenge."

Chapter 29

"They look like they're planning a war, don't they?" Rachel made that remark over the rim of her coffee cup. Her gaze stuck on the table across the packed dining room of the little deli. The ominous observation had Hailey glancing in the same direction, fearing Rachel had it right.

Kyle and Cole announced they needed a "guys' night out" when she showed up at the shop not a half hour before. The declaration wouldn't have unnerved Hailey half as much if Kyle would have appeared himself just once or if Cole would have stopped smiling.

Between the two of them, they were acting really odd. Always quick with a grin, Cole had twisted into a near giddy state. It wouldn't have shocked her in the least if the man actually giggled. Giggled over her, because both of them were acting like it was Christmas morning and she was the last present under the tree.

Not that Kyle giggled or even truly smiled. His grin always so full of humor and happiness had settled into a twist hinting at a mind more intent then distracted. The predatory confidence of a hunter who'd cornered his prey gleamed with mirth in Kyle's gaze, making Hailey pretty damn nervous.

"Something is up. That's for sure." Hailey sighed, glancing over at where the horde of Cattlemen had pushed a whole bunch of tables together. They gathered around, leaning secretively in as they whispered amongst themselves. "No good comes from a pile like that."

"Look at them." Rachel shook her head. "There are eight of them. It makes me almost itchy to call Patton and warn her."

"I don't think we're there yet." Hailey tasted her tea and purposefully ignored the huddle of men. "In fact, they're just trying to screw with us. They don't know anything, or they'd be over here accusing us. They probably just sense something amiss and are trying to rattle us, Rachel. Stay firm."

"I don't know," Rachel muttered. Setting her cup down, she leaned in to whisper. "I'm telling you something bad is coming."

"Why you giving me that look?" Hailey leaned back in the booth, not at all appreciating that look.

"Because, honey, I think you are stuck in the middle of this." Rachel glanced back at the men. "I mean, look at them. You think they're talking about sports?"

Hailey hated to glance back over at that table but couldn't seem to help herself. This time Kyle caught her gaze. He didn't look half as happy as Cole. In fact, he looked a little pissed.

"Don't be dramatic," Hailey snorted, breaking Kyle's glare. "You're just all antsy because you guys just got back together."

"No. I'm antsy because of Kitty's call, and you should be, too," Rachel shot back. "Or aren't you the least bit concerned that Cole made a lunch date with her tomorrow?"

Hailey was more than concerned, but she wouldn't let that faze her. Not now when her fears appeared perfectly justified. "It's his decision to make."

"Oh, spare me." Rachel rolled her eyes. "Fine, you want to pretend like it doesn't matter, go ahead, but I know the truth. I can see it in your eyes. You care about that man."

"I do not." The denial came out instantly as always, but this time a blush heated her cheeks, making a liar out of her.

A fact that didn't go unnoticed by Rachel. "No?"

Sighing out the weight of her objection, Hailey's shoulders dipped under the press of the truth. "It doesn't matter. I mean, if he cares more about a car than me. Why should I care about him at all? It's his decision to make."

"He's a man, Hailey." Rachel groaned with obvious impatience. "They don't think like that. You know if you put a chunk of chocolate cake and a slab of lemon pie in front of a man, he doesn't choose between them. He eats both!"

"Then how am I supposed to ever trust him? How the hell do you trust Killian? Or Adam?"

"Well, it certainly isn't conspiring with another woman to seduce one of my men," Rachel snorted.

"And is it by telling them all your secrets?" Hailey asked. "Maybe that's what all the hubbub is about."

Rachel went still enough for Hailey to regret her flippant response. "Are you accusing me of betraying you? Because despite the fact that I think this whole thing has gotten completely out of hand, I still wouldn't rat you out, even if that does mean lying to Killian and Adam."

Hailey helped by keeping her mouth shut. Yes, she knew. This whole plan had gotten out of hand. The whole ball of yarn started to unravel, but that didn't mean Hailey had a clue about how to stop it.

"I'm sorry, Rachel," Hailey finally sighed. "I know you're in a hard spot right now. I know what you're saying. I just have to make sure I know who Cole and Kyle want to be sleeping with."

"That would be you." Rachel waved a hand over Hailey's objection. "Please, don't feed me any of that crap about you sleeping only with Kyle. I don't buy it, nobody else does. We can all see quite clearly that Cole is a well-laid man, and there isn't any other woman he's been rubbing up against. So that just leaves you."

Hailey licked her lips and broke Rachel's stare. She'd been denying it for weeks now, and people had been asking. Patton, Heather, Rachel, they all pressed, worrying her with concerns about how sleeping with Cole changed the whole game. Hailey didn't want it changed. She wanted her damn answer.

"Listen to me, Rachel, and listen good. I am not now, nor have I ever, slept with Cole Jackson."

"You are a liar!"

Hailey's head hit the table as much to hide the blush flaming over her face as in defeat to Rachel's barked accusation.

"I know you've been sleeping with that man, and now he's going to go rub all up against Kitty Anne. In the short order, you are going to be sobbing your heart out. What I don't know is why? This game was supposed to get Cole, not you."

"So? So what?" Hailey gave up arguing the lie to argue the truth. "So we call off the game, and it's what? A month, two, maybe five, but somewhere down the road, Cole will rub up against some woman if that's what he wants. I'll be crying then but probably a whole lot harder. So why not know now?"

Typical Rachel, she ignored that argument in its entirety. "You tell Patton you slept with Cole?"

"Are you insane?" Hailey snorted. "No."

"You do realize that even if he gets caught, Cole isn't going to be repentant once he finds out your hand in all of this," Rachel warned her. "If you're already sleeping with him, he's going to take this as a full-on betrayal, and his response won't be pretty."

Hailey knew, but her gut told her she could outdo Cole's outrage. Hers would be motivated by true emotion, not just injured pride. "He won't have any right."

"That isn't going to change anything." Rachel shook her head before pinning Hailey with her look. "Now I'm asking. This is the last chance, Hailey. You really want to go through with this?"

"I just need to know, Rachel."

They shared a moment of understanding. It ended with Rachel glancing back over at the table their men were sharing. "I wonder why Devin is with them? I thought the Davis boys kind of considered Cole and Kyle punching bags."

* * * *

That question stuck with Hailey a half hour later as they watched the huddle of men break up. Cole split from the group to come swaggering over, still wearing that cocky grin. With every step he came closer, Hailey could feel the knot tightening down in her stomach.

Rachel excused herself, leaving Hailey completely undefended. Not that her friend's presence would have changed Cole's behavior. As if the whole world knew they were a couple, he pushed up along her side and looped an arm over.

"Hey, princess." Just like that, he kissed her, a quick brush of their lips. "How was your dinner?"

"I get a feeling not as entertaining as yours," Hailey retorted before pointedly looking at the hand he folded over her shoulder. "Uh, Cole? You trying to make a statement here?"

"Yes, I am." Instead of trying to charm her around his possessive contact, Cole acted more drunk than sober when he pushed back out of the booth to declare to the whole damn dining room. "I just want everybody here to know that I love this woman."

He pointed at her. Like he aimed an invisible gun and pulled the trigger, Hailey could feel the impact of his gesture, and it about killed her. Her body certainly flooded with enough heat to scorch her very skin as he went on.

"Hailey Mathews," he went down onto his knees to ask her, "will you wear my collar?"

The crowd went wild behind him, egged on by the overwhelming number of Cattlemen hooting and hollering. One voice separated itself from the mob as it lobbied for Cole's plight.

"Ah, come on, Hailey, don't leave the man on his knees."

"Shut up, Aaron!" Hailey shouted back, finally finding her voice and her ability to move. Snatching Cole's earlobe between her fingers, she pulled him unkindly back onto the seat. "And you, I don't know what it is about this place, but behave yourself!"

The cheers ballooned into a raucous roar of laughter that pitched up as Cole pulled his head to the side, freeing his ear to rub the sting from it. Giving her a pouty look as if she'd been the one to do wrong, he griped at her.

"You know you just killed my reputation."

"You killed your own reputation," Hailey shot back. "And I don't particularly appreciate the joke."

Cole's grin flattened out, and his gaze locked on her with a certain stillness that changed the tension in her stomach back into butterflies. "I wasn't joking, Hailey. I was asking, but I guess I got my answer now."

"Everybody heard that answer," Kyle slid into Rachel's abandoned seat. "I'd say you just got dethroned, sire."

That brought the laughter back to Cole's features, and even Hailey shared his smile this time. She didn't even object when he put that possessive arm back around her shoulders. For some reason, he'd gotten into a touchy-feely mood this evening. It went well with his grin, making it even harder to be mad at him despite all the reasons she had.

Cole really was a goober underneath all that arrogance. It played out as smug assurance too often, but Hailey learned to see beneath the surface. He didn't take life half as seriously as Kyle did, evident by the sour look he still wore.

"I take it your dinner wasn't as good."

"What?" Kyle's brow furled into a full scowl.

"Kyle's constipated," Cole declared with such grandness it earned him a dirty look from his partner.

"I am not."

"He certainly looks it," Hailey agreed over Kyle's objection. "But I have a feeling you have more to do with that than a lack of fiber."

"Me?" Cole laughed. "Oh, princess, you got that wrong."

"That's my seat." Before Hailey could press either man on Kyle's dour attitude, Rachel reappeared. She didn't appear appeased when Kyle simply scooted over to give her a little room on the wooden bench. "Let me rephrase that. Get out of my seat."

"Oh, come on, darlin'," Cole cajoled her. "Just smile and join the party."

Not the least bit amused, Rachel turned a hard look on Cole. "What did you call me?"

"Hey, Killian, your woman's about to get mean over here," Cole called out across the room, sending Rachel into a fit.

Hailey might have joined her, but her gaze caught on Devin shoving out the door. He'd been there when Cole made his scene, and Cole certainly did seem intent on making as many scenes as he could.

Devin didn't hit Cole, and Kyle's glaring at us like we killed his dog.

Something was definitely up.

"Shut up, Cole." Adam's annoyed snap had her glancing back to the sight of the big deputy shielding Cole from a flushed and obviously irate Rachel.

Kyle held out her purse to her, and with a knowing look in Hailey's direction, she snatched it up before storming off. With a dirty comment in Cole's direction, Adam trailed off after his woman looking like a man who knew he was about to get chewed out.

"You're welcome!" Cole called out at the couple, drawing Hailey's attention back to his smirk. This time she didn't share his good humor.

"What did you say to her?"

"What? Me?" Cole actually managed to look confused. "I just offered to pay for your lady's dinner, and your friend just took it the wrong way."

"I'm sure it had nothing to do with the way you said it." Hailey snorted. "Nothing at all."

She could almost envy the way he lied with such ease. A bad trait, lying, but she couldn't hold it against him, not with that grin. Rolling her eyes, she looked back over at Kyle, who still studied her with a brooding gaze.

"I take it your boys' night is over?"

"Nah," Cole shook his head. "We're all headed out to the club to have a little fun."

"The club?" His grin belied his intent. He wanted to prick her jealousy. Knowing his game didn't make her immune from the effects. "I thought you two didn't belong to the club anymore?"

"And how would you know that?" Kyle perked up, asking his question with the speed of an investigator lunging in on a suspect who just slipped up.

Hailey didn't appreciate being accused, especially on this subject. "You told me."

"No. I told you I resigned, but nobody told you that Cole didn't belong to the club anymore," Kyle corrected her. "So how did you know that?"

Hailey shrugged, not about to rat Patton out. "I assumed."

"More like somebody told you," Kyle retorted.

"Somebody probably named Patton," Cole tacked on. "Which kind of makes you wonder, doesn't it, Kyle? You been checking up on us, princess? Having your friend paw through the club files to find out all our secrets?"

"I don't know what you're talking about." Hailey dismissed him and his accusation with a lightness that earned her a growl from the other side of the table.

"I don't know, Cole. If Hailey had read our files, I don't think she'd be so relaxed about what's coming her way in six days."

The savage hunger in Kyle's tone matched the wicked intent that curled his lips up. He enjoyed thinking about what she had coming, a change from his attitude for the past three weeks. A change from just that afternoon when he'd been all cajoling with double-dimpled grins.

"Counting your chickens a little early." No point in playing nice if Kyle didn't.

Cole burst into laughter, and even Kyle managed to put some true humor in his grin. "After three weeks, you still clinging on to that hope? You know what I think, Cole?"

"Hmm?"

"I think we should take the little princess out to the club." Kyle's gaze darkened on her even as his voice dipped into a husky purr. "Show her what consequences are coming her way."

"That's not a bad idea." She could sense Cole's chin turning in her direction, but Kyle held her gaze trapped with its intensity. He actually looked dangerous. "What do you say, princess? Want to go get a peek at how the other half plays?"

"I'm not that dumb." It popped out of her more in response to Kyle's look than Cole's suggestion but drew laughter from both men. Scowling at them for having so much fun at her expense, Hailey huffed. "Besides, don't you two have plans?"

"We got about an hour before the games start."

"Games?" Hailey glared at Cole, reading into his answer all sorts of salacious misdeeds. "What do you mean, games?"

"Poker, why?" Cole shot back, all smug. "What did you think I meant?"

"Nothing."

"You know, Cole." Kyle pondered her with the same arrogant smirk. "I think our little princess is jealous."

"I am not," Hailey shot at Kyle.

"I do think you're right."

Turning her chin, she scowled at Cole. "He is not."

"Why don't you just admit it, princess?" Kyle drawled, bringing her frown back to him.

"Just say it, and we'll respect your wishes and not go to the club," Cole murmured in her ear, making her feel that much more cornered.

She wanted to give in, but her pride just wouldn't bend to their smiles. "I am not jealous."

"Okay then." Kyle leaned back, seeming to go instantly relaxed as he cast Cole a curious look. "You know, I'm thinking I could do with some dessert."

"Oh, they got some sweet treats out at the club."

Hailey started growling as Kyle nodded, sliding toward the edge of the bench. "Oh, yeah, I'm thinking the chocolate dipped kind."

"With a creamy center." Cole's arm disappeared as he shoved away from her.

"And some whip cream." Kyle grinned in anticipation of something that had nothing to do with dessert. "You know how I like to lick things."

"All right!" Hailey snapped, unable to take it anymore, even as she remained firmly convinced they were teasing her. "I'm jealous, now sit back down."

Cole's ass hit the seat the same second Kyle's did across they way. Then she had two grinning idiots on her hands.

"That wasn't so hard, was it, princess?" Cole looped his arm back around her shoulders and snuggled her in close to his side.

"Maybe we should hold out until she volunteers to be our dessert," Kyle offered. "That seems more like a fair trade, doesn't it?"

"That it does." Cole nuzzled her ear to growl the temptation into her soul. "What you say, princess? Ever been dipped in chocolate?"

"Stop it, Cole." Hailey shoved him back, giving him a dirty look. "I don't know what's gotten into you, but I think you should remember we're six days away from when you get to be that kind of lewd."

"Six days?" Cole snorted. "Try twenty-four hours, princess, or don't you consider our porno-date nights lewd?"

"If I say no, you'll take it as a challenge, right?" Hailey shot back. "And you think I'm dumb enough to do that and screw myself out of my dinner?"

"Dinner?" Cole glanced over at Kyle. "What she talking about?"

"You didn't tell him?"

Kyle shrugged at both their questions. "It didn't come up."

When Kyle didn't continue, Hailey explained the rest to Cole. "You're cooking me dinner, and we're doing the proper date night tomorrow. You know, the one where you pick your underwear off the floor before I come over'?"

"You mean I got to clean?" Cole actually managed to sound outraged at the very idea.

"And cook." Hailey didn't show any mercy. "Don't forget, I expect to be well fed."

Cole snorted at her threat, turning to glare at Kyle. "You agreed to this, and you didn't even tell me?"

"What's wrong, Cole?" Hailey jumped on his question before Kyle could respond. "Got other plans?"

He gave away his answer by the second of stillness that flashed over him before he cocked his head. There was that charm, the old Cole smoothness she hated. "Plans? No plans. Why you ask?"

"I don't know." Hailey shrugged, returning his brittle smile. "I guess I figured you for the type that might like to eat dessert before dinner."

No more laughter swirled in his gaze. It went deadly still as he leaned in, his voice dipping to a rough whisper. "You know, darlin', after all these weeks, I'd think you know me better by now."

"Maybe Hailey just needs to be taught the lesson," Kyle suggested, drawing a quick glance from her. He looked about as pissed as Cole sounded, and she didn't understand that at all.

"Is that what it's going to take?" Cole asked. "You want us to prove it to you?"

Hailey didn't really know what the hell they were talking about then, but she knew her answer. Meeting his gaze dead-on, she nodded. "Yes."

Just like that, Cole relaxed back, shooting a grin over to Kyle. "You hear that, man? I guess we're going to have to find some way to prove it to our princess."

Kyle didn't smile. He just stared hard at her, making Hailey's muscles tingle with the need to bolt. "I guess we are."

"Well," Cole pulled his arm back and shoved out of the booth, "we gotta get to that game."

"What?" Hailey's head snapped in his direction. "I thought you said you weren't going to the club."

"The club?" Kyle snorted as he shoved up to his feet. "We're playing poker at our house. Really, Hailey, where do you get these ideas?"

"She's just paranoid," Cole commented as the two men started to strut off. "I'm thinking we've hitched our wagon to a crazy lady, Kyle."

"Yeah." Kyle cast her a look over his shoulder. "But she does look good naked."

Whatever Cole's responses, she didn't catch them over the din of the fading dinner crowd. Glaring at their backs, she watched them disappear through the deli's door before releasing her breath. Something was up. They couldn't know about the plan, which meant they started their own game.

Not a good sign.

Chapter 30

Wednesday, May 28th

Kyle stared down at the burgers, not even seeing them. He still couldn't get over it. Yesterday when Cole skipped out on lunch, he hadn't been worried about anything. Then Adam had showed up and ripped all of Kyle's hopes to shreds.

Taking a deep breath, Kyle reminded himself that it would all be all right. They had a plan. They had help. Lots of help because Hailey had gone too far this time. Not just Hailey, the whole damn lot of them.

There is a war at hand, men. A revolution that threatens to overthrow the entire order of things in this town. This is the second offense, and if we don't step up and put this thing down now, it will only be a matter of time before you all fall.

Devin Davis made that proclamation last night as he governed over the impromptu meeting he called of the Cattlemen. To a man, each ducked out of their night's previous engagements to huddle around their house and construct a plan.

Pissed off and alarmed, men rallied to Chase's arguments that they had to pool together and make a statement. They'd put this revolution down and remind the women of just where their place was.

Lust clenched into his anger as Kyle reminded himself of just where he and Cole agreed Hailey's place was. In their bed, bound, naked, and at their mercy. She'd be offering that up along with all the words Kyle wanted to hear. Then they'd savage her little body all night long, all day long, for days.

"Hey." Hailey's head popped out of the kitchen door to snatch him back into the moment.

He forced a smile as she stepped out on to the patio, but the gesture did little to actually ease the tension in his body. All day, he'd been working hard on being his normal, relaxed self. Hailey still seemed hesitant around him, not appearing to buy into his act.

As much as she might doubt his performance, hers didn't come off too well. For all the smiles and pointless chatter, she remained tense, edgy. Kyle knew why, but he left it alone.

"I set the table. How long until we eat?" Hailey rubbed her belly in a pointed statement, but he could hear the uncertainty in her voice. It had been there all evening. "I'm starved, and you know how I get when I get hungry."

It took all his effort to actually make his body relax and slouch back into a not so battle-ready stance. "Yeah, I know, princess, but you're just going to have to survive a few minutes more."

"Don't you mean you'll have to survive me for a few minutes more?" Hailey offered with a desperate tint of humor. "And don't even think of suggesting we wait for Cole. I take it that was him on the phone, and he's just started on his way home."

Home. Kyle wondered if she realized how often she used that word anymore. He knew she didn't mean it terms of any house or street address. She said the same kind of things about her own place because home had slowly come to mean where the three of them were together.

Only Cole wasn't coming home, and he knew Cole's absence put the worry in her gaze. It had been there since lunch yesterday. "No. Uh, something came up with a car. He said he'd probably be pretty late."

"Oh." All the joy drained out of her voice with that one simple word. "I guess he's chosen to eat dessert first, after all."

The bitter anger in her comment pleased Kyle as much as it pained him. Neither emotion made it into his response. "He's looking at a car, Hailey, not a woman. You know, I think Cole's right about you. You're getting paranoid."

"I'm not paranoid," she snapped instantly.

Ignoring her objection, Kyle continued on, talking as much to himself as her. "Of course, it kind of makes me wonder why you care. I mean, you bet the man he couldn't be faithful. Sort of takes away your right to be mad if he isn't. Doesn't it?"

"You're really trying to piss me off, aren't you?"

"No." But she was doing a good job with him. "I'm just trying to figure this out. If you're jealous, that means you care. So do you care?"

"I care about getting fed because this is not exactly turning into the pleasant dinner you promised." With that, she stormed back into the house. Kyle took that as a yes.

* * * *

Kitty Anne's picture hadn't done her justice. As beautiful as she looked in the image, the blonde was downright mesmerizing in person. Even the way her lips kissed out to embrace the butt of her cigarette lured a man in, and Cole didn't care for smokers.

Nor did he get into the film noir scene, and this woman definitely came from that genre. Folded gracefully into a darkened corner, she exuded a mysterious air. Her hair shinning, her long legs glowing, those sky-lit eyes shifting, everything about her read "on the make," but this wasn't a two-bit bar hussy. No, she had the grace and elegance to pull off the old movie star look and not end up being cheap and tacky for it.

"Jacob said you might share an interest in some of my...hobbies." Smoke slowly slipped out with each husky note as her full lips slid back into a seductive smile.

That smile, that body, her whole act, even knowing it was one, should have triggered the battle cry of a worthy challenge in his body on any given day of the week. Cole always wondered how his dad resisted all those women who had been so quick to flirt with him.

It seemed to him a hard challenge. One that he always feared he failed. Even finding out that Hailey set him up hadn't triggered any sour feelings because he figured she had some right to worry. God's truth, he'd never be the type of man who didn't notice a pretty woman, and flirting just sort of came as second nature to him.

Now, though, he knew what his father meant when he said it would all just be skin deep if it wasn't with the right woman. That's all he felt for Kitty Anne. A little awareness, a certain appreciation, but definitely wishing he was with Hailey instead.

Kyle, that son of a bitch, got the fun part of the equation. While Cole had to go plaster on a fake smile and make sure he didn't cross any line, Kyle would be dicking it up with their woman all night long, laying it on nice and thick until the little princess purred.

God, but I love to hear her purr.

"Am I boring you, Mr. Jackson?"

Cole blinked and then threw up a quick smirk to cover his slip in attention. *Focus on the now, dumbass.* "Sorry, darlin', I just got lost in the moment."

Her gaze narrowed on the "darlin'," and he could see her jaw tighten ever so slightly despite the smile that forced her lips up. "Not a problem, Mr. Jackson, but you still haven't answered my question."

Shrugging, Cole knew how to work the game. "I might, but then again, I might not be."

"If not, then there's the door."

Cole didn't even look in the direction Kitty Anne nodded. Instead, he leaned in to drop his own voice in the range of a lover. "I guess it all depends on whether or not I've heard right about you."

Kitty met him over the table, her lips fluttering very close to his. "And what have you heard?"

"That you have a very big fiancé who might take objection to your hobbies."

"Scared?" She offered him a slow smile that followed with a soft brush of her lips over his as she purred on. "You don't need to worry about him."

Cole snapped back when she bit his lower lip. Instinctively, his hand when to his lip, looking for blood as he growled out. "Damn it, woman, that hurt."

Kitty chuckled as she settled back into her seat. "Can't take it, but you can dish it out. Is that it, Mr. Jackson?"

That had Cole's eyes narrowing on the woman. She might look like a goddess, but she was clearly a bitch. "Maybe you should ask yourself that, Miss Kitty, or are you not willing to try something new?"

One perfectly arched eyebrow lifted. "Is that a challenge, Mr. Jackson?"

"Only if you take it as such." Cole ducked a second direct answer, not about to be hemmed in by this one. For all the theatrics, the woman had her own agenda. "You might consider it a chance to explore a little more of life's pleasures."

"Maybe I've already been down that road."

"Not with me," Cole assured her with his best grin. "Trust me, darlin', I can show you scenery you never dreamed of."

Instead of retreating, Kitty Anne's smile took on a true touch of emotion. "That's what they all say, Mr. Jackson."

"I can do more than say." Cole leaned back in, daring another damn bite and promising it would come out of Hailey's hide if her friend pulled the rude stunt again. "I can show you. I'm even willing to pay for the trip."

No bite, just a smooth retreat and a slow consideration. "Perhaps this is a conversation that would go better in private."

Shit. He didn't want to have a private conversation with the crazy lady. Private meant she might push for things he didn't intend on delivering. Cole knew he walked a fine line here because whatever he did would be getting back to Hailey. He needed to be clean enough to command the guilt he wanted.

Kitty didn't leave him any choice in the matter. Apparently they had a date, and he had better hope Hailey hadn't required actual fooling around to make this show go down. If she had, then it would be her ass, and he'd tan it good.

Pressing the napkin on which she scrawled out an address in his direction, Kitty gave him another one of those sultry smiles. "Fifteen minutes and then follow."

* * * *

It became harder and harder as the night ticked by for Hailey to fake being even slightly happy. She thought she did a good job through dinner, despite her earlier outburst. Kyle must have sensed he pushed too hard because he returned back to her sweet, understanding lover.

It left her believing that he knew. He knew what Cole was up to, and that's why he'd been so mad this past day. Knowing Cole would be crashing their relationship, Kyle must have become desperate to try and save it.

As desperate as Hailey became to hear the sound of Cole's truck in the drive, the only thing that filled the air was the movie. She'd been able to stare more at the screen than at the little clock keeping time on the DVD player through the first movie. The second movie became her downfall.

Hailey couldn't even concentrate on the plot. All she could do was watch those little digital numbers turn over until they fell squarely over the eleven o'clock line—well past the time when Cole could legitimately claim to be working on a car deal in Dothan.

That little, stinking, son of a bitch hadn't just gone to see Kitty Anne. He stayed with her. With her when he could have been here with Hailey, but she guessed after three porno-date nights, the idea lost its charm. She'd show him a loss of charm whenever he brought his cowardly butt home.

As if to echo the very grim and violent nature of her thoughts, Rachel's cell number lit up Hailey's phone. That couldn't be good. Sparing Kyle a half-ass, fake smile, she straightened up from where she'd been curled into his side to answer it.

"Kitty just called." Rachel didn't even bother with a greeting. There wasn't even a touch of sympathy in her tone as she droned on, causing Hailey to tense more with each word. "She says Cole just left her house with a promise to meet her at the motel tomorrow night."

"Why am I not shocked?" But why was she hurt?

Rachel's voice dropped into a conspirator whisper. "I'm getting really worried that this entire thing is about to go haywire. Are you getting any kind of weird vibes?"

Yeah, the sinking feeling she'd fallen in love with a complete asshole, which kept her mind focused on her own worries. "Did they already..." She couldn't finish that painful thought.

"No." Rachel's mercy showed itself to be very hard. "I don't know. I didn't ask for details, but if you want them—"

"No." Hailey's gut answered for her a second before her heart got out its response. "Yes."

"What? Which is it yes or no?"

"Yes."

"Fine." Rachel sounded disgusted. "I'll get back to you tomorrow night, somewhere around seven. That's should be when your heart's breaking anyway, and I always love to kick a friend when they're down."

With that brutal goodbye, the line went dead, leaving Hailey to stare at the little device. Rachel had it wrong. Hailey's heart already started to break. There would be no stopping it now unless Cole stopped it.

"What's going on, Hailey?" That calm tone couldn't hide the worry or the demand in it. For as soft as Kyle's touch was as he brushed the hair back over her shoulder, she could feel the panic hiding in the moment. Maybe it wasn't his. Maybe it was hers.

Swallowing down that grim thought, she dropped her phone back in her purse as she tried to roll over the magnitude of what just happened. "Nothing. Just Rachel with some gossip."

"Why you lying to me, princess?" She hadn't wanted to look at him, but the fingers sliding under her chin to turn her gaze to his left her no choice. "I can see it in your eyes, Hailey. Those beautiful, witchy eyes." His thumb brushed over the circles so many sleepless nights had left on her cheeks. "There is pain there."

Because all she had left were sleepless nights, except for this one with him. In so many ways, Kyle and Cole blended together, but they were not the same man. Kyle had the gentleness, the tenderness, and the loyalty. No wife of his would ever worry because his love consumed his world.

When he settled down, it would be to a life defined by nothing more than work and family. He'd need nothing more than that and want for nothing more. His wife would be one of the lucky ones, but it wouldn't be her. She couldn't build that life with him beneath the painful shadow of Cole's betrayal.

"Hailey, you know you're kind of worrying me right now. I'd really like you to tell me what's going on."

Letting out the breath she'd been holding, she leaned back across the couch to try and kiss his concern away. It didn't work. With his hand still spanning her jaw, he barely let her get the softest of brushes before he lifted her lips back a fraction of an inch.

"Hailey?"

She didn't want to talk about it. She didn't want to try and work it out. She just wanted this one last night, this one last fantasy. "Make love to me, Kyle."

That had him going still, and his gaze drilled into hers as he asked for the truth behind that request. "And would it be love, Hailey?"

"Yes."

He groaned her name as his lips broke open over hers. Like the gentle whisper of brushed leather, his mouth pressed hers open, leaving her defenseless against his slow inspection. Instead of feasting, he savored, drawing her taste, her breath, her very soul into his body as he melted the whole world down to nothing more than his sweet exploration.

When his mouth finally lifted, the air that rushed in felt painful. She didn't need air to live, she just needed his breath. Pressing in, this time she claimed his mouth, wrapping her arms around his neck to assure he had no retreat. Kyle didn't seek any, but pulled her tighter to him as all the soft emotions gave way to the burning need that always lingered just beneath the surface.

With the hungry desperation of a person who knew the moment couldn't last, Hailey clung to it. His arms scooped her up, and in one smooth motion, lifted her off the couch as he shoved up to his feet. Just like that, he carried her off to his bedroom.

* * * *

Kyle could feel the goodbye in Hailey's kiss. The sensation wound around his heart, tightening it into a painful vise because he knew what that phone call had been about. It had started.

Hailey's heart was breaking. He could feel the truth in the hungry desperation of Hailey's kiss. She wanted to escape the pain.

No longer soft and pliant in his arms, Hailey's inner savage reared its passionate head as her kiss became demanding, consuming, leaving no doubt that she wanted to possess more than just his body, but his very soul. She just didn't understand she already owned it.

If she did, then tonight would have been a celebration instead of the beginning of all out warfare. Determined to be the victor and not the conquest, Kyle broke the kiss. He wouldn't be dominated or rushed tonight.

Brushing back the hair from her face, he let her legs slip back down to the floor. The same hand that stroked over the softness of her cheek also held back muscles that flexed in her neck as she went to her tiptoes to find his lips.

"Relax, princess." Kyle brushed a soft kiss over her lips. "Let me show you what it means to be loved."

Chapter 31

With that, Kyle claimed Hailey's mouth the way he intended to claim her body, with the delicate appreciation for the woman who had become his heart. With slow precision, he discovered and memorized all the different textures and flavors of Hailey's kiss. She offered it all up to him freely, pressing into his body as her fingers clenched into a fist, pulling on his shirt.

No matter how much he wanted to linger, to savor every moment of their kiss, he couldn't hold back that passion that always flamed out of control when they came together. The need to breathe was the lone thing that could break them apart.

The kiss ended with ragged, panting breaths as they stood there, clinging to each other. Kyle inhaled the intoxicating scent of cinnamon and feminine desire. It sank into his blood stream, pumping liquid lust through his whole body.

He fought back against the sudden rush of urgency, forcing his hands to loosen their grip and give him the ability to step back. She looked so beautiful with her swollen lips and eyes gone all soft and chocolaty. His savage princess. There was nothing more beautiful than the sight of her desire.

Holding her gaze, he reached forward to work each button down the front of her sundress free. One at a time, the little, white buttons gave way under the blunt direction of his fingers. With each sighed release, another inch of the thin cotton dress relaxed open.

The pink lace of a bra brought an unexpected smile to his lips as it peeked out at him. "You wore underwear."

Hailey licked her lips and offered him a tentative, almost uncertain smile. "Patton says underwear sets the mood."

And Hailey hadn't come here with her panties off to fuck. She'd come dressed in the delicate veil of sexy lingerie to make love. To him. Kyle pressed another kiss to her lips. A quick, soft brush that feathered off over her cheek and down the arrogant slope of her jaw.

The delicate muscles of her neck contracted beneath his lips, and he paused to chase the shivers away with a soothing lick. A nip of his teeth brought the tremors back. Flexing slightly into him, she whispered his name in a breathy plea for more. The husky caress warmed through his lust, rounding the edges with a need far greater than any physical desire.

They became addictive, those little whispers. He pulled them from her with the slow massage of his kiss over her shoulders. She almost purred as he rubbed his hair-stubbed cheek against her skin. He hadn't shaved, and the rough caress left an angry red line for his lips to follow.

His chin bumped into the thick strap of her little, yellow sundress, and then dug into the velvet of her skin as he nudged the barrier over her shoulder. Tasting the blushing path of skin back over the gentle round of her shoulder led him to the thin, silky pink strap that remained as the last obstacle.

Clamping it in the vise of his teeth, Kyle tugged until the little plastic ring down the back gave way. Just like that, her bra strap floated down over the creamy slopes of her breasts, giving him an entirely new path to follow. Very sweet. He didn't need the warming lotion to make the delicacy of her plump swell any more delightful. All he needed was her hands digging into his hair as she tried to force his kiss over the frilly lace cups that hid her most tender flesh. Kyle resisted the invitation, making her moan his name as he traced over the wispy curves of her bra.

"You're as bad as Cole." Hailey groaned that soft complaint out as his lips discovered the virgin territory of her other shoulder.

Kyle smiled at that, rubbing his cheek into the graceful curve of her neck until she shuddered and mewed. "Am I your king, Hailey?"

That got him a giggle—a rough, ragged one that peeled down over her labored breath. "You want me to call you sire now?"

Despite her teasing, Kyle took the comment to heart. Hailey wouldn't be lightening this moment and making it safe. There could be no safety left for little Miss Hailey. He wanted her to be honest about what she risked with her games. That started with waiting for her big, cloudy eyes to finally blink open.

Hailey always closed her eyes during sex, and Kyle had begun to think it was a way for her to hide that last little part from him. He let it go, but not tonight. Tonight, he wanted her to look at him and know just how much he loved her. The way her lower lip rolled in and she swallowed assured him the message had been received.

"You know what I want, princess." And he could only wish she'd finally give it to him.

"I thought you were going to show me." Ragged with lust and tinged with fear, her barely-there voice matched the whirl of emotion in her beautiful eyes.

"If that's what it takes, Hailey. Whatever it takes."

He issued that promise against the curve of ear before making love to the fragile shell. Such a simple thing, and yet it made her crumble into him as her head curved to offer up the lush landscape of her neck for his feasting. Delighting in her rich flavor, Kyle took his time, treating her shoulder to the same teasing caresses he had its twin.

By the time he snapped her second bra strap with his bite, the urge to follow its sigh down the full breast panting against his chest became almost irresistible. Only a need deeper, one that pulsed straight out of his soul, overrode the boiling desires of his lust.

Stepping back, he let her dress fall to a puddle at her feet. Instead of ogling the body he ached for so much, Kyle waited through the second it took her eyes to finally lift back open. Only once their gazes caught and locked did he slowly go to his knees.

He thought she might give him what he wanted when she saw how much she needed, but Hailey's expression only turned sad. "Kyle…"

He didn't want to hear it. Whatever excuse or defense she'd come up with this time, it didn't matter. Not to him. Wrapping his arms around her hips, he pulled her into the shelter of his body and just held on, not wanting to ever let go of the soft, smooth feel of her pressed against him.

Built so differently than him, his little princess tried so hard to be tough and rugged, but these velvety curves betrayed her as sweet and delicate. A man just had to peel away the armor to find the most decadent of treats. It was a feast just for him, just for his hands. They spanned over her body, recording the feel of every inch of her rounded curves for fear this would be the last time he held her.

The muscles flexed beneath the satin of her flesh as thumbs slid into the graceful ravine of her spine and followed its path to the sweet dip at its base. With a moan, she arched and flexed, showing him the pleasure he gave her as his fingers lingered there, teasing her sensitive skin.

The musky scent of her desire thickened in the air around him, condensing into every breath he took and drugging him with the need for a taste. He rubbed that need out on the quivering mass of her stomach, trying to squelch it even as he flooded his system with the exciting aroma of cinnamon. There could be no escape for him because this need would never be vanquished.

Kyle felt helpless as his tongue snaked out, giving in to the roaring demand. Fanning down and over her stomach, he drugged himself on her intoxicating taste. Sweet and spicy, just like his savage princess. Only now the savage had been lulled into a thing of soft, mewing need.

Beneath his cheek, he could feel the soft pillow of her gently rounded stomach flutter and convulse as her hands dug into his hair and tried to press his lick lower. Over the indention of her belly button he paused despite the insistent push of her palms.

A gentle, nibbling kiss had her fingers digging, pressing him against her rubbing stomach in a demand for more. A plea that echoed out of her lips as she moaned his name. He'd have kissed her stomach for a lifetime if she'd only moan his name like that forever.

Her gasping sped up into pants as his kisses trailed lower. The scuff of his cheek left red streaks trailing in his wake. Lapping at the small wounds, he savored her taste and the soft feel of her stomach's gentle curve. All the way down, his kisses trailed lower until his lips scraped over the crisp edge of her panties.

He teased her, nibbling his way along the elastic band. Resisting the insistent imploring of her hands, Kyle delighted in making her twist and arch each time his tongue slipped beneath the edge of her panties. Over the sexy dip of her waist, Kyle paused to tickle that delicate stretch of skin, reveling in the way she gasped and jerked back. Digging his fingers into the fleshy globes of her ass, he held her still as he tormented his delightful find.

Over and over, he scrapped his chin along the sweeping indention. Nibbling and licking the small red mark he left, Kyle felt the tremors roll down her legs and her body start to cave inward. Only with the help of his hands coming to brace her waist did his little princess stay on her feet.

Holding her quivering, mewing body in position, he snagged the pink band stretching over her hips. She stiffened and stilled as he tugged the edge of her panties down the bony outcropping of her hip, over the rounded flare of her thigh to bring them to a rest under the hard ridge of her knee. His hand made the same slow journey, catching the elastic band pinching into the middle of her other thigh to lower it down over her knee.

With a whoosh and a plop, the little lacy panties fell to the floor, leaving Kyle eye level with the sweet, rounded mound of Hailey's pussy. Beneath the shadow, her pink, little lips had swollen and bloomed, giving him peeks of the delicate flesh hidden in her folds. It cried out to him, weeping slow streams of cream down the insides of her thighs as her voice quivered above him.

"Kyle?"

Slowly his eyes lifted, taking in the lush landscape he could call his own. His little princess bore the marks of his possession. The angry red streaks where he bruised her tender skin with his kisses and caresses made him want to growl, want to show all the world so everybody could know who her passion belonged to.

They would all see it as clearly as he did in the molten mocha of her gaze. Filled with want and need and thickened with love, that look belonged only to them, him and Cole. Nobody would ever see it, though, because it only shined out when they came over her to claim their princess's body.

Lowering his gaze back to where her bra clung to her breasts, Kyle reached up to snap the last clasp hiding any of her from him. With a pop, the feminine garment slipped back, revealing her swollen globes. Flushed with need, her breast ached so bad she strained forward, offering puckered tips to him. Kyle ignored the offering.

Instead he rolled his hand back down the trembling curves of her body until they hooked around her knees. In one smooth move, he lifted her into his arms even as he rose to his feet. Catching her gasp with his lips, he fed her the fiery passion of the lust boiling just beneath his calm surface. He got lost in the addictive flavor of her kiss and almost fouled up. Banging a knee into the mattress, he nearly dumped her onto the bed. He tried to cover the clumsy motion with an appearance of aggression by following her down.

It didn't matter how hard he pressed her into the sheets, she still managed a giggle. "Smooth move, sire."

He didn't retreat from her challenge but assured her with his narrowed gaze he intended to show her just how smooth he could be. It started as he broke the clasp of the hand wound around his neck. Catching one tiny wrist in his broad palm, he turned into the fingers that he pressed against his cheek.

They slid down, tenderly cupping his jaw even as he pressed a kiss into her palm. He tasted the differences between the callused pads at the base of her fingers and the still soft skin that ran down their length until they curled, trying to catch his kiss.

Instead, he melted the strength from her bones. Her arms went limp beneath the inspection of his lips as they explored the smooth glide down to her elbow. A scrape of his teeth over the delicate stretch of skin had her muscles stiffening, contracting. Her moan turned into a soft murmur as he loved on the small wound, making his apologies even as he turned her arm so that his cheek could scrape along the side of her breast and turn those gasps back into more heated, husky sounds of need.

Exaggerating the motion, his tongue dipped down to lap at her softness even as his stubble teased over her puckered nipple. Hailey's entire body responded with wanton welcoming as his kiss traced over the curved crease where her glorious breasts rose out of the solid plane of her rib cage.

As he nuzzled down, ignoring the feast rolling over his cheek, her fingers threaded back into his hair to try and drag his head up to where he knew she must ache. Just like she did lower, where her legs twined around him to hold him hostage as she rubbed the tantalizing heat of her pussy along his erection.

The denim in the way was the only thing that kept Kyle from taking up that invitation. Only his determination to force as much pleasure on Hailey as possible kept him from accepting the one her hands issued. Instead, he turned his cheek into the arm bent around the side of his head.

Capturing the new morsel in his hand, he ignored her cries and even curses as he began exploring the differences between her sweet limbs. The soft curve of muscles thickened a little more along this arm, and the pad of her palm was a little rougher, but her long, slender fingers still curled with the dainty sweetness of a woman in love as they molded around his cheek.

Pressing a final kiss onto her palm, his gaze caught hers. Open, swirling with dark, molten need, she watched him. In that second, he forgot all about the game, all about pressing her into saying what he needed to hear. Kyle didn't need that anymore because that look said it all.

Murmuring her name, he felt helpless as that gaze pulled him down into her kiss. Breathing in her very breath, he sank into the kiss with nothing but the warmth of tenderness in his heart. That emotion burned away almost the second her teeth opened up to capture his lower lip.

With a nip, his savage little princess pricked his own inner primate awake only to lure it to the surface as her tongue sank in to claim his mouth. Rallying to the battle, the kiss turned into a passionate mating of mouths that unleashed the lust wrapping around him as her body clung to his.

Kyle could feel the need in the hard, pebbled nipples rubbing into his chest. Her hips flexed and rolled against his in a sensual dance that he had little will to resist. Her moan faded into a smile that had his hand stilling at the edge of his shirt. Her hands still raced over his abdomen, pushing the cotton up until it rolled over her wrists.

Kyle helped her, tugging the shirt over his head to let it shrug down his arms and fall where it may. There came that little smile again as Hailey ogled him with wicked intent. An intent carried in the message of her fingers biting into his side as she tried to pull him back down.

Very nicely done, my princess.

Kyle kept that compliment to himself, letting his always-in-a-hurry love think she'd gotten the better of him. Giving in to the insistent demands of her hands, he lowered himself back down to take her lips in a kiss that promised all the fiery passion she craved. Rubbing that message into her breast, he massaged her tender tips with his chest, delighting in the way her lips broke from his to gasp.

"So...*good.*"

Kyle watched as her head rolled over the pillow, chanting that mew as she arched into the rough caress. He didn't even bother to chase down the hands that slid along his waistband to tug with clumsy impatience at his belt. No, Kyle let the little spitfire wind herself up tighter and tighter in the belief that her satisfaction lay almost at hand.

So lost in her own frenzy of need, Hailey paid him almost no attention as he stilled above her. Offering no help, he reached instead for the pillow hanging on the edge of the bed. Two tugs on the case and the pillow plopped out of it. Just in time.

Giving up on his stubborn belt, Hailey wiggled her fingers beneath the tight bind of denim to find the swollen head of his cock trying to push up past his jeans into her grip. One searing touch and Kyle's whole body contracted with the force of pleasure whipping out of his balls. The motions sucked in his stomach, and he almost didn't catch her hand in time as it dove into the gap.

"*No!*" Convulsing into rabid curses, she fought him as he dragged her hands away. The objections only drew louder as he made short work of leashing both wrists together with the taught cotton of the pillow case. One more knot and he had her bound to the bed frame.

"Damn it, Kyle! This was not part of the bargain."

Kyle smiled down at the indignant little princess spitting fire at him. Flushed, sweaty, naked, vulnerable, and best of all, so wet he could smell it. That's just the way Kyle would like to keep his savage princess, bound and in need.

He didn't waste a second on her curses. Diving into the feast of skin her ached neck provided, he greedily tasted his way down to her straining breasts. Her protests turned to mewed encouragements as he ravaged her tender peaks. Nibbling from one to the other, he dallied only long enough to make her beg for more before turning back to her abandoned breast.

By the time he brought his hands up to torment her swollen and puckered tits, she'd lost all control. Her head snapped wildly about as her thighs tried to crush his hips. Heated desire penetrated the thick denim of his jeans as her pussy ground over the bulge of his erection.

She stilled only when his hands slid down over her side, lifting her up and bringing that little pussy higher and higher, closer to his lips. All the while, his thumbs circled over her stomach, casting out over her mound until they rested on the edge of her swollen folds. Just an inch from his kiss, he held her still, knowing she waited for the delight of his mouth.

Instead, he pressed down with his thumbs, capturing her swollen clit with her own lips he rubbed over the tender bit of flesh, loving the way she cried out and bucked into the caress. Over and over, he ruthlessly toyed with her sensitive bud, using her own weeping folds to torment her.

"*Kyle, please!*"

He gave her almost what she wanted. Lowering his lips, he tasted all around the sweet flesh hidden within her puckered pussy lips. Never releasing her clit, he drove her cries into incoherent babbles as he traced over every smooth indentation and sexy dip without sipping from the very well of her desire.

Leaving her with just the thought, he explored the smooth, rounded curve of her inner thigh, trailing his kiss into the dip behind her knee. His hands followed, releasing her hips to float back down to the mattress as he discovered the graceful flow of her calf into her ankle.

Slowly, her denials quieted into ragged breaths as he watched her writhing peter out until she finally lay near still. Heaving with pants, she shifted slightly, lifting her gaze to his. His little princess. He could see the iron clad determination shinning out at him.

"You done playing, yet?"

Rubbing his cheek along the arch of her foot, he held the little treat still as he tasted the ticklish skin there. She groaned over the assault. Her leg bent as her ass slid down as far as her bound wrist would let her. The motion spread her creaming cunt wide, and Kyle stared at it until her voice prodded his gaze back up.

"Go on, cowboy, and have yourself a taste." Cocky and arrogant, she grinned back at him as she bent her other leg wide, splaying herself open for his feasting. She wouldn't be able to hold that smile for long. When he finished with her, she wouldn't be able to speak. She'd scream her voice that far away.

Releasing her foot, it thrilled him the way her smile flattened out as he leaned back over his wanton princess. Bringing his lips to rest nearly on hers, he growled out his only warning. "Every five minutes."

"Every five minutes, what?" Hailey whispered back, but her breath broke over free air because Kyle already started to slide down by the time she got that question out. Eyes locked, she didn't have to ask again as he slipped between her breasts to dip even lower. "*Oh, God. Kyle!*"

Chapter 32

Hailey tried. She really tried to hold Kyle's gaze as his breath washed over her pussy, but the intimacy of the moment had her lids lowering in protection. He growled his disapproval out over her mound, but she wasn't ready to give him this moment.

The fear of the tangled web she'd woven and the disaster screaming toward them reared their ugly heads in that moment. For as real as this moment might be, it wouldn't last. That sad thought sank into her heart as Kyle's kiss consumed her cunt.

The pain, the pleasure, both so extreme and exquisite, tore her apart. It didn't even take the five minutes he'd warned before her whole body convulsed with a rapture that wiped out any rational thought. Heaving with the strain of her long sought release, she didn't get a second to savor it as he relentlessly rushed her into a second.

Ecstasy trapped her body within its vise just as Kyle trapped her clit in the liquid pull of his lips. She couldn't escape, not his tongue, nor the pleasure. It whipped through her in hard sheets of rain that cracked with thunder then bolted with lightning as his fingers invaded her sheath.

Hailey lost all sense of the world or reality as she drowned under the avalanche of rapture. Again and again, Kyle drove her through one release and into another. Crushed under the weight of so much pleasure, it became agony to strain for the next release and the one after. Pain turned to anguish as the pleasure mounted, building toward an orgasm of epic proportions.

Sobbing with her need, she begged him with words that lost all meaning to her. All she knew of the world echoed through a body that had become so sensitive the very air against her skin felt like a caress. His tongue felt like a liquid flame as it danced over her weeping flesh.

Then, just when she felt sure she could take no more without being driven into complete insanity, he lifted. Solid, inflexible ridges ground over her until the scent of her own arousal breathed down into her face, and the bulbous head of his cock lodged against her clenching sheath. Like a flower lifting to the sun, she rose to his invasion, their sighs mingling as he pumped all the air straight out of her lungs with one smooth glide.

"I love you, Hailey Mathews."

A fresh bolt of terror had her eyes flying open to meet his as her one word response fell from her lips. "No."

Kyle didn't listen, didn't give her a chance to marshal her defenses. Burying his chin in her neck, he murmured on with the same easy rhythm he stroked into her with.

"Love you."

"Kyle, please."

She didn't need this, didn't want it. As desperate as her heart beat with the need to escape, her body melted beneath the slow seduction of his rolling hips. Instead of the ravaging that would have kept her safe, he loved her with the steady determination of a man intent on stealing her very soul.

The wicked glide of his cock along the tender walls of her sheath sparkled out mesmerizing tingles that thickened into dangerous bands of warmth as he sank back in, each time murmuring of his love. With each grinding return, he stoked her further and further into a winding storm that threatened to tear her to pieces.

Even as she began to sob with her pained pleasure, her legs clung to her tormentor, reveling in the very words that lashed her soul bloody. With each blunt statement, he drove himself into her, resisting all her attempts to rush him beyond loving into fucking.

"I'm going to love you forever, my princess. You. Only you because I'm ruined. Ruined, Hailey. I could never be like this with another. Never. But I could live here always. Always with you. Only you."

"Oh, God. Kyle, please stop."

"Love you."

"*Damn it!*"

"Love only you."

"You sneaky son of a bitch."

"Love me?"

"Yes." Hailey couldn't hold it back, couldn't take being suspended in this exquisite moment anymore. Her defenses worn, her reason obliterated, she gave into the truth even as she felt her soul begin to split wide around it. "You're just an evil bastard, but I can't help it. *Yes.*"

Her snarled answer turned into a scream as his hips picked up speed, revving into a relentless pounding that began to shear her soul free of her body. His low whispering soothed over the fear that always lingered in these moments as his cock tried to hammer Kyle's very soul into hers.

A husky murmur, it rippled through her mind, releasing the ties that kept her soul bound to his. Even as he sank into her body, she could feel her spirit sinking into his until they beat as one, repeating the same truth over and over even as the sharp claws of ecstasy started to rip through her.

"Love you."

* * * *

Oh, damn! Kyle carried that thought with him as he flopped over onto his back. Pulling free of Hailey's moist heat, he welcomed the chill from the night air as he sank into the mattress. The sheets felt sticky and warm, or maybe that was just his skin.

He lay there panting, feeling the pain of trying to get air into lungs that expanded too quickly with the racing of his heart. With no ability to form coherent thoughts, he just stared straight up at the ceiling until the crack above him came into focus.

It crept from under the molding, weaving a shadow of a curl all the way down the wall. A fresh fracture and Kyle knew who caused it. Lassoed to the frame, Hailey had pounded the old metal bars into the wall with the violent force of her release.

Apparently she left her mark in the near century-old plaster. The very idea of which made him grin as he rolled to his side. He won. Tonight the victory went to him because he'd ridden his little princess through the walls of her defenses into an honest admission. He put the screws to his little princess, and she buckled.

Just like he'd planned. God, he loved it when a plan came together. Feeling giddy, almost like he drank too much champagne, Kyle nuzzled her neck. "Hailey?"

"Don't talk to me, you bastard." Kyle laughed outright at that cranky response. His mirth earned him a look, not exactly the kind most women gave a man who had just loved them so well. "Kyle?"

"Huh?" He couldn't wait to hear what followed that impatient prompt, but he didn't get a smart answer. Instead he got a pointed look above her head to where the pillowcase still snarled around her hands. "Oh. Sorry, princess."

"Still as smooth as ever, *sire*."

"Still as tart as ever, *princess*," Kyle shot back without any of the heat that came from her scathing remark. Releasing her wrists from their binds, it didn't surprise him at all when she snatched her hands back and continued on grumbling.

"And that was not fair. In fact, it was against the rules and you know it."

Hailey and her rules meant nothing to him anymore. A lesson he preferred to demonstrate than explain. That pleasure would come soon enough. Rolling out of the bed, he offered her the easy dismissal instead of the truth.

"Well, seeing as this is the last porno-date night, it doesn't seem like there really is any consequence to breaking the rules."

"This wasn't supposed to be a porno-date night, Kyle," Hailey spat. "Maybe I made a mistake here."

"Oh, Hailey." Kyle shook his head with mock sadness. "That kind of challenge really should be issued fully clothed and legs closed. This way is just too easy."

Kyle proved again what a dumbass he could be when she snapped those legs closed with a growl and started pulling the sheet over her luscious, little body.

"Fine! Maybe I will sleep with you again, but next time I'll tie your ass up and see how well you take to being bound. What are you doing?" For all her spit and vinegar, Hailey still curled into his arms as he lifted her out of the bed.

"Well, I thought a shower might be in order."

"It is," Hailey snorted as she snuggled her head into his shoulder, still bitching. "Of course, just stepping into your bathroom leaves one with the feeling of need to bathe."

It continued on all through the shower. She complained about the lukewarm water, the trickle coming from their rusted shower head, the astringent smell of straight soap, how the towel felt like sandpaper, and how she was afraid she was going to get warts on the bottom of feet from just standing on the floor.

All the way back to the bed, she belabored every little thing in a ceaseless tirade. Kyle knew it hid her fear and worry. Like a miser who had just been robbed of her gold, Hailey knew he'd stolen her heart, and she wanted desperately to figure out how to get it back. He could almost see the thoughts swirling in her gaze as she glared at his bed—that offensive thing that had been her downfall.

"I am not sleeping on those sheets."

Kyle cocked a brow at that loud declaration. "Why not? You were willing to fuck on them."

That earned him a dirty look. "And that's why I'm not sleeping in them. They're icky."

"Well, what do you want me to do about them?" He knew. He just delighted too much in the flush of her cheeks and the crackle of green lightening in her gaze to not prod her temper along.

"Get. New. Sheets. Dumbass." She tacked on the last bit with a mutter and an eye roll.

"There. Are. No. Fresh. Ones. Smartass."

"You know I'm coming over tonight, you know what's going to happen. You'd think a smart guy like you could figure out to do the laundry." Adjusting the towel wrapped around her, she preened in only the way a pissed-off princess could. "This is just why I don't need a man mucking up my space."

"I love you, too, Hailey."

Her jaw clenched at that, and he could see real fire almost shoot through her face as she glared him down. He expected that to be the "set and match," but he forgot about the dark horse not in the room.

"Fine. I'll sleep in Cole's bed."

"Uh, Hailey?" Kyle snapped into motion but didn't beat her to bathroom door or through the other one. Heart racing with the sense of helplessness coming over him, Kyle watched as Hailey made herself comfortable in Cole's bed.

As comfortable as she could. He could see the stark pain in her gaze even as she tried to cover up her fury. "Don't look so worried, Kyle. I know Cole doesn't like sleeping with anybody, but I don't think that's going to be an issue tonight. On the off chance he actually finishes up his business, he can sleep in your bed, on the stained sheets for all I care."

"Yeah." Kyle didn't see that going over well with Cole, especially given that Cole's business had been instigated by Hailey herself. "I tell you what, princess, why don't we just swap the sheets?"

"Swap?" That idea intrigued Hailey enough to let him escort her back out of the bed. As if the question needed to be asked as he started to pull the sheets off, Hailey still seemed puzzled. "You're going to put your dirty sheets on Cole's bed?"

"Yep." Kyle even snatched up the pillows.

"Isn't that going to piss him off?"

With the bundle all wrapped in a ball and tucked under his arm, he paused to give her a curious look. "You care suddenly?"

"I just thought it was sort of the 'united we stand' kind of deal."

"It is," Kyle grunted. Before Hailey could question that, he pressed a quick, hard kiss into her lips and stormed off through the bathroom.

That let Hailey reach the wrong conclusion. It would only help Kyle out. Changing out the sheets, he considered just how smoothly everything had gone that night. Hailey jumped to the bait and assumed the worst of Cole. It made her as vulnerable as Kyle predicted, and he'd easily been able to swoop in under her defenses.

Now, though, Hailey didn't have the molten waves of lust ruling her mind or even the sharp spikes of betrayal distorting her thinking. The desperation to rebuild the fortress walls around her heart played out in her endless search for something else to complain about.

The time had come for him to level her with his best blow yet. Dumping the pile of dirty sheets on Cole's bed, he glanced around the abandoned room. Time had run out on him and Cole. They'd been good boys, appeasing all of Hailey's insecurities, and still it had come to this. So be it.

Braced with that determination, Kyle still got thrown off his intent when he stepped back into his bedroom. The overriding scent of his own cologne hit him before he even cleared back through the bathroom. Coming to a stop in the doorway, he stared in amazement as Hailey nearly emptied the bottle all over the sheets.

"What the hell are you doing?"

A dirty look over her shoulder, that's what he got for asking a reasonable question. He guessed she figured the answer should have been obvious because she didn't respond. Capping the bottle, she tried to storm back into the bathroom to return it to the counter.

Kyle held firm, refusing to let her pass. Another dirty look, but this time it was his turn to retort with just a raised brow.

"I'm getting rid of the stink. Okay?"

He let her shove past him with that, turning to watch. "Not clean enough?"

"No." This time she intentionally bumped into him, muttering as she pouted past. "They smell like Cole."

The small hint of sulking hurt made Kyle's heart clench. All the instincts he had to cherish and protect urged him forward, but Kyle spared himself the effort. Hailey wouldn't understand tenderness. The little hardhead would probably mistake it as sympathy, and she was crabby enough.

Crabby, but not terrified. Not yet, Kyle smirked to himself as he jerked open his sock drawer. It took him less than a second for him to find the old, black canister that had once held a roll of film, back from the time when people actually used film. He used it to store the one piece of jewelry he ever owned.

Given to him by his grandmother, he tucked the little gold chain and cross into the plastic holder over fifteen years ago. That's where they stayed until tonight when he finally popped the lid open. Offering up his apologies to God, he let the cross slide all the way down the chain to drop back into the plastic canister.

Tucking Jesus safely back under his socks, he carried the cross over to his nightstand, aware of Hailey's gaze tracking every motion. She tucked herself back in under the covers, and he knew as much as she bitched the last half hour, she waited for him.

His little princess didn't sleep well unless he held her. A truth she'd never admit to, but Kyle figured it out. He figured out quite a number of the secrets she didn't want revealed, like what she really feared.

"What are you doing?" Kyle cast her a quick smile as he settled onto the edge of the bed. Hailey didn't smile back. "You got me a necklace?"

"No." Kyle pulled open his nightstand drawer to extract the box he tucked in there earlier. "I picked this up from my mom this afternoon."

"What—" Her voice choked off at the snap of the jewelry box's lid opening. Kyle pulled the modest, but definitely sparkly, diamond ring free, knowing it held Hailey totally petrified by its significance.

"Kyle?"

Stringing the ring onto the chain, he turned to his princess. Shock, fear, and maybe even a little hope held her still as he latched the necklace around her throat.

"Now." Settling back he stared into the wide eyes gazing at him in confusion. "The question's been asked, Hailey. You take as long as you need, but there is only one answer. Only one answer I'm going to accept."

Chapter 33

"Okay, Cole." Riley pulled the glass out from under Cole's nose. "I have washed, stocked, and tucked every last bottle and glass all into their beds. I wash this, and I go home. You know what that means?"

Cole grinned. "I got to go home."

"No. You ain't got to go home. You can go any damn place. Go nowhere and just sleep it off in the lot outside for all I care. There is just one place you can't be."

"Right here."

"You got it."

"Yeah, yeah, yeah." Cole sighed as he turned on the bar stool. He got it all right, and finally for once, in time to save his ass. Sauntering toward the door, he considered whether he should bunk down in the bed of his truck and let Hailey assume he'd been dicking around all night.

It would serve the little spitfire right for playing this stupid game, but Cole had something else he wanted tonight. Tonight, tomorrow morning, he wanted to prove a point to her about love and fidelity.

"Oh, and Cole?" Pausing with his hand on the door, he gave Riley a look back over his shoulder. "You came in at midnight. I know, and if Hailey comes around asking, that's what I'm going to tell her."

Riley wouldn't be covering for Cole, but he hadn't asked him to. Nodding his head, he pushed on through the door. Riley was a good guy, but he wasn't a Cattleman, and his loyalty belonged first to those he called friend. Hailey fell into that category, like she did with a lot of the fine citizens of Pittsview.

That had always been his problem. He'd been fighting a lone war against a well-protected opponent. Those loyalties had shifted, though, and now Hailey had few allies left. Riley's truth wouldn't be able to stop the tide from crashing down on his princess.

Whistling as he spun his keys around his finger, Cole considered all the fun possibilities of how this game would end. He wanted his victory to be absolute, to be unprecedented and heralded in the legends of the Cattleman. Cole intended to make sure Hailey's memory lived on forever just by virtue of what he'd done to her.

Peppered with all sorts of perverse musings, the drive home gave him an erection. He'd been good at the bar, keeping his thoughts on the tactical. Now with every inch of asphalt that slipped past, the Mr. Man grew until he swelled to a full-length pant. For all his anticipation of getting home, Cole savored every moment. This is what it would be like for the rest of his life.

That was a victory Cole didn't waste time to savor when he pulled into the drive. Kicking open his door, his heart pounded with the thrill of battle. Inside that house awaited his savage princess. Kyle had it right with that endearment.

Savage, as in she'd probably rip him to shreds if he ever did cheat on her. Bad enough that tonight she probably thought he already had. It made him pause with his key in the lock to consider where he should go find a protective cup before daring to go in his own house.

Caution, not cowardice, had him opening the door slowly to peek in and ensure that he could enter without damage to his person. Nothing greeted him but the clink of weights being lifted and the muted murmur of music coming down the hall. Kyle was working out, which meant Hailey had to be passed out.

Either that or she left, Cole thought as he chunked his keys onto the console table and sauntered off to find out how Kyle had done that night. Snatching the milk from the fridge, he went to face the music.

It was AC/DC, set low, no doubt, to keep from disturbing the little princess. It left more than enough stillness in the air for Kyle to have heard him come in, but he didn't even look Cole's way when he sauntered into the room.

"Aren't you supposed to bench press with a spotter?" Clicking off the stereo, Cole turned his grin on Kyle.

"Better to have no spotter than an unreliable one." Straightening up, Kyle wiped the sweat from his face before dropping the hand towel back over his thigh.

"Mighty big words from the man working off his extra energy. What happened, Kyle? Couldn't get the precious to give you the three little words you were after?"

Rising from the bench seat like a king from his throne, Kyle held his arms up in a dramatic splay of victory. "Who's the king?"

"Oh, really?" Cole couldn't help but laugh at the spectacle Kyle put on with that big grin. "So she coughed it up, huh? And how many orgasms did it take to wring that admission out of the princess?"

"Not even one." Kyle's hands folded down to let his hands rest on his hips as he gloated over that victory. "And that makes me the king. I got our princess, who is irrationally afraid of commitment, to say 'love you.'"

Cole admitted it. He was impressed, but he kept the celebration to himself lest Kyle's head swell up enough to float off the floor. Instead, he snickered and cast Kyle a look of disappointment. "Love you? That's the best you could come up with?"

"The best?"

"Where's the 'I?'"

"Screw you, Cole," Kyle snorted out over Cole's laughter. "I'd like to see you do better."

"And you will. Tomorrow. At lunch." That's when Cole's turn came to deliver the killing blow before they crashed Hailey's game down around her head.

"Yeah." Kyle's grin gave away to a scowl. Cole could guess where that lead just as easily as he could guess why Kyle had chosen weights over cuddling with the princess.

"Don't start feeling guilty now, man." Cole straightened off the wall with that stiff bit of advice.

"You weren't here." Kyle slouched back down onto his seat. "She got that call, and I could see it in her eyes. We broke her heart, Cole, and we just got started."

This time Cole gave the drawn-out sigh. "This was your plan, man."

"I know and if we confront her with the truth, all it would do is embarrass her a little, and it certainly wouldn't make her any more inclined to giving in to the obvious. In the long run, her insecurities and trust issues will just result in another game."

"Not another, man." Cole couldn't take another round. "I can live through this one, but I'm kind of looking forward to getting beyond it."

"Bullshit," Kyle snorted out over a chuckle. "You're looking forward to getting to relish the end game."

"Well, yeah, but, believe it or not, Kyle, I'm more looking forward to the after. Actually, I was thinking about that tonight at Riley's. By the way, he's not covering for us."

"It doesn't matter. I think the call Hailey got did the damage. Right now, I don't think she cares about the details." The guilt obviously weighed on Kyle's shoulders, even as he tried to shrug it off. "You'll be lucky to get to first base."

"Luck doesn't have anything to do with it, my friend. It's called skill and inevitability, which brings me to the point I was making. We should be thinking about the after."

"The after?"

"Yes, the after. We need to be negotiating the details now before we just run into them and Hailey takes the advantage."

"Details? What details?"

"Okay. I'm just putting this out there." Cole gestured to the entire room with his milk carton. "I ain't changing no poopy diapers."

"What?" Kyle gasped either from shock or indignation. Cole couldn't tell which.

"I'll mow the yard, do gutters, anything, but when it comes to biological waste, count me out."

"You are seriously shitting me, right?"

"No, my friend." Cole slid onto the bench seat of the Bowflex across from where Kyle sat. "Think about it. We both know Hailey is going to make one of us wipe ass, and I'm just saying we should start negotiating now."

"Negotiating now over our children." Kyle couldn't keep the grin off his face. "That doesn't seem, perhaps, a little premature?"

"It's only nine months."

"Nine months?"

"And you got to figure between the two of us, we'll keep the princess pretty rounded for the next ten years."

"Ten years?" No doubt. This time Kyle's jaw unhinged. "How many fricken kids are you talking about here?"

"Well, I figured at least six."

"Six? At least? What are you? Breeding an army?" Kyle shook his head in disgust, giving Cole that look he knew only too well. "I am not having six kids, Cole."

"Well, point of fact, you ain't having any. Hailey's going to have them." Cole tacked the last bit on as he took another swig of milk.

"Oh, yeah. I'd like to see you sell this load to her."

"Don't you worry about that." Cole wiped the mustache he could feel on his lips away with his wrist. "I'll be taking that issue up with the princess tomorrow."

"Oh, I see. You're going to perform some kind of miracle, is that it? You're going to confess to an infidelity, then sweet talk her into saying she loves your sorry ass and agree to have six of your kids."

"Our kids."

"You're delusional."

Cole ignored Kyle's smirk to offer a very reasonable retort. "Actually, I figure five will be mine and one will be yours."

"Excuse me?"

"Well," Cole stood, "I am the king."

That seemed like a great exit line, and he really would rather be messing with Hailey than messing with Kyle. Kyle wouldn't let it go, though, and Cole couldn't let him have the last word.

"Okay, smartass, where we going to put all these kids?"

"Oh, about that." Cole turned in the doorway. "I was looking at the real estate section of the paper, and the old Gravey place is up for sale."

"That thing's a rotted piece of shit."

"It's got nine bedrooms."

"Its plumbing dates from the civil war."

"And more than enough land for a shop."

"You could fall through the floor just stepping on the porch."

"They're only asking three hundred for it."

"Thousand?"

"You know, Kyle, you take the fun out of everything," Cole snapped before storming off. Sure, the Gravey place was a pit, but it had potential.

Sitting on the hill with the sweeping porches looking out over the grassy slopes—that was the place to raise a family.

Despite Kyle's predictably rational reaction, Cole knew Hailey would love it. He would fix it up any way she wanted, and it would be perfect. With nine bedrooms, they could have eight kids. Eight kids. That would be one hell of a Thanksgiving dinner.

He could already hear the thunder of conversation and imagine the long stretch of table, piled high with food while the kids elbowed each other and complained. With eight kids, he could end up with eighteen grandkids. They'd need two Christmas trees, if not three, to fit all the gifts.

What other house would accommodate three Christmas trees but the Gravey place? No place that Cole knew, and he'd sell that case to Hailey before Kyle poisoned her mind with a bunch of details. Turning into his room, he considered the issue settled.

If Kyle didn't want to do the sane thing and work out the agreements ahead of time, then Cole would just make the deal with Hailey. Given how much Hailey liked to deal, he figured she'd jump at the bait. Once he got her to agree to having the kids.

Cole considered how hard that might be as he ignored the obvious ball of sheets making a statement on the middle of his bed to saunter into the bathroom. He'd need to wash the stink of Kitty's perfume off along with the stench of smoke from the bar before he could crawl into Hailey's bed.

The pathetically short supply of hot water told him how many showers Kyle had already taken, which let him conclude how worn out their princess probably was. Too bad about that. The Mr. Man definitely didn't want to have to wait till morning for his treat.

He would, though, Cole decided as he padded into Kyle's room. The sight of Hailey passed out in the carnage of bedding brought a smile to Cole's lips. In sleep, at least, Hailey looked sweet and innocent, completely incapable of conspiring to publicly ridicule him.

His little savage. Cole understood why she did it. He could even understand why she worried. He didn't have the best track record when it came to women. That didn't mean he couldn't be trusted. With all the women who had come before, he only ever promised his loyalty to Serena, and he kept it.

Hailey just needed to learn to trust him. She could do it. The way she snuggled back into his warmth as he settled into bed spoke volumes of how much she already trusted him. That was her heart. When she woke up, the cynical little part of her mind would start to sow new fears and worries. Cole had the cure for that—one night, his way.

Wrapping an arm around her, his hand went in search of hers only to find it fisted beneath her chin. Peeling back her fingers exposed the ring she'd been clinging to. Cole smirked at the sight. He'd have loved to see her reaction to that gift.

Threading his fingers through hers to curl her fist in his, Cole let the scent of cinnamon lure his cheek into the soft tresses dampening the pillow. This is how a man should go to sleep, with his little woman tucked into her place. He'd been an absolute fool to pass it up until now.

A fool, Cole finally figured that out along with the best weapon to bring Hailey down. Up until now he'd been working just as hard at keeping his distance, and that had given her all the room to retreat. It also gave him the advantage of knowing all her defenses intimately because they had been his own.

Cole intended to use that knowledge tomorrow to perform a small miracle. Yawning, he burrowed his cheek deeper into her pillow and drifted off, dreaming of just how glorious tomorrow would be.

Chapter 34

Thursday, May 29ᵗʰ

Hailey woke to a world of pleasure and confusion. The sultry seduction of Cole's kisses working over her breasts made it almost impossible for her to latch on to a rational thought. Only the intimate knowledge of a lover gave her the certainty that Cole, not Kyle, forged a thick, hairy thigh between hers.

Lost in the haze of pleasure, she moaned her appreciation for his slow invasion, grateful for the quick ease to the ache burning up her womb. Arching her back, she dragged her thigh up toward his hip, pressing down on another two delicious inches.

A hand latched on to her thigh, jerking her down his entire length as Cole growled into her ear. "Like that, little one?"

"Oh, yeah." Hailey surely did. Especially when a second set of hands settled over her sides to swoop in and cup her breasts. The slow heat of a lover's kiss began to massage all the strength from her neck. Kyle.

He made love to her with all the gentle tenderness he'd shown last night while Cole fucked her with the smooth, steady rhythm that provided no real ease but instead inflamed the fires licking over her sheath until she felt ablaze. Like skilled craftsmen, they worked her body up to the very edge of ecstasy's pinnacle and then kept her bound there.

Even though it was Cole's hands holding her hips steady, she begged Kyle for release, knowing he broke easier. For a second, she sensed victory when Kyle's hands dropped to push Cole's out of the way. Lifting her off his partner, he barely left her feeling empty for a second before Kyle's thick width began pressing into her spasming pussy.

Not near as long as Cole, but damn close to being twice as meaty, she loved the feel of Kyle sinking into her body. Her leg sank as she tried to close herself around every scrumptious inch, but Cole's hand snagged her by the knee, jerking her back up along his length.

Even as Kyle began to twist her world into a new knot with his easy strokes, Cole began to grind his erection over her clit. Kyle riding her from behind, Cole teasing her from the front, they offered her no reprieve from their sensual torment. They drove the wild desperation for release higher and higher until they turned her into a thing of naked need.

Clawing, twisting, begging, doing anything she could to share her disease, Hailey tried everything she knew to break them of their slow determination. It didn't work. Nothing worked as they passed her back and forth, sharing her body even as they shared the role of her tormentor.

When Cole lifted her off Kyle to slide her back down over heated cock, his mouth lifted, leaving her breasts to Kyle's returning touch. Five, ten, fifteen strokes later, Kyle's turn came again as Cole passed her back. Trapped between them, there was nothing Hailey could do but writhe and whimper as her body welcomed either man with the same pulsing need.

She lost count of the number of times they shared her, lost the ability to tell one from another as her world merged into a single streaming tide of pleasure. Made of pure, molten lava, the rippling waves melted her bones and muscles even as they flooded down toward her heart and soul.

Those wounded things, they felt the pain of betrayal even if her mind couldn't fathom the reasons. The rapture wrapping around her heart only made the ache within seem more poignant, more painful. It wouldn't stop, and, as the vise tightened even further with their sweet loving, the despair began to roll out from under her lids.

"Oh, no, princess, don't cry." Cole's lips brushed over her cheeks, catching her tears even as his murmured words scratched fresh wounds onto her soul.

Digging her nails into his shoulder, she tried to drown out his compassion with the gasping mews of her own wanton desires. Hailey didn't want this tender loving, didn't want to sink beyond skin deep into either of her lovers.

"Fuck me." That's all she wanted from him.

"Hailey?" The confusion in Cole's voice had her blinking open her gaze to glare at him. The concern she could see in his features only made her ache even worse. The pain rallied an anger she didn't understand or bother to question. Instead she just unleashed on him.

"Save your charm for a woman who cares, Cole. I just want the fucking."

In an instant, the lines of worry deepened to a hardened scowl across his face, echoing the sudden bite of his fingers into the fleshy sides of her ass. Even as he growled out his warning, he matched the threat by slowly spreading her open to the swollen cock head burrowing into her from behind.

"You're going to pay for that one, princess."

"I don't care." Moaning out that honest response, her back arched as her hands lifted toward the metal rails of Kyle's bed frame. She needed that cool, solid anchor in a world that shifted constantly around her. Cole's chest flattened her breasts, the rough hairs of his thighs scraped against her, and all the while Kyle's invasion ground her against the long, hardened pole of Cole's cock filling her ass. With every single breath she felt them all around her and in her.

Hailey's eyes rolled back as Kyle seated his full length deep into her pussy, leaving not even a breath of motion that didn't cause her two channels to spasm and pulse with a ridiculous amount of pleasure. Racing up from her nether lands to explode across her mind and blow her brain to complete smithereens, the rapture shredded the last of her decency.

Physical pleasure overwhelmed any emotional resistance she had as the men sandwiching her started to grunt and shift as they began to hammer her with pounding blasts of ecstasy. There wasn't enough room for both of them, not at this angle. They went in and out in opposite strokes that never even gave her a second of relief from the release building faster and harder with each delicious glide.

Panting, mewing, Hailey clung to the headboard as her hips popped and pulled, driving her lovers into a full gallop. As the thundering pound of their merciless loving rolled over her spine, Hailey screamed and pumped her hips even harder, desperate to milk every single drop of ecstasy from this moment.

Then, just like that, both men forged straight into her, hard and ruthless as they stretched her to the very extreme. Her world shattered around her, leaving her body limp and lifeless for the whirling hails of rapture buff her about. In the mist of the chaos, Hailey could feel her lovers' releases flooding into her body.

In a slow creep downward, her orgasm unwound around her, leaving her a heaving, sweaty mess still stuck between Cole and Kyle. Cole, that slimy little bastard. She hadn't intended to let him touch her ever again, not after what he'd done last night.

Not that he left her any choice. She didn't even have one now, pinned as she was between them. It felt almost intolerable to her bruised heart, and she tried as much as she could to retreat. Those few inches gave her no room at all. Thankfully, Cole withdrew.

Unfortunately, he did it with a great deal of glee as he rolled from the bed to bound up onto his feet with way too much energy. "Now that's the way to start the morning, but you made me late for my parts run. I'll see you at lunch, princess."

With that and a quick kiss on her cheek, he whistled away as if everything was just fine. Maybe for him. Hailey glared at his backside. For her, this morning was a horrible revelation of just how out of hand things had gotten.

This was supposed to have been the easy part. The part where she triumphed and proved once and for all Cole didn't have a heart in his cold body. Well, she might have been right about the heart, but her victory turned into a bloodletting of her own soul.

She told Patton she couldn't love a man who betrayed her because how could she love a man she didn't trust? Hailey didn't understand how, but that hadn't stopped her from falling victim to it. As she stared at the door that closed behind Cole, she faced the horrible truth that she'd fallen in love with the bastard, fallen for him despite him being a bastard.

"Hailey?" Kyle's arms tightened around her even as he shifted free of her body. Turning his hold from passionate to caring, he snuggled her into his warmth, and Hailey was grateful for the shelter.

"Is everything all right?"

She couldn't tell him because she wasn't even supposed to know anything. Even if she could have complained to Kyle about Cole, Hailey wouldn't have. She didn't want to ruin this moment, for it seemed like it would soon fade completely away. In one day, this day, everything would change.

"Hailey?"

"I'm just tired, Kyle." Hailey gave the easiest lie she knew.

"Hmm," satisfaction sounded in his growl as he nuzzled his cheek into her hair, "I guess I can understand that, but I got the cure."

Hailey couldn't help but smile at that suggestive assurance. "I don't think that helps, Kyle."

"I was talking about a hot shower with a cup of black coffee and big breakfast waiting for you when you're done."

"Mmm, keep talking."

"How about I get some clothes on, and we get cleaned up enough to go back to your house and take a nice, long shower together. Between me and those steam jets, you'll be so relaxed that I'll have to carry you back to the bed."

"Mmm." Hailey rubbed her backside into the cock she could feel rallying to the game again. "Then what you going to do?"

"I'm going to give you a massage."

"A massage?"

"A full body rub down," Kyle growled. His hands spread wide and dipped down to her sides to begin working some of that magic into her tired and sore muscles. "I'm talking hands and mouth."

As his fingers began to work the tiredness from her lower back, his lips came to melt the muscles in her neck, making her go all limp and soft in his arms.

"Then, when you get to all moaning and begging, I'll take care of the rest of your urges." Kyle couldn't hold his chuckle back, and he forgot his smooth moves to give her a big hug. "How's that sound, princess?"

"Like it didn't include any coffee or food," Hailey retorted, breaking into laughter when his arms pressed down tight over her stomach and yanked her into the nibbling bites he growled over her shoulder.

"I said I'd take care of all your urges." Releasing her, he rolled off the bed. "Now, come on and let's get cleaned up so we can go shower."

Hailey didn't argue with him, didn't even fight the good cheer he smothered her in as they washed off quickly in the shower. She didn't want to fight it because when the sun rose tomorrow, Kyle would be wanting his ring back. Once he knew what she'd done to his best friend, Hailey knew he'd side with Cole.

Kyle made that quite clear twice. When he told her he wouldn't hold Cole back a second time after she called him a whore, and then last night when he said they stood united, she'd gotten both messages clearly. If this was to be their end, then she wanted it to be an end worth remembering because she would anyway.

* * * *

Kyle played along with the plan. Cole had a lot of errands to take care of that morning before he could get to his lunchtime surprise for Hailey. Instead of taking her to work and giving her the space to shore up any kind of mad, Kyle took Hailey back to her place and then back to bed.

Keeping her naked and satisfied also kept her from having the energy to worry or scheme. Not that Hailey gave him any resistance. She seemed all too willing and eager to waste away the entire morning in bed with him, especially given she didn't have to bathe at his place.

Kyle admitted it. Hailey's house had the nicer shower, the bigger rooms, the better maintained kitchen. It would be a perfect place to live, and it had two extra bedrooms for the two children they'd be having. Cole could just take the Gravey place and shove it up his ass because Kyle knew how that'd end up.

Sure, Cole's plans would be amazing and glorious, but to be completed it would be Kyle slaving over the hammer. He knew that story, and Kyle didn't have any interest in sweating out his days off at the Gravey house when he could be sweating them out in bed with Hailey.

"Well, that's an awfully big scowl. Feeling guilty?" Hailey murmured, nuzzling her head into his shoulder.

At the small motion, Kyle's arm contracted reflexively around her back, pulling her in closer. "Guilty? What do I have to feel guilty over?"

"Skipping out on work." Hailey made a show of lifting her head to glance at the clock. "I know you had Buck's Pinto on the rack, and I thought that had to go out this morning."

"Buck can wait till this afternoon," Kyle retorted with a yawn and a stretch to show how little he cared.

Hailey snorted at that and rolled away, taking the sheets with her. "That's an excellent customer service attitude. You put that on a business card?"

"Hailey, it's a Pinto."

"You're such a car snob, Kyle." So decreed the princess all wrapped up in toga sheets. "I'm going to take a shower, and you can go make lunch."

"Oh, I can?" Kyle smirked, not at all ashamed to be laying there butt-ass naked as she lectured him.

"Yes. It will make up for the breakfast you failed to produce."

Kyle let her think she got the last word as she sauntered off, but when he finally rolled to a sit, he had no intention of getting her lunch together. She locked him out of the bathroom, a clear sign that she needed food, not sex. As grumpy as she got when hungry, he really hadn't done Cole any favors by not feeding her.

Then again, Cole was the king. Kyle smirked at that thought, heading off for the second bathroom and a quick shower. He really couldn't wait to see this show. Whatever Cole planned it better be good because Kyle knew a thing about pissed off women.

He might have drained some of the vinegar out of Hailey's mood, but sex could only go so far. Not that Cole worried. Kyle could hear him moving about in the kitchen as he came out of the second bathroom. His friend's sheer excitement at being in the crosshairs of chaos showed on the grin he greeted Kyle with.

Casting a glare back at Cole's confidence, Kyle grunted. "How long you been here?"

"Just got in." Leaning back slightly against the counter, Cole let him pass to the refrigerator. "She in the shower?"

"Yep." Hailey didn't tend to keep a whole lot of milk on hand, so Kyle went for the orange juice. "And I didn't feed her so she's kind of crabby."

"Thanks, man," Cole snatched the orange juice out of Kyle's hands before he could tilt it over the cup he pulled off the drying rack by the sink. Just like that Cole tipped it back and took a swig from the damn carton before passing it back with a belch.

"You're disgusting." Kyle snatched the carton back. "And Hailey will have your ass if she sees you doing that again."

"That's why I even brought along glasses for our picnic." Cole smirked. "I'm going to show her how reformed I am."

"I thought you said you weren't going to lie to her."

"And I ain't. I'm not going to promise her to use glasses, I'm just going to show her I'm capable of hearing, understanding, and responding to any issues or concerns she might have about our relationship." Cole's chin went up in an almost scholarly gesture as he laid out that crap.

"Where did you read that?" Kyle asked as he overturned the orange juice in the sink. He just couldn't do it, just couldn't drink it or put it back in the fridge for Hailey to drink later. He had to kiss that woman. "In some *Reader's Digest* when you were waiting in line?"

"Actually I heard it on some talk radio show on the drive over here." Cole shared Kyle's laugh before sobering up to give him a concerned look. "You know, man, there are a lot of weird people in this world."

"Yeah." Kyle nodded. "Hailey being one and you being another."

"Are you saying you're not a little screwy, too?"

Kyle didn't dignify that with an answer. "Are you saying you aren't?"

"I'm not the one pouring a whole container of OJ down the drain," Cole snapped back with that look.

"Yes. Why are you pouring my orange juice down the drain?"

That sharp question had them both starting as Hailey came full force into the room with a scowl. Far from looking like the well-loved woman she was, the little princess looked ready to do battle. Unfortunately, her dark gaze narrowed in on him.

"You know how expensive that stuff is? You owe me three bucks, Kyle."

"Cole owes it to you." Not about to go down for this crime, Kyle willingly threw Cole into the garbage along with the container. "He drank straight out of it."

"That's disgusting." Hailey turned her sharp retort on Cole. "And I'm sick and tired of asking you not to do that, so you know what, Cole? I'm going to roll up a nice, thick section of the paper and duct tape into a good whack-stick. Then, whenever I see you misbehaving in my house, I'm just going to hit ya on the nose like a dog."

Cole blinked that in before turning to give Kyle an annoyed look. "Yeah, she is crabby."

"Told you."

"And you'd think with all that loving." Cole shook his head. "That's why you're not the king."

"Oh, don't even start with that shit," Hailey spat. "Unless you want to start explaining where my lunch is because I don't see any sandwich."

"Lunch?" Cole puffed up. "I got that covered."

"You?" Hailey finally turned her glare in Cole's direction. "I'm not eating with you. I'm mad at you."

Kyle envied Cole's ability to actually pull off looking insulted. "Mad at me? What did I do?"

Hailey went still. The kind of still that warned a violent eruption was coming. "Why don't we start with where you were last night?"

"Worried?" Cole grinned down at her, and Kyle wondered if he really did want to lose a nipple.

Hailey showed restraint, though just barely. Eyes narrowed, tone tight, arms battened down over her chest, she looked like a grenade missing its pin. "Given our deal, I do have a vested interest in knowing just what you were up to last night."

Cole took that just as seriously as he had her question. He snorted out a dismissal. "You need not worry, little princess, I was just working on a car deal last night."

"Yeah, right."

"Yeah, right," Cole mimicked back with a smirk. "You just keep on being a smart ass, Hailey, and your tab will get longer and longer."

"I don't know what the hell that means," Hailey snapped, finally breaking into motion. Instead of going for Cole, she went for the refrigerator. "But you ain't welcome to any of my sandwiches today."

Kyle didn't know if Hailey understood the hidden challenge within her bold one, but Cole did. Their gazes met, and he could see the laughter Cole struggled to hold back. The bastard was having himself a grand time.

"I wouldn't even think of it, princess."

A grand time. Kyle shook his head as Cole stepped up behind Hailey. Before she could even straighten up, he had an arm hooked around her stomach, and just like that, he hefted her off her feet. All shrill squeaks and squeals, Hailey fought him as Cole worked to get her over his shoulder.

Stronger, bigger, even perhaps a little more determined, Cole won the spontaneous battle. Dumping Hailey over his shoulder, he ignored her cusses and threats to throw a quick smile at Kyle.

"I'll catch up with you later, man."

Chapter 35

"*Ow!*" Cole grunted.

Hailey took great delight in that howl of pain, even if it didn't liberate her from her humiliating position. There were times when Cole's superior strength was sexy and exciting. Then there were times when she wished she could do the Incredible Hulk morph and beat his sorry ass into the pavement. Right now all she had were the fingers to pinch his ass as hard as she could.

"*OW!*" That one bought her some freedom, about as much room as the truck cab Cole stuffed her into with an insulted grunt. "You got some crab in your blood, woman?"

Hailey ignored that to try and kick him backward out of the door so she could escape. "Screw off, Cole, and let me go."

"Ah, come on, princess." Cole pressed in between her flailing legs to rest his chest on the edge of the seat and trap her. He had a knack for pinning her into tight corners. Like right now. She didn't want to have anything to do with him.

Actually, that wasn't true. She wanted to rip him from stem to stern, but she couldn't. She didn't know what she knew, and she wouldn't be allowed to know it until tomorrow. That just added to her frustration and fueled her anger as she tried to shove him backward.

"Back off, Cole."

"But I got a special lunch planned for you, princess."

Flowers for the wife after he finished porking his mistress, Hailey knew his story. Not that she'd ever been a wife or a mistress, but men learned this game well before matrimony. They perfected it on girlfriends.

Of course, none of those times ever hurt like this. "I don't want to eat your stupid lunch. I got work to do."

"You wasted all morning in the sheets with Kyle, and now you won't waste an hour to eat with me? That hardly seems fair." He actually managed to sound not only insulted but hurt. As if he had any right to either of those emotions.

"Get out of my way, Cole."

Giving over his puppy dog look, he straightened up to give her a much more considering one. Hailey didn't like it. She stiffened beneath his look, holding herself still and straight as he measured her.

"You know, you seem really pissed at me today." Cole finally found a serious tone.

The scowl she wore to mask her pain didn't crack at the tiny taunt. Instead, she held firm, not allowing any of the emotions boiling beneath the surface to peek through as she growled back. "I am."

"Just because I missed last night?" Cole cocked a brow at that. "I'm sorry, Hailey, but it was business, and I honestly didn't take you for a clinger."

"I'm not a clinger, you ass," Hailey snapped, not at all liking that accusation. "And I'm not an idiot. There is only one business that keeps a man out of his house till past midnight."

"Is that so?"

"Yes."

"So despite the fact that I'm telling you nothing happened last night but me working toward getting a car, you're accusing me of cheating, right? That's what you think happened, but you don't have any proof beyond the whisperings of that suspicious little mind of yours. Right?"

"I don't need proof to know a dog when I meet one. I just need my eyes, Cole."

"I was working on a deal for a car, Hailey."

"Then where is the car, Cole?"

"I'm getting it tomorrow morning."

She bet he was. Tomorrow morning, after he went to sleep with Kitty tonight. It didn't matter anymore that Kitty wouldn't actually touch Cole. The fact was Cole would be willing to sleep with another woman for a fricken car. That's all she needed to know.

But she wasn't supposed to know any of it. Not yet.

"So, who are you getting this car from?"

That made the smug bastard smirk, and she knew why the second he answered. "A woman."

"So then you were with a woman last night."

"Well, I didn't say I wasn't."

That did it. If she had a gun, he'd have been dead. She'd have shot him right there in her driveway, and all she would have done is stepped over the body. "Get the hell out of my way, Cole."

"Now see, there you go with that dirty little mind of yours again." Cole caught her legs in his hands as they kicked back out at him. It really annoyed her the way he could just force them into the truck, making her ass spin to face forward. "I get you have concerns, and there are things we need to talk about. That's exactly what we're going to do over lunch."

With that proclamation, he slammed the door on her. It would have served him right if she'd thrown it back open in his face, but Hailey didn't because the bastard had it right. All she could have now are suspicions. Tomorrow, she could have her accusations.

Until then, she had to play along at some level with Cole's charade. Besides, a sick, demented part of her wanted to hear Cole's lies. They would help harden her heart and remind her of who he really was so that in the nights to come she could remember. Hopefully, that would break her love for him and this pain she carried.

"I hate you." It popped out of her the second the driver door opened.

Not bothering to look in his direction to see how he took the insult, she still sensed his pause before he slid up onto his seat. "That's going on the tab."

"What the hell is this damn tab?" Hailey roared, finally provoked into turning on him.

"You'll find out."

"I swear to God, Cole—" Kyle knocking on her window cut her off and Hailey let the rest go, having giving him enough of a threat. Wrenching down the window handle, Hailey didn't spare Kyle her bad mood. "What?"

He dangled her keys in front of her nose. "I locked up your house."

Thrown off by the considerate gesture, Hailey managed a begrudging "Thanks" as she accepted the keys.

"Yeah." Kyle's head dipped to the side as he cast his gaze over at his partner. "I'll see you later?"

"Yep. You coming with me tonight, right?"

"What?" That had Hailey's head snapping toward Cole to wrench back on Kyle in absolute shock. "Where are you two going tonight?"

"I'll explain it over lunch."

Like Hailey trusted Cole, but she had trusted Kyle. Glancing at him, she sought some reassurance. "Kyle?"

"Don't look so worried, Hailey." Kyle gave her a warm smile that until that moment had always made her melt. "It's just one night, and Cole needs some help on this car deal."

Reaching in, he brushed a quick kiss across her numb lips. "See you later, princess."

* * * *

In the face of the obvious gloom radiating from the other side of the bench seat, Cole clicked on the radio. Feeling more than good enough to sing along, he left Hailey to brood all on her own. For as much as she might think he should feel loaded down with guilt, Cole actually felt kind of high on jubilation.

Hailey's dark mood fed Cole's good cheer. His little princess was jealous, angry, and hurt—the holy trinity of a woman betrayed—but she couldn't be that unless she cared. Cared about him, Cole Jackson.

Not even the fact that it required such extreme measures to get such a small response from Hailey upset Cole. She'd set the ball into motion. He had a right to defend himself and see after his own interests. That's just what Cole intended to do as he cut the truck off the main road and down a long, bumpy dirt track.

It impressed him when she didn't even voice a complaint but clung on to the door as they pounded through the deep ruts in the road. Around the first curve, it evened out and the tall walls of pine thinned into a vast rolling plain that rolled out from the large, stately porch of the Gravey house.

Pulling to a stop beneath the branched canopy of an oak, Cole tossed Hailey a smile as he bounded out of the truck. Ten steps and he bounded up onto the porch to swing around and survey the quiet stillness of the countryside with a full grin.

"What do you think, Hailey?"

She met his happiness with a scowl, lumbering down from the truck with little enthusiasm. "What do I think about what?"

"About this place," Cole gestured to the house behind him, "isn't this great? It's—"

"It's the old Gravey place, I know." Hailey came to a stop at the bottom of the steps to glare up at him. "I know everything about this house, Cole, including the fact that you're tempting fate standing there 'cause you're likely to fall through."

"Well, since you know so much about this place, how come you didn't know we were going to buy it?" Cole paused at the bottom of the steps to finish off that question before pushing on past her. He made it to the bed of the truck before Hailey caved and came trailing up behind him.

"You're going to buy this place?"

"Yes, ma'am."

Cole lugged the cooler he brought to the edge of the bed and then over the gate. Piling the picnic basket on top, he pulled out the store bag he tucked the blanket into.

"Why?"

"Why what?" Cole retorted, going with confusion as a way to pull her deeper into the conversation. Pulling the cooler with the basket balanced on top of it into the bright sun, he again left her to follow.

"Why would you buy this house, Cole? It's a dump."

"It is not." Dropping the cooler's handle, he straightened up indignantly. "This is a great house."

"It's plumbing dates from the early nineteen hundreds, and it isn't even wired for electricity," Hailey shot back. "Not to mention the condition—"

"You haven't got any imagination." Cole shook his head. "This house is perfect. Look at this yard. You could have a shop, a pool, a barbeque and still have room for soccer games and throwing balls. And this house isn't just old, it's a piece of history. It's got that charm, that grace, that—"

"Mildew and rot."

"Fine." Cole let it go. "I can see you need food first."

Turning back to spreading out the blanket, he ignored Hailey's glower until she finally muttered something to herself. "At least it's not pink."

"What's not pink?" Cole paused over smoothing the final edge of the blanket out to cast her a confused look.

"The blanket. Kyle runs around with a pink one." Hailey's nose wrinkled as she scanned over the comforter he spread out on the grass. "That just looks dirty and old."

Cole looked down at the blanket in his hands before patting the edge out perfectly. "It's a quilt, and my grandmother made it like eighty years ago, so you'll have to forgive the stains."

"Oh." He could hear the pause in her voice and knew she hated him for that response. Now she felt guilty, and it showed in her snap. "Well, if it's so precious why you going to eat on it?"

"Because," he toed his boots off before settling onto the blanket, "this is a special lunch."

Hailey eyed the way he gestured to join him. "I just came for the food."

"And I have a lot to offer."

That got her feet shifting as she nudged off her own shoes. Ignoring his hand, she settled down onto the far of edge of the blanket. "It better be good food."

"I have wine," Cole popped the cooler to pull out the bottle, "chilled, and even glasses made out of real glass."

He clinked them together before offering her one. Hailey didn't take it but glared back. "I don't like wine."

"I brought apple juice, too." He waited patiently until she folded with ill grace and snatched the glass from his hand. "I got this cheese, port salute I think is what the lady said, but she said it was the best, and she even recommended these crackers, some kind of grain and then there's—"

"I like my cheese in individually wrapped slices." The chunk of funny cheese that cost him over ten bucks got tossed back into his lap even as she turned her wrinkled nose in the direction of the crackers. "Low sodium. That means why bother."

"You are just bound and determined to be difficult about this, huh?"

Hailey shrugged at that accusation as if she hadn't given him attitude for days. "It just seems to me you put a lot of effort into this."

"I did, and most women would be grateful."

"Gee and here I am a woman thinking you're just acting awfully guilty."

Cole met her sneer with a direct look, about to put the screws on to his little princess. "I'm not guilty of nothing, Hailey, but loving you and trying to make this moment as—"

"That's a lie." It came out a second late, but Cole could see the way she snapped from shocked to mad in the flash of red that stained her cheeks. "And I'm not going to be falling for any false declarations until you tell me where you were last night."

Hailey levered up onto her knees to threaten him with a finger in his face. "And you better tell me the truth because I'll find out if you lied."

"Lying really isn't my style, Hailey," Cole retorted. "I'd have thought you'd figured that out by now. You want to know where I was last night, I was schmoozing a lady named Kitty Anne."

Just as he suspected, that answer had her stilling. Those pretty hazel eyes widened and full lips quivered, but his savage little princess didn't make a sound. He finally, for once, rendered Hailey speechless. Cole knew when to take advantage of a miracle.

"Now, if you don't mind." He folded her finger back into her fist, then used that to push her slowly back into a sit. "I'm going to explain everything, but would you do me the favor of maybe eating a little of this chicken I picked up from the Bread Box? I mean, you do like Heather's fried chicken, right?"

"What game are you playing, Cole?"

"No game. I'm going to tell you the whole truth and nothing but the truth. I swear to God, Hailey. Now go on and have some chicken."

He placed the carry-out bucket down in between them and waited. Begrudgingly, she gave in. With a sigh, she held up her glass, and he accepted that she wouldn't be asking him for anything. Silently filling it up with juice, he gave her the time to consume at least a whole leg before he brazened into the conversation once again.

"Okay." Helping himself to some juice, he settled back against the cooler. "I get that you're pissed and you probably actually have a right. I should have told you four weeks ago when Bavis brought his deal to me, but—"

"Bavis." She choked the name out over a piece of chicken before dissolving into a fit of coughing. Cole waited for her to get control of her breathing before responding.

"Yeah, Bavis called about his Fastback." Her eyes rounded into oval disks, and he could feel the tension shifting in her from anger to worry. He didn't let her reaction change his plans but remained relaxed. "You might or might not know, but I've been hankering after his Fastback for a while."

"I know," Hailey stated very softly, her gaze diverting from his to get lost in the blanket. "Everybody knows you want it, and he won't sell it to you."

"That's right." Cole nodded. "Been three years I've been after that car, and he hadn't budged until four weeks ago."

"Why?" Hailey cut in, confusing him for a moment.

"Why what? Why wouldn't he sell it to me, or why is he willing to now?"

"No." Lifting her eyes back to pin his with sultry swirl of molten chocolate, she showed him her pain. "Why do you care about that car so much?"

"Ah." Cole's head dipped back as a realization hit.

To this point he thought this was all about the other woman, but Hailey wasn't jealous of Kitty Anne. Kitty Anne was her friend, and she had to know nothing had happened or would happen. It was about the car.

"You ever been in love before, Hailey?" This time she broke, turning her attention to the chicken with a shrug. "Well, I was. Not with a woman, though."

"What? With a car?" For the first time that day she offered him a smile. Admittedly nothing more than a shadow of one, but Cole counted it just the same.

"Actually, with a baby."

He left it there, and it wasn't long before Hailey couldn't resist. "Uh, Cole? You know how that sounds?"

He gave her a dirty look for her dirty thoughts, clarifying, "My baby, Hailey." Looking back up at the sky, he sighed. "You know, when I was growing up, I was one of those kids that kind of looked at my dad like a hero. He flew helicopters for the Army. That's how he met my mom, down in Enterprise."

"Then Aaron and Jacob are related to you on your mother's side."

"Yeah," Cole nodded. "My dad didn't really have any family, just a mom, and she passed on decades ago. That made our family really important to him, and I guess he sort of raised me with that same view. Nothing more important than family."

Hailey considered what he said before shaking her head slightly. "I'm not following? What does this have to do with the Fastback and Bavis? And are you saying you have a kid somewhere?"

"I'm getting there, Hailey. It ain't an easy road to trace back over." Holding his level gaze for a moment, she nodded, giving him his room as she picked over the chicken. Cole relaxed back and looked up at the Gravey house.

"You know our house kind of looked like this place. Oh, not as grand, but we had one of those little white-plank wood houses. It had the wraparound porch with all the old mill work. At some point, somebody had added on a carport. You know the kind where you got the green plastic roof. My dad and I used to work on his Fastback under that green shade."

The heat of the late summer sun melted the cool out of the juice bottle. It perspired, dripping long rolls of drool down its side as the birds and insects twittered all around. Just like when he'd been a kid, except nothing shaded him from the glare of light raining down.

"When I was growing up, it was always my brothers working on something in our garage." Hailey shifted slightly, relaxing just a hair. "They were always having their friends over. Before cars it was go-karts, potato cannons, that sort of thing."

"Potato cannons?" Cole smirked.

"Yeah, ever October they'd build pumpkin hurlers. My brothers used to invest a lot of time in building things to smash things." Hailey smirked. "And trust me, that went with cars, too. They use to have an on-going relationship with Jerry down at the junkyard."

"And you were there with them," Cole guessed. "Weren't you? I bet bothering them every step of the way."

"As only a little sister can." Hailey nodded, not the least bit ashamed. "I guess you could say I was one of those kids that worshiped their older brothers."

"Not much older, though, are they?" Cole had heard quite a bit about her older brothers.

"Only a few years, but don't tell them that. They got a bad case of parental obsession when it comes to me."

Cole could hear the heavy burden she felt at that observation. "Never grew out of thinking of you as their *little* sister, huh?"

"You'll see soon enough."

Her smile warned him she meant her assurance as threat. Cole just smiled, already aware of the fate coming his way. "I will?"

"Oh, yeah. I talked to Brett not two nights ago. Him and Mike are already headed home. They're stopping over in Vegas for some fun and should be here by the end of the week."

"And you think they're going to beat my ass," Cole finished for her.

"Oh, I know they are."

"I take it from that grin you're not going to try and stop them."

"I get a feeling after last night you probably deserve the beating."

Cole's chin lifted, and his gaze rolled back over the old plantation house looming above them. "I dreamed of owning a house like this and having a yard full of kids and commotion. I'd given anything for that, Hailey."

He caught her glance, wanting her to believe him on this, if nothing else. Unsure if she did, she scowled back at the house. "I get the grim sense you're about to tell me a story where you sold your daddy's Fastback, but something went wrong." Cutting her gaze back to his, he knew she got the point, got it on the head. "Didn't it?"

Cole nodded. "The woman's name was Serena. When she told me she was pregnant, it didn't even take me a day to ask my dad if it was all right to sell the car. I even had our house picked out."

"You must have been planning that family with her before she got pregnant to have everything so well mapped out." Hailey's comment held a dark tinge of pain to it, but Cole couldn't change the past or the truth.

"Yeah, I'd thought about it, asking her to marry me, but it would have been a mistake. She wouldn't have said yes, anyway. She didn't even when she was pregnant, and then she wasn't even that. I felt like a fool."

Cole laid it out there. It would be the only time in his life he'd own up to the emotion, and he only did it to let Hailey know he meant what he said. She could have laughed at him, could have used his admission against him, and a part of him braced just for that.

With a sigh, Hailey smirked. "I guess that's why you've been chasing every skirt you could, huh? Some woman broke your heart, and you use that to justify breaking any heart you want. You know how pathetic that sounds, Cole?"

"It certainly does sound sad," Cole admitted, giving her a dirty look for taking the cheap shot. "Of course, that doesn't sound like me. You can lobby all the attacks you want, princess, but I have never lied to a woman. I never promised, never suggested I'd commit, never gave any woman the slightest hope I'd be anything other than what I am."

"But you did promise me four weeks of fidelity," Hailey shot back. "And somewhere at the end of this sob story is a woman named Kitty Anne."

"No it ends with a woman named Hailey Mathews," Cole shot back. "If you wouldn't be so stubborn, I'd get to that point."

"Then get there already."

"Fine. Bavis offered me the Fastback, but he won't sell unless I break up his nephew's wedding, which, by the way, happens to be in five days. Now he put that offer out there four weeks ago, and I sent Jacob and Aaron to take care of the matter."

"Jacob and Aaron?" Hailey burped up a laugh. "You tell Kyle about this?"

"Not then," Cole shrugged. "I figured I had it handled. Besides, I'm not buying this car to sell. I'm buying it for me."

"So you're still going through with this." Hailey waved a hand to emphasize her point. "You got Jacob and Aaron on seduction duty, but something went wrong, right? I mean, I'm going to take a guess Bavis's soon to be niece-in-law is this Kitty Anne, and if your slick cousins could finish the deed, then you wouldn't be spending past midnight with her, right?"

"Kitty Anne is a prostitute, Hailey."

Cole gave her credit for playing her part well. She didn't even try to fake shock but went with a rolled eye and muttered response. "Oh, this keeps getting better and better."

"I'm not going to sleep with her." Cole wanted that on the table before she lit into him. "Even if you weren't in the picture, I don't pay for sex."

"Well, that just makes my heart glow with warmth," Hailey shot back. "You know, I don't even think I need to hear anymore. Just the fact that you got involved in this crap in the first place tells me everything I need to know."

Cole bet, given she set the whole mess up. Hailey couldn't claim indignation at her own idea, but neither could he point that fact out to her in this moment. Still, he went with annoyance. "Why? What is so wrong? I mean, some man is out there about to marry a whore, and don't you think he has a right to know that? Hell, I'm doing him a favor as well as myself because I want that car."

Hailey went still, her glare beating into him with the kind of violent energy he could feel rippling in the air around her. "Why you telling me this? You want me to give you my blessing to go seduce some other woman? For a car?"

"No. Not your blessing." Cole shook his head. "I gave that car up once for my dream and that hasn't changed. I still dream. I dream of this house and our kids. What I need to know is if that dream has a chance of becoming reality."

Hailey's head tilted from side to side in a slow shake. "I don't understand what you're saying."

"I love you, Hailey Mathews, and I want to build a life with you. Now what I need to know is that what you want?"

Chapter 36

Hailey wanted to say yes, but the word just wouldn't pass her lips. His confession swamped her ability to reason through a response, leaving her the victim of emotion. For as much as her heart swelled and pounded, it couldn't overwhelm the fear roiling in her stomach.

He told her the truth and put the decision back into her lap, but Hailey couldn't make it. For as much as she wanted to dream the same dream as him, she couldn't believe it would ever be more than that. How could she?

Cole said it himself. He believed in that dream once before and it had been a mistake. What if five years from now he woke up and thought the same thing about her? What if he wished one day he had chosen the Fastback?

"Hailey?"

She couldn't answer him. Not with words. It was his decision to make, and he would have to make it. Either way, Hailey would still love him. That wouldn't change. The only thing that would was whether her love became the thing that made her days whole or hollow in the future.

Right now it made her desperate, painfully aware of time and how little she had left with Cole. Not wanting to waste it talking down a painful road, Hailey moved her glass to the grass and then stretched across the distance to press her answer against Cole's lips.

The soft brush went unacknowledged and he pulled back. Hailey knew the question forming on his lips and didn't want to hear it asked again. He would have to trust her for her to trust him. Catching the first break of sound, she didn't give him a chance to withdraw a second time.

Devouring his mouth, her tongue plundered his meaty depths as if he were her captive. The dominant master in Cole couldn't ignore the challenge for more than a few seconds. His question disappeared in the hands that wrapped around her head, holding her still for his retribution as he dueled her tongue back into her mouth and began his own pillaging rampage.

This was not the tender display of affection Kyle treated her to through the night and into the morning. This was an unleashing of raw, violent emotion that clashed as their hands dropped, fighting to work each other free of the clothes that kept them from each other.

The buttons on his shirt bounced off her stomach as her own whipped up over her face. The cotton broke apart their kiss, but for barely a second, and then they were skin to skin, rolling across the quilt as he fought with her bra and she fought to capture his kiss again.

Her lips collided with the hard, taught, sweaty roll of his shoulder and she sucked down on the skin, tasting and nibbling her way over the hard planes of his chest even as he grunted over the back snap of her bra. The little clasp gave him hell, distracting him enough for her to push him onto his back. With another roll, she came up over him, spreading her legs out to straddle his hips as she reared up to handle the bra herself.

A feast of tanned skin and rippling muscles, she barely spared the second it took to snap the bra open and shrug the garment free. His hands lifted, catching her breasts even as she dipped her head toward his chest. In an electrifying scrape of calloused fingertips, the sensitive slopes of her breasts slid free of his grip as her mouth settled over the cut ridge of his pectoral muscle.

Licking a path that had his hands digging into her hair, Hailey discovered the pebbled disk of his nipple. Cole never let her play, never risked that much of his control. Today, Hailey punished him for it, just as he taught her how.

Calling on all the tricks he used to torment her body, Hailey nibbled over the edge of his puckered flesh, lavishing the peaked tip with long licks before she sucked hard and left her mark. Cole groaned, his fingers biting into her scalp as he tugged her lower.

Hailey knew just what urge drove him. Even as she latched down on to his nipple in silent defiance to his demand, her palm pressed down over his bulging erection, massaging it through his jeans. Over and over, she molded her fingers to the thick width and squeezed her hand down his length until Cole snarled.

Abandoning her hair and giving her the freedom to torment his other nipple, Cole's hand brushed hers out of the way to fumble with his zipper. He had better luck with his own clothing than hers, and it took him less than a second before he was shoving her hand beneath his waistband, forcing his zipper to roll down as her bare fingers glided over his pulsing heat.

His smooth, heated length nearly burned her palm as it jerked and throbbed in her hold. Cole's fingers pressed over hers, teaching her how he liked to be stroked and pumped before he released her to wind him up to a fevered, panting pitch. It served him right when she stopped suddenly.

For all the times he held her helpless in his lap or in his arms, she didn't have the ability to force her will the way he did. Hailey only got to savor her victory for a bare second before he growled, his hands shifting. Taking the power from him before he could follow that thought, she slid down, arching her own back and letting her breasts nuzzle his cock in an intimate brush.

Cole froze, his gaze focusing on hers with a sudden clarity as she repeated the motion. Lust sharpened his features, his jaw tensing in time with the slow rolling caress she treated him to. Grinding the edge of herself into his velvety strength, Hailey rubbed her breasts over his thickness until her nipple brushed along the ridge of his pulsing vein.

Right down the center of his cock, she teased her swollen bud to a delicious glide that had her lids rolling closed as she savored the pleasure. Cole muttered a cuss, his hips lifting into the motion. The slight shift had his cock slipping down into the valley between her breasts.

Hailey didn't hesitate to capture him there. Folding her breasts around his dick, she sandwiched his hardness within her softness. Holding him there with her fingers rolling over her own tender nipples, she met his tormented gaze. Caught by the need she could see there, she slowly began to stroke her swollen globes up and down his cock, giving him the most wicked treat she knew of when she dipped her chin and took a taste of the bulbous head rising to meet her lips.

Cole gasped, his muscles tightening with every inch of skin she licked down over. Dancing over the blind eye that wept for her kiss, she tasted the earthy flavor of his desire, the heated silk of his head as it sloped toward the flared edge. Trapping the sensitive tip in her lips, she treated it, and only it, to a tongue lashing.

Her teasing ended in deep suckling pulls that had his hand fisting back into her hair. She learned in that instant Cole did not take to being commanded, and he was never without the power to force his authority.

"Lick it." He growled, the sound more animal than human.

He didn't leave it for her to obey but forced her mouth down over his length by the sheer strength of his hands pressing against her head. Choosing to obey in her own way, Hailey's lips folded down, running a kiss down his length instead of trapping his heat within the kiss.

Cole snarled, sounding close to a barbarian. Before he could revert back to a primitive state, she rounded the base of his cock to latch on to the tender sacks of his balls. Then she sucked him into seeing things her way.

His hips jerked, his body going instantly tense as he panted through the torment she unleashed on him. Emboldened, Hailey licked over his balls, teasing them before letting her suckling kisses explore the interesting arc of his hardened cock. All the way to the top, her tongue led her lips on sensual journey.

Delighting in her own discovery, she gave in to the temptation to taste him, all of him, to pull his body tight as an archer's bow and then cut him off just as he had her so many times. With that thought smiling through her lips, they parted and down she went.

"*Oh, shit.*" Cole's hands came again to direct her movements, forcing her all the way down until the flared head of his cock butted into the back of her throat. Doing to him as she had to Kyle, Hailey swallowed, and Cole cussed, his fingers digging in to yank her back up his length just so he could press her back down.

Over and again, faster and harder, he fucked her mouth with groaned encouragements and snarled curses. Hailey gave over all authority to him, letting him guide her motions even as she reveled in her power over Cole.

Just as his muscles tightened down and his body went taught, she'd have pulled free if hadn't yanked her head clear. Dragging her up his chest, he brought her within an inch of his kiss to gasp out heated breaths over her cheeks.

"You don't think I don't know what you're doing?" Cole growled. "If you want to show me how you feel, then show me. Give me all control, let me bind you, blind you, and show you true freedom. Trust me, princess."

Tempted, she couldn't give him what he needed. Not until he gave her what she needed, proof. Proof that he would choose her no matter what. Without that, she couldn't trust.

"Give me the words, princess."

Licking her lips, Hailey met his gaze and gave him what she could. "Fuck me, Cole."

His lip curled slightly at her words, his gaze narrowing as his big hands brushed back her hair to cup her cheeks. "Oh, princess." The gruff, gravelly texture of his voice sent wicked thrills down her spine. "You're in for it now."

* * * *

Cole didn't care what stubborn reason Hailey had for holding out on him. Hailey wanted to play her game, and that was just fine by Cole because he already had every move she made countered. Including this one.

Keeping her hips bound to his with a hard grip, he rolled until she lay pinned beneath him. Holding her gaze as he leaned back to pop the top button on her jeans, he gave her one more opportunity to save herself.

"You know, princess, I admire your stubbornness." Her second button popped free. The frilly edge of her panties tickled the backs of fingers as he worked on the third. "But is it really worth all the pain when you could just trust me?"

She swallowed, her gaze clearing slightly as she locked in on his. "If you wanted me to feel punished, then you wouldn't make suffering feel so good."

The fourth button slipped free along with his grin. Come tomorrow morning, he'd show her just how good punishment could be once there were no restrictions. Today, he would just tease her.

Sliding his palm over her mound, he pushed her jeans out of the way as he cupped her heated flesh. With his fingers molding over the swollen folds pressed against her panties, Cole smirked at her whimper before moving on to the last button.

"What's our record?"

She knew just what he threatened. Her darkening gaze narrowed and gave her away, even if she didn't answer. Silence wouldn't save her, not with the final button slipping free of its hole. Rubbing his fingers back to the flimsy lip of her panties, he curled the tips under, pausing only to answer his question.

"I believe it was eight."

Trembles shook over her abdomen beneath the scrape of his palm as he settled his free hand along the waistband of her jeans. The instant catch in her breath sucked in her stomach just enough for his fingers to slip beneath the rough denim and begin the slow glide down. Capturing her panties in his grip, he walked both her jeans and her underwear down her legs.

Backing up to pull the last of her clothing free, Cole's gaze instantly narrowed in on the plump, swollen pussy creaming just for him. The sultry lure of her desire had him crawling back between the sexy curves of her legs to breathe down over the very treat he planned to feast on.

"I think we'll go for twelve today." Cole lifted his grin to her flushed face, offering her no reassurance. "What with your Prince Charming not here to save you from my evil clutches, I might just push you to fifteen."

Hailey's swallow told him she believed him, and Cole's grin only grew bigger. "Of course, you could save yourself. Last chance, princess."

Instead of doing the sane thing and looking even more worried, Hailey actually appeared to relax slightly. Her head dropped back to the blanket as her lids closed and a whisper of a smile stretched over her lips.

"Like you wouldn't make me endure fifteen orgasms if I agreed to let you tie me up." She actually laughed at the idea.

Laughed up until he lashed her with his tongue. Pressing his lips along the folds of her pussy, he licked her slit straight up until her clit got trapped under the fury of his response. Then she moaned, her legs tensing, her hips arching, her hands digging into his hair. Cole made damn sure she didn't even have a hint of a chuckle left in her tone before he released her.

Sitting back on his knees, Cole figured she misread his intent when he gripped her thighs and slid her straight up over his. Hailey's head rolled as she muttered out encouraging little fragments, not resisting at all as he lodged the thick head of his cock against the clenched opening to her sheath.

So tight, so wet. Cole groaned as he sank himself into heaven. It took every ounce of his control not to plunder but instead savor the liquid glide of her velvety sheath sucking in every last inch of his cock. Panting through the exquisite pleasure, his fingers tightened on her hips as Hailey bucked and twisted in obvious impatience.

Cole waited through her tantrum, waited until she calmed down enough to lift her lids and pin him with an annoyed stare. By then, Cole found his breath and his will to give her a slow grin in response.

"I believe we were going for fifteen."

* * * *

He couldn't possibly be serious, and Hailey complained with a whine at his teasing. "Cole."

Shifting to pull the picnic basket closer, he pumped her just enough to make her choke on his name. The glorious thrills racing up the walls of her cunt exploded out over her spine like the sparkling, burning spray of a firework settling back to Earth. Hailey gasped through the sensations, twisting with the rolls of pleasure until they finally shimmered back into an aching throb.

"I guess I won't be getting to use these today."

That sad sounding comment had her eyes blinking open to take in the watery sight of sticks and straps. Trying to blink through the haze of lust, it took her a moment to focus as he dropped the pile with a clack onto the quilt. *Stakes.* They were stakes with leather straps threaded through the tops and the very idea of what he intended to do with those had her going still.

"You planned this."

The realization whispered out of her as her gaze lifted to focus on his. His hand fell in her path, and she saw something disappear into his fist. The motion went by so quickly it had her looking back before finally meeting his grin.

Leaning over her, he treated her to a smooth, even stroke solely intended to make her squirm, which it did. Letting the ragged breaths roll out of her as the burst of rapture settled back into a simmer, she couldn't help but tense as lips nuzzled her ear.

"Of course I did, princess. So you never wonder again, let me assure that for the rest of my life, my plan will always be figuring out how to get you naked, wet, and at my mercy. That's my only goal in life, and I'm going to hold on to it for the next fifty years plus."

Swallowing down the glut of emotion his vow clogged her throat with, Hailey watched warily as he rose back to his knees. Stretched out over his lap, with her ass cushioned on his thighs and her pussy impaled on his dick, she might as well be staked to the ground because he held all the power.

Cole only handled power one way—ruthlessly.

"What's that?" She knew he held something in his fist, just as she knew by his grin he wouldn't answer. Cole always preferred to show instead of tell. Hailey's eyes fluttered as he got to the showing.

Heated fingertips pushed her pussy lips wide, exposing her clit to the gentle brush of something softer than the callused tips of his fingers, something she'd become all too familiar with since he gifted it to her three weeks back.

Groaning in anticipation of what came next, she twisted as she felt him leash that damn butterfly to her clit. From practice, Hailey knew to breathe now because in just a few seconds she'd be screaming.

"Now, where did I put the switch?"

Cole shifted again as he released her little bud to rummage into the picnic basket. The soft clip of the butterfly held her in its vise, a warning and a threat that only made her muscles tighten down on the cock filling her.

A cycle she'd come to know and love, every little motion echoed, from her clit to her womb up her spine and then in a liquid rush back down her front. It never ended and always felt good, which was why she greeted Cole's grin with a smile when he held up the magical little button.

"Last chance, princess. I have the stakes here."

Hailey smacked her lips and stretched, letting him know she didn't scare easily. "I guess fifteen it *is*."

Hailey's smartass comment ended in a shriek as he hit button and lit up her pussy with a devastating spasm that rolled on endlessly. Screaming, bucking, when his lips closed over one tender nipple, she gave herself over to the glory of his rough loving and flung through orgasm number one.

Number two bloomed out of the collapsing clouds of ecstasy that billowed through her body. Driven by the relentless vibrations of the toy, her pussy clenched and pulsed, desperate for any tiny bit of friction it could wring out, but Cole's steely length held still, leaving her to scream through one orgasm and into another without really tasting any satisfaction.

She lost count of the number, her eyes opening, seeing nothing but the bold strobe of lights circling before her, faster and faster until they exploded, racking her with another storm of shudders. Hailey screamed her pleasure to the heavens as her hips jerked in demand against his cock.

Abandoning the breasts that felt swollen and sore from his ravaging kisses, Cole finally gave her a moment of calm, clicking off the toy to let her body roll through her last climax to wash up a limp ragdoll on the shores of his thighs. Panting through the burn in her chest, Hailey's gaze finally focused enough to take in Cole's taut features.

"What number was that?"

She didn't even have the energy left to argue with that taunt. Shaking her head with a weak roll, Hailey cringed to hear him chuckle.

"You know the rules, princess. If you don't know the number we start over at the beginning."

"Cole." She wished she could believe he was kidding, but she knew him too well by now.

"Mmm." The thickness filling her shifted, pressing into her side and making her moan. She could hear him rooting through the basket, that damn thing he'd obviously packed with more toys than food.

"Ah, here it is."

She would have paid more attention to that declaration if he hadn't started to pull back. Biting down on her lip, Hailey arched under the lash of pleasure that whipped out of her cunt to scald her entire spine with its fiery caress. The brilliant sensation ended with a painful gasp as Cole actually slid completely free of her body.

The sudden loss had her eyes going wide only to narrow a second later. Her lids dipped with the pressure of a sweetly rounded cock head pushing back into her heated depths. Not Cole, but a toy, smooth, cool, plastic, a pathetic comparison to the real thing. Hailey whimpered her complaint as she refused to greet this new invasion with any real enthusiasm.

Cole noticed. "Not as good, is it, princess?"

"No." Hailey put the pout into her response, knowing it would taunt him into making it better.

"Well, then, maybe this will help."

He hit that little button and brightened her life back up with the sheer rapturous thrills cascading out of her womb. This time she got her fucking, a hard, ruthless one that drove her mercilessly over the edge. Catapulting through Utopia's sky, she could have just kept on sailing if Cole hadn't blasted her out of orbit by pulling the dildo free of her spasming pussy to press its sticky head against her ass.

A pop and it pushed in, searing her inner muscles as Cole fed her every single inch. Never once did the butterfly skip a beat. Vibrating out endless rolls of ecstasy, the pleasure crashed into the pressure radiating out of her ass. Hailey hadn't grown accustomed to the full sensation, but that didn't mean she didn't love it. She loved it more when two men pressed her between them.

This moment didn't feel like the soul giving union of three bodies but scorched with all the glory of unleashed fantasies. Wickedly erotic, the sunlight warming her skin made her revel in the return of Cole's own heated length as he filled her aching pussy with more thickness than she thought she could take.

As always the slender stretch of skin separating the two dicks got caught in the endless grind of friction. With every breath, every slight shift, electricity shot across that sweet swath to thunder out as white-hot lightning bolts.

They cracked across her body, piercing into her soul, hammering that last inch by Cole's own cock shifting forward as he bent back down to her. The moist heat of his breath tickled over her puckered nipple, warning it of the torment to come.

"Now we start back at the beginning."

Chapter 37

It was too much, too intense. She lost count at number six and just needed a moment to catch her breath, but no such moment came. No amount of wiggling or thrashing offered her escape from the endless, relentless vibrations of that damn toy.

Worse, every slight motion only intensified waves of ecstasy crashing down on her, highlighting the bold strokes of orgasms with intense colors as her ass and pussy spasmed and clenched over the rock-hard cocks holding still deep inside her body.

Screaming and bucking as roll after roll of rapture washed over her, Hailey fought the tide of bliss, trying to survive the pleasure that would surely kill her. She couldn't breathe, could barely see.

One climax fed into another until her heart threatened to give out and her muscles began to cave inward. Tightening down around the toy, around Cole, the aching need for just the slightest bit of friction had her writhing on both hard, unforgiving lengths.

Then, finally, as she felt the tears start to roll down her cheeks, Cole moved. Leaving her breasts aching and sore, his kiss slid up her neck even matching the smooth, slow glide of his hip.

Inflaming her tormented pussy, he stoked the fire burning in her womb into an inferno with his easy fucking. Just like his partner before him, Cole murmured tempting fantasies into her ear with each stroke.

"I love you, Hailey Mathews." Her head rolled to the side, trying to escape the intimacy of his declaration, but his lips followed, his hips punishing her by dragging out his already leisurely strokes. "I love you and I want to make a baby with you. Let's make a baby, princess."

His rough palm scorched over her skin as it slid over her hip to rest on the small birth-control patch that kept him from his baby. A bolt of fear lanced the fog of pleasure clouding her mind. It gave her no clarity but sparked an instinctive urge that had her hand flattening his over the patch.

Cole reacted instantly, snarling as his hips punished her with the sudden change to a hard, fast tempo. Pounding out his revenge on her, Cole grunted above her, using his whole body to force her pleasure to the limits.

Pressing down, forcing her ass to bounce the toy while his pelvis ground the butterfly right against her clit, even his chest scraping over her nipples drove the wild beat of primitive lust through her blood until finally she snapped. An animalistic urge rose up and claimed control of her body, and she began to fuck him back.

Bucking into the incoming hammer of his cock, she growled orders for him to go faster, push harder, to give her the satisfaction and release her from the pain of pleasure.

The quiet afternoon filled with his groans and her hollers, the air thickened with musky scent of their sex, then the bright light of the sun burned down into her soul. The lust intoxicating every cell in her body exploded, jerking her hips up even as her head flung back and a scream ripped out of her chest.

Then everything went peacefully silent. Like an anchor sinking into the ocean, her body collapsed into the still slumber of oblivion. It seemed as if she floated through the soothing waves for but a moment before washing back up on the shores of reality, but as the buzzing whirl of the world slowly ordered itself, Hailey roused disoriented by her long nap.

The chirps and snaps of birds and insects filtered themselves into distinct sounds as the heat surrounding Hailey condensed into the hard scrape of a hairy body pressed along her back. An arm weighed heavy over her stomach. Cole and the sun had shifted from above to behind. She had slept for quite a while.

A well-earned sleep by her reckoning. Reality settled back in along with the rush of memories, memories that came to a sudden end. Hailey smirked to herself as she burrowed back against Cole. Blacking out tended to be the best way to screw Cole out of victory.

He could brag all he wanted about fifteen. Her body didn't go beyond ten consecutive orgasms without shutting down. Even better, Cole wouldn't, couldn't admit defeat and take his damn pleasure. Inevitably he screwed himself over, like today, which explained the still fully packed erection poking her in the back.

That put her in a very precarious situation. Sweaty, sticky, limp, and sore, Hailey didn't feel up to round two on the hard ground. A nice comfy bed, some pizza, then she could just forget all about the appointment he had with Kitty Anne.

Finally focused, Hailey's world snapped into place with crystal clarity, and it only left her confused. Cole had confessed and blown her plans to hell. His honesty made her confront things she would rather just ignore.

If only Cole turned out to be the shallow, narcissistic pig she'd always accused him of being. Instead, beneath all the bluster and attitude lurked a sweet kind of guy who dreamed of white picket fences and kids. Hailey believed him. Cole wouldn't lie about love.

That didn't change his definition of it. Hailey looked at the stakes lying off in the grass, tucked up along the side of the picnic basket. After she passed out, he must have piled everything up into a heap so he could roll them up in the quilt. That was her Cole. He packed sex toys for a romantic picnic.

Patton thought the same as Kyle—that she was afraid of commitment. Hailey didn't deny she had trouble trusting a man, not just for a moment, but for the next fifty years. That didn't mean she couldn't have borne the worry and confronted the fear.

With a nice, ho-hum kind of fellow, she probably could settle down and have the kids and the house on the hill. Even knowing it might all fall apart around her, she could find peace there, would be thankful for the family and the memories even if they one day disappeared.

The last thing Cole or Kyle would ever be was ho-hum. In this fantasy of family and home, they'd carve out a nook, a hidden room for their dark desires. If she let them take her into that room, they wouldn't just take possession of her body or even her life but her very soul.

What then would happen if they ever decided to leave her? Hailey feared that answer. She couldn't go in that room, and that's why she couldn't stop Cole from going to see Kitty Anne. That meant she only had one move left.

Rolling out from under his arm, Hailey held her breath when Cole flopped over onto his back with a muttered protest. A smack of his lips and a slight shift to drag the quilt up his chest and Cole fell back asleep. Not once, not before last night, had Cole ever actually slept with her.

It left Hailey unsure of how far to trust his slumber, and she rushed through dressing. If he woke, she'd have to face decisions she'd rather just leave him to decide on his own. Decisions she knew exactly how he would decide.

When Cole woke, he'd assume her absence as consent. He'd go for the car and fall into her trap. By tomorrow morning, her name would be mud in his book. As much as that would hurt, she'd be saving herself worse pain in the future.

That assured knowledge didn't make this moment any easier. With her sneakers laced back onto her feet, Hailey towered over Cole, trying to hold this moment as long as she could because it would be the last of the sweet memories she ever carried of Cole.

Going to her knees, Hailey brushed back his hair to study his features. He really was a good man, but still a man. Pressing a kiss to his cheek, she whispered her goodbye into the afternoon air and then left, never once daring to look back.

* * * *

Cole lifted his lids barely a fraction to watch Hailey strut off down the field. He stayed perfectly still until she disappeared behind the tree line, but she never once looked back. That didn't dampen his mood as he hopped up to start dressing.

I do love you, Cole Jackson. I am the king.

Too bad Kyle wasn't around for Cole to gloat to. Nobody but him got to enjoy his grin, and he did enjoy wearing it. All the hoo-ha aside, he'd gotten just what he came for.

Cole had gotten Hailey's confession, really more like permission. Permission for him to do what he wanted because now he knew he owned her heart and soon enough her body as well.

It didn't phase Cole's ego a bit that she kept the rest of her secrets to herself. Truthfully, he hadn't wanted to hear her confessions. Not when his revenge would be so much sweeter to enjoy.

Enjoy, indulge, devour, he'd be getting to all those notes come tomorrow morning. That was a whole week earlier than their agreement, and that just went to prove he really was the king.

His princess. Cole flipped the gate of his truck down to pack everything back in it. He'd known Hailey wouldn't confess, and not because he bought into Kyle's theory that she had daddy issues. Maybe her father leaving might have left her a little nervous about trusting a man, but the Hailey he knew didn't live in fear.

She lived it free, not bound, and Cole bet that's what really had her walking away. Popping the gate back up, Cole paused to glance back at where Hailey had disappeared. Behind the long line of pines was the Davis land.

They bought up almost all of the Graveys' old land, and Cole knew there was a dirt track back there that connected the old house with the ranch. About an hour's walk and Cole suspected it would be well traveled over the years. Not just but Hailey, but their kids as well.

Their kids...and Patton's spawns...it'll be like Lord of the Flies. It would probably be a damn good thing that there were five fathers to mind over the entire brood. Of course that would mean making peace with the Davis boys.

A treaty had already been signed the other night when Devin agreed they'd handle Patton and Hailey would be left to Cole and Kyle. Then again, that might be a death sentence because Devin warned Hailey's brothers would be arriving at the end of the week.

If Cole didn't want to die, he better make Brett and Mike Mathews' little sister a very happy woman. Fortunately, Cole knew just how to make women very happy. Unfortunately, Hailey wouldn't let him use any of his best tricks, but that would change tomorrow morning.

Checking his watch, Cole got his ass into gear. He had three hours before show time and a whole bunch of things to get done before then.

* * * *

Patton glared at the phone in her hand as she hung the receiver back onto the base unit suspended on the wall. The aroma coming from the oven actually smelled tempting, not that Chase believed her. The damn man knew she'd gone to the effort to have Heather come over and teach her how to cook just so he'd stop grumbling about his empty stomach. Then what did he do? Called and said he and the rest of her men would be eating out tonight, the night she'd gone through all this effort to surprise them with a good dinner. Patton could have just told him, but she didn't see any fun in that. Instead, she decided to put out the whole dinner and let it sit.

When they walked in, they'd know.

The *ratta-tat-tat* at the front door drew Patton from her planning to find Hailey, looking pretty raw, standing on the other side.

"Well, check you out." Patton stepped back, opening the door to let Hailey through. As her friend passed, she peeked out to look for the car she hadn't heard pulling into the yard. "Where did you come from?"

"Over by the Graveys' place," Hailey answered, heading straight on to the kitchen. "Wow. Something smells good."

"Dinner," Patton explained, shutting the door to follow in Hailey's wake. "Where's your car? It break down at the old house?"

"No." Hailey rounded the kitchen counters to take a pointed whiff of the oven door. "Smells romantic. Am I interrupting something?"

"You would be if Chase hadn't just called and ditched me." Patton paused in the doorway to watch Hailey. Despite the roughed over look, her friend appeared a little lost. A highly unusual state for Hailey. "So where is your car?"

"At home." Hailey straightened up to turn and look straight at Patton. "Cole took me out to the Gravey place. I left him there."

Patton waited, but Hailey just stared. "Is he dead?"

Hailey shook her head. "No. In fact I heard his truck start up, so I imagine he's on his way to see Kitty or getting ready to go see her."

"Oh?" It clicked then, just what had Hailey acting like her dog had died. "You know, there is still time to call everything off."

Not a lot of time, but enough if Hailey finally felt like owning up to a few honest emotions.

"No." Hailey's head just kept on shaking. "You know he confessed."

"What?" Uncertainty on what Hailey meant pulled Patton into the room. "Confessed to what?"

"To everything." Hailey turned, keeping her wide-eyed gaze locked on Patton as she slid into one of the island stools. "He told me all about the deal

Bavis offered him and about meeting Kitty Anne and why he wanted the Fastback, everything. He told me everything."

"Well, shit."

Patton didn't know what else to say about that. In all the possible moves she'd run through her mind, Cole confessing hadn't been on the list. He really didn't come off as the type to rat himself out. It just went to show, in Patton's mind, how much he must really care about Hailey.

Patton could tell how much Hailey cared back, but that left a very big question in her mind. "So, what are you doing here?"

"He asked me decide," Hailey answered but not the question Patton had asked. "He basically gave me an ultimatum. Agree to be with him on his terms or he'd go after the car."

Wincing, Patton knew how she'd take an ultimatum like that. "And you said?"

"Fuck me, Cole." Patton blinked at Hailey's shrug. "What else was I supposed to say?"

Patton knew a whole bunch of better answers than that one, but she kept them to herself. "So, now what?"

"I don't know." Hailey looked around the room before settling her gaze on to the counter. "I guess it's over."

Patton gave her a moment to really think that answer through before responding. "That's it. It's just over?"

"Well, I figure by tomorrow, Cole with be both so pissed and so hurt that he won't have anything left to say to me. I mean, even if he does, it'll be nasty and I'll deserve it, but then I figure it will be over. I mean, he won't plan revenge. We've kind of moved beyond that."

Hailey explained it all to the counter. Patton figured the counter probably understood better than she did because Patton didn't think Hailey had a clue. Cole not respond? Not seek revenge?

"You're delusional." The second the words popped out of her mouth, Patton's hands went up in surrender at the look Hailey pinned her with. "Okay, maybe it's me, but I think tomorrow it's going to be Hailey Hunting Season for Cole and Kyle. I'm going to ask you again. This is the last chance. Do you want me to call this off?"

"No. I want you to be a good best friend and help me watch the clock."

Patton nodded, knowing just what Hailey meant. Sighing, she shoved off her stool. "You know, you're really making me regret helping you out with this in the first place. I get the distinct feeling when this all goes down, I'm going to get blamed."

"Why?" Hailey scowled. "It wasn't your idea."

"And I'm sure Cole and Kyle will buy that, but Chase, Slade and Devin think you're just all that's pure, and I'm the one always corrupting you," Patton retorted as she came around the counter. Her comment actually drew a laugh from Hailey.

"You know Brett and Mike share that opinion. In fact, I'd say they encourage it."

"Great, and they're due home when?"

"Depends on how long they stall out in Vegas." Hailey accepted the plates Patton pulled out from the cupboard. "I talked to them two nights ago, and they'd hit it big so they were going to hang over until the end of the week, but you know them. They change their minds about as many hours as there are in a day."

"Either way," Patton dumped silverware for five on the plates Hailey still held, "they'll be here in time to make everything interesting."

"I don't even want to think about what they'll say over all the gossip." Hailey's nose wrinkled before she cocked a smirk at Patton. "Hell, it would probably be easiest for me to just blame it all on you."

Patton paused with the napkins in her hands. "I didn't make you sleep with Cole or Kyle." Taking the plates from Hailey, she started for the table. "And I'll thank you to thank me for not nagging you about the fact that you've been lying to me all these weeks."

"Lying?"

"Yes, lying," Patton shot back without even looking in the direction of Hailey's insulted tone. "You've been sleeping with Cole all this time, and I warned you not to do that."

"Yes, you did, and for once, I wish I had listened to you."

That complaint brought a grin to Patton's lips, and she cast Hailey a curious glance. "That good, is he?"

"Patton."

Despite Hailey's blush, or perhaps because of it, Patton pressed. "You let him tie you up?"

"*Patton.*"

"That's a no," Patton sighed. Turning her attention back to setting the table, she expected the conversation to be over. Mostly because she didn't intend to needle Hailey further.

"I can't."

The soft admission caught Patton off-guard. She paused to turn and find Hailey scowling at the counter again.

"I just can't. What if he does something I don't like? Or what if he does something I don't want but do like, and I have live with that knowledge? Hell, how am I ever supposed to let Cole Jackson treat me like a sex toy and then be able to look him in the eye next day with any sense of dignity or self-respect?"

Patton understood. She didn't agree, but she got Hailey's point. She just hoped Hailey could get hers. Stepping up to the other side of the island, she drew Hailey's gaze to hers with the boldness of her question.

"You ever pick your nose, Hailey?"

"What?"

"Ever pick your nose? Bite your finger nails off and spit them across the room? Maybe you have places you don't want nobody to know you grow hair there, so you shave, but never admit to it."

Hailey blinked once, and only once, as she stared at Patton. "That's disgusting."

"Yeah and we all have some disgusting habits we hide from the world, private things, things we'd be horrified for others to know much less imagine us doing. It doesn't stop anybody else from waking up every day and going around being who they are. It's not going to stop you, trust me."

"It's not the same."

Patton lifted her shoulders in disagreement. "You know maybe you should just try—"

"Maybe I should just go home," Hailey snapped. "I didn't come here to feel worse, Patton. I just came here, because…"

Hailey's voice faded off, but Patton understood. Coming around the counter with a groan, she looped an arm around Hailey's shoulder. "Ah, I'm sorry. Say, why don't I make a batch of cookie dough and we can veg out in front of the TV?"

After a second, Hailey relaxed with a nod of her head. "That sounds good, but what about the roast?"

"Oh, that? That's not to be eaten."

Chapter 38

Cole whistled as he stepped on the curb and pulled open the office door. The little run-down motel had a distinctively dirty feel to it just by the age and weather on the building. Stepping into the stale-smelling little room crowded in by wood paneling didn't help the impression.

It didn't stop him from whistling. Blood pumping, outfitted with two tiny, wireless cameras, he felt like he was enacting some boyhood game of good guy versus bad guy. The best part was he got to play bad while being good.

That's what brought his grin to the little brunette sitting behind the counter. Busy with her emery board, she looked up through a forest of fake lashes to cock a brow at him.

"You have a reservation?"

"Yes, ma'am, I do."

That had her wrist going limp as her gaze dropped over her fingers to scan the ledger open in front of her. "And what's your name?"

"Cole Jackson."

"Oh, yeah." She nodded. "I got you right here. That's going to be two hundred dollars."

He noted she didn't say for the night, but he didn't press the point as he dug out his wallet. Instead, he held on to his card even after she took the end he extended to her. Giving her a curious look, he widened his grin. "You know, I only reserved the *one* room, but I was kind of feeling like I might need more space."

A little scrapper, the way the brunette snatched his card from between his fingers warned him she probably had a knife or a gun on the other side of that counter. "Is that right?"

"You wouldn't happen to have any extra vacancies, would you?"

"We might. I guess that depends on what kind of room you're looking for."

"I was thinking something with a red rug and maybe a set of queen sized beds." Cole waggled his eyebrows. "Hell, if you have the room, I'd even take a third one because I do like diversity, and I certainly love a dark, mocha-kind-of-setting to help me relax."

"You want three rooms?" That got him a look over followed by a smirk. "And just how long were you planning to stay with us, Mr. Jackson?"

"However long a thousand dollars lasts."

"Make it two and you can have all three rooms for the night." The girl smiled, tacking on, "The whole night."

"Sounds like a deal to me. Go on and charge it up, darlin'."

A business woman at heart, the little brunette didn't waste a second to burn up his credit card. Cole just hoped getting the money back would be as easy as Killian promised. He didn't need to waste two thousand on any whore, even three of them.

Passing the card back along with a key, she offered him another smile. "That key opens up all three rooms, Mr. Jackson, though it might take a few minutes for the second and third room to be ready."

"Not a problem." Cole slid the credit card back into his wallet and pocketed it before nodding to the woman. "Thanks."

"Certainly, and have a nice night."

Whistling down the breezeway, Cole found the habit kept him from laughing. He really wanted to laugh. Just the idea of what Kitty Anne had coming to her in the next few minutes made him want to howl, but if he did, then he wouldn't get to enjoy the joke. Not that the cops all waiting for their moment thought this was a joke.

Glancing over the packed motel lot, everything seemed silent and still except for the noises coming from the windows he passed by. Even though he knew he was surrounded, watched, Cole couldn't spot a single man as he pulled up to the door number matching his key number.

Not bothering to look for what he couldn't find, Cole slid the key in the little gold knob and looked forward to seeing just what a dominatrix's den looked like. A little cheesy and kind of tacky. Cole's nose wrinkled as he stepped into the overly perfumed air of Kitty Anne's room.

Pulling the key free and letting the door slam behind him, Cole took in the motel room's shag carpeting and velvet-covered walls. It really tried too hard in his opinion. Stepping up to admire the leather whips and bondage garment hanging from the walls, Cole couldn't help compare the quality and quantity to what the Cattleman's Club offered.

It was like comparing a Motel 6 to a five star resort. One got what one paid for. Eyeing the long line of candles thickening the air with the overly sweet floral scent, Cole wondered if they kept the room basked in candle light to hide the dirt that he felt sure lingered in the corners.

Hell, he'd want a black light before he'd even sit his ass down on that bed. When it came to running a reputable sex club, everybody knew linens were everything. They could only be washed so long before they had to be replaced, and Cole figured the sheets on the queen sized bed dominating the room should have been tossed years ago.

"Is the room up to your standards, Mr. Jackson?" The low-toned, husky question drew his gaze to the blonde bombshell filling out the door to the bathroom. He had to give Kitty Anne one for knowing how to make an entrance.

The see-through lace robe floated open as she strutted forward. Thigh highs, a garter, and a teeny-tiny thong, Kitty Anne obviously wasn't shy about showing off her body, but Cole wondered how she'd feel when she realized more than half the Dothan police department got to enjoy the show.

Just because he was the kind of bastard who enjoyed that thought, he met her right in front of the bed, giving her a once over and his patented grin. "It leaves more than a little to be desired, but this outfit surely doesn't."

Kitty Anne struck a pose, breasts out and hips in. "So you approve of this at least."

"I'd approve more without the bra," Cole growled, reaching for the front snap just before him. He knew she'd stop him, but he figured the boys outside were probably wishing she wouldn't.

A little hand settled over his wrist. "Lest you forget, Mr. Jackson, I'm in charge here."

Catching the steel in her gaze, Cole shrugged back with a smile. "Naw, I didn't forget, darlin'. In fact, I've been thinking about nothing but your particular interest."

"Is that right?" For as bored as she looked, Cole could hear the slight tension in her voice.

"It is." Sauntering off to slouch into the one little chair tucked in along the far wall, Cole relaxed back. "You see, I know we agreed to this show and tell. You tie me up, and then I give you a taste of the same medicine, but for my money I figured I'd like this to be a little more exciting."

Worry flashed through her eyes and straightened up. "We already settled on our terms, Mr. Jackson and our price."

"Ah, don't sweat that, darlin'. I renegotiated with the clerk at the counter." Cole paused to let Kitty Anne consider the ramifications of that before prodding her. "She does, after all, run this little motel, right?"

"She might represent the owners, but we all work here on a freelance basis, Mr. Jackson. She can't speak for me when it comes to services and pricing."

She'd regret that line if she didn't fold on it in the next moment or two. "No? So you mean the fact that I paid for three pussies don't mean I'm going to get them?"

Disgust pinched in Kitty Anne's features, making Cole's grin just grow bigger. "No, but it doesn't guarantee you mine. If you're that interested in an orgy, I'm sure Robin can handle that for you."

"Robin?" Cole scowled in mock confusion. "I didn't come here to play with any Robin, I came to play with a Kitty."

Not amused or relaxed, Kitty closed her robe for all the good it did. "Robin handles the room assignments. Vanessa made a mistake when she implied this one was a double occupancy."

"Triple," Cole corrected right before a knock echoed through the motel's hollow door. "Ah, and here are the reinforcements."

Before she could object, Cole hopped out of his seat to go open the door for the two women in matching maid outfits. Just as he ordered, one was a redhead and one was an African queen meant to bring a man to his knees.

"You requested extra services, sir?" The redhead asked him that as she brushed past, carrying a load of towels with her.

"I did indeed." Cole nodded, letting both ladies past so he could shut the door and enjoy the sight. "And I must say, I am quite pleased with the offering."

"We aim to satisfy." And they didn't wait because Cole had an arm full of woman on either side of him the second the door clicked closed.

"Well now, ladies, I'm going to have to ask you to take a step over to that bed and make yourselves comfortable."

Every hooker in the world knew that code, but Cole didn't bother to watch as the two women moved off, stripping out of their clothes. Instead, he focused his smirk on Kitty's outraged face.

"See, Kitty, I was thinking we could kind of have ourselves a competition. You pick your lady and I'll pick mine, and we'll see who gives the best orgasms."

"You're disgusting," Kitty spat, unable to keep to her role. "And I'm not taking part in any of this."

Just as planned, that refusal sparked an argument between the two other whores, who didn't want to see a good night's wage flushed down the toilet. It didn't even take the women five minutes to call the Madame herself. All Cole had to do was settle down and let the spying eye on his belt buckle play back the scene to the men in blue.

Sure enough, Robin appeared at the door, and Cole had to admit she kind of surprised him. Looking more like a soccer mom with her blonde hair cut into a boy's bob, the whore house master lit into her troops. It took her maybe a minute to incriminate herself once the door closed behind her.

Given the cat fight brawling in front of him between Kitty Anne and Robin, it kind of disappointed Cole when the police rolled over the little motel like a tsunami. Everything snapped so fast he didn't know which came first, the roar of voices shouting, "Police, open up!" or the crash of doors being blown out all around.

What came next muddled the moment even more as women screamed, men shouted, and suddenly Cole's face was pressing way too deep into the shag carpeting. He didn't have to get arrested, but he'd asked to. Still, he hadn't really been prepared to be shoved around, arms wrenched behind his back, guns aimed at him, and then being lifted and dragged like a piece of meat to be pushed into the back of a paddy wagon along with a whole bunch of other men.

It took only a few minutes for him to go from being comfortably seated to being cramped on a metal bench with his fist pressed into his ass. At least he had his clothes on, Cole smirked to himself, more than comfortable with the moment since he knew it was all for show.

* * * *

Eight thirteen. Hailey stared at the clock trying to feel the number. Eight thirteen, an hour and thirteen minutes had passed since the official end of her relationship with Cole and Kyle. After three hours of consuming nearly a dozen cookies and half pound of batter, the only thing Hailey felt in that moment was bloated.

She certainly didn't feel like a woman whose heart had broken, but it should have. Her brain reasoned it through almost every second of the way. This was the moment Cole would be smiling at Kitty Anne and then that was the moment she'd kiss him. All of it went noted and ignored by her heart that just blatantly refused to notice anything more than it was 8:14, and she was getting kind of bored of watching TV with Patton.

Maybe it was time for her to go home, sit in her own house, and stare at her own clock. Then she could wait for what she'd been waiting for all night—the call. Somebody had to call, Rachel, Cole, Kyle, at some point one of them would call and then maybe, just maybe, her heart would begin to understand.

A flash of headlights through the den window broke the silence between her and Patton as Patton glanced up from the movie she'd been watching. "I think Chase, Slade and Devin just got home."

Hailey followed Patton's lift off the couch, but stretched instead of going to peer out the blinds. "I guess that means my ride is here, huh?"

"I could have given you a lift home." Patton let the blinds snap closed as she glanced back at Hailey. "But are you sure you want to go home? All alone?"

Hailey smiled, about to tell Patton it would be better than staying here, listening to Patton and her men enjoy themselves. The ringing of her phone cut off her comeback. The little cell started vibrating on her hip, and finally her heart sank.

Forgetting all about Patton and paying little attention to the pounding quaking across the floors as the Davis brothers came up the porch steps, Hailey sank down as she stared at the number flashing on the cell's screen.

Bavis. She hadn't expected him to call. "Hello?"

"Hello, Miss Mathews." Bavis's words sounded like they caught on either a cough or a chuckle. The difference was hard to tell in the old man's gravelly voice. "I wanted to be the first to congratulate you."

"Congratulate?" In a reversal, her heart began functioning, understanding all too clearly the implications of that word. Now it was her brain that flat-lined, appearing unable to understand the obvious.

"I admit I added on something special for your friend Rachel's story, and it was spectacular." Definitely laughing, Bavis did end up hacking over the sound and gave Hailey a moment to digest.

"What did you do?"

Clearing his throat, it took the old man's breathing a moment to stable and let him answer. "Cole's been arrested."

Heart, head, time, everything just stopped with that revelation. "No."

"Oh, yeah. I just had me a nice talk with him in his cell. I have to give it to you, Miss Mathews, you got that boy so wrapped up he just plum out wouldn't believe you had anything to do with this."

His words twisted the knife slowly deeper into her gut, holding her paralyzed with pain as he gloated on. "I'm having the Fastback dropped off as we speak because I know he's going to come looking for it."

"No." She said it too softly, too much to herself for Bavis to even bother to recognize that she made a sound.

"Enjoy the car, Miss Mathews. You earned it."

Before she could repeat her objection, the line went dead, leaving Hailey sitting there, holding her phone and feeling nothing at all. It felt like she'd been sucked into a vacuum cleaner and the whole world existed some distance from her. The sounds of the Davis brothers, the commotion of their entry, everything felt disconnected as she stared down at her phone.

Cole had been arrested.

That changed everything. What could have been pawned off as a joke gone too far had just turned into a disaster for which Cole would have every right to seek justice.

"Hailey?" Slade's hand folding over hers to close the cell phone in her grip brought her focus to the man settling into the couch beside her. "You okay?"

"No." She answered honestly without thought.

"Wanna talk about it?"

"No." That time she managed to answer with some real emotion—horror at the thought.

"Well, then how about I take you home?" Slade's head dipped so he could catch her gaze. "You look like you could do with some sleep."

She could, but Hailey didn't think she'd find any tonight. Being at home, alone, didn't actually sound like a good idea given Cole would be released from jail sometime tonight and Kyle was out there freewheeling around. All those thoughts came to her but didn't actually transmit into action as she allowed Slade to help her up and escort her to the door.

Still caught somewhere in the trance of shock at Bavis's stunning phone call, she didn't do anything but follow as Slade led her out of the den and through the living room. They cleared the porch and just started down the path when Patton's sudden holler echoed out of the house behind her.

The high pitched words came out muffled and almost inaudible, but Hailey ears caught on what she thought she heard. *It's a set up!*

Her feet stumbled over her steps as her mind tried to figure that message out. Slade dragged her along, not even appearing to notice Patton's screams or the way they just suddenly stopped.

"Slade?" Hailey didn't know what she wanted to ask him, but confusion clouded her mind.

It didn't his, and he brought her to a stop by his truck without even recognizing she'd spoken. Opening the door, he stepped back to offer her a hand up. "Here you go."

"I don't think I want to—"

"Here you go." He repeated himself but this time latched on to her waist. Before Hailey could figure out his intent, Slade boosted her into the seat before slamming the door.

Hailey might have objected. She might have jumped out and stormed in the house to find out what Patton yelled. She might have done a lot of things right then if fate hadn't conspired against her and lit her phone back up. Worse than Cole or Kyle, the number that flashed across her screen had her going cold.

"You gonna answer that?" Slade asked as he slid up behind the wheel.

Hailey couldn't. She couldn't do more than stare at the phone, tracking it as Slade picked it out of her hand and answered it for her.

"Hey, Brett. What's up, man?" Pulling his seat belt on, starting the engine, Slade chatted it up with her older brother, pinching the phone between his ear and shoulder. "Yeah? I hear we are going to be throwing a welcome home party in the coming week...Yeah, actually she's right here...Nah, man, she's just having a rough night. One of the guys she's involved with just got arrested at whore house and—"

The scream that bled her own ears shrieked out of her with such violence the truck actually swerved down the drive as Slade flinched in reaction. His fumble gave her the second she needed to rip the phone out of his hands and rush to reassure her brother.

"He's only kidding, Brett."

"He better damn be," Brett shot back, obviously believing her.

"He is. I'm not even dating anybody right now."

That lie popped out of her from force of habit. Since she'd been a teenager, it had always been better if her brothers didn't know about her personal affairs. Unfortunately, it wouldn't even require them to be nosey to find out the truth this time. All it would require was them finally getting home.

"When are you going to be home?"

Bret didn't answer her sudden question, but attacked it. "Why you asking that now? I want to know about this man you've been dating, and don't think I didn't take note of Slade's comment. He said one of the guys, which means you got more than one bothering you, and I want names. Now."

"Don't take that tone with me, Brett." She might have made a complete disaster of her love life, but Hailey knew Brett's involvement would only make it worse.

"I'm not taking any—"

"Hey, Kiddo." Mike must have jerked the phone away from Brett because her other brother's cheerful voice sang across the line with his normal good humor.

"Hey, Mike."

"Why you picking a fight with Brett? Huh, Kiddo?"

Happier he might be, but Mike always agreed with Brett, and he liked to throw just as many punches. He just threw them with a grin on. "I'm not picking a fight with Brett. He's picking one with me."

She could hear Brett yelling in the background, his voice fading away as Mike obviously moved away from his irate twin. "Now, you know Brett just loves you to pieces and wants you to be happy, so I'm betting you aren't happy if he's upset."

That twisted bit of logic could only come from an older brother. It had the usual benefit of making her so frustrated she didn't know how to respond with anything other than a snarled, "I am happy."

"Well, see, you don't sound happy."

"That's because you're annoying me."

"And that's it?"

"That's it."

"Because you know I can always make a call or two and—"

"Fine." Hailey had enough. If Mike wanted to hear it she'd give it to him. "I was dating this guy and his best friend, but then he just got arrested tonight at a whore house, so the wedding's off and I'm not really in the mood to hear about what you think of all of this."

"You were dating two best friends?" Mike didn't sound so happy now.

"It's over, Mike. O.V.E.R. Over. So, I don't want to hear any more about it."

Silence greeted her, and Hailey wished her brother stood before her so she glare back at the stare he no doubt drilled into something through those moments. Finally, when he did respond, his tone came out tight and crisp, more like the military commander he'd been trained to be than the big brother he'd always been.

"It's going to stay over, Hailey."

Normally, she'd have told him to kiss her ass, but right then she had no problem agreeing with him. "Don't worry, Mike. The only reason I'd ever see them again is if they forced me to endure their presence."

That wasn't really true, but Hailey knew better than to tell her brother exactly who was at fault for her boyfriend being arrested. They'd figure out those details soon enough, which made Hailey suddenly consider the virtues of taking a sudden vacation.

"And we're going to be having a long talk just as soon as we get back into town."

She had no doubt, but if she wanted to take a spontaneous vacation, timing would be everything. "And just when are you arriving in town?"

"Maybe we should just leave that at soon."

The conversation went downhill from there. Slade didn't even defend himself, just grinned as if he knew something she didn't. It made her suspicious and nervous as he pulled into her drive.

Slade didn't help her anxious state when, instead of getting out to escort her to the door, he just beeped his horn and backed out the second after she shut the passenger side door. Never before had any of the Davis brothers left her standing in her dark driveway as they drove off. Hailey just watched Slade's taillights disappear in absolute amazement.

He'd left her, left her out in the dark where anybody could be hiding. Swallowing as that thought occurred to her, Hailey's eyes started darting over the shadows. It was impossible to miss the biggest shadow filling out the driveway. *The Fastback.* Bavis must have had it delivered before he called her because there was no way it had been towed here in the past half hour.

It didn't matter when it had come. What mattered was getting it out of her drive. Carefully, quickly, keeping an alert eye out, Hailey unlocked the garage. Turning on the light reminded her of another grim fact. Her Studebaker was still parked over at Cole and Kyle's.

No way to get out of town fast without a set of wheels, and Hailey wasn't dumb enough to go within a mile of their place—not tonight. That meant instead of fleeing, she had to bunker down. This would be the last time she stepped out of her house until she knew she was safe.

Rushing through her chores, she covered the Fastback with a tarp, failing to get it to budge into her garage. She picked up all the hidden rocks that held keys, double checked every window and even latched her doors. Even the idea of turning on a light and letting anybody outside know where she was inside seemed like a risk in that moment.

Between Cole's arrest, Patton's warning, Slade running off on her, and her brothers' call, Hailey knew something was coming. She just didn't know what or who. Hunkering down in her bedroom, she took up a vigil, waiting for whoever showed.

Chapter 39

Hailey woke with a start, unsure of what snapped her from sweet oblivion back into a world flooded with sunlight. Cramped and stiff, she still wore the same clothes from last night. That fact put everything back into focus. She tensed and looked again for the sound that woke her.

Straining to hear, the only thing that echoed around her was the silence. Still, she had to check out every room, double check every window, peer out them before pulling the blinds back down. By the time she circled back to her room, Hailey told herself she could relax, everything was fine.

The problem was she didn't believe herself. Hailey couldn't escape the feeling that she should be bracing herself for Cole's reaction, but it would help if she had a clue as to what that reaction would be. Hailey didn't have any idea of what to expect but figured a shower and food would help her handle it better than being stinky and hungry.

A great idea in theory, bathing required a great deal of vulnerability with the removing of clothes and the loss of hearing by the rushing water. Hailey had never before been so aware of just how dangerous the simple act of showering could be. Rushing through her daily luxury, Hailey even dressed in the steamed-over room, too afraid of what may lurk on the other side of the door.

Never before had opening her bathroom door been such a nerve-racking experience, but Hailey peeked out, making sure nothing had changed while she'd been insulated in the shower. Silent stillness still reigned over her house, and she peered around the corners like a cop on a TV show as she made her way to the kitchen and the coffee pot.

A half hour and two cups of coffee later, Hailey started to feel a little silly. She was acting like the CIA was after her, but neither Cole nor Kyle would ever actually hurt her. Fortified by sunlight and growing impatience with her fear, Hailey began to rationalize just how good her situation actually was.

Yes, Cole had gotten arrested, but really, whose fault was that? His own. So what if Hailey had put the offer on the table? Only a total butthead would have taken it up. That had been Cole's choice and just as she'd always said, it was his to make.

It didn't sound good to her ears, but Hailey couldn't take just sitting in her kitchen waiting for something to happen. Still, for all her silent bravado, Hailey peered out of windows, scanning her yard and street before she dared to unlock the front door.

Dashing out as if the boogie man might just out and grab her at any point, Hailey rushed for the newspaper. Making it back through the front door safely, she slammed it, leaning against the solid wood surface as she panted from her exertion.

Locking it back up, she carried the plastic wrapped paper into the kitchen where she dropped it onto the table. She'd need another cup of coffee before she could face the headline article. Folded over as it was, Hailey could already make out the first bold words.

Local Man. She knew who that referred to. Armed with a full mug, settled into her seat, and braced for the worst, Hailey dumped the paper out onto the table and flatted out the front page.

Local Man Helps Police Breakup Prostitution Ring.

Hailey finally heard something as her eyes traced back over the letters— a high pitched ringing. It started in her head, buzzing right out her ears as she read the small print.

A local man, Cole Jackson, went undercover to help the Dothan police infiltrate a motel long suspected of operating a prostitution service through its rooms. The sting last night...

She read it over and over again, just that sentence. Rachel hadn't written this article. Andy Anderson had, so where was Rachel's article? Where was Rachel? She hadn't called once in the last day. As the thought occurred to her, Hailey reached for her phone.

She got Rachel's voice mail on her cell and counted on getting the same on her home number when on the fifth ring a man finally answered. "Hello?"

"Uh," Hailey couldn't place the voice in the moment and it left her fumbling slightly. "Is Rachel there?"

"Hailey?"

The question almost sounded like an accusation, and she snapped back her own. "Who is this?"

"Adam."

"Oh, hey, Adam." Hailey almost laughed as the stress released out of her with that answer. "This is Hailey. I was just trying to get in touch with Rachel."

"She's tied up right now," Adam drawled with a certain smugness that had Hailey stilling.

"What?"

"She gonna be tied up for a few days, Hailey, but I'll let her know you called."

He didn't even bother to say goodbye before the line went dead. Staring at the phone, Hailey didn't know what to make of that strange call. It left her almost feeling the need to call back and demand answers, but instead she dialed Patton's number. Unfortunately, Slade answered.

"Hello?"

"Slade? It's Hailey."

"Oh, morning, Hales. How's it going?" He sounded way too damn happy.

"Not good." But she bet Slade knew that already. "I don't suppose you'd let me talk to Patton for a moment."

"Ah, sorry, Hailey. She's tied up right now."

"And I bet she's going to be that way for the next couple of days," Hailey muttered.

Slade laughed in the face of her misery. "You got that right, Hailey. Now you have to excuse me, I have a busy morning ahead."

"Yeah, great." Hanging up, Hailey just stared at the paper until she couldn't take it anymore. Dialing the number she knew by heart, she waited four rings for the son of a bitch to answer. When he didn't, that just riled her temper another notch and had her fingers scorching over the numbers to his cell.

He answered on the second ring, and she didn't even wait to hear his greeting. "Can't bother to get out of bed to answer the phone? Do I have to ask what it is you're doing?"

"Mornin', princess." Cole sounded ready to laugh. "I wouldn't bother with the good part because I can tell it ain't going that well for you."

"No, it isn't, and you know damn well why," Hailey snarled. "You think you are so clever. Don't you, Cole?"

"Clever? I don't know about all of that, but according to the paper, I am a hero."

Oh, he loved saying that. "How?"

"How what, princess?"

"How did you figure it out?"

"Is that really important right now, Hailey?" Cole retorted. "Or aren't you calling to find out what it is I want in retribution?"

Just the way he asked the question told Hailey the answer. "I know what you want, Cole."

"Is that right?" His voice dropped into the husky tones of a lover. "So, tell me, then, you going to give it to me?"

Hailey swallowed. He'd take it if she didn't, and she didn't doubt that. "Where is Kyle?"

"Holding the leash, princess," Cole growled. "If it had been up to me, you'd have woken up with dick holding you still for the torment you got coming to you, but your Prince Charming wanted to give you a chance to surrender with dignity. So tell me, Hailey, how do you want to end this game?"

Hailey closed her eyes and went with the nuclear option. "I love you, Cole."

Silence hung on the other end before he muttered. "Oh, that's low, Hailey."

"I think I'll call Kyle and tell him I'll put his ring on."

"Oh, don't you—"

Hailey hung up on his yell and dialed Kyle's number as fast as she could. He picked up on the third ring, and she could already hear Cole yelling in the background.

"Don't you let that woman sweet talk you out of our deal!"

"Shut up, Cole. Hello?" His voice went up as he turned back to the phone.

"Kyle?"

"What?"

That sharp response had her feeling her way slowly. "I guess you know about the Bavis deal." She rounded the statement out when he didn't help fill in the pause.

"You promised, Kyle. She earned her due, and you aren't going to stand in my way."

"You realize he's getting ready to head over to your place." Cold and detached, Kyle's tone sobered Hailey up more than his words. Cole might be all fired up and ready to bring the battle to her doorstep, but his outrage was all bluster. An act he planned to use to corner her into giving him his night, his way.

Kyle, though, sounded honestly remote, and that had her hesitating. "I'm sorry, Kyle. I didn't mean to hurt you."

"No? Let me ask you this, why did you do it? I mean, I know you and your buddies came up with this plan about the time Cole and I tore up the Bread Box. I get that you might have been mad back then, but we gave you *every* chance to confess yesterday. So, why didn't you?"

All her answers felt lame and limp in the face of his anger. Hailey didn't have the courage to air them now. Instead, she tried to gloss over them all with a muttered, "I don't know. I guess I just got scared."

"Scared?"

"Yeah, I mean I figured you'd be mad."

"And so you reasoned we'd be less so after the fact?" Kyle snorted.

"Okay, fine," Hailey snapped, goaded by her own guilt into rash truth. "I know one day you two are going to move on to your next victim, and I can't...I won't..."

She stopped trying to say what she couldn't. Sighing, her shoulders slumped forward. "I do love you, Kyle. I just know love doesn't last."

He didn't respond for a long moment. When he did, his voice didn't carry an ounce of sympathy or understanding. "Hailey?"

"Yes?"

"Be naked and in bed by the time we get there."

* * * *

Kyle managed to hold on to his laughter until after he disconnected the call. "This is almost too much fun. You know?"

"She said she loved me." Cole laughed.

"Hailey's really desperate right now."

"Yeah." Cole appeared to consider that for a moment before cocking a brow at Kyle. "You think she's going to be naked and in bed?"

Kyle could wish. "No."

Sighing, Cole straightened up. "Well, then I guess we better get a move on it. We got a lot of work to get done today."

"A lot of work," Kyle echoed as he lifted the gym bag Cole already had prepared and followed Cole out the kitchen door. He felt good about the coming confrontation. It felt like a cleansing. After today, they could finally start their life together.

Pulling in behind the tarp covered car in the drive fifteen minutes later, Cole sat with the truck idling staring at the Fastback hidden under the blue cover.

"I can't believe I actually own it, man." Cole shook his head and laughed. "I got the car and the girl. I really am the king."

"We don't have the girl yet." Kyle pushed open his door. Hefting the gym bag over his shoulder, he paused before jumping out. "What do you want to bet I have to break down the back door?"

"Why don't we just use the key?" Cole's question came a moment later as he cleared the hood of the truck to fall in step with Kyle as they went up the drive.

"You think Hailey left those rocks out?" Kyle snorted. "She ain't that dumb."

"Neither am I." Cole produced one of Hailey's house keys from his pocket. "I swiped it out of the rock yesterday before lunch."

"I guess you really are the king," Kyle snickered as they turned around the path that led up to the back porch. The shuffle of their boots over the pavement came to a pause as they both stared up at the wide-open kitchen door.

"Will you look at that," Cole murmured.

Kyle looked, even as he leaned in to whisper to Cole. "You think she's still in the house?"

"Yeah," Cole nodded.

"You think it's a trap?"

Typical Cole, he just grinned at the idea and started back up the path. "Only one way to find out."

For all his cockiness, Cole didn't strut but peeked through the door, moving into the kitchen much like a man who expected a banshee to jump out at any moment. Nothing stirred but the whine of the door as Kyle pushed it even farther open with the gym bag.

"What do you think?"

Cole didn't answer but tossed him a shrug before he began moving down the hall. Neither man called out to Hailey but crept along for all the stealth the hard wood floors provided. Cole veered toward the living room, and Kyle ducked into the longer hall the bedrooms fed off. He looked one place, and he only needed to.

"Cole." Calling his best friend back to his side, Kyle waited until Cole crowded in the hallway to see the sign Hailey left for them. Stuck to her closed bedroom door was a little brown square patch Kyle recognized instantly. Dangling from behind, the gold chain hammered in the message.

"It is a trap." Cole shook his head, starting down the hall. "The little wench, she trying to throw the damn game."

Barging into her room, Cole came to a short stop, forcing Kyle to push around him to see Hailey sitting in bed wearing nothing but a sheet and his ring. The sight took Kyle's breath away, and the gym bag thunked down onto the floor.

"Well, well, well." Cole circled the bed but didn't draw Hailey's gaze or smile from Kyle.

Ah, but she looks like a goddess.

With her hair glowing in the sunlight, the golden rays warmed over her shoulder and arms, making her fairly radiate with sensual appeal that all but lured Kyle to his doom.

Cole blocked Kyle's view as he stretched one arm over the headboard and the other across Hailey's hip to lean in and threaten her. "Don't think all this ceremony is going to stop me from taking my revenge, princess."

A hand with his ring glinting on her finger circled Cole's neck and pulled him down over Hailey. With a hoot, Cole rolled over her and, from all the laughter, it sounded like his friend had fun wrestling with a naked Hailey. Kyle certainly liked the show, especially when she crawled over Cole and spread those legs so he got a nice view of the heaven he'd soon be delighting in.

Mesmerized by his own lustful thoughts, Kyle barely paid any attention to their commotion as Hailey pounded Cole with a pillow. His friend hollering all sorts of obscenity-laden threats didn't even disturb his pleasant contemplations.

Not until Hailey leaned back and Cole didn't follow did it even dawn on Kyle that something was wrong. Blinking away his erotic musings didn't come easy when Hailey turned, crawling naked across her bed.

"Kyle, damnit! Do something!"

Cole's outraged demand still didn't draw Kyle's gaze as his mind considered just what he'd do with the sexy little woman coming his way. With that look in her eyes, he should probably consider what it was she intended to do with him.

"*Kyle!*"

Sighing over that impatient demand, Kyle did what he didn't want to look over at Cole. Cuffed to her headboard, just like some part of him had known for minutes. Still, he didn't feel like doing anything more about Cole's predicament than wrap his arms around the warm, soft, naked woman pressing all her sweet curves into him.

"I knew you set a trap." Kyle turned back to accept the kiss Hailey brushed into his mouth. Returning the gesture, he kept his just as teasing as he murmured between the caresses. "You don't really think a few kisses are going to trick me into letting you leave him like that, do you?"

Hailey pulled back with a pout on her full lips. "We both know Cole's going to punish me."

"You got that right, princess," Cole shot back instantly. "And your tab is just going up, so why don't you save yourself and undo these cuffs now."

Cole didn't sound happy or amused anymore. In fact, Kyle hadn't ever heard him sound more pissed. Hailey didn't appear too concerned. She didn't even appear to notice Cole's interruption, probably hoping to distract

Kyle, too, with the subtle rubbing motion that kept him very aware of all the naked curves at his fingertips.

"And he doesn't really have any right."

"I have all the right in the world, princess," Cole snapped. "You gave me that when you and your little girl squad teamed up with Bavis to make a joke out of me."

"But he didn't make a joke out of Cole," Hailey pouted in a little girl voice she'd never unleashed on him before. Like salt water to metal, it eroded his strength. "We made him a hero."

"I made myself one, and don't be trying to twist the facts. Kyle knows the whole truth."

"All I wanted was for Cole to know what it was like to be bound." Hailey gave Kyle a hopeful little smile. "Don't you think I should get to enjoy a little of that before I suffer for it?"

Kyle smiled. She argued a good point, especially to the man who didn't have metal bracelets on.

"Don't you dare, Kyle. I swear to God—"

"Besides," Hailey looked back at Cole. "I bent the keys, so you either have to cut through the metal poles of the headboard or call somebody."

"You're assuming we don't have our own set of keys," Cole snarled.

That challenge had Hailey straightening away from him to give Cole the classic head-roll of a pissed off woman. "Did you bring them?"

"Son of a bitch."

"So," Hailey turned her grin back on Kyle. "I guess that means you have to leave Cole with me while you run off to get the key or, of course," Hailey pressed herself back against him, "you could just stay and enjoy the moment."

"The moment?" Kyle smiled. His little princess really did think he was the Prince Charming, but Kyle wanted to be king. Maybe it was time he explained that fact to Hailey.

Chapter 40

Hailey held her smile as Kyle moved back. He'd fold. Her whole plan relied on him folding. It had all come to her the moment Kyle hung up and she realized just how deep she sank her ship into the mire.

Hailey accepted it. She couldn't win the war. She'd been fighting and fighting, but she could go on her whole life and they'd still be standing there, waiting for her to finally tire out. For all the bluster, Hailey admitted she'd come to that point.

Being tired didn't mean just accepting defeat in Hailey's mind. She meant what she said to Kyle. If she was going to accept the punishment, she wanted to commit the crime. So Cole could stay cuffed to the bed, and she'd let Kyle make a meal out of her.

A risky move given Kyle didn't always choose her side, and it kept her gaze focused on the slow motions of his hands as he undid his belt. As the thick strap of leather slipped through the loops, it became harder to hold her smile and not give into the urge to run in the opposite direction. Especially when he held on to the long tail and beckoned her.

"Come here, Hailey."

Cole's silent brooding from behind only added to the tension. Even as she slipped her legs over the foot of her bed, Hailey's mind had already started to scream at her to flee—now—before he used that belt against her. With her feet bearing her weight, Hailey's eyes darted to the door, stalled out over her indecision.

"Hailey."

Licking her lips, eyeing the belt, Hailey just couldn't move forward without any reassurances. "You're not going to tie me up with that belt, are you?"

"I might." Kyle smiled. "Of course, you really have to ask yourself where are you going to run to naked?"

The bathroom.

With its solid wood door she could barricade Kyle out if she could only make it in time. The thought hit her feet before it received any proper approval from her brain. What might have been hailed a victory turned into a battle of sheer force as she cleared the threshold and swung the door right into Kyle's head.

With a grunt, he put his full force into shoving her bare feet back over the tile. It really didn't require much effort for him to push his way into the bathroom, and Hailey gave up almost instantly to retreat to the other side of the large room. That gave her barely six inches beyond his arms reach, not nearly enough to feel secure as he snapped the door shut.

Smile still in place, Kyle rested against the door, paying more attention to the belt he was roping round his hand. "I guess I had that answer coming, huh?"

Heated and hungry, his gaze betrayed his relaxed stance. It slid up to connect with hers briefly, warning Hailey the worst thing she could do right now was make any sudden movements. The predator was annoyed, and she was trapped.

"You know, every time I think you haven't any room left but to see reason..." Kyle shook his head as he snapped the belt taut between his hands. Again, his gaze lifted for a moment to pin her with lust darkening his eyes. "Maybe that's my fault. I've been very lenient, too lenient, too considering and patient. Now you've become like a stray cat. You come to eat my food, but you don't ever let me pet ya."

Shoving off the door, he measured his steps until he had her cornered in the farthest reach of the bathroom. Boots to bare toes, he loomed over her to declare, "No more, princess. No free meals for you and don't be thinking you can sniff around anybody else to beg a meal from because I will whop any man who so much as puts his hand on your arm.

"I'm talking bloody, princess. So you got a choice. You can either walk your naked ass out of this room and start obeying, or you can starve to death." Kyle leaned in to growl over the bridge of her nose. "And I mean it, Hailey Mathews. You will die a lonely, horny old woman because it's either Cole and me or nobody."

He'd only given her two options, but Hailey went with a third. Throwing herself straight into his arms, she forced him to release his threatening hold on the belt in order to catch her, which he did. Wrapping his arms around her with a long, suffering sigh of a man who had put up with too much, Kyle still let her duck the ultimatum—for the moment.

Aware of the little time she had to lobby her case, Hailey went to the main point. "What if I don't like it?"

"Hailey," Kyle groaned as if she'd asked the most annoying question. "You like everything we do. Don't you think you can trust us by now?"

"I mean the tying up." Hailey ignored his complaint, too consumed with the importance of her own point. "What if you do this and it bothers me, then I have to do it for the rest of my life? And what if I don't? Will you be slipping off to your club to find women who do? I mean what if we're not compatible in this way? What if—"

A heavy hand clamped down over her mouth, his grip consuming most of her lower face. "Hailey. You have two choices. And let me make this quite clear, you don't get to argue or reason or persuade. We command. You obey. Understood?"

She nodded just to get him to lift his hand but couldn't help voicing another concern. "And I'm not calling you master. All those women call you master, but I'm not some pet—"

"Oh, the hell with this." Kyle grunted, more to himself than her. She got the message when his hand clamped down on her arm and yanked her into the shoulder he lowered into her stomach.

Without so much as a huff of exertion he lifted her off her feet and carried her out of the bathroom. It didn't shock her in the slightest when she got dumped onto the mattress. Not even bothering to run for it a second time, Hailey huffed as she pulled the sheet out from under Cole.

"Plan backfired, huh, princess?"

"Shut up, Cole," Hailey snapped, not taking her eyes off Kyle or the bag he chunked onto the foot of the bed. Whatever he looked for inside the oversized duffle, he didn't pull anything out to give her a hint of the fate waiting for her.

"You just can't stop digging your grave." Cole appeared to have passed through being pissed and moved into a more contemplative mood. "So what did you say to piss him off this bad?"

"Nothing," Hailey snapped. "And don't start with all the threats, Cole. I figure you came over here planning to do your worst, so how much more afraid should I really be now?"

"A lot." Kyle's crisp answer drew her gaze to him and her breath out of her chest at the sight of the rope in his hands.

The belt lay discarded across the bed given over for the softer threads of braided black. "Is that velvet?"

"You don't think we use rawhide, do you?" Cole snorted.

"Well, I just—"

"Come here, Hailey."

Kyle apparently didn't want her to finish any sentence this morning. Giving him a dirty look for his rude behavior, she really didn't have any choice but to obey. Taking the sheet with her, she scooted down the bed until she once again stood before Kyle.

With a sigh, he reached out to yank the sheet away, leaving her to curl her toes into the hard wood as she stood before him naked. This time her unrobed state made her feel keenly aware of his power and strength. Perhaps because he'd pulled the sheet away. Though it might have had something to do with the rope still dangling from his hand.

"Listen up, princess, because I'm only going to explain this all to you once. From this point on, you do exactly as you are told. Any hesitation, any refusal, any attitude whatsoever, even a look, gets your ass whopped. And you can keep all your sass silent because if we hear it, you suffer for it."

The scuffed tips of his boots loomed dark and dangerous beneath her nose. The crisp cut of his words matched the deep creases on his jeans. He towered over her with his body heat soaking into her through the distance. Hailey felt a wicked curl of heat unfurl in her stomach.

"Now, I'm only going to ask you this once, and I want you to really consider the answer. Did you really bend the cuff key?"

She'd sunk it into the bottom of a jar of lotion in the bathroom, but that answer didn't make it out of her mouth. Instead, Hailey bit down on her bottom lip and accepted Cole's truth. She just liked digging her own grave, liked the thrill a little too much.

"All right, then." Kyle stepped back and nodded toward Cole. "Go on and crawl up him."

Hailey swallowed at that command, doing just what Kyle told her not to—hesitating and sending him a look. Like a snake striking, he responded so fast she didn't even have a chance to realize she issued the challenge. The soft bite of the velvet rope pressed hard into her back as he bent her over the edge of the bed.

Smack!

Hailey sucked in a mouth full of comforter at searing smack that lit her ass up like a candle. He didn't give her a chance to understand, to reason, or feel anything other than the scorching lick of the flames flaring out of her ass as he whopped her with the flat of his palm.

One, two, three, all the way to five and even then her flesh still vibrated with the aftershocks. They rippled over her, rolling the air out of her lungs in gasps that matched the heated waves of cream dripping down her thighs.

"Now, up."

Not another spank, more of a pat, the hand pushing that order into her back end had her wobbly legs coming up to obey. Only Cole's smug smirk put the moment back into perspective, making Hailey hesitate to spread her legs over his and reveal just how much she actual enjoyed Kyle's paddling.

Not that she had any control. The sharp smack to her already smarting backside broke over her with Kyle's equally harsh command. "Now!"

She might have had the spirit left to disobey, but her body didn't have the energy. Weakened with lust and trembling with anticipation, she crawled over Cole's straightened legs and bore the impact of his incoming smirk as she settled onto all fours.

"Higher, princess," Cole beckoned with just enough gloat to again make her hesitate long enough to earn another spank.

"Higher."

Hailey's heart jumped at the feral sound of Kyle's growl. Something changed in her Prince Charming. His halo had darkened. Why that turned her on so damn much, Hailey didn't understand. She simply obeyed.

Unable to break Cole's jaded gaze, she moved slowly upward. Tensing in anticipation, her breasts passed mere inches above his face, but he let her pass without torment. Neither man ordered her to stop until the very heat of her desire hovered dangerously close to Cole's smirk.

"That's good, man." Cole's hands stretched up to grip the top of the headboard. With the cuffs clinging against the metal rods, he pulled himself to a sit, washing a tantalizing spray of breath over her mound, up her stomach, all the way till his lips almost rubbed against hers when he spoke next.

"That's perfect. Just tie her off here."

Before she could guess at what he meant, Kyle showed her by pulling her wrist right up to the top rail and tying it tight to the metal bar. The panic she always feared at being bound began to race her heart, but the exhilaration only fed her lust.

The scorching flare of desire burned through her chest, making her pant in a desperate attempt to get enough air. The ragged gulps heaved her breasts against Cole's chest, rubbing her tender tips into the heated cotton. She arched, reveling in the decadent pleasure.

"That's it, princess," Cole murmured in her ear. "Enjoy what you can, while you can."

The threat buried in his satisfied tone didn't stay there. Kyle delivered on it a second later as he snatched up her other wrist and stretched it all the way across the back of the headboard. He pulled her so tight she had lean in, all the way in, until her chin brushed against Cole's shoulder.

Kyle tied her up just like that, like a sacrifice for his best friend who had already started to indulge in his position. Nibbling his way across her shoulder, Cole nudged her hair out of the way with his chin to point out a fact she was already vividly aware of.

"See, no hands and I can still play with whatever part of your body I want." He cut the last few words out with a hard bite that had her swallowing as shivers raced down her spine.

"You're going to have to go a little wider here, princess." A big hand pressed her inner thigh out. Her back arched as Kyle spread her legs just as wide as he wanted them, leaving her that much more vulnerable to him. To Cole, who chuckled over her defenseless position.

"This is going to be so much fun."

In that second, Hailey thought he meant what he intended to do to her. In the next, she realized he meant what Kyle intended to do to her. Her eyes bulged at the thick round feel of something too smooth and very hard being pressed into her sheath. There had been no warning for the motion, and her mouth unhinged to suck in a long gasp.

"More than wet enough to take all ten inches." Kyle's tone had started to take on the same arrogant hardness Cole's had as he fed her a slow, steady diet of cock. "And we haven't even touched you yet, princess."

If Hailey could have formed the words for a comeback, she'd have shared it with him—despite the threat of punishment. With the full length of the dildo settling into her, she didn't have the air or the reason left to think any words other than, "*Oooohhhh.*"

That drooled out of her and over Cole's shoulder as Kyle's fingers reappeared. The evil genius focused in on her clit, pinching and toying with the little bud. The sparkles of pleasure that blossomed out of the tiny nub radiated through the stretched muscles of her pussy, making them clamp and tighten around the toy.

Amplified by the small motion, the pleasure rolled into compact balls of rapture that bubbled up her spine with such delight she just had to taste a little more. With little room to move, the best she could do was a slight sway, giving her only a paltry thrill.

The big dose came when Kyle's hand retreated, leaving something small and soft pressed up against her clit. Hailey knew that feel. She'd been here yesterday but had a sick feeling this time there would be no passing out as a means of escape.

Sealing that fate, Kyle's hand slid up her spine as he walked along the side of the bed. Coming to brush the hair back from her face, he gave her a chaste kiss on the cheek before murmuring, "I'll be back in a half hour."

"Don't rush on my account," Cole retorted, accepting the button Kyle pressed into his hands. "The princess and I will be just fine, won't we?"

Hailey swallowed, her gaze shifting to Cole's. Pressed close enough together, she could see the shards of green darkening in his eyes. A passing glance, his gaze dipped out of sight as with a rattle of cuffs he slipped down. His kisses laid down a path of liquid heat that flooded into a river as his lips settled over her nipple.

Like being lit up with a live wire, the second his tongue curled around her puckered bud, he pressed the button and set the entire brigade of fireworks off in her cunt. Not a dildo, a vibrator. That's what Kyle had packed her full of, and it went into full-spasm mode, right along with the damn butterfly.

"*Oh, shit,*" Hailey squealed, her knuckles going white as her fists curled around the headboard. With almost no room to move, she could little more than pant and melt as Cole tormented her. Taut with pleasure, her muscles couldn't take the strain, and she collapsed into Cole's hard body.

The velvet binds at her wrists wouldn't allow for her to rub as she wanted, to grind herself into his strength and power. Hailey could only tickle herself with the decadent feel of Cole's clothed body pressing against her naked one.

Just knowing he held all the control made the pleasure avalanche through her, washing away all resistance as she gave herself over to his authority. Resting her chin on the top of the headboard, Hailey flexed her whole body into Cole. Letting the wanton need boiling in her blood drive her body's motions, her climax began to spiral tighter and tighter as it took her to the point of pure oblivion.

"*NO!*"

That denial ripped out of her throat as the promised Utopia blinked out at the sudden stop of Cole's torment. Cole and all his toys might have gone still, but Hailey went wild. Thrashing so hard she actually made the headboard bang against the floor and wall, she still couldn't pull free of the binds that only tightened the harder she wrenched.

Futility meant nothing to the rage that spurred her body into a fit. Fed by the lust that turned painful, Hailey unleashed her frustrations until her arms ached and she had no more curses left to bombard him with. Not that Cole took any offense.

Vibrating her breast with his laughter, he smoothed his cheek between her two aching globes only to pull himself back up once she quieted down. Hailey flinched against the pleasure as he began to leisurely taste his way up her neck.

"New rules, sugar lips. We ain't playing how many orgasms can Hailey take today." Cole pulled back, showing off his grin as she panted and tried one last time to twist her wrist free of its bind.

"That ain't going to work, princess, so maybe you ought to pay attention now." Eyeing him with distrust, she really didn't have any choice but to obey. "Very good, princess. See, you're learning. The next lesson is very, very simple. You don't get to come until I say so."

He let those solemn words hang there for a moment before his grin broke loose and spilled into a chuckle. "And I got to tell you, sugar lips, I ain't exactly feeling charitable toward you, so we start at the beginning."

Chapter 41

Cole twisted Hailey's entire world into an endless orgy of rapture and pain. He brought her to brink of release only to snatch her treat from her grasp. The Denier and that's just what he did. He denied her at every point, twisting her mind and body into nothing more than a toy for him to play with.

God, but she loved to be played with. That thought drooled out of her as the sweet friction of the vibrator slowly fucking her began to harden into delightfully hard punches. So good, her moans morphed into elongated rolls of laughter as body tensed and prepared for the final act.

"Just a little harder, a little faster." The words slipped from her lips as the only thoughts in her head. The consequences of speaking them, not to mention the reality of Cole's hand still cuffed to the bed, didn't register until a hand cracked hard over her ass, bringing all the delightful motion to an end.

"I see she hasn't taken to the lesson."

Freezing driblets of sparkling thrills raced down her spine at the hard sound of Kyle's tone. *He's back.* And now there were two of them. Now Cole would be unleashed. That thought barely settled over her lust fogged brain when a hand dangling a key came up from under her arm to work on the cuffs' lock.

"Yeah, man, well I wasn't exactly teaching the princess anything," Cole grunted back, shifting beneath her as one hand came free. "I was just having some fun, giving the princess a little warm up."

Just like that he slipped from beneath her, leaving her to collapse on the bed. Held up only by the velvet ropes, she couldn't even turn around to watch the two men she knew watched her. The heightened sense of fear that came from being so vulnerable before them only shaded her arousal into the darker, deeper hues of wicked wants.

They didn't help, talking about her like she had no ears.

"Warm up, huh?" Kyle actually sounded annoyed. "So what does that mean? You didn't explain any of the rules?"

"Not yet." For being a Cattleman, Cole sounded unconcerned with the rules. "I thought we might settle a different score first."

There came that smug note in Cole's tone. It sent another round of shivers as Hailey regained enough sense to turn her head and spy on them over her shoulder. Just as she'd known, they were watching her. What she hadn't expected was for Cole to greet her look with more than just a smirk. He held a blindfold in his hands.

"See now," Cole settled down onto the edge of the bed, "we've got punishment and training on the schedule today, but I was thinking we could start with something a little more fun."

She had no clue what he meant by fun, but she didn't need details to set off another ripple of fear. It crashed through her arousal, showering in a tingly rain of excitement. Instead of fading into tiny aftershocks, the tremors doubled down as Cole stole her sight. Slipping the soft mask over her eyes, he tied the string tight behind her head before leaning in to whisper in her ear.

"Your chin points this way." The instruction came with a hand turning her chin back into the pillows. "That's a good girl, and don't even think about closing those legs. I like the sight."

With that, he disappeared from a world he reduced to nothing more than sound and feel. Having only those two senses to help track their movement made the very words coming from behind her that much more of an aphrodisiac.

"I was kind of looking forward to the training," Kyle complained with enough pout to make it sound like Cole had stolen his favorite treat.

"And you can keep on looking forward to it because we have more than enough time to get to all that," Cole shot back. "There is just one thing I think we need to settle."

As they talked, a hand appeared to pull the vibrator. The slow motion buzzed her head with a whoosh of pleasure as her sheath clamped down, hungry to savor every inch of friction. Then with a snap, she was achingly empty and the joy of the second before back lashed into spiky shards of pain.

"I figure we time each segment and then see who here in this room really rules." Cole's voice waned back in as the riot of sensations faded back into a dull hum. She caught only the end of what he'd been saying, and Kyle's husky chuckle warned her that she missed the best part.

"I like it." Which meant Hailey would love it. And hate it.

She breathed deep as they shuffled around behind her. Whatever they'd agreed on, it required moving furniture. That made her all the more nervous and even more aroused. The ropes loosening around both her wrists at the same time tickled her almost at the idea of two such capable and strong men working to control her.

They had every advantage. Bigger, stronger, clothed, they could even see what they were doing, but Hailey refused to give up. Mostly because she knew it would rile them both up, she gave it all the effort and energy she had to try and pull free of their grips.

It didn't even take a grunt for them to wrench her arms behind her, but they still treated her to unnecessary force, which did actually tickle Hailey in all sorts of deviant ways. With her new position came all sorts of deviant kinds of pleasures, like the feel of a calloused palm running straight down her spine as if he was sizing her up.

The he turned out to be Kyle. "You know it really only makes us harder when you fight."

Hailey turned her face in the direction his voice came from, hoping he would catch her smile. "I know."

"Up on your knees, sugar lips." Cole's command cut through any humor in the moment. Traditional Cole, he didn't wait for her to obey but pulled her upright with a tug on her ropes. "We're going to put that sassy mouth of yours to work."

The bed shifted and jolted as a set of rough, denim clad thighs slid down around hers, and she could feel Cole settling into a sit in front of her. Even without her gaze, Hailey knew the sound of zipper being lowered and just what that meant.

It left her more than prepared for the hand that stretched around her cheek to press her head down but not at all prepared for the hands that pulled her ass back down toward the edge of the bed. Still on her knees, Kyle kept her hips arched and quite clear a second later why.

"Here, let me get this first."

His words brushed along with his hair, teasing the inside of her thigh before his mouth broke over her pussy. Despite the mask, Hailey's eyes bugged wide as her jaw went slack at the feel of his lips closing over her clit. He didn't tease or toy with her, but freed the butterfly with his teeth.

"Oh, sugar lips." Cole chuckled, his fingers biting a little harder into her scalp. "If you could see the way you look right now. The only thing that would look better is watching you suck this."

The sticky heat of a rounded cock head bumped into her lips as he dipped her head downward. Hailey followed the motion, intentionally ignoring his command to nuzzle her cheek down his long, hard length. His dick pulsed and bounced with his growl.

"I said suck, sugar lips. Not tease."

"Hey." Kyle's head, a warm, silent threat still snug between her legs, made its presence known with that snap blasting against her cunt. With her pussy lips swollen and split, nothing offered her any protection from his words. "Let the princess play. You have to put up with it all."

Hailey had no idea what he meant, but Cole understood. His fingers tensed in her hair a second before disappearing. "Fine, but just remember, Hailey. I have a *long* memory."

He could threaten all he wanted. It was her turn to play, and she didn't need a long memory to justify tormenting him. She only needed the burn that still scorched through her veins to make her think revenge. Revenge on Cole would be bringing him to his knees in less than five minutes.

"I think our girl is having naughty thoughts." Cole chuckled. "You just are so cute, smiling like that. Makes me wonder just what—"

Hailey didn't want him to wonder. She wanted him to feel. With no ceremony or finesses, she opened her lips and sucked him all the way back to the end of her throat. Like he'd been whipped, Cole jerked and cussed. That was all the encouragement it took to feed her ego and set her motion into a full-blast gallop.

Up and down, and over and over again, she twirled her tongue around his velvety hardness as her lips ate up his strength. She pulled Cole's wire tight, locked on a rhythm she had every intention of taking him over the edge with.

With a tempo especially meant to drive Cole insane, she felt certain he'd come at any second, which was just when she crashed over the notes of her symphony. Choking on Cole's dick, her head flew back to gasp in air as a set of lips closed over her clit and scraped her tender little bud over the hard edge of his teeth.

Hailey shrieked, pumping her hips down toward the mouth that began to spiral her passions back toward the peak of the heavens. Moaning over Cole's cock, she forgot all about showing him any of the love Kyle lavished on her.

Kyle was a true master when it came to knowing just how to roll and when to suck and even how to lap. *"Ooohhh, Kyle!"*

"Don't be 'oh-ing' him," Cole snapped, his hand reappearing to fist into her hair. "Be 'mmm-ing' some of this."

Cole's definition of "this" had a very short run, and so did his patience. Not leaving her to obey that command, his hand took control of the issue. Hailey didn't resist as he pressed her mouth back down and over the swollen head of his cock. It wept for her return and pulsed eagerly into her kiss.

With his fist controlling her motions, she didn't have to worry about rhythm or speed. All she had to do was suck and wallow in the gluttonous pleasure of Kyle's kiss. His tongue had a mesmerizing quality. It danced and lured her into forgetting the game of the night—denial. Just as the whirlwind of release started to clip through her, Cole tensed, his fingers tightening painfully in her hair.

"Now, Kyle!"

The world whirled around her. Cole's cock popped free of her lips as Kyle's disappeared. She came to a panting, sweaty stop on her side, jerking with the throes of unrequited passion.

"That was eight minutes."

"Bullshit."

"I'm telling you, man. You didn't even last longer than the little princess."

Hailey blinked, taking in Kyle's satisfied laugh, but the world remained a dark mystery to her. Their plan, though, became clearer by the moment.

"Yeah," Cole snorted, shifting off the bed. "Well, sugar lips has quite a suck on her, and eight is still three better than five."

"Eight with help."

"Oh, it's going to be like that, is it?"

"Yeah, it is, man. We're fighting for the title, so don't be thinking you can just talk your way into it. You got to earn it, boy."

"Title?" Hailey licked her lips and dared to ask, "What title?"

An arm shot down from behind her, rough hairs tickling over the tips of her breasts before his palm sank into the mattress. She expected Cole's voice to growl through the heated breath fanning over her ears, but Kyle's came instead.

"To see who you're going to be calling sire for the rest of your life, princess. What else?" With that warning issued, he disappeared.

They're serious.

That panicked thought added adrenaline into the rush of volatile hormones raging through her body. They argued about this before, but she hadn't ever actually conceived of what it would mean to them. Apparently it meant a lot.

"Now stop whining." Kyle settled back into the bed in Cole's old place. Hailey could already guess what came next without Kyle's instruction. "It's my turn, and we'll see just how good you are with that mouth you're always running."

A set of hands settled on her waist. Cole. He leaned in to murmur something clearly directed at Kyle. "Give him hell for me, sugar lips."

With that, he rolled her back onto her knees, and she didn't need any instruction to figure out her position. With her hands bound behind her, she did need help maintaining the position to not fall face first into Kyle's crotch like a drunk. Thankfully, Kyle provided the same support Cole had—a hand fisting in her hair.

"I got you, princess. Just give Cole a moment to get in position, and we'll start from the beginning."

That was an expression Hailey had really come to fear, but there was no time to panic. Not with Cole settling down between her thighs, his breath heating the path for his devilish tongue. Unlike Kyle, Cole dined on her entire pussy, making a feast out of every intimate inch.

In those moments she forgot all about Kyle and just indulged in her own glorious pleasure. Kyle didn't take to being ignored anymore than Cole had. With a near identical motion, he tugged her down to his waiting erection. Thicker, definitely a stout boy, Kyle's cock stretched her lips wide as he began to pump her up and down.

Keeping her pace steady, Kyle played out the moment, making Cole play out her pleasure until her toes curled and her legs began to cramp with the tension. She couldn't stop it from cresting, all that frothy goodness.

"Son of a bitch!"

Cole's roar blasted away the thrills that had just tingled out of her cunt to sprinkle their fairy dust over her body. He jerked away from her, leaving her to collapse and giving all control to Kyle, who continued to fuck her mouth with grunted pants. Even as the tide of rapture receded into a whirling pit of need deep inside her womb, Hailey gave herself over to racing Kyle's hand.

Neither of them paid any attention to Cole, cussing up a storm behind her. She got the point. He'd lost the round, but Kyle didn't care, and neither did she. Too consumed in their own passion, Hailey's hips began to bump and grind with the same rhythm as Kyle's, her need feeding off of his.

"Now, Cole!"

The world did the topsy-turvy thing again, but this time she ended up in an oriented heap, capable of understanding every nuance of the male harassment that broke out around her.

"That one is a draw." Crisp, sharp, Cole's bite had the sharp edge of a man already entrenched in his position.

It contrasted sharply with Kyle's almost breathless laughter. "Oh, bullshit. That was my win by a mile."

"Try three minutes, pinhead," Cole shot back. "And I got the little princess off in five, so it's my win by a mile."

"That's crap." Kyle still didn't have much energy in his tone. He shifted on the bed, slowly away. "I warmed that cunt up. You were just riding my coattails."

"Your coattails?"

"My coattails."

A tense moment of silence followed Kyle's satisfied retort. He'd lifted completely off the bed, and Hailey silently imagined the two of the nose to nose, ready to go fist to fist. For some sick reason that just heightened her arousal all the more.

The sound of fist hitting flesh didn't break the stalemate, but Cole's snarl did. "I'm getting the clamps."

The clamps? Hailey swallowed. He wouldn't be clamping anything of Kyle's. Apparently he wouldn't be hitting his best friend, either. That meant all of Cole's aggression was coming her way. The very idea had her breath stilling so she could strain over the sound to listen for his movements.

She heard nothing but the hum in her own mind. Like they'd disappeared, everything had gone perfectly still. Starting to quiver with anticipation, Hailey felt assured that any moment she'd be touched, anywhere and everywhere. The only thing that touched her was the warm wash of Kyle's words as they appeared out of the silence behind her, giving her a start.

"Nervous?" The ropes around her wrists began to loosen.

Never much, but not dumb enough to say so. "I take it I can't make fun of you for being the five minute man anymore, huh?"

"Scared, but never cowed," Kyle murmured, releasing her wrists altogether.

"It's hard to be cowed by pleasure, Kyle."

"Not cowed, but spoiled. That's just what you are, sugar lips." Kyle's use of Cole's newfound endearment had her letting him position her just as he wanted. The Kyle she'd known all the nights they'd come together, her sweet Prince Charming, had turned into a dark knight.

Hailey had never factored on what happened. It made him feel like more of a threat. Just the simple act of him rolling her onto her back to stretch her wrist up toward the headboard had her fighting back a squirm. God, but she ached and itched in all the best ways.

"You see, princess, down at the club we have this tradition when it comes to new members, both male and female." As if they were discussing the weather or the morning paper, Kyle continued on in casual tone as he circled the bed to pull her other arm toward the opposite end of the headboard.

"Everybody is, shall we say, evaluated to consider best how to train them as either masters or pets."

He dangled that last bit out with a slow drawl that matched the smooth slide of his hand down her slick inner thigh. All the way down her ankle, with the same tender touch he used not two nights ago. This time, instead ending with a seductive lure, he pulled her ankle all the way before lassoing it to the footboard.

The feel of the velvet tightening down over her skin, of her arms stretched way overhead, being completely bound, open before them, it almost overwhelmed her good sense. The drowning, though, triggered panic and she had only one anchor left to hold on to.

"This is just a onetime deal, Kyle." Weak, squeaky, she didn't sound sure of that statement, prompting her to repeat it to find the right tone. "Just one night."

"How about we discuss that tomorrow?" Kyle suggested. He sounded sure, almost smug. Why shouldn't he?

Tightening down the rope on her last ankle, he had her spread out over the bed like an offering. Knowing Kyle probably stared didn't make her as nervous as knowing that Cole still lurked somewhere out there in the black abyss, waiting with his clamps.

The very idea of which fortified her nerves. "Just one night. That's all I agreed to."

"You know, sugar lips, you're beginning to annoy me with that." Kyle sounded it, too. She expected a follow up order or maybe even a spank to her pussy, fully opened for the blow.

Instead, she got a shot of pure, intense pain. It streaked like fireworks shooting up into the night sky, but this molten trail sank deep into her cunt before exploding. It didn't stop. With the clamp holding her nipple in its vise, the sensation continued to pump out of her chest, flooding her pelvis with such heat she couldn't stop thrashing.

Hailey screamed as she jerked on her binds, desperate to escape this new torment. There was no release to be found, only acceptance as her body slowly adjusted to this new level of rapture. Bit by bit, her breathing calmed back down and her body stilled as her definition of "doing fine" started to recalibrate.

She didn't have to breathe in so deep and press her tip deeper into the clamp's grip. Shallow pants helped her finally came to a twitching stillness. As if she hadn't spent the last five minutes going crazy, Kyle picked up their conversation with a very matter-of-fact tone.

"There are a lot of rules and traditions that go along with these kind of games. It would be unreasonable of us to expect that you learn them all in one night, but certainly you can grasp the concept."

Kyle's voice was moving, rounding her to the left, and her chin followed his motion. He made it easy to track his movements, sliding a hand along her side as he continued on.

"It's pretty simple. You, as the woman, are to be gracious and welcoming. And while I admit you have welcoming down," his hand curled around her thigh to let a stray finger stroke through her slick folds, "it's the graciousness that needs a little work."

"I think I'm being very gracious given the fact that the two of you barged into my house and—"

A second thunderbolt of pain shot out of her other nipple as her words got clamped off. Knowing it had been coming, even knowing what to expect, didn't help the rush that consumed her. She lost touch with the world around her, existing only in the rapture consuming her body until it lulled back into a boil.

There waited Kyle, smoothing a gentle hand over her head as he brushed her hair back from her face. "See, that wasn't very gracious, sugar lips, and after what we've put up with."

"You?" Hailey could almost laugh at the insult in Kyle's tone. "I'm the one who has been harassed, hounded, hunted, threatened, and made a spectacle of. I mean, look at me."

Maybe that hadn't been the best ender, but it rolled at naturally, bringing her to a sudden stop and Kyle to laughter. "Trust me, I am looking. I could look all damn day, but we have those rules and pesky traditions to keep after."

"Perversion has traditions?"

Hailey felt safe to argue with him. She had her breathing down so that barely a trickle of pleasure leaked down to the cauldron burning in her womb. Accustomed to the vibrations, she felt confident they'd done their worst. That arrogance split open into a scream that rang her throat raw.

Softer, not as tight, the third clamp clipped over her clit and sent her crashing into the sea of madness. Her whole pelvis felt on fire, and she fought for any inch in her binds just to rub her tender folds together. They needed something, to be licked, to be fucked, anything to wash out the intense ache shredding her apart.

Kyle didn't wait for reason to surface through the tide but shoved her deeper into the undertow with a simple growl. "Now come the chains."

Chains? Hailey barely had a chance to suck in that concept before the fever consuming her flared up to unleash a billion tiny, licking flames as something tugged on her nipple, on the clamp. From one peak to the other, the burn in her tits blossomed out into a rioting inferno. When the pull stretched both tips slightly down, running a straight line of lava straight to the center of her being, Hailey screamed out at the horror.

"Oh, God. NO!"

"Yes." That response came in the simple action of clinking the tiny chain against the clamp on her clit and then latching it down. It was pure evil what they did to her because nothing that felt this good could be right. They robbed her of all decency and sanity, leaving her writhing in a screaming fit as the pleasure reduced her down to a thing of savage need.

Chapter 42

Cole smiled at his handiwork, watching Hailey squirm. The view couldn't be better. From her cream glistening cunt to her berry red nipples, she just looked beautiful. He'd never seen her so wet, so wild. It made him want to growl with contentment.

He'd been fantasizing of this moment for years. As often as dreams tended to be better than reality, he found himself captivated by how good this moment felt. *Better than anything I'd imagined.* And they'd only just started on their sugar lips.

The pet name fit this side of Hailey. She got aroused, and her whole body flushed, those lips swelling slightly, becoming lush looking with her tendency to lick them. They beckoned to be fucked, a promised joy they could deliver on. Cole grunted with the thought, his gaze dipping down to her pussy and the memory of the absolute best thing he ever fucked. They'd get there, eventually.

"I think it's time to settle up the score. Don't you, Cole?"

Cole waited for her to calm down enough to hear him quite clearly. From the whimpers, she had. That was good because he had more to say. Circling around the bed, he came silently up onto her side. Even as Kyle lifted off the other side, Cole settled onto the bed.

"We got a lot to settle. Don't we, Kyle?"

Kyle answered with a nod, intentionally keeping his silence. It kept the princess a little more wired if she didn't know. Even though she did because Cole told her.

"Kyle here owes you for all the heartache you've put him through. Teasing him, trying to demote him into nothing more than your little sexual puppet…"

Cole let his tone fade off as if he actually contemplated what he said. Really, he just let Kyle get into place. It pleased him, though, that Hailey was incapable of filling the pause with anything more than mews and whimpers. The thin chain connecting her tits to her clit shimmered in the sunlight as she squirmed. He imagined it just felt too good for her not to.

Cole leaned down to whisper in Hailey's ear. "You really made us dance on the end of your strings for the past three weeks, so, you know what? It's your turn. Dance, sugar lips."

That's just what she did. Squealing loud enough to make him cringe, she danced in her binds, futilely trying to escape the cold wind Kyle unleashed on her pussy. He blasted her for a good thirty seconds, and she went wild for a good minute beyond, only slowly coming down to pant "Oh, crap" over and over again.

"Yes. 'Oh, crap' it is." Cole chuckled, eyeing Kyle as he moved. "You want to know what that was, sugar lips?"

"You're a pervert," Hailey shot back.

"Yes, we are." And so was the little princess because she didn't ask them to stop. Cole knew she would, too, if she didn't really like it. Hailey liked the torment, but she really loved earning it. A good match because he really loved doling it out.

"That was an air duster can, only used by us serial, professional perverts. You like?"

Kyle blew her answer away with another shot from the can. This time the freezing wind whipped over her nipple and set her chains back to dancing as she cursed and writhed. As much as Cole hated to give in on his own control, the Mr. Man had become violently angry at watching but not indulging in the feast spread before him.

For as much as his tormenting Hailey made her pussy fill the room with the intoxicating scent of her desire, it also made Cole's unruly cock weep. He just had to be petted, and Cole could offer him with the tight squeeze of his own fist because he certainly wasn't going to give up his fun.

As she finally quieted down, Cole nuzzled her ear. "You didn't answer me, sugar lips. Failure to answer is a punishable offense."

So Kyle punished her.

Back to her pussy, Kyle got the long red nozzle till it almost kissed her clit before he let the wind fly. She screamed herself hoarse, twisting hard enough to make the headboard bang against the wall.

He didn't wait for her to come down before demanding an answer of her. "Tell me, do you like it?"

He knew she wouldn't have the breath to answer. That's just why he asked, giving Kyle all the justification to make her cry out again. They played the game four more times before an answer roared out of Hailey, honest and blunt to her core.

"You sons of bitches! *My pussy's cold!*"

"Well, let me take care of that for you," Cole responded instantly, dropping a hand to cup her pussy with the warmth of his skin. The pebbled bud of her clit and the plastic indention of the clamp pressed into his palm. With all her squiggling, it wasn't his fault that the tender bud got a healthy grind. Not that she didn't blame him.

"Oh, God, Cole! Don't! I can't stand it." But she did, and she just kept going, crying and dancing against his palm.

Cole egged her on with a few healthy words of encouragement. "You feel hot and wet to me, sugar lips, more than ready for Kyle's punishment. What do you think?"

Incoherent babble answered Cole and Kyle took that as a "yes," unleashing all his pent-up grudges in a barrage across her tits. Boy did she dance, so sexy and luring. Cole swore they were going to enroll their princess in some belly-dancing classes. Just like that, a new fantasy was born to replace the one he was acting out.

It was so nice he had to give the Mr. Man a few pumps just to keep him on his leash. Otherwise, the damn cock would have gone and buried itself in the sultry welcome Hailey's cunt laid out. She was wet, wetter than she'd ever been. So damn wet, she made him ache to go swimming. Cole grunted over the very tempting idea and tried to pet the Mr. Man back into only a pulsing pant and not an outright drool.

Not that he was the only one sweating. Trickles of moisture beaded all over Hailey's golden skin. Rivulets streaked down from under her mask as her head rolled from side to side, slowing down along with her whispered mantra.

"Please. Please. Please…"

Over and over again, she begged so softly Cole had to lean into hear. Pressing his lips close to her ear, he asked just as quietly, "Please what, princess?"

His attempt to lure her into begging him just as he wanted backfired because apparently Hailey hadn't suffered enough.

"I want to come, you son of a bitch."

Cole growled over the rebuttal, his hand shooting to the clamp on her nipple as he planned to punish her by giving her just what she asked for. The rash, impulsive slip of Cole's control almost cost them, but Kyle caught his wrist before Cole went too far. In the moment, Cole didn't appreciate Kyle's aid because he wanted to go too far. That way he could punish Hailey for making him go there.

Punish. He'd do it anyway. She pushed more than him far enough for that because he could tell from Kyle's smirk his partner had something special in mind. Nodding at the finger Kyle held up to ask for a moment, Cole turned back to take care of the princess while Kyle prepped their response.

"Is that right, sugar lips?" Cole drawled, evenly and calmly now, letting his hand rub down over her stomach. The thin chains bit into his palm, catching and tugging her back into a squirmy little thing of need. "So tell me, how do you want to come?"

"*Please*," she whined in response, her body arching into his hand. "Want to come."

"Yes, I know, but how? Do you want to come by my kiss, my touch, my cock?" Cole grinned at the way her mouth opened wide, gasping in all the possibilities.

"Yes."

She still didn't grasp the concept, but Cole did when Kyle walked in.

* * * *

Awash in a sea of rapturous torment, Cole's voice sounded distant, murmuring and unclear. His words came in spurts and pieces, disconnected, but still sounding so good. He was talking about coming and cocks, making Hailey smile as she twisted on the tight leash of the vicious lust in control of her body.

He asked her something and she just said "Yes" to everything. Whatever he wanted because this just felt too good. So hot and pulsing, she just twisted with the need. Oh, the need. Hailey's eyes bulged and her neck strained on the scream that lifted her head right off the mattress.

Arms flexed painfully behind her, stretched to the very limit, she couldn't stop the shrieks as something very hard and extremely cold fucked itself all the way into her cunt. It felt beyond words to finally be filled even if the chilled, glass cock muffled the delight.

The chill froze over the edges of the waves of pleasure, sharpening them to claws. At same time, the cool sensation invaded the inferno of her lusts, clearing away almost all of the sensual fog that enveloped her. Hailey panted out shrill whines as she coped with understanding Cole's words now.

"A glass dildo chilled to the right temperature stops a naughtily little girl like you from stealing her orgasms."

His words made sense but didn't tell her what to expect. Not that anything he could have said would have prepared her for the sudden release of one of her nipples from its clamp. Like a geyser, blood rushed up to fill her breast, but she couldn't find a release.

Instead, it flowed over itself to pound into a tidal wave that washed over her pussy. Tightening every muscle in its path, the rush of ecstasy clamped down on the frozen cock filing her and suckled. No release came. No matter how hard she tried to flex herself into one.

The cold wouldn't give her the satisfaction, but Cole certainly intended to test that theory. Releasing her second nipple, he showed her just how high she could go and still not touch the stars. They sparkled so close, and she burned so bad, but even the seizing pleasure of her clit being released couldn't span the distance.

Hurling curses, she strained to find some miracle strength that could snap her binds and release from their control. Then she'd have as many orgasms as she could stroke herself into.

"Damnit all to hell!" Hailey hurled that curse at the world as her body collapsed, unable to sustain the energy it took to fight.

"Doesn't work that way, sugar lips," Cole drawled, all smug and happy as he lifted off the bed. "You don't get to demand orgasms or take them…though you can always beg. That helps."

"Screw you, Cole."

Smack!

"Ahh!" Hailey howled over the bare-palmed slap that lit up her pussy. "That's not fair!"

Smack!

"Ahh!"

"Of course, it is." Sounding no less smug, Kyle responded calmly and that just made her growl all the more. "This is all perfectly fair. You know the rules. You obey or you get punished."

Not that she could match his reasonable tone, but she managed to cling on to a thought or two. "I don't know the rules."

"I guess she has a point." Kyle's voice trailed closer, his weight settling into her side as he sat down on the bed.

They were trading off again. Cole had gone silent and disappeared. That couldn't be good. It made her nervous and edgy on top of being painfully wound around desire's tight coil. She didn't want to be distracted by Kyle, but she couldn't avoid his words.

"Of course, most women don't need to be told that betting a man to stay celibate for four weeks and then setting him up to be not only seduced but made the butt of every joke in town in the process—most women just know that's against the rules."

He might be right on every point, but Hailey wouldn't give in. "It isn't as if you knew all along. You could have said—"

It clicked in that second, all the strangeness over the past few days. They'd set her up for this guilt. "Oh, you sons of bitches."

Kyle laughed at that. "Yeah? Really you should—"

The loud, shrill ring of a phone blasted through whatever witty thing Kyle meant to say. As the sound clipped out, it seemed as if the air itself thickened enough to hold everything frozen. The second blare had a hand clamping over her face as Cole's voice barked out.

"Yeah?...Who the fuck is this?...Whatever, man. Hailey's tied up right now, and she's looking to stay that way for a long while, so you can just forget this number."

Hailey heard the crash of the receiver banging back into its cradle before a second ring ripped through the air. Her cell. Given that the hand didn't lift from her mouth, she half expected one of them to answer that. The anticipation of hearing Cole's voice at a distance left her unprepared for his words as they cracked over her face.

"Why is some strange man calling you, Hailey?" The warm breeze of his growl prickled every one of her pores as it washed over her face. "Let her go, man. I want my answer."

Hailey sucked in a cool breath the second she could. She needed the air to answer, but Cole's jealousy showed as impatience. "Answer me, Hailey. Why is some man calling you?"

"You ever think it was one of my brothers?" This time Hailey got to smirk at the silence that greeted her. Cole's hello-idiot button had just gotten pushed. It figured it would only make him more annoyed, and given her vulnerable position, she probably shouldn't have smiled.

"Well then," Kyle sounded very amused. "I guess it's going to suck for you then to explain what Cole was doing answering your phone."

That took away Hailey's smirk.

"Yeah, I thought you'd see it my way, but let's not get distracted by boring conversation about siblings." The intermission finished. Act two opened with Kyle leaning in to whisper kisses over her neck and re-electrify her tired muscles.

"Because you still have some answers to give us, and while we have you in this coherent state, why don't we try for a few."

Hailey licked her lips, wondering what Kyle wanted to know when he already seem to know everything.

"And just for a little motivation—"

Kyle's words cut off at her gasp. The cock that warmed inside of her finally moved. Its smooth glass surface didn't give her half the friction she wanted, but still her hips followed, her need taking any crumb it could. Cole fed it a whole dick, giving her one good pump to make her mad before pulling the damn toy free.

It didn't disappear, but the rounded head trailed down until it lodged against her ass. Then Cole fed her another delicious dick full, making Hailey moan and grind as her ass joined the bonfire and went up in flames. The fiery licks echoed back through her cunt as a second cock joined the game.

The vibrator reappeared to stretch her sheath so wide, Hailey felt sure she would soon die a very happy woman at the hands of the most amazing climax. All he had to do was give a few pumps and she'd be sailing, but he didn't. Instead, Cole disappeared back into the ether while Kyle's dark purr growled through the veil of lust taking over her again.

"And just so we're clear on this, smartass remarks, cussing, actually anything other than the truth will get you this."

The crisp slap of leather left a scalding imprint over her clit, making her writhe with the sudden rupture of pleasure. The bubbly foam of pure ecstasy only frothed up for a moment before collapsing back into that painful tide of need.

"Now, let's start with that ring on your finger?"

"The ring?" Hailey's finger curled around its weight, instinctively holding on to it.

"Yes, princess, the ring and the birth control patch. Was that just to avoid your punishment?"

She'd be wise to be sincere. "If it was, it didn't exactly work, did it?"

She wasn't wise, but she was certainly in love. Hailey's eyes rolled back into her head as her whole body lifted into the blow she knew was coming. Just a few more and she'd be there. All she had to do was taunt them enough.

"That would be an awfully big bluff, sugar lips." Kyle commented when she settled back into a pant.

"Not so big." Hailey moaned out her disagreement. "After all, I'm not really getting the sense that either one of you grasps exactly how to make a baby at this moment."

That did it. Cole unleashed a barrage of whips, dancing the leather from cunt to her tits and back again until her whole body clenched and rolled with the exquisite pain. It kept her tethered to the edge, tied to the wrong side.

For all brashness in the world, Hailey couldn't hang on anymore to dignity. Not when the vibrator started to spasm and the slaps kept coming. She could bear no more. She needed them, and she needed them now.

"Uncle!"

All motion came to a stop, though it took her several minutes to follow suit. She'd barely wound down enough to breathe without the air flaring the flames licking through her body. For as hot as her skin flushed, Kyle's breath felt almost cool across her cheek.

"What was that?"

"Uncle. Enough," Hailey panted, turning her head in Kyle's direction to beg. "I don't want to play anymore. I want to make babies. Please."

"Is that right?" The deep baritone drawl of Cole's had a hard cut to it. "You wanna make a baby. You think that pretty plea is going to make me forget about the debt you owe me?"

He didn't sound amendable, but the rope loosening around her ankle did made her rush to beg. "Baby now, debt later."

"There's interest," Cole warned.

"Don't care." And she didn't.

Hailey only cared that one ankle now lay free while the ropes loosened around her other one. Kyle disappeared, but she knew where to when the ties at her wrist started to come undone.

"Don't care, huh?" Cole's hand trailed up her leg as his chest pressed between them. He'd taken his shirt off, and the satiny heat of his skin made her knees flex and rub against his sides.

"No." Hailey smiled wide as his breath fanned over her pussy. Tempted into forgetting her plans, she slid her knees over his shoulders to arch her pussy blindly up toward his mouth.

"I'll give you whatever you want for an orgasm," she promised in what she hoped was a sultry purr. It sounded more hoarse and broken to her, so she slid the hand Kyle freed into his head to add a little pressure.

Cole answered her with a lick straight up her slit, letting his tongue bounce the vibrator in her before making her squeal as he lapped at her clit.

"How about a lifetime?" he growled that suggestion against her tender bud before sucking it into his mouth.

"A. Whole. Lifetime." Hailey panted out each word on a separate breath as he took her to paradise.

Her second hand came free, and she folded it over Cole's head, trapping his face against her pussy as she began to ride the vibrations that erupted out of the vibrator. Galloping straight into the blinding horizon, she didn't take almost any note when a set of hands rolled her over.

A clumsy move, she rushed to right herself, releasing Cole's head to lift herself up on her hands. From clutching Cole to her pussy to grinding down onto his tongue, it felt even better on all fours.

Especially when he adjusted his position to right beneath her, his hands biting into her hips as he held his treat in place. He didn't have to. Hailey wasn't going anywhere but on an airborne trip straight to the sun. She could already feel the rays beginning to incinerate her, when, suddenly, the bubble popped with the cock sliding free of her ass.

"Oh, *no*."

Falling face first into the mattress, Hailey became convinced they were just teasing her even more. Cole kept her burning, moaning, unable to even crawl away from his ravishing kiss. It didn't matter that it only added to the pain. It felt so good.

Not that they'd let her escape. A hard hand fisting in her hair yanked her back up. Kyle's growl greeted her ear a second before he nipped the lobe. "A whole lifetime, Hailey. Not just one night."

Whatever that cryptic vow meant, the worry didn't have a chance to set as Kyle jerked her back with a hand wrapped around her stomach. She cried out at being denied the pleasure of Cole's feast, but the sound quickly turned into a moan as the sticky head of a real cock pressed against her ass.

Hailey didn't need any lead in this dance. Forgetting all about Cole and loving the vibrator buried in her, she pumped herself down onto Kyle's waiting dick. The flared head stretched her tiny entrance so wide she could feel the tension all the way to her soul.

It tunneled deep into her channel as she worked herself back onto every swollen inch, so thick he made her whole world light up with joy. She just loved taking Kyle this way, especially when she already had a packed pussy.

Losing herself in the vibrating beat of the toy buried in her cunt, she seesawed herself back and forth over his delicious hardness. His hand, holding her steady as she fucked herself on him, tightened finally to add a little oomph to the bounce.

"Oh, fuck! Yeah!" Hailey loved that. Her palms pressed deeper into the mattress as she matched his quickening tempo, letting him beat out a massage of pure ecstasy into her ass. "Fuck me...harder...harder in the ass...*oh, Kyle!*"

Yes, she had become like all the other women, and she'd be happy to sigh his name for the rest of her life as long as he didn't stop now.

"Will you two get off!"

Cole's hand pressed into her chest, forcing her to roll and taking Kyle with her.

"You two really aren't that smooth for Cattlemen," Hailey groaned as she wiggled about, trying to find a position where she go back to fucking the dick still trapped in her ass.

"Hold on, baby girl," Kyle panted as he righted her over his chest. He kept her from enjoying a good squirm with his arms lassoing her stomach. "We got to get to making them babies, after all, or didn't Cole tell you he wanted six."

"I upped it to eight."

In some realm of her mind, she had a sinking feeling Cole wasn't kidding, but she didn't argue with the man pulling the toy free of her pussy and lining her up for the main course. He fed it to her one slow inch at a time. With Kyle making her stretch almost beyond her limits he left Cole so little space.

Hailey didn't mind the burn, the tinges of pain that flowered over the sweet grind of friction. She loved it, loved it when they took her like this. It was the darkest, most wicked drug, and they'd addicted her. She couldn't be made whole without them, the both of them.

Settling his full length into her, Cole brought the weight of his chest down to squash her breasts and the breath right out of her. "I'm not going to make any babies with you, princess, until you tell me what I want to hear."

"Want to hear?" She tried to flex in their grip, teasing them as well as herself with how good it would be with just a little motion.

"You know what I want to hear."

It clicked then, and even in the thrall of it all she almost laughed. Keeping her voice somewhat even made it a challenge just to get the words out. "Please, master, fuck me."

Her lips quivered and she rolled them in to keep the smile from her face as Cole grunted above her. "You're going to pay for that smirk later, sugar lips. Right now we got a baby to make."

"I'm going to make you a girl, Cole. Just to get even for today."

His only response to that challenge was a flex and bang that drew his cock out only to pound it back in even faster. Apparently, Cole's prescription for guaranteeing sons was to fuck her with an unleashed aggression that spoke of a primitive man on a testosterone overdrive.

She loved every inch of it going and coming. Clawing at his back, she almost forgot about Kyle all still and steady at the rear. Almost, except for the poignant echo of the pleasure thundering out of her pussy coming from her ass, and then he shifted and took her to that special place.

Coherent words of praise melded into incoherent babble as Kyle began countering Cole's thrusts. Smooth and steady versus the relentless race that possessed Cole to drive himself that much faster into her. The mismatch of beats left her crying out as her orgasm danced all around her but wouldn't embrace her.

"You son of a bitch!" That didn't come from Hailey, but from Cole, who snarled it through his clenched jaw.

"You're going to come without us." Whatever Kyle was talking about, she didn't understand. All Hailey understood was that the winds of chaos brushed painfully over her soul, teasing it with the obliteration to come.

"*Please, Kyle.*" Hailey ground out, buckling under Kyle's threat.

"Who is the king?"

"You are."

Her answer didn't appease him because he didn't pick up speed. Instead, he left her twirling at the very end of her rope as she tried to claw her way to release along with Cole.

"Who is the king, Cole?" Kyle gloated.

"You are, you son of bitch, and you can consider your title challenged. Now fuck!"

Hailey took the heat of Cole's roar, but she didn't mind. Bless his soul, Kyle caved and began hitting all the right notes. Just fast and merciless as Cole, Kyle pounded his dick deep into her ass, matching Cole stroke for stroke as Cole pillaged her pussy.

Then they were hitting just the right spots together, one single, hardened force pounding away at her domestication until all that was left was a primitive need to mate. Lassoing Cole in her arms, she found his mouth by simply crashing her head into his and kissing her way over to capture his lips with hers.

He was just as hungry for her taste and they fought for control, him taking hers as he began to plunder her mouth just as he did her body. Pressing her down with the kiss, he trapped her in the binding embrace of two male bodies. With each thrust, they ground her between them, giving her a full body massage of heated muscles and hard angles.

That was the way the path to heaven lay—in the sweaty, writhing, grunting strain to the finish. All around her floated the whispers, "*Love you princess.*" Cole, Kyle, and even her own voice blended into the sea of pledges as their souls merged into one.

Hailey's eyes rolled back in her head as the cauldron of desire they brewed to such an explosive level detonated and the whole world liquefied around her.

* * * *

Cole couldn't hold on anymore, not with Hailey going wild in his arms. More than he wanted the babies or his dignity, he wanted this moment with Hailey, when she took him past the stars and showed him all the colors in the universe. So he held on—to her.

Giving himself over to the pussy pulsing all around him, Cole let himself be swept away by the beautiful violence of his release. Roaring through the heavens, he felt his soul shearing into pieces, but it was such a wonderful thing. So warm and healing, he crashed back to Earth, clutching it to his chest and taking it with him as he rolled over to his back.

Kyle grunted, probably in objection to being left all alone with his cock hanging in the wind. Cole had the comeback for that. He just didn't have the breath. It probably would have helped his chest to heave if he'd shrug Hailey's weight off, but he just suffered.

"Well, that was fun." Kyle sounded tired and exhilarated at the same time. The hint of smugness in his tone prompted Cole to remember what he wanted to say.

"You aren't the king."

"Prove it."

"Are you two arguing again?" Hailey groaned, pulling away from him only to snuggle back into his side.

"Tired, princess?" Kyle asked, shifting to his side so he could pancake Hailey between Cole and him.

"And sore," Hailey muttered.

"Oh, poor little thing," Kyle growled, making her squeal slightly as he tickled her in some way. "I guess you're going to ask for a little break before round two."

Hailey jerked free of Kyle's hold to climb over Cole and reach the safety of his other side. Cole didn't object. He did try to take a nibble at one of the tits she shoved in his face, but she moved too fast. Fortunately, fast enough that she didn't catch his motion and just kept on arguing with Kyle.

"And sticky."

"You need a shower?" Kyle raised up on his arms as if he were about to go over Cole. Cole really didn't want anything of Kyle's hanging down in his face, so he shoved him back as he sat up.

"Stop playing around, man." Shoving straight down the bed, he escaped both of them. He jerked the jeans he still had on back up. "If the little one wants a shower and a nap, might as well give it to her. You and I have other business to address."

Not about to take that order lying down naked, Kyle jerked out of bed, snatching his own jeans off the floor as we went. "Oh, we do? And just what is that?"

"A little matter of a title and a challenge being laid down," Cole smirked, "or do you just want to save the princess all the exercise and admit defeat now."

"Yeah, right." Kyle had his shirt in his hands. "Fine, we'll have our talk."

"That's great," Hailey yawned. She rolled herself up in the top sheet and scooted back to the pillows. "Just do it somewhere else."

Cole shared a look with Kyle. They'd really worn Hailey out because she didn't seem to be getting the message. Not that Cole saw any benefit to explaining the details to her now. He and Kyle had to come to agreement on just what each individual challenge was and how they'd rank who did better. To take the title of the king it would mean a tedious testing of almost every skill they possessed.

That could take a while, which was why he shook his head when Kyle started toward Hailey. "Let the little one sleep. It will be fun to wake her up."

"Just don't do it too soon," Hailey murmured into her pillow.

Chapter 43

Brett pulled his truck to a stop across the street from the house he'd grown up in. Home, it was his even if he hadn't lived there in years. All the memories, all the nooks and crannies where stories of the olden days lurked, none of that peaceful pull had him parking across the street to admire his old home. His gaze didn't linger over all the old familiar sights but focused in on one that was definitely not part of the traditional scenery.

A truck hogged the driveway, and it didn't belong there. Jacked up with jackass lights across the top, Brett could smell the redneck from across the asphalt. Belonging to that pack didn't make Brett anymore tolerant of his brethren. Especially not when the only light on in the whole house was Hailey's bedroom.

Probably the same bastard who answered the phone yesterday.

As a general rule, Brett felt morally obligated to hate and annoy any man that dated his kid sister. With this one, he wouldn't have to work at it. Hell, his need to pound some respect into the fellow was what had him more than willing to drive in non-stop shifts just to get home and revel in the moment.

The idiot was not only present, but he was up to something that Brett couldn't wait to break up. With his elbow, Brett nudged Mike awake. Mike came to just as the Marines trained him—alert and taking in his surroundings. It didn't take his twin more than thirty seconds to focus in on the pick-up truck.

"Why is there a truck in our parking space?" Mike asked as if Brett could actually answer. His twin didn't expect one, evident by the way his second question rolled immediately out. "And why are all the lights—oh."

Brett guessed Mike was a little groggy for it to take that long to recognize the obvious. With no answers to give to his brother, Brett offered him an assurance as he pushed open his door. "Wanna go make little sis's night miserable?"

"Oh, hell yeah." Mike paused only long enough to shoot Brett back a grin before pushing open his door.

They left their bags and everything with the truck, crossing the street fast and silent. Not about to let the couple get any kind of warning, they communicated silently with hand gestures and pointed glances. That's all Brett needed to know his role.

Heading straight down the drive, he didn't even have to pause as he reached out and bent the truck's side mirror back. It cracked behind him and he figured he'd broken it pretty good. That made Brett happy, even happier thinking just how he'd explain to the little prick about getting in Brett's way, because—

"Oh, God! No! You son of a bitch!"

The strangled screech sliced through the night. He knew that voice. That was *his sister*. Brett froze with a fear that cemented his feet to the driveway. For the first time in his life, he choked on the horror as one nightmare sped through his mind after another.

The rounding sound of male chuckles pounded away his paralysis, leaving only raw, violent rage in its place. There was more than one man in there with his sister. Brett didn't need to run for the back door. He knew how to go through the window.

* * * *

Hailey's wrist twisted in the cuffs binding her to the headboard. Her fingers curled into her palm, digging her nails into her own flesh as she fought against the magic of Cole's mouth. They were on round three of the pussy eating challenge, and Cole was second up, with one round used as warm up and somewhere along the way she'd forgotten all about the competition and lost herself in the delight of so many orgasms.

Too many and slowly rapture turned to anguish as Cole's tongue drove toward yet another horizon. The stretch to reach it felt like it would snap her in two. For all her whimpering and pleading, it just drove him harder and drove her faster and faster until the world started to shimmer all around her.

"Oh, God. No! *You son of a bitch!*"

The insult pierced the air at the same moment her release crashed into her soul. She was coming, and the world was crashing in around her with a shower of glass. Through the delirium of release, Hailey watched her nightmare unfold as Brett tumbled across her bedroom floor onto his feet only to tackle the nearest man to him—Kyle.

Even without the high of an orgasm everything would have played out too fast in those moments for her to track it. Brett was screaming curses interlaced with punches. Yelling his own profanities, Cole tackled Brett and somewhere in the distance it sounded like a tree had fallen on the house. Not a tree, but another brother rushed into the room, needing no incentive to join the fight.

From there time morphed into a trickle that played out to be the worst half hour of her life. Cuffed to the bed, naked, nobody paid her any attention. The fight might have started with some warped misunderstanding, but it continued on within a fever of testosterone that had the men crashing through her room and then out of it to tear up the rest of her house.

There was nothing she could do but yell her own curses at the lot of them. They became more profane and high pitched as the shrill wail of sirens wobbled into screams. The police, and if one of the four numbskulls still bloodying up her floors didn't get his ass into her room to untie her hands, she'd come back to haunt all four of them right after she died of embarrassment.

That's when time performed its most infamous trick and almost stopped. Eyes trained on the door, she could hear every second pass in the beating of her heart. She could also hear the squeal of breaks, the pounding of heavy footsteps across her porch, the new symphony of male voices that added themselves to the chorus and still nobody came.

She could hope and pray they'd forgotten all about her, but Brett shattered that faint aspiration with an accusation that made her flinch.

"He was raping my sister."

I'm going to kill him. Bad enough that he and Mike invaded her bedroom so rudely or that they beat the crap out of her men, but now she'd have to explain it all to the cops.

"They have her cuffed to the fucking bed, and she's screaming no!"

It would have to be a painful death.

"Go and see for yourself."

Very, very painful. Hailey unleashed that sentiment on the head that popped through the hallway door to glance down in her direction. "Get your ass out of my house, Killian, and you take that baboon-brain brother of mine because I swear to God—*are you listening to me?*" She screamed the last part at him when he disappeared with a smirk. "And nobody else better be sneaking a cheap look, either!"

"Um, Hailey?" Killian's shout didn't hide the laughter bubbling underneath. "Uh, somebody's got to take a look or who is going to undo you?"

"Send Kyle!" Silence greeted that demand and she waited, straining to hear Kyle coming forward. "Killian?"

"Uh, yeah. Brett says Kyle can come, but his dick can't leave the kitchen, so you sure you want Kyle?"

"Now, Killian!"

"But Brett—"

"Tell Brett anything he takes off my boyfriend, I'm going to take off him." Again silence greeted her, but this time it was broken by a hard thud. "Killian?"

"Okay, Kyle's out."

"What?"

"He's passed out," Killian yelled back an explanation that still left it up to her to figure out what had happened. "You want Brett to knock Cole out, too?"

"Don't let him do that!"

"Uh, Hailey? Given his size, there isn't much about *letting* Brett do anything."

"You have a gun." So did she, but Hailey couldn't reach it.

"Like I'm going to shoot my buddy." Killian laughed outright at the very idea.

"Well then cuff him." God, did she have to tell the man how to do his damn job. She might shoot his ass, too.

"Why'd I do that? After all, he's not the rapist."

Hailey let forth a litany of profanity that cursed every descendent Killian had or ever would. It still didn't get her anywhere. They argued it around one bend and back through another before finally Brett roared down the hall at her. He did a better job with the profanity, and the threat that he'd becoming down that hall if she didn't start behaving had everybody agreeing the best answer would be to call in Patton.

Patton meant adding to Hailey's humiliation by including all three Davis brothers in the night's high drama. Cole and Kyle probably lived through the night only because Killian had the sense of mind to drag them down to the police station before it became a five against two fight. Not very fair, especially with Kyle dreaming of daisies.

The only time a two against five fight was even fair when it was her and Patton against all five arrogant asses they called family. All she had to do was endure another half hour wait until her friend came to Hailey's rescue. Time went back to playing its old tricks and warped everything around her until she felt at least ten years older by the time Patton came charging into her room.

Hailey knew exactly what thoughts lurked in her friends mind with those twinkling eyes and full-on grin. Just the idea brought a growl to Hailey's chest. She wasn't in the mood. Not that Patton ever cared. She gave her friend points for holding it in until she shut the bedroom door.

"Oh, my *God*, Hailey."

"Will you just undo these damn cuffs and spare me the commentary," Hailey snapped. "I am so not in the mood."

"Well, you better get into it," Patton retorted, coming around the side of the bed. She pulled the sheet with her, giving Hailey at least that little bit of dignity back. "Because you got two full-size jarheads pacing through what used to be your living room, preparing for the fight."

"This is bullshit." It felt so good to lower her arms and get some blood back to her fingers. Hailey worked the feeling back into her hands as she glared at Patton. "I wasn't doing anything I should have to explain to anybody. Hell, Brett is the one who should be explaining himself, busting in like gang-busters. Will you look at my window?"

"I see." Patton tossed Hailey's jeans at her, along with a pair of underwear she snatched out of the drawer. Hailey didn't wait to put them on, tired of feeling so naked.

"It just isn't fair, you know?" Hailey tugged her jeans up her legs under the safety of the sheet, only bothering to stand at the last minute so she could button them up. Accepting the T-shirt Patton handed to her, she let the sheet fall to the floor as she continued complaining. "Things were going really good here. It was like everything was finally falling to place and now," Hailey gestured to the window as she sat back down, "I just can't win."

"So stop playing," Patton suggested, settling in beside Hailey. "Killian told Chase that Kyle and Cole had been taken to the police station, but I imagine they'll be released soon enough."

Hailey's shoulders slumped. "After I give a statement."

"After you fail to file a report," Patton corrected. "Only Brett is crying rape and not even that numbskull believes it. He's just being a dick because he's your older brother, and he can get away with it."

"That's the part that's not fair," Hailey mumbled. She could grow up, but she could never outgrow her brothers.

"Well," Patton sighed. "I see an open window and a long walk to Kyle's and Cole's in your future."

Hailey glanced at the window, tempted, but it would just be another game. Besides, Brett would show up on Cole's doorstep, and it would round two of the night. She really didn't want her brother knocking both her men out in one night. Though it probably would stop Cole from using this incident to claim the title of King once he got over being beaten up by her brothers. Brett and Mike could pretty much take anybody they wanted, especially fighting together. There was probably only one person in all of Pittsview who could beat them.

Smiling at Patton, Hailey stood up. "Nah. I'm going to walk out that door right there and explain to the police that I expect my men to be released and released immediately. Then I'm going to explain to my brothers that they aren't to be using my fiancés as punching bags, that they are to use doors and use them properly, and that this is my life and what I do with it is not open for comment. I'm going to set them all straight."

"Yeah?" Patton smirked. "Good luck with that."

"Thanks." She would need it.

* * * *

Kyle watched the patrol car's tail lights disappear into the night. He owed Killian big time for letting Brett clock Kyle while he was cuffed. It violated the rules of fair play. While there may be no rules during the fight, there sure as he were rules after. Like being clobbered by two deputies on top of Mike. *Mountain of a man he is.*

Kyle had never had any beef with Brett and Mike before, but they made his short list tonight. It didn't matter what he'd been doing to their sister. That might have bought them a punch or two, but the trouncing had gone a little too far.

"Give it up, man." Cole nudged him. "It's been a long night, and tomorrow we have to get our truck and our woman back from those trolls without getting pummeled a second time."

With one last dark glower at the end of the road, Kyle started shuffling up the driveway behind Cole. "You think it's going to be easy to get Hailey back? Because I'm thinking she just got handed two very big weapons in this war."

"They might be big, my friend, but we'll find a something even stronger on our side." Cole appeared more worried over the fact that the front door was locked than the two apes guarding their princess. For as cool as he sounded, Kyle could read the tension in Cole as he got angry at the door. He kicked it and then immediately winced, bending slightly at the waist. "Damn those assholes!"

"I think I left the backdoor open," Kyle offered, completely understanding Cole's frustration. Shoving off the porch railing, he left Cole to follow as he curved back around the house and up the drive.

"You know everybody warned me," Cole muttered. "Everybody said they were as big as mountains, but—damn, Kyle. How the hell are we going to get around them?"

"We'll think of something," Kyle assured him, not sure what it was they'd think of. At least the backdoor knob turned easily in his hand. "See, open."

"Thank God for little mercies," Cole grumbled, following him into the kitchen. "I could go for a nice long soak in Hailey's steam shower right now, but I guess the best I'm going to get tonight is a hot towel wrapped around just the worst spots. Hey, man, are you listening to me?"

No, and Kyle didn't intend to take the time to answer. A piece of blue, dark blue, edging around the entrance from the living room into the dining room caught his eye. It stood out against the hardwood floor as a beacon out of place. Lulled by curiosity through the dining room, Kyle blinked in the sight of a pair of jeans discarded on the floor.

Cole could have done it if he'd been half the size. Those were women's jeans, and they matched the pair of female sneakers kicked off by the side of the front door. Breaking into a grin, he followed the trail to the tiny T-shirt puddle in the hall. No bra, but a pair of pink panties hung from Cole's bedroom door knob. Just the sight filled him with such satisfaction. He hadn't been sure earlier when Hailey put on his ring. Given her rash and competitive nature, she could have done it for all the wrong reasons. Only the right ones would have led her back to here tonight.

"I guess we don't have to figure out how to go around those jackasses, huh?" Cole's smug comment snapped Kyle back to the moment as he realized Cole had followed. More than follow, he shoved past Kyle, apparently not interested in savoring the moment.

He should have because the moment Cole opened the door Kyle's romantic illusion popped. Like in his fantasy, Hailey was there where nothing more than a sheet, but true to her own nature she didn't wear a come-hither smile. Instead, she blasted them the second the door opened.

"I'm not having six kids."

Kyle didn't know exactly what to say to that, but thank God. He cast Cole a smug look only to break into a real grin at the one Cole shot back. They might not agree on everything, but they were thinking alike right now.

"And I'm not cleaning up after you two. If you want somebody to wash your underwear, hire a maid."

Cole went right and Kyle went left, both shedding their clothes as Hailey continued down a list she'd obviously spent too much time building.

"And this house isn't going to do, not without a major remodel. I cannot bathe in that bathroom on daily basis. Of course, we can't stay at my place because that's now infested with brothers, so we're just going to have buy or renovate. And I expect my own room, something with a solid wood door, and at least three dead bolts for when you piss me off."

On and on she went, working herself up as they stripped down and crawled into bed. She even managed to sound grumpy as Cole snuggled her into his chest. This wasn't the first time Cole had taken the dominating position. Kyle let it slip, giving Cole his moment, for now.

Snuggling into her back, Kyle nuzzled his way through her hair to her ear to whisper, "Hailey?"

"Yes." She actually sounded scared and hesitant.

"Shut up."

She did for a moment, but Kyle didn't mind it so much when she whispered this time. "I'm sorry my brothers beat you up. I won't lie and say that they feel sorry for it, but I did set them straight."

"Really? And how did you do that?" Cole didn't sound particularly convinced that she handled her brothers. Kyle hoped she hadn't because he had some handling he wanted to take care of. That thought got lost, though, when Hailey answered, back to sounding mousy.

"Well, I told them that I loved both of you and that we were going to make a life together and they could either be a part of their nieces' lives or they could go suck a lemon. Then I walked out."

Kyle couldn't keep from squeezing her tight, feeling the warmth of her confession clean down to his soul. "I love you so much, princess."

"That goes double for me," Cole grunted, jerking her back closer to him.

Not discouraged, Kyle made Hailey giggle with a quick tickle. "Does this mean we get to tie you up whenever we want?"

Hailey cast a mischievous grin over her shoulder. "Maybe."

"No maybe about it, princess," Cole snorted. "Unless either of you forgot, we still have a competition to settle."

"I didn't forget." Hailey did that rubbing thing, grinding her ass against Kyle's rousing cock while arching her breasts into Cole's chest. "And maybe we should start over from the beginning, Cole. I think you need the practice."

THE END

www.JennyPenn.com

ABOUT THE AUTHOR

I live near Charleston, SC with my two biggies, my dogs. I have had a slightly unconventional life. Moving almost every three years, I've had a range of day jobs that included everything from working for one of the world's largest banks as an auditor to turning wrenches as an outboard repair mechanic. I've always regretted that we only get one life and have tried to cram as much as I can into this one.

Throughout it all, I've always read books, feeding my need to dream and fantasize about what could be. An avid reader since childhood, and as a latchkey kid, I'd spend hours at the library earning those shiny stars the librarian would paste up on the board after my name.

I credit my grandmother's yearly visits as the beginning of my obsession with romances. When she'd come, she'd bring stacks of romance books, the old fashion kind that didn't have sex in them. Imagine my shock when I went to the used bookstore and found out what really could be in a romance novel.

I've worked on my own stories for years and have found a particular love of erotic romances. In this genre, women are no longer confined to a stereotype and plots are no longer constrained to the rational. I love the 'anything goes' mentality and letting my imagination run wild.

I hope you enjoyed running with me and will consider picking up another book and coming along for another adventure.

Also by Jenny Penn

Cattleman's Club: *Patton's Way*
Tasty Treats, Volume 1: *Rachel's Seduction*
Sea Island Wolves: *Mating Claire*
Sea Island Wolves: *Taming Samantha*
Tasty Treats, Volume 3: *Claiming Kristen*
Deception
The Cowboys' Curse: *Sweet Dreams*
Tanners' Angel
Jamie's Revenge
Kansas Heat

Available at
BOOKSTRAND.COM

Siren Publishing, Inc.
www.SirenPublishing.com

LaVergne, TN USA
28 September 2010
198751LV00012B/174/P

9 781606 018279